Praise for Anne E

Praise for *Fenian Street*
"Emery does a fine job integrating Shay's personal story with the larger Irish political issues of the period. Adrian McKinty fans will want to check this out."
— *Publishers Weekly*

"Fans will be delighted to see the return of such characters as Father Brennan Burke from earlier books in the series, and she adds depth to *Fenian Street* by depicting the politics of the era, giving a full sense of the Irish community."
— Shelf Awareness

"I always look forward to the next Anne Emery. They are always impeccably researched, richly atmospheric, and with a spellbinding plot that keeps me hooked until the very end. She is a true Irish treasure on both sides of the Atlantic!"
— Jim Napier, author of the Colin McDermott Mysteries

Praise for *The Keening*
"The intricately developed story may appeal to fans of Cora Harrison's 'Burren' mysteries."
— *Library Journal*

"Halifax author Anne Emery has superbly blended two fascinating storylines in *The Keening*, a splendid murder mystery with characters you wish you knew."
— *Winnipeg Free Press*

Praise for *Postmark Berlin*
"Emery has twice won the Arthur Ellis Award (both for earlier installments in this series), and readers who have not yet sampled her tough-edged crime fiction are advised to rectify that immediately. A fine entry in a consistently strong series."
— *Booklist*

"As in the earlier novels, this one relies on two particular strengths — immaculate research and moral worthiness — and along the way, it slides expertly around a whole slew of narrative conundrums."
— *Toronto Star*

COUNTED AMONG THE DEAD

COUNTED
AMONG
THE DEAD

A Mystery

ANNE EMERY

Published by ECW Press
665 Gerrard Street East
Toronto, Ontario, Canada M4M 1Y2
416-694-3348 / info@ecwpress.com

Series design: Tania Craan
Cover design: Jessica Albert
Author photo: Mick Quinn / mqphoto.com

LIBRARY AND ARCHIVES CANADA CATALOGUING
IN PUBLICATION

Title: Counted among the dead : a mystery / Anne Emery.

Names: Emery, Anne, author.

Series: Emery, Anne. Collins-Burke mystery series ; 13.

Description: Series statement: A Collins-Burke mystery ; 13

Identifiers: Canadiana (print) 2024036502X | Canadiana (ebook) 20240365046

ISBN 978-1-77041-711-3 (softcover)
ISBN 978-1-77852-272-7 (ePub)
ISBN 978-1-77852-275-8 (PDF)

Subjects: LCGFT: Detective and mystery fiction. | LCGFT: Novels.

Classification: LCC PS8609.M47 C68 2024 | DDC C813/.6—dc23

This book is funded in part by the Government of Canada. *Ce livre est financé en partie par le gouvernement du Canada.* We acknowledge the support of the Canada Council for the Arts. *Nous remercions le Conseil des arts du Canada de son soutien.* We would like to acknowledge the funding support of the Ontario Arts Council (OAC) and the Government of Ontario for their support. We also acknowledge the support of the Government of Ontario through the Ontario Book Publishing Tax Credit, and through Ontario Creates.

PRINTED AND BOUND IN CANADA

PRINTING: MARQUIS   5   4   3   2   1

In honour of those who survived and
those who died in my Halifax neighbourhood,
the Devastated Area, on December 6, 1917.

PROLOGUE

"Gentlemen, our task is to do something that has never been done before. To develop a bomb based on fission, the splitting of the nucleus of fissionable material, uranium or plutonium, to set off a chain reaction. This will, of course, release a colossal amount of energy. Let's look at some previous explosions before we talk about the size of the blast. In 1917, in Halifax, Nova Scotia, two ships collided in the harbour. One was a munitions ship, carrying a huge cargo of flammable and explosive materials: TNT, picric acid, benzol, gun cotton. The ships collided and sparked an explosion, which was massive. Nearly two thousand people were killed, thousands more injured. I have photographs here. As you can see, a large part of the city was obliterated. And it's been reported that people living on Prince Edward Island, over a hundred miles away, could hear the blast."

"My God, Oppenheimer! And we're looking for something more destructive than this?"

"Yes, we are. What we want is a fission weapon that can produce an explosion bigger, even more powerful, than the one in Halifax."

SEPTEMBER 1993

Normie Collins

That wasn't really Robert Oppenheimer talking. That was the opening scene of the play we wrote at my school. It was Father Burke talking like an American, reading out the part of the great scientist, J. Robert Oppenheimer. Well, Oppenheimer made the atomic bomb, which was evil, but he was a brilliant scientist to be able to do that. So, in that way, he was great. Anyway, at our school, Saint Bernadette's Choir School, we wrote a play about the Halifax Explosion. My science teacher played the part of the scientist who asked Oppenheimer the question. We put Oppenheimer in because, when he was figuring out how to design the bomb, he really did tell the other scientists that they had to study what happened here in Halifax on December 6, 1917. It was the biggest man-made explosion that had ever occurred, before the atom bomb itself. The main characters in the play were Mike Kavanagh and Lauchie MacIntyre. They were real boys, twelve years old, who lived in Halifax at the time of the explosion, and we had the notes they made before and after the blast. The name of our play was *Devastated Area*.

Last night, I was sitting up in bed with a copy of the script, and it was as if I could hear Lauchie and his friend Karl talking:

NORTH END, HALIFAX, NS. MORNING, DECEMBER 6, 1917
LAUCHIE MacINTYRE, a schoolboy, stands on the doorstep of his friend KARL NEUMANN'S house.

                    LAUCHIE
We'll only be gone for a minute, Mrs. Neumann.
There's a ship on fire in the harbour!
Everybody's out looking at it.

MRS. NEUMANN

(Sighs.)

Boys! All right, Karl. Run out and have
a quick look and then come right back
and get ready to be at school on time.

KARL

I know, I know!

The boys run from the house and head towards the
corner with Richmond Street. KARL stops.

KARL

Needham!

They turn and head in the opposite direction, run
up the slope of Needham Hill. Other people are running up the hill, then turning to look out to the
harbour. Fire bells are ringing.

LAUCHIE

Look, that's Pier Six! A whole wall of
fire! Can you believe all the colours of
those flames?

KARL

And look how high that cloud is, that
cloud of smoke!

LAUCHIE

There's going to be nothing left of that
ship! They should move it away from —

CHAPTER I

OCTOBER 1993

Father Brennan Burke

It was cool and clear, a fine evening, and Brennan was out walking with his father, Declan, who was in Halifax on an extended visit from New York. They were on their way to see Monty Collins and Maura MacNeil at their house in the centre of the city. Declan was in his seventies, but he had no trouble keeping pace with Brennan.

"You remember Monty and Maura's daughter, don't you, Da? Normie."

"Of course I do. She'd be how old now?"

"Ten, going on eleven. She is very involved in a play we're putting on at the choir school."

"Is that so?"

"She'll be on stage for a bit, but her main role is playwright. She and two other students are doing most of the writing. The story is about a cataclysmic event that took place on the morning of December the sixth."

His father turned to look at him. "They're doing a play about the feckin' Treaty?"

Brennan had anticipated his father's response. He laughed. "No, not the Treaty." The treaty between the British government and a delegation of Irishmen to end the Anglo-Irish War of 1919 to 1921 did not give Ireland all the independence it wanted from the British Empire. It led to a bloody civil war in Ireland. The Burkes of Ireland were anti-Treaty republicans, although they knew as well as Brennan did that the British were not going to cede, or concede, anything more at that time. The thing had been signed on the morning of December 6, 1921. "Nor is it about the creation of the Irish Free State." That had occurred exactly a year later, on December 6, 1922.

"So, what else happened on December the sixth?" Declan asked. "Surely, nothing as dramatic as those two events."

"You've heard of the Halifax Explosion."

"I have." He turned to his son again. "Right, of course, I'd forgotten the date. December the sixth, oh accursèd day!"

"Exactly. We're performing the first act two days from now, on the seventh; the second act in December. So, you'll get to see at least one part, and maybe both." Brennan turned to him. "You will be staying on for a good while here, Da?"

His father didn't answer that but said, "Have you a role for yourself in it, Brennan?"

"My only role is to impersonate J. Robert Oppenheimer in a prologue to the play. And I'll be projecting some images above the stage. Aside from that, it's all the students' show. And they're outstanding. Wait till you see."

"Looking forward to the play. And yourself as Oppenheimer."

"I considered adding a bit of scriptural interpretation."

"Oh?"

"Yeah. 'What God has joined together, let not man put asunder.'"

"Eh?"

"Those uranium atoms, billions of years old, their nuclear particles held together all that time by an unimaginably strong nuclear force. Then they were split asunder, a rip in the very fabric of creation, of our world. Scientists now know of a naturally occurring nuclear fission in Africa, which occurred some two billion years ago. But the Manhattan Project, as it was called, the making of the atomic bomb, that was done by the human hand. Done to create the ultimate weapon of war. At the same time, who could not marvel at the brilliance of the men, and women as well, whose work over the centuries led to this? Oh, and we can't leave out the Irishman who got there before Oppenheimer and the Manhattan Project."

"The Walton fella. Won the Nobel Prize. And somebody else?"

"Ernest Walton and an English physicist named Cockcroft. They succeeded in splitting the atom in the 1930s and won the prize in 1951. Of course, the Manhattan Project took that to an entirely new level!"

"You'll be a fine Oppenheimer, my lad."

When they arrived at the Collins-MacNeils' grey shingled house on Dresden Row, they were given a warm welcome by Monty and Maura, Normie and her little brother, Dominic. They enjoyed a nice visit, though they knew it would be a short one because Monty, Maura, and Normie had another engagement to attend. They all said goodbye to little Dominic and his babysitter and headed out. Brennan said that he and his father would walk with them and continue on to the Midtown Tavern for a draft or two.

"Hope you'll be able to get a seat," Monty said. "The Midtown will be packed, everybody there to watch the Blue Jays on the screen. First game against the Sox for the American League championship. A Canadian team with a chance to win the *American* League pennant for the second year in a row."

"And you'll be missing it?" asked Brennan.

"Oh, you can be sure I've set the VCR to record it. Good thing you scheduled act one of the play for the seventh. That's the only time from now to the end of the week when there's no game on. Even the most dedicated parents would be torn between the Jays and their own kids on stage!"

"Sheer luck we picked the date."

They enjoyed a nice brisk walk, and once again, it was clear that Brennan would not have to slow his pace for his father to keep up. Age had never held the oul fella back. And he didn't have the appearance of a man in his mid-seventies. His hair was white but still thick, and his blue eyes were clear; those eyes didn't miss a thing. There wasn't a great resemblance between father and son; Brennan was taller and he looked more like his mother's side of the family with his black hair and black eyes. He glanced over at his father as they walked along. No, age was not holding him back. Brennan appreciated the irony of it; the reason Declan was in Halifax now was precisely so Brennan could *hold him back*.

A pal of Declan's — an Irish immigrant like the Burkes — was under threat in New York. From what Brennan's brother Terry had told him, there was a vendetta against the man because of something that had happened years ago. The man's name was Fiach Colum O'Flynn, so it was inevitable that his nickname was "Flying Colum," after the Old IRA's flying columns in the early part of the century. Those men would hide out on the land, carry out an ambush or a barracks raid, and then fade back into the night. This Fiach had been a long-time member of an Irish crime gang, the Irish mob in Hell's Kitchen, New York. In recent years, he had been taken on as an employee of Declan's company, Burke Transport. Declan had never been all that forthcoming about whatever connection he — Declan — had to the old Irish mob, but Brennan knew he had been on friendly terms with the gentleman gangster Mickey Spillane of Hell's Kitchen, until Spillane was murdered in 1977.

Like Spillane, O'Flynn had stood firmly against any move to sell drugs in the Kitchen. But others were not so particular, not so concerned about the devastating effects of drug addiction. One of these men, Cavan McGarrity, had sided with a faction that was determined to bring the lucrative trade in narcotics to Hell's Kitchen. McGarrity was arrested, tried, and convicted of selling heroin on New York's West Side, and he was sentenced to eight years in prison. Now, he was out. McGarrity had always believed — on what evidence, Brennan didn't know — that O'Flynn had somehow set him up for the arrest. McGarrity was determined to exact his revenge. And he wasn't a lone nut; he had a gang around him, willing to assist in the quest for vengeance. There hadn't yet been any threats made against Burke Transport itself, but Declan was on edge about it. The Burke family's fear was that Declan would try to interfere in some way, call upon some old pals from Hell's Kitchen to take action, and in doing so put himself in the way of danger or arrest.

Whatever the case, Brennan's brother Terry — an airline pilot in New York — had put their father on a flight to Halifax, in order to provide Declan with a distraction, a nice protracted holiday with Brennan that would prevent the paterfamilias from embarking on some kind of escapade to assist his friend.

Brennan managed to get some of the story in his father's own words, which dovetailed with the information from brother Terry, as Declan and Brennan walked the streets of Halifax with the Collins-MacNeil family. Brennan attempted to lighten the mood. "Monty, Maura, and Normie are headed to a little hooley at Government House, the lieutenant governor's residence. Which makes me think, speaking of governors, it's too bad you don't still have an Irishman as governor of New York State. Governor Hugh Carey. If I remember correctly, his mother was a Collins." Brennan pointed to the Collinses walking ahead of them. "If you still had Carey as governor, you might have enlisted him to help O'Flynn. Carey might have, I don't know, issued Cavan McGarrity a retroactive pardon and set him up with a cushy job on the governor's staff. He'd be so well placed, he'd put aside his campaign against O'Flynn. Or, alternatively, Carey might have come up with something that would land McGarrity back in prison. Powerful men, the state governors."

"Yeah, right, Bren. He would have come down from the governor's mansion, waded into the muck of these sordid shenanigans, and saved the day for all of us."

"A missed opportunity for yer man," Brennan agreed, in the same spirit of make-believe.

It was a short walk from Dresden Row to Barrington Street, and soon they arrived at their destination: a magnificent Georgian house made of stone in a light brown colour, with symmetrically placed windows and twin chimneys on the roof. Brennan pointed to it. "Brilliant, isn't it?"

"It is, so," his father replied. "You've always had an eye for the great buildings, Bren. Hope you're not regretting your change of career." Before his call to the priesthood, Brennan had been on the road to a career as an architect.

"No regrets."

"Let's hope the Pearly Gates are up to your standards whenever your time comes."

"I'm sure they will be. If not, I'll put up some scaffolding and set things right."

"So this place," Declan said, "who did you say lives here? The governor?"

"This, Da, is the home of the lieutenant governor of Nova Scotia."

"If that's the lieutenant, where does the governor himself live? Will you be showing me a palace next?"

"Not unless we take a detour to London."

"London?"

"Buckingham Palace."

"I'm missing something here, Brennan."

"You are. The lieutenant governor of Nova Scotia is the Queen's representative in the province."

"What century are we in?"

"Her Majesty the Queen is Canada's head of state. You're not in a republic now, Da." Declan Burke had a long and colourful history as an Irish republican.

"Right, right. I knew that, but somehow it had slipped my mind."

"You repressed the memory. The head of government of the province is the premier."

"What kind of grand estate does he live in?"

"Just his own house, like anybody else's."

"There's something skewed about that."

Monty and Maura had a good laugh and assured Declan that even though he would be missing *the* event of the season at the LG's, they would be sure to tell him who was there, who wore what, who said something unforgivably gauche, and what brand of champagne had been served.

Normie

On Tuesday night, I was at the lieutenant governor's house! A big stone mansion. We got invited because my grandmother Evelyn, dad's mum, knows Mrs. Runcey, the lieutenant governor's wife. They used to live close to each other in the south end of the city, and went to the same school. Grandma Evelyn was already there when we arrived, and we all went over to talk to her. Mr. Runcey's son Thane had just got married to Caroline, a girl from Toronto, and that's where the wedding had been. Now the family was having a party for the bride and groom. Yes, we got invited. But I knew I'd probably never get invited again. And it was my own fault.

The inside of the house was beautiful. There was a high twisty staircase that I wanted to climb. The room the party was in had huge windows with purple curtains and mirrors and pictures with gold frames. There was a big fancy light in the ceiling, with crystal things dangling from it. I knew the word for it from one of my Nancy Drew books: chandelier. Nice word, eh? There was a big tall wedding cake with dolls on the top, dressed like Thane in his black suit and Caroline in her pretty yellow dress. There were also a bunch of little-kid dolls and baby dolls on it, too, and somebody called over to Mr. Runcey, "If this cake is any indication, Your Honour, you may be a lieutenant granddad soon!"

And he answered, "Can't come soon enough! But that's what I get for marrying so late in life!"

He must have been old when he got married. Thane laughed and said, "We're all the better for it, Dad. Age brings wisdom, and you were always the wise old owl."

Thane's big brother was at the party too. He was the one who made the wedding cake and a whole bunch of fancy food because he was a cook. A chef. His name was Edwin and he had his girlfriend with him. She had long dark wavy hair, some of it bunched up in curly bangs over her forehead. Her dress was even fancier than Caroline's, silver and silky, and she had on a big necklace with blue stones. I heard somebody call her Wanda. Everybody was teasing her and Edwin that they would be next, the next ones to get married, and they laughed and said maybe they would. And Wanda held her hand out and showed everybody the great big ring on her finger. And somebody said, "Wow!"

I was watching all that, but then I noticed something on one of the walls, a picture of a huge house made of stone, a light brown colour. It had pointy peaks all along the front; it looked like five different houses with pointed roofs, but they were all attached. It was all one house. It had chimney pots like some of the Hydrostone houses and beautiful windows with a whole bunch of windowpanes. And there was a big lawn out in front of it. "That is beautiful!" I said, and Thane's mum, Mrs. Runcey, heard me and said, "That's not all. Come with me. I think you're going to like this." I followed her into another one of the rooms, and I couldn't believe it. There was that beautiful house right there on a table. A dollhouse exactly like the picture! And I could see inside the windows. There was some little doll furniture, couches and chairs and tables, and even a little bookcase with tiny books on the shelves.

"That's amazing!" I said.

And she told me, "The house is in England."

"Who lives there?"

"Some of our relatives."

"Wow! Can you go and visit them?"

She laughed and said, "We have visited, actually. It is lovely."

Another lady asked her, "Is it your family's place, Mrs. Runcey?"

"My husband's mother, Cordelia, her family."

The other lady smiled at her; it was almost a mischievous look she gave her. "Will that be your house someday?"

Mrs. Runcey laughed again and said, "Oh, now, that would be getting ahead of things!" Then, "But Cordelia had no brothers, so . . ." And the other lady laughed too.

When the other people had finished speaking, I asked Mrs. Runcey, "Can I show my mum?"

"Of course, dear."

So I went back to the party and saw Mum and said, "Mum, you have to see this! It's a dollhouse just like a big beautiful place in England that their relatives have."

Mum came in to have a look. A little girl had heard what I said, and she came in too. So did the bride, Caroline. And Wanda, too, the brother's girlfriend, the one who had been showing off the big flashy ring on her hand. She said she was getting married to Thane's brother. Somebody said she'd never go hungry, and she laughed and said, "Yes, we certainly eat well!" She said Edwin was such a good chef that he was always being hired away from one restaurant to another one. I was hoping their wedding would be soon, so there would be another party in this room! We all stood around, gawking at the amazing dollhouse. I knew the little girl was like me; she was dying to play with it. She stood there with her hands behind her back as if she was afraid she'd touch it if she left her hands free. I said to Mrs. Runcey, "It's so great that you've gone to visit this place. That must have been so much fun!"

"Yes, we certainly enjoyed it."

Then Wanda said, "How much is a place like that worth over in England?"

And Mrs. Runcey didn't answer; she just looked at Wanda as if she'd said something rude. I remember seeing Grandma Evelyn looking like that when somebody asked the price of something. So it must be rude. My mum must have thought so, too, because she raised her eyebrows up the way she does when she is surprised by something.

I decided to change the subject a bit, so I said, "Imagine being able to make something like this, all the little chairs and glasses and books. I can't make anything! I get a B minus whenever we have an art project in school!"

But then, later on, I was the one who was rude. I didn't mean to be. Mum and Dad and Dad's boss, Mr. Stratton, were talking to Mr. Runcey, the lieutenant governor, and Dad introduced me to him. Mr. Runcey was old but he didn't look it; his hair was still there and his face didn't have a lot of wrinkles. They were all talking about a meeting last summer between the premiers of the Canadian provinces in the eastern part of the country and some of the governors from the eastern United States. And that got me thinking about what I'd overheard Father Burke's dad talking about on our walk over, about the real reason he was visiting in Halifax now. And something about a governor, and how he could save Mr. Burke's friend. I said, "Mister, um, Lieutenant Governor," and he smiled at me and said, "Yes?"

"If the leaders here have meetings with the leaders in the States, maybe somebody could help a friend of ours."

"Oh?"

"Our friend, well, it's his father, his father's friend —" And I stopped and I knew my face was turning bright red because I was making a mess of what I was trying to say. I felt like crawling away, but I didn't. I tried again. "There's a bad man who got out of prison in New York, and he wants to hurt our friend's friend."

Dad put his hand on my arm and said, "Normie . . ."

But Mr. Runcey said, "What do you mean, dear?"

"They said that a governor could give the bad guy a job and a nice house, so he would forget about hurting the friend. Or maybe put him back in jail. So maybe the governors from here could talk to the governor in New York. Our friend's friend is a good guy even if he lives in Hell's —"

"Normie," Daddy said again, and it was his serious voice. I shut up. And I saw that the lieutenant governor and Mr. Stratton, both of them had looks on their faces as if somebody had said a bad word or brought something stinky into the room.

I turned towards Mum, but she wasn't mad. She looked as if she was trying not to laugh. "Normie," she said, "let's go look at that doll-house again. It's not every day you see something like that."

So I followed her away from the men and I didn't dare look at any of them.

"I thought Runcey was going to have a stroke right then and there!" Monty and the family were back home after the wedding party.

"Rowan Stratton didn't look any better," Maura replied. Rowan was the founding partner of Monty's law firm, Stratton Sommers. "Our dear, sweet little daughter asking the Queen's representative to help a member of the Hell's Kitchen Irish mob. With the oh-so-English Rowan Stratton looking on. Priceless."

"I couldn't tell which one of them was more shocked and appalled." Monty imitated his boss's oh-so-English voice and said, "This calls for a letter to the *Times*."

"Wait till Brennan hears this!" And they both enjoyed a laugh.

Before they went to bed, Monty checked to make sure the VCR was recording the game between the Toronto Blue Jays and the Chicago White Sox. He resisted the temptation to peek at it. "It's going to go late," he said, "so we'll watch it tomorrow." They were delighted early next morning when they fast-forwarded the tape to see the highlights of Toronto's 7–3 win over Chicago.

Monty had supper with Brennan and Declan Burke at the Athens restaurant that evening. As they enjoyed their beer and a meal of moussaka and kleftiko, Monty recounted the story of Normie's diplomatic endeavour the night before. He told the Burkes about Normie overhearing their conversation on the way to the party and her speaking up on behalf of Declan's friend. But Monty left the best part to the last, that being the identity of the person Normie tried to enlist in the rescue. Monty knew of Declan's history as a member of the IRA, the Irish Republican Army. That history had led to the Burke family's sudden midnight exit from the old country decades before. Declan had set neither left foot nor right on Irish soil ever since. But his loyalty to Ireland, to the goal of a united Irish republic, had never faltered. Brennan had often expressed the view that it was long past time for Declan to put old disputes and misunderstandings behind him and make a return visit to Ireland. Unless there was even more to Declan's history than mere misunderstandings. Was there another reason he felt he couldn't return to Ireland? Some kind of legal trouble, perhaps? But that was for another day.

Monty looked at Mr. Burke across from him in the restaurant and said, "So, Declan, my little girl engaged in some high-level diplomacy to get the threat removed from your pal. She went right to the top and asked the English Queen's representative in Nova Scotia to assist an Irish, um, member of the Hell's Kitchen community."

It was the first time Monty had ever seen Declan Burke — or any of the Burkes, as far as he could remember — choke on his beer and spew some of it out. "What?!"

Brennan threw his head back, laughing. "Mother of God, that's brilliant!"

Declan asked again, "What are you telling us here?"

Monty explained, "The premiers of the eastern provinces of Canada have regular meetings with the governors of some of the eastern states of the U.S. Known as the New England states, as a matter of fact. Somebody mentioned these meetings, and Normie thought with these high-level Yanks and Canucks getting together, maybe our lieutenant governor — he doesn't actually go to the meetings, but that wasn't clear to our little diplomat — he could do something about your friend."

"God bless her," Declan said. "It's a remarkable little girl you have, Monty."

Brennan raised his glass. "To Normie." And Declan and Monty raised theirs and toasted little Normie Collins.

"So, Montague," Brennan asked, "what was the Queen's representative's response to Normie's diplomatic intervention?"

"Ah, well, he . . ." Monty began. Then he said, "You should have seen the face on him. He looked as if something unpleasant had entered the room and his nose had caught it."

"A whiff of cordite," Brennan said, and Declan gave him a dead-eyed look.

CHAPTER II

Normie Collins

We wanted to do a project at school about the history of our own city, Halifax, and that's how we ended up writing the play, *Devastated Area*. We called it that, because that was the official name given to the part of the city that was wrecked in the Halifax Explosion. Father Burke — he is in charge of the school — said it was a great idea. And Mrs. Graham is fun to work with; she's the teacher who's directing the play. I was especially happy to be writing it with Richard Robertson. He's two years older than me, in grade eight, and he has red hair too. Darker than mine, so it looks better. And his eyes are almost the same colour as mine: hazel. Don't get me wrong. I don't have a crush on Richard! He's just a friend. He hangs around with the older kids, his own age, but he also hangs around with me and Kim sometimes. Some of the guys in grade eight tease him about it, but he just says "I'm a big hit with younger women. Eat your heart out!" He told me once that he always wished he had little brothers and sisters, but me and Kim aren't really that much littler than he is! Kim is my best friend, Kim Kennedy; she's in my own class, grade six. She is beautiful with long blonde braids. The three of us got together and came up with the idea. Lots of kids in the school would be actors in the play. And the best thing is that me and Kim and Richard got hold of some inside information about the explosion!

This past April, my mum and dad bought a second house, even though we already have one. They bought it to rent out, and then it will be there for me or my big brother, Tommy Douglas, if we want it when we're older. The new house is on Young Street, which was one of the streets that had a lot of damage, the eastern part close to the harbour. The explosion flattened the north end of the city and killed almost two thousand people and hurt many others so badly they may have wished they were dead. And, of course, thousands more became homeless; their houses were destroyed. The house on our property was badly wrecked in the blast. I mean, the house that was there in 1917 got wrecked. A new house was built to replace it a couple of years later. The lady who sold us the house — Lilith Stewart — was born around that time, and she is still there. Mrs. Stewart told Dad the house was "getting to be too much for her" and she's going to move out to an old folks' home sometime soon. But Mum and Dad told her she can stay as long as she likes.

And so it made sense to write this play because my family now owned a house that was part of history! And this gave us a chance to do some research.

"You know that house Mum and Dad bought," I said to Kim and Richard in April when we were back at school after the Easter break. "Remember what I told you about it?"

"Yeah," they both said.

"We should dig around in the garden!"

"Really?" said Kim.

I said, "My dad has a friend, Don, who's a good gardener. Dad was talking to the guy the other day. He lives in the north end, and he calls the earth around his house 'explosion rubble'! And a friend of mine lives around there, too, and she was helping her mum dig for a garden, and she found bits of broken dishes and stuff. My friend wanted to keep them, but her mum told her it wouldn't be right. So they took everything to the museum, or to some professor or somebody, and were told that these were things that had been blown apart in the explosion."

"From way back then!"

"Right, nearly seventy-six years ago. If we find anything, we can put it in our play. And we'll give it to the museum afterwards. So our story won't just come out of a bunch of history books. It will come right out of the ground! And the lady living there, Mrs. Stewart, told Dad she doesn't mind if we dig around."

Richard and Kim both shouted, "Yes!"

"Let's hop on the bus after school tomorrow. Bring some tools with us."

So that's what we did. I got a trowel from Mum, and Kim got one too. We got on the bus downtown, and it goes up Gottingen Street and stops right near Young. We got off and walked down the street, in the direction of the harbour, and then we saw the house. Ours was made of wood shingles like the one next door, ours yellow and the other one grey, both with white trim. The grey one had a big roof that slanted way down over the front of the house, like the ones nearby in the Hydrostone district. Our yellow one had a nice front porch.

"Aw!" Kim said. "These are such sweet houses! I'm glad your mum and dad got one, and that nobody's going to tear it down for a condo building!" That's what was happening to other old houses in the city.

"We have to go to the door and remind Mrs. Stewart about what we're doing."

We knocked on the door and rang the bell, but there was nobody home. I looked out in the back and saw a big square of dirt. It was a garden, obviously, or it used to be. There were no flowers, even though it was springtime. We could dig in that and then put the dirt back where we found it. Richard said we'd have to dig deep because other people could have found anything close to the surface. So we started to dig down into the dirt. But Kim stood up and said, "Look, that lady is watching us. She may think we're robbers or something."

I looked over at the house beside the one next door — two doors away from ours going down the hill — and there was an old lady in the window of her back porch. She had the window partway open, so maybe she could hear us. I called over to her. "Hello! My mum and dad just bought this house, and we're, um, we're just checking out the garden."

There was no answer at first, but then the lady said, "The Stewart place? You're the new owners?"

"My parents are." I turned to Kim and Richard. "Let's go over and meet her. We're going to be neighbours, after all. Sort of."

So we put down our garden tools and walked across the backyard of the middle house and into the lady's yard. She was old and skinny with a sweet old lady face. "Hi. I'm Normie Collins, and this is Kim Kennedy and Richard Robertson."

"Oh?"

"Um, my dad is Monty Collins, and my mum is Maura. They just bought Mrs. Stewart's house."

"Oh, yes. Lilith told me she felt the time had come to sell. I've been avoiding that decision myself! I'm Miss Kavanagh. Ellie Kavanagh. Come in, come in." I saw then that she was leaning on a cane. She moved back from the porch door and invited us in. "Have a seat in the kitchen there. Would you like tea?"

We looked at each other. Was it more polite to say yes or to not make her do any work? She was old, and she tripped on the leg of one of the chairs. We moved towards her, but she got a grip on the back of the chair and didn't fall.

"I have tea made. You're welcome to some."

"Sure," said Richard.

And she reached up into a cupboard and brought down some cups and then poured tea from her kettle. She brought a bottle of milk from the fridge and got a bowl of sugar and put them on the table. "Help yourselves." And we did and thanked her. She sat down and smiled at us.

"I heard you out there and wondered who it was. Turns out, you're the new lady of the house! And you like to work in the garden."

She meant me, so I told her about the house, our digging plans, and the play we were going to write. "It's called *Devastated Area*."

"Good name for it. Right now, you are sitting in part of what was designated the Devastated Area."

"Right," said Richard, "we are!"

"The area started two blocks over from here, on Russell Street," Miss Kavanagh said.

"And," I told her, "if we find anything interesting, we're going to put it in our play."

"Oh, good for you. People should remember. Yes, everything around here was destroyed or terribly damaged. There may be things out there for you to find. Objects certainly came flying this way when it happened. Or things were blown out of the houses. And, of course, glass was shattered everywhere." She pointed to her eyes. "That's how I lost my sight. These are artificial eyes. I was standing upstairs looking out the window. Not here. If I'd been upstairs here on Young Street, I would have been blown sky high, would not have survived! No, I had spent the night with our cousins on Gottingen Street, the northern part of the street. It was my cousin's birthday, and I'd been invited to stay over. That house was damaged, no question, but it remained standing, and nobody else in the house was injured. But I'd heard somebody talking about the ship burning in the harbour, and I hoofed it upstairs to take a look."

Oh my God! Had I said anything mean, even though I hadn't meant to? Had I said anything like *you see* or *it looks*? "I'm sorry, Miss Kavanagh. I didn't know. I'm sorry."

She smiled and reached out to where my voice was coming from, trying to find my hand. I put it by hers and she took it. "No need for you to be sorry. It was a long time ago. And, as you can see, it didn't stop me from living to a great old age! I'm eighty-two years old now."

Richard said, "You were just a little kid back then, Miss Kavanagh."

"I was six years old. I'm grateful that I had six years of seeing the world, the beauty of the sun and the moon and the stars, the flowers, my parents, other children, all that before everything went blank."

I felt as if I was going to start crying, and Kim looked the same way, as if she was going to cry too.

"There were dozens of people who ended up like me. We never saw another thing. Ever."

I did start crying then, and so did Kim. Richard kind of cleared his throat and looked away from us.

"You are very sympathetic young ladies," Miss Kavanagh said. "You care about other people, which is a good way to be. There's plenty who don't."

"Thank you," I said.

"I do too!" Richard blurted out, and then his face turned red.

Miss Kavanagh smiled and said, "I'm sure you do. Now, listen to this." She leaned forward in her chair and said, "You're interested in the history, and you're writing a play. So you may be interested in the diary."

"Diary?" me and Kim asked.

"My brother Michael, he was six years older than me, and he had a friend named Lauchie MacIntyre. They used to go up to Michael's bedroom and look out the window and watch the shenanigans in the neighbourhood. Those rascals, they were supposed to be doing their lessons for school! I'd hear them laughing and carrying on, but why not? Two young boys, what would you expect?" She was smiling when she said it. "And I have to say they were particularly interested in the goings-on in the house next door. The house in between yours and mine. Michael would scribble notes on scraps of paper. I was that much younger that I didn't understand what was happening, what it was that had captured their interest. But later I realized that the house next door to us here was a . . . There were a lot of girls, women, in that house. So, as twelve-year-old boys, my brother and his friend were interested in watching them."

Richard looked as if he was going to say something, but then he didn't.

"Now, I never had the chance to read the notes myself. By the time I would have been old enough to be curious about them, I, well, I had lost my sight. Michael either stashed the notes in the cellar at some point, or they ended up down there after the explosion. Whatever the case, my nieces and nephews found the pages and tried to read them. They were able to make sense of some of them, I know. Some are notes by Michael, and others by Lauchie. Lauchie must have handed over his pages, or a portion of them, to Michael. You're welcome to look at them if you're doing research about the explosion."

"Wow!" That was Richard. "Notes written at the time of the explosion?"

"Well, mostly about other things, but there's a bit about the blast. And some written afterwards."

"Maybe the history people would want a copy," I said. "The colleges or the museums."

Miss Kavanagh laughed. "My sister, the oldest of us, made her views known on that question. She died quite a few years ago, God rest her, but on the question of handing those notes over to anyone to study or preserve? She was having none of it! She wanted to throw the pages away. After all, it wasn't the sort of thing you wanted publicized, living next door to a . . . People here in Richmond, the north end, were looked down upon by the 'wealthier, more respectable' people in the south end. That didn't put my sister in a frame of mind to reveal the notes. But other members of the family hid them away, and nobody gave it much thought after that.

"They're here somewhere. I've always lived in this house. Well, the house before and now this one. I . . . I was to be married back in wartime. The second war, I mean. But the man I was to marry, he was killed in the first year of the war."

"Oh, Miss Kavanagh," I said, "that is terrible! I'm so sorry!"

"Yes, it was terrible. I never found anyone again who . . . Nobody else measured up, at least in my mind. My heart. But," she said and got up out of her chair, "enough of that. I'll let you go off and see if you can find those papers."

"Um, how would we go about finding them?" I asked her. "We wouldn't want to go rooting around in your house, like burglars."

"Oh, I don't think Normie — Collins, did you say? — I don't think Normie and her friends are burglars. The notes would be either in the attic or the basement. My niece told me they are in a box, some kind of container." She told us where to find the stairs up to the third floor and down to the basement.

We decided to try the basement first. We found all kinds of boxes and cookie tins, but no diary or notes in any of them. So we climbed up a steep set of stairs to the attic. It took some searching, and some sneezing from all the dust, but we got them! A big stack of pages of different sizes, some lined, some without lines, some pages warped as if they'd got wet. But they were notes in ink and pencil, in the names of Mike Kavanagh and Lauchie MacIntyre. We said thanks over and over again to Miss Kavanagh, and we promised to get the notes photocopied, and we would bring the originals back to her.

When we were standing outside the house, Richard said, "You know what she was talking about, don't you? About the house with all those girls in it."

I thought I knew, but I wasn't going to say it.

"What?" Kim asked him.

"A place where men pay women to . . . be with them. You know, in bed."

Right. That *is* what she meant. Mum and Dad had told me about that, after we watched a movie and that kind of house was in the story. I didn't want Richard to think I was stupid, so I said, "Oh, yeah, I know about that."

"So," Richard said then, "that's why those two guys, Mike and Lauchie, would be gawking out the window, watching all the goings-on next door."

Just as we started out for the bus stop, a car pulled into Lilith Stewart's — our — driveway. A guy got out of the car. He looked like a high school guy, or maybe college, around that age. He was tall and had light brown hair, which was short on the sides, but kind of long in front.

Richard looked at him and said, "You're Kirk Rhodenizer! You played for the Buoys!"

The guy turned around. "Yeah, that's me, and I did. Hoping to play again."

"I used to catch as many Buoys games as I could."

"Boys games?" I asked them.

"The Halifax Harbour Buoys, Junior A hockey team."

"Oh, right." I remembered then. Dad and my brother Tommy used to go to their games.

"Do you play, yourself?" Kirk asked Richard.

"Only the odd pickup game. I'm not good enough to go anywhere with it, but I love to watch. Especially Montreal or Detroit."

"Yeah, it's the greatest game in the world. What other sport requires so many different skills, eh? Shooting, passing, defending, skating . . ."

"And skating backwards," I put in, "and you don't know who's behind you!"

"That too. So, are you looking for somebody? Or . . ."

I explained about the house and who we all were.

Kirk said, "Right, well, I go with Janice. She's my girlfriend. You know, she looks after Mrs. Stewart. Janice has the old . . . She has the lady out for some errands and stuff, so I'm going to wait here till they get back."

"Okay," I said, "maybe we'll see you again."

We started to walk away, and he called out, "I'm assisting at a hockey clinic for some young fellas at the Forum on the weekend, if you're interested. We've got the rink for a couple of hours Saturday afternoon."

Richard's eyes got wide; he was really excited. "Yeah, definitely!"

"Just call the Forum to check the time."

"Cool. I will!"

On the way to the bus stop, Richard told us that Kirk Rhodenizer was such a good hockey player that he could have played in the most important hockey league, the NHL. "He's a forward. He wouldn't ever be a big star like Gretzky or Lemieux, but I think he's good enough to make the big leagues. He didn't score that often, but that's not what he was known for. He was a goon."

Me and Kim laughed. "What do you mean, Richard? A goon?!"

"Enforcer, a fighter, a tough guy. Sure, you have some scrapping in junior hockey. But he was too much of a scrapper, too rough. So the Harbour Buoys let Kirk go."

"Oh, that's too bad," I said. "He should promise them he'll never fight again, and they'll let him back on the team."

"Uh, it's not that simple."

But we forgot all about him after we got to my house on Dresden Row and said hi to Mum and told her that we had a project to work on, and that we'd be asking her to make some photocopies for us at the law school where she teaches. Then we went down to the family room and opened the pages of notes. "Shit," Richard said, "there's dates on some of the pages but they're out of order. Some of the paper is crumbly. And some of that writing, we won't be able to read it."

"But some of it looks clear," said Kim. "Let's give it a try."

"Yeah, you're right," Richard said. "There's the name Mike, and there's Lauchie. It will be cool to see what it was like for kids back in those days."

We passed the notes around so we all had some to look at. Mike's were in blue ink, in nice clear handwriting, while Lauchie's were printed in pencil. The pencil ones were kind of faint, but I could make almost everything out. And the boys had made some drawings, like cartoons. There were funny-looking guys and girls, and soldiers and army tanks.

And as we read the notes, we knew that's what we would put in our play. The stars would be two boys at our school playing the parts of Mike Kavanagh and Lauchie MacIntyre.

NOVEMBER 15, 1917

Lauchie MacIntyre

"Are we going over to Mike's after?" Lauchie asked Karl as they headed into their school on Roome Street.

"Doesn't that all go on at night?" Karl asked.

"No! Mike says they come to the house all hours of the day."

"Good. We'll go."

"Maybe we'll go in there ourselves!"

"Not if his mum catches us! All we can do is watch."

"I was making a joke. I wouldn't want to go in there. But it's fun to see who *does* go in there."

So, when school was over for the day, Lauchie MacIntyre and Karl Neumann headed over to Mike Kavanagh's place on Young Street. But they didn't get far.

"Karl!" It was his big brother, Johann. "Where are you going?"

"No place. Just around."

"Dad's going to be painting again, and he needs us to keep the little brats out of it. He came home early from work to get it done."

Lauchie said, "Tell him you'll do it if he gives you a bowl full of sugar." Karl's dad worked at the Acadia Sugar Refinery, down on the harbour.

"Ha, ha," said Johann. "You should be on the vaudeville stage, MacIntyre. Karl, come on."

Karl rolled his eyes but knew he had no choice. "You go ahead without me, Lauchie."

So it was Lauchie at Mike's doorstep on Young Street.

"Michael! What are you boys up to?" Mike's mum asked.

"We're going to play cards in my room," Mike told her.

"And your lessons?"

"That too."

Mrs. Kavanagh gave them a look that said she didn't believe them, but she had the little kids to look after, the two that were younger than Mike, and they kept her busy. So the boys ran up the stairs and into Mike's room and closed the door behind them. Then they jostled each other for the best view out the window, the best view of the house next door where men came and went, and sometimes the girls came out too.

"Guess who's back! I saw her the other day."

"Who?"

"Your girlfriend, Lauchie!"

"Ha! She's everybody's girlfriend!" It was the blonde one. "Where was she all this time? Haven't seen her since the spring. Maybe she was entertaining our boys overseas!"

"Well, now she's back and she was out doing the shopping. Must have gone for groceries."

"Booze, you mean! And rouge for her cheeks because she used up all her supply getting ready for the boys!"

"Guess what, Lauchie."

"What?"

"I know her name. I heard one of them over there, calling out to her. Minnie is her name. Someday we'll be calling out 'Minnie and Lauchie, Minnie and Lauchie!'"

"Ha, ha."

The woman was young. Minnie. Mike always teased Lauchie about liking her. She really was pretty. She was short and had blonde hair curling down the sides of her face. And there she was! She had on a bright blue coat with a fur animal wrapped around her neck like a collar. She went into the house, and a few minutes later a man came out. He had his collar up around his face, but Lauchie knew he had seen him there before.

"There's the guy with the Case," Mike said. "He's back again. Wonder if he was away fighting."

The boys laughed when they saw the man's eyes shifting all around before he took off walking at a fast clip. It wasn't long before another man came out, younger with wavy dark hair.

"Look at that fella. I saw him before," Mike said then. "Down by the docks, in uniform."

"Yeah, he's a sailor. But doesn't he look like Charlie Chaplin?"

"I think that sailor was at the party they had a few weeks ago," Mike said. "The one I told you about. All the singing and shouting, and somebody threw a rum bottle out over the fence and it broke in our yard. And one of the other sailors came out with one of the other girls, the big one with the puffy black hair, and they were kissing and laughing out in front of the house."

"We should sneak in there some night!" Lauchie suggested.

"Or put caps on us like the police," said Mike, "and peek in the windows at them and scare them, make them think they're going to be arrested."

"Yeah, that would be fun."

They stayed at the window until they heard Mrs. Kavanagh calling up to them. "Boys! Are you doing your work?"

"We'll get it done!" Mike replied. "I'll get the cards," he whispered to Lauchie. "You close the curtains." It was getting dark now, and there was a blackout order in effect because of the war. Light from the Kavanagh house mustn't be visible outside.

Lauchie pulled the curtains across and said, "You're right, the Kaiser might fly over and see us."

"Yeah, I saw him myself the other night, flying all around the neighbourhood in circles, in his Zeppelin."

"Looking for a place to escape to, but I don't think he'll want to come here. Our boys captured Passchendaele! Old Kaiser will be on the run now!"

"But, Lauchie, a whole lot of fellas died, thousands and thousands of them. Ours and the British, Australians, New Zealanders. And what they had to go through to take the place! My dad heard about all the shells and torrents of rain coming down on them and them nearly drowning in the water and the mud. He even heard that bodies of soldiers who'd got killed there came rising up again out of the swamp!"

"It must have been horrible. But, despite all that, our guys took the place. We're going to win the war, Mike, and the Hun won't ever mess with us again!"

"Yeah," Mike said, rummaging in his desk for his pack of cards.

The door flew open, and Mrs. Kavanagh gave them a stern look. "Lessons, then cards, or your pal will have to go home."

They didn't want to press their luck, so they agreed and opened their schoolbags and took out their notebooks, pens, and pencils, and Mrs. K left them to it. Mike went to the Catholic school, Saint Joseph's, between Kaye and Russell Street. Lauchie went to Richmond School on Roome Street.

Lauchie liked school, especially science class. A few of the kids started up a science club and their teacher, Mr. Finlay, often came in and joined them. He was brilliant. But not only that, he was fun to have in the club. At first, the club was only five boys. Then the first girl joined up.

Now, in the Kavanaghs' house with Mike, Lauchie said, "I didn't tell you about the day the first girl joined our science club. Mr. Finlay said to us, 'I know you boys will give a warm welcome to Mademoiselle Chartrand.' That's her name, Hélène Chartrand. French family from New Brunswick. Mr. Finlay said, 'I think that, for the purposes of this club, we'll call her Madame du Châtelet. Does that mean anything to you?' he asked us. 'Émilie du Châtelet?'

"Nobody knew the answer, so he told us. 'Émilie du Châtelet preceded Einstein's famous equation by more than a century and a half, bringing together existing theory and experiment to confirm the relation between energy, mass, and velocity. Velocity *squared*. The *c* part of the equation, of course, the speed of light, came just a few years ago with Einstein. Émilie was one of those brilliant women of science that many people don't know. But in a science club, we want to know those things, don't we?'

"We all answered, 'Yes, Mr. Finlay!'"

Mike said, "I'm going to work that into my own science class one of these days and impress everybody with how smart I am! Do you have work to do for science class tomorrow? I have to finish my grammar lessons. We'd better get at it in case Mum comes up again."

Lauchie knew he had better go along with Mrs. K's wishes, or he wouldn't be allowed to come and visit. There would be lots of time to spy on the place next door, with all the fancy girls and the men coming to see them.

Mrs. K made supper for them, and they did their lessons and played cards, and then they turned to what they most wanted to do: turn off their light and spy on the place next door. "They're playing music, and somebody's laughing. Open the window," Lauchie said, "so we can hear better." Mike wrenched the window up a few inches and the boys leaned down to catch the sound coming in. A man was singing "Pack Up Your Troubles in Your Old Kit-Bag."

"He thinks he's a vaudeville star, that fella," Mike said. Soon the man brought his act outside into the backyard; he drew a girl out with him and danced her around the yard. They were both in fits of laughter and none too steady on their feet. "They've been into the rum and the beer tonight." Mike turned to Lauchie. "What do ladies drink? Not beer."

"They're not ladies!"

"That blonde curly one, Minnie, will be your lady when you walk her down the aisle at Grove Presbyterian!"

Lauchie gave his friend a playful punch in the arm and said, "No, I'll be too busy being best man when you walk Mary Catherine Malone down the aisle at Saint Joe's." Lauchie knew that Mike liked Mary Catherine. She was in the girls' class at Saint Joseph's school and went to Saint Joseph's church like the Kavanaghs, and she lived on Russell Street two blocks over from Young. Mike and Mary Catherine had both asked for roller skates last Christmas, and they liked to put them on and go flying down the steep Russell Street hill. Mrs. Malone always said the same thing: "You two will break your legs and end up in the hospital!" No broken legs so far. Lauchie was going to ask for a pair of those skates for his birthday in February.

The two boys watched the next-door hijinks for a while longer, until it was time for Lauchie to go home.

DECEMBER 3, 1917

Mike Kavanagh

"You should have heard the ruckus last night!" Mike said to Lauchie when they got together after school on Monday. "The men were coming and going at the house as they always do. One guy stumbled down the front stairs, and a girl came out after him and you should have seen what she had on! Or didn't have on! Little skimpy pieces of ladies' underwear!"

"And I missed it!"

"But that wasn't the main thing that happened. I went to sleep and then way later, I heard hollering out behind the house."

"What happened? Some fella tried to walk out without paying?"

"It was a fella, yeah. You know *Mr. Important*, the guy with the Case. It was him and Minnie, and they were having a barnburner of a fight. An argument, I mean."

"That guy with the case — didn't you tell me he had a row with somebody else too?"

"Yeah, he was squabbling with that sailor we've seen there, the one you said looks like Charlie Chaplin. They were in each other's faces, looked as if they were cursing each other to hell that night. But this time, Mr. Important was arguing with Minnie. They woke me up, and I climbed out of bed and went to the window, and there they were yelling into each other's face. He said something about 'Tabby,' or that's what it sounded like. And she said, 'He's mine!' And the guy shouted back that he wasn't."

"Tabby? She had a cat?"

"I never saw one, but she must have. He took it away from her, and she wanted it back. She started crying, and he told her to shut up. And he shouted at her, I think about something else he said was his, and then 'Don't you ever come around my office again. Or I'll have you arrested.' She yelled back at him, 'I'll have *you* arrested!' And they said some other stuff, and I can't remember it all. The things people fight about, eh? It was a wild scene!"

"That's for sure. I miss all the action. That's what they'll write about me, 'Lauchie MacIntyre, missing in action.'"

"Oh! I remember he said something nasty to her. 'Who are the police going to believe? Me or a little whore from Richmond?'"

"Richmond!" Lauchie said, and he made his hands into fists.

Richmond, the boys' own neighbourhood, where the MacIntyres and the Kavanaghs and a whole lot of other good people lived. That man calling the place down! Well, Mike should not have been surprised. He knew there were rich people in the south end who had never set foot in Richmond and never would; too *good* for the *poor folk* in the north end! He would never say this to Lauchie, but Mike had often heard his dad say that the rich people — his dad always talked in a snooty British accent whenever he spoke of them — didn't like the people in Richmond because they were "poor old Irish Catholics."

Well, then, the Kavanaghs were "poor old Irish Catholics," and that was nothing to be ashamed of. Mike loved being an altar boy at Saint Joseph's church, wearing the black cassock and the white surplice over it. It was almost like being a priest, serving Mass (and God) and saying all those responses in Latin, with so many of his friends and his family watching. And the church suppers were always fun because he knew so many of the other kids who came to them. The ladies made chocolate squares to eat after the sandwiches that had no crusts on them. Mike always hoped they threw the crusts outside to feed the birds. But the best thing about the suppers was that he got to spend time with Mary Catherine Malone. He'd die before he'd tell anybody this, but his heart always did a weird little flip when she walked in the door. (The Malones were always late for everything.) Mike was pretty sure she liked him, too, because when she came in, her eyes went all around the place and stopped when they saw Mike. And she'd wave and smile at him, and they'd talk to each other and plan their next time to go roller skating together. She always looked so pretty, with that long shiny red-brown hair and eyes that sometimes looked brown and sometimes green. She was shorter than Mike, and she always joked when they were putting on their skates, "Let me put mine on first, so for a whole minute I can be as tall as you!" Yes, he sure did like her. Was it all right to say you *loved* a girl when you were only twelve years old? Well, he did: he loved her! And that was nobody else's business.

But he had other things on his mind today. He said to Lauchie, "After Mr. Important made that nasty remark to Minnie about Richmond, one of the other girls came out, the one with the long hair down to her bum. And Minnie called over to her. 'You'll see something in my room,' she told the long-haired girl. 'Hide it for me!'

"And the man hollered at her, at Minnie. 'What did you keep?' And then a couple more people came out of the house to see what the yelling was about, and the guy took off running."

"That was quite the row, eh, Mike?"

"Yeah. Sounds as if she went right into his office to argue about getting the cat back. She must really love it. But you can always get another pet."

"I guess we can't get out of our lessons tonight. Loads of studying before they set us free for Christmas. You in the pageant, Mike?"

"Just in the chorus. Danny McArdle is going to be Joseph, and Janna O'Dell is Mary. And the Butchers' little baby, Peter, is the Baby Jesus."

"I'm in the chorus for ours, too, but Mr. Campbell told me if I don't learn the music better, I'll have to just mouth the words. I should fool him when I get up on the stage and bray like an ass!"

"I'd love to hear that! Now, let's get to work, so we can have a card game after."

After they'd been at their lessons for a while, Mike heard his dad coming home. And then he heard him climbing the stairs.

"How are things in the Tin Pot Navy today, Dad?" Michael Kavanagh Senior was in Canada's navy, which had only been formed a few years ago.

He saluted the boys and said, "Aye, aye, sir, all is well and all hands are on deck. Sir!" He said it all in that British accent he liked to use, and the boys laughed. He was making fun of all those people he called "British toadies," and members of the Conservative Party, who hadn't agreed with Canada having its own navy instead of just supporting the British one. That's where the "Tin Pot Navy" insult came from. "You two sailors are following orders, I hope," he said in the same kind of voice.

Mike and Lauchie saluted and said, "Aye, aye, sir!"

Mr. Kavanagh left the room, and the boys scrambled to finish their lessons.

CHAPTER III

Normie

I t took us a long time to write the play. Good thing we started writing and rehearsing parts of it in the spring before the last school year was over. Now it was September and nearly all the kids at school wanted to be on stage as actors. Except Richard! All of a sudden, he was too shy to be on stage? But he was one of the play-wrights, along with me and Kim, and he said, "That's enough glory for me." So, two other grade eight boys would play the parts of Mike and Lauchie. Other kids had roles as parents and kids, ships' captains and sailors, and others. But there were only so many roles to be filled. There was a place, though, for some kids just to lie down and "play dead" on the stage because so many people got killed. Father Burke found a bunch of photographs of the two ships that crashed into each other, the big cloud that rose up above the harbour, and the wreckage of the harbour and the city's north end after it happened. They would be projected onto a screen above the stage.

And Richard did something that was so cool. We were all collecting information about the explosion, all the destruction, deaths, and injuries, and all the people here and from away who were so helpful afterwards. Richard read something about the first season of the National Hockey League, which was brand new back then. Two teams in Montreal, the famous Montreal Canadiens and the Montreal Wanderers, played an exhibition game and the money they made, they gave to the Halifax Relief Fund. It was really nice of them to do that. So we decided to get that into our script.

Richard had gone to play hockey a few times with Kirk Rhodenizer last spring and again a couple of weeks ago. And he asked Kirk if he would like to be in the play. Richard said there was some joking between the two of them about Kirk maybe wearing a Canadiens jersey someday. He said yes, he would be in the play for a little short scene about the game. Richard told him he wouldn't have to attend the rehearsals; he would just rehearse it with Richard and come for act two.

The play was going to be in two parts because we had so much stuff to write about, it wouldn't fit into just one play. Act one would be on Thursday, October seventh, and act two not till December ninth. We had so much to do at school in the fall that we wouldn't have the second part ready before then. But it was good because it was just after the anniversary date, and our second act was about the aftermath of the explosion.

DECEMBER 6, 1917

Lauchie MacIntyre

"Karl, come on down to the harbour! There's a ship on fire!"

Lauchie was standing in the doorway of Karl Neumann's house on Veith Street.

"But I never got that last question of my math lesson done!" Karl said. "The teacher will kill me."

"If I don't get to you first," Karl's mum called out. "Now get back to the table and finish your sums."

Friedrich and Stefan, Karl's two little brothers, came up behind him in the doorway and chanted, "Teacher's going to kill you, teacher's going to kill you!"

"Boys! Get back in there and clean your teeth and get your schoolbags ready."

"What did Lauchie say?" one of the boys asked.

"Never you mind. Now, do as I say and get ready for school." They turned and walked back into the house.

Lauchie said, "We'll only be gone for a minute, Mrs. Neumann. There's a ship on fire in the harbour. Everybody's out looking at it."

She sighed and said, "Boys! All right, Karl. Run out and have a quick look and then come right back and get ready to be at school on time. You'd better come up with a good excuse for your teacher, if you don't get that lesson finished."

"I know, I know!"

The boys ran out of the house and headed towards the corner with Richmond Street, which would take them down to the harbour. But Karl stopped and said, "Needham!" and turned on his heel and headed in the opposite direction. They could see the pier from Veith Street, but they'd get a great view of the ship and the harbour from being up high, on the slope of Needham Hill. It was only a short run, and when they got up on the hill, they saw that lots of people had the same idea and were running up the slope. Fire bells were ringing from all directions.

Lauchie looked down towards the pier and there it was: a wall of flames in all kinds of colours, red and yellow and green and blue. And there was a great cloud of smoke shooting up from the ship. "Wow! Karl, can you believe that?"

"There's going to be nothing left of that ship! They should move it away from —"

It all happened at once: the biggest loudest rumbling sound of thunder Lauchie could ever have imagined, and he could feel the thunder moving through the ground beneath him. A rush of wind blew him up into the air. He came down on his left side, and his elbow and hip flared with the pain. He heard people on the hill screaming and shouting words that would normally get you a belt across the arse, but not today. He pushed himself upright and looked to the harbour. He couldn't believe his eyes. There was an enormous cloud of smoke rising so high it seemed it was miles in height. What on earth was happening?

He turned to Karl who was lying on his back, staring with his eyes and his mouth gaping open. Lauchie froze, staring at his friend's motionless body. Karl blinked then, and Lauchie felt himself sagging with relief. He was about to speak to Karl when he saw something fly down onto Karl's coat. They both looked up, and Lauchie cried out as something hot burned into his face. It felt like a hot knife searing the skin of his cheek. He covered his head with his mittened hands. Everywhere on the hill, people were shouting and crying. When he looked around again, he saw a sailor lying on the ground above him, his dark blue jumper bunched up around his neck, one leg of his trousers gone. His face was smeared with black stuff, and he was muttering to himself, "Where am I? Where am I? Where's the boat?" Another man got up and walked over to him. Lauchie heard them talking, and he realized the sailor had been working down by the pier and had been blown all the way into the city, up the hill.

Karl pushed himself to his feet, and he and Lauchie walked to the top of the hill. All around them they saw scenes they could never have imagined. "Hell," Lauchie whispered. "Hell." And it wasn't a curse; it was a description of the city below, or what they could see of it through the smoke. Where houses had been, now there were yards filled with broken timbers, lumps of concrete, roof shingles, everything busted. All that remained of the houses, as far as Lauchie could see, were a few jagged broken walls and open cellars.

"Oh God, oh God, I have to get home!" Karl said. He was crying. They both were. The two of them started running down the hill. A black oily rain was falling, marking their faces and clothes with dark greasy splotches. When they got to the street below, they saw wreckage all around them. Houses were flattened or partly collapsed. Some of them were in flames. The boys' neighbourhood looked like a great big junkyard, with the broken planks and people's chairs and beds, stoves, and pots and pans, all lying around the ruined houses along with blackened fallen trees and telegraph poles. Things were twisted, broken, burnt. And there were people on the ground, grown-ups and children, covered with soot, some bleeding, some without their clothes on. Where were their clothes? Lauchie wanted to help them, but he had to see his family, his home.

"The Germans!" he heard someone shout. "There's more to come!"

Karl was from a German family himself; lots of Nova Scotians were, from their ancestors coming here many years ago. Karl didn't say a word, just turned and ran towards his own street, Veith Street. But Lauchie called out to anyone who would hear. "No! It was a fire; it was the burning ship!" But was it? With everything destroyed around him, and the thunder and the cloud and the raining down of hot things from the sky, could he even be sure of what he had seen? Had he really seen a ship on fire? A shipboard fire could not cause destruction like this. What had started the fire? *Were* the Germans bombarding the city? Halifax was a seaport, a garrison town. The navy was here, the army, and this was the harbour where the ships gathered before sailing out to the war in Europe. Halifax would be one of the enemy's first targets. Had the war come at last to North America?

But all Lauchie could think of now was home, his mother, his sister, his father at work at the drydock. He kept on running until he tripped over what looked like a stovepipe. Where had it come from? He looked around and upwards, and wished he hadn't. Dangling from a bent and broken telegraph pole was something long, burnt, and black with two small pointy things at the end of it. Lauchie lurched forward and threw up the contents of his stomach. What he had seen was somebody's arm hanging there. Three fingers missing. Who? Where did the . . . He did not want to know. He had to get home. He was running so fast he could barely catch his breath.

But when he got to Duffus Street, what he saw was flames, the flames devouring his own house. No! He ran towards it, calling out, "Mum! Heather!"

"There's nobody there, Lauchie!" It was one of his neighbours, standing alone beside his own ruined house.

"What? Did they —?"

And then he remembered. Thank the Lord, his mother had taken his sister to an early morning appointment with their doctor on Windsor Street. Windsor Street, Lauchie told himself, was a long way from the harbour. But what about his dad, down at the drydock? No, the men would have gone in somewhere safe, wouldn't they? And what about Karl? He'd be at his own house by now, if . . . If Lauchie's house had been destroyed, how could Karl's house still be standing? And what about Karl's mum and dad, his brothers? What was he seeing right now? And Lauchie's other friends at school. What about Mr. Finlay? Hélène and the others in the science club? Lauchie had seen the houses where everybody lived, kids from school, from church, families of the navy men. Could anybody survive their house crashing down? He doubled over and cried as he had not cried since he was a baby.

Mike Kavanagh

Mike's dad had already left for work on his ship, *Niobe*, by the time Mike finished his breakfast. His little sister, Ellie, was lucky; she'd been invited to stay overnight at their aunt's place on Gottingen Street because it was their cousin Deirdre O'Donnell's birthday. She turned six, same age as Ellie. Mike's younger brother, Patrick, was seven, and he had never stayed at anybody else's house and thought that would be fun. But they were having some fun of their own down in the cellar trying to build a toy barn out of wood scraps. Their mum had sent them down there after they'd heard the neighbours outside talking about a burning ship at one of the piers. Mike and Pat had wanted to run out and watch, but their mum distracted them with the idea of building a toy barn for Pat. So that's where they were. But when it came time for breakfast, she wanted them upstairs. "We'll be up in a minute," they kept saying. But they were keen on their building project, till their mum finally marched down the stairs to collect them. Patrick was boasting about the barn and the toy animals he hoped Santa Claus would bring him for Christmas.

Suddenly Mike was on his back on the concrete floor, his ears throbbing from the loudest boom of thunder he had ever heard. He put his hands up to cover his ears. He felt a sharp stab of pain in his left shoulder, which had landed on a rough piece of wood. He rolled over on his side, feeling the grit of the floor through his clothing, and saw his mother and brother lying a few feet away. His mum was on her back, staring up, her mouth open wide with no words coming out. Patrick was on his tummy, legs and arms spread out; his right leg was trapped under a fallen beam. He started to wail. Mike heard a strange rumbling, buzzing sound under the ground. It was as if thunder was down in the ground instead of up in the sky. He looked up to see cracks in the ceiling, and dust floating down into the cellar. He heard the cracking and crashing of things falling and breaking above them. Patrick's crying grew louder. Their mum stood up and seemed to be all right except she was gawking around as if she had no idea where she was. "Mother of Mercy, Mother of God," she was muttering, and she and Mike bent down and pushed the beam up off Patrick. Just as they did that, a cat came streaking in through the cellar window, which hardly had any glass in it. The cat landed on the floor and started tearing around in circles, screeching as it did.

"How are we going to get out?" Pat whimpered. "How can we get out?"

Mike turned in a circle, staring all around him at the broken beams of wood, the crumbling plaster, the tools fallen from their shelves. His mother stood, immobile, her gaze fixed on the window where the cat had come in.

Mike rushed to the window and peered out. "Oh, my God! The houses!" The other houses on the street were wrecked, battered down. His mum came up behind him. She cried out, "Ellie! Clare! Michael, we have to get out, find them! Help me clear out this window."

He picked his way through the debris to where his dad's tools had been shelved and found a hammer on the floor. He took it to the window and smashed the remaining shards of glass, clearing the edges as best he could with a rag. "Pat," he said, "you're going out first. Here, we'll lift you up. Stay right out there where we can see you." He helped his mum lift his sobbing little brother out through the window.

"Ow, my hand!" Patrick cried.

Patrick held up his right hand, and Mike saw blood seeping from a cut on the palm. "We'll fix you up, Pat. Mum, you go now."

"No, you, Michael."

He hoisted himself up and through the window, his left shoulder throbbing with pain, his hands stinging as they scraped across the tiny bits of glass in the window frame. Then he turned and assisted his mother as she pulled herself out.

He gripped his aching shoulder as he turned to look down the once-familiar street, and he was stunned by what he saw: it looked like a war zone, a street bombed by a Zeppelin. Many of the houses had been blown down; others had only a wall or two left standing. Where some houses had been, there were only piles of beams and boards and shingles. Bright orange flames shot up from some of the battered houses. The smell of smoke was overpowering. And up in the sky, an awesome and terrible sight: a huge billowing cloud rose as high as Mike could see, hovering over the harbour. A black shower of hot things was falling from the sky, and cries of pain echoed through the wreckage. Men, women, girls, and boys, their clothes and faces covered with soot, were standing around the ruins of their homes. Some people ran back into the ruins, screaming the name of a daughter, a son, a grandmother who had not emerged from the wreckage. Mike didn't know how long he stood there, stock-still, his mother and brother at his side. He had no idea what to do.

He was jolted by the sound of Clare's voice. His older sister. She was shouting to someone or to everyone. "The ceiling caved in at school! The floors fell down! Collapsed!"

Had Michael heard her right? Saint Joe's was wrecked too?

Then Clare was at her family's side, panting for breath. "Run!" she urged them. But where? There was nothing left intact, no place to find shelter.

"Clare," Mike started to say, when she burst out, "The school, the windows! Pieces of glass like arrows came flying in at us! They went into Colleen's face and her throat, and there was blood pouring out. Some of the girls are *dead*!"

The girls at school! What about Mary Catherine? Was she at school? Was she one of the girls who . . . No, he couldn't let his mind go there. Maybe she was late, as she often was. Please God, let her be safe! But the other girls . . .

"We couldn't stay in there," Clare said. "'We're under attack!' That's what Sister said. 'The Germans are here!' Sister stayed, tried to help Colleen, but she told us we had to get out."

"Atta-attack!" their mother stammered. "Your father! Did they attack his ship?! Oh, please, no!"

From all the way across the ocean, the Germans had actually arrived and bombed Halifax! The city was in the war! Mike had to know, had to find out right now, that Ellie and Dad had not been . . . not been hurt.

"Thank God," their mum said, "that at least you are all right, Clare! Those poor girls at the school, their families . . . Now, we must go to the O'Donnells to get Ellie! Pray that the O'Donnells' house —"

Clare stared at her, tried to speak, but nothing came out.

Mum told the boys, "You go to Uncle Frank's!" That was another relative, Dad's brother. He lived up at the top of their street, Young Street. "You two go there now and stay inside the house! Clare, you're coming with me."

"But, Mum," Mike said, trying to keep his voice from quivering, "maybe his house is wrecked too!"

But his mum just grabbed Clare's hand and pulled her, and they started running. Mike and Pat started up the hill after them.

Patrick was gawking at all the destruction. Then he let out a yelp and pointed at something lying on the ground. It was a big dog, burnt to a crisp, and its head was . . . just bare bone, a skull with its huge teeth bared. Mike grabbed Pat's hand and pulled him along. Behind them, Mike heard someone wailing, keening. He turned around. He saw a woman, face and clothes blackened from the falling oily soot, holding a child in her arms; two small legs dangled down, not moving.

"Pat, don't look! Keep your eyes straight ahead. We have to get up the hill."

Amazingly, Uncle Frank and Aunt Mary's house, at the top of the street, was still standing. Their house and those of their closest neighbours had suffered very little damage. Mike said, "Thank Christ!"

Frank was out in his front yard when the boys arrived. He came running and threw his arms around them. "Thank God in Heaven you lads are . . . You're bleeding, both of you. Come inside and we'll patch up your hands."

"It'll be all right, Uncle Frank. It's just from the glass in the window."

"And Mary will try to wipe that stuff off your clothes. All that black rain falling on you!"

And he asked about the family, and Mike told them about their house. And told them Ellie was at the O'Donnells'.

"Ah, they're a few blocks north of us," and he pointed in that direction. "So maybe . . . maybe their house . . . Come on inside."

They followed him in and saw their aunt standing by the living room window in tears. Frank walked over to her, whispered something in her ear, and she turned to the boys and said, "Your house?"

"It's crashed down into the cellar!" Mike said. "Houses at our end of the street are wrecked or badly hit. Did everything get bombed? Are the Germans really here?"

Frank shook his head. "No, it wasn't an attack. It was a ship on fire. A couple of men ran by here; I called out to them, and they told me the ship blew up. An explosion down on Pier Six. The few houses right along here were protected by Needham Hill."

"But you're up the same street as us. How come our places weren't protected?"

Frank put his hand on Mike's shoulder. "Geography, Mike. It's as simple as that. You and your family will move in here with us. Now, you boys are to stay inside. No going out. I'm heading out to see the damage, find out what's going on, see if I can be of any help." There was a bit more conversation, and then Frank got ready and left the house.

He worked in the late afternoons and evenings in one of the taverns downtown, so he would be able to help people for much of the day. Aunt Mary told them they were welcome and could stay as long as they needed to. Frank and Mary only had one son, and he was grown up and living in Montreal, so there was room. Mike and Patrick, who knew their manners, said, "Thank you very much, Auntie Mary."

Pat whimpered when their aunt bandaged his hand, and then she gave the boys a soapy cloth to wipe their faces. Of course, Mike and Patrick were desperate to go outside and walk around and see what all had happened to their neighbourhood. They didn't want to be disobedient, though, so they looked at some books Auntie Mary had brought out for them. But after they'd been there a while, Mary stuffed a bunch of white cloths in a bag and said she was going out to see if she could help anyone. She told the boys to stay inside. Then she left the house. The brothers looked at each other, waited for a couple of minutes, then made for the door. Mike opened it, peered about, and said, "Be quiet, Pat, and we'll slip out for a bit."

They tiptoed out of the house. Patrick said, "I want to go home!"

But they had no home.

"We have to go see Mum and Clare and Ellie!"

He was right; they had to. But they couldn't, because their mum had told them to stay inside Frank and Mary's house; she hadn't brought them with her all the way up Gottingen Street to the O'Donnells'.

But if they sneaked out for a short time, she wouldn't know. So they headed out to stare at what remained of their house. Two walls were still upright but sheared off near the top, and the roof had caved in. Mike knew that the first floor had crashed down over the cellar, and he and his mum and brother were damned lucky to have escaped. Some other houses were smoking, some in flames. At least the remaining wood of the Kavanagh house had not caught on fire.

Mike looked over to the place next door, where all the girls had lived. The *brothel*. The top storey of that house had collapsed into the first, which also had a lot of damage: walls were bent and broken, the windows open to the air, glass all gone. Where were the girls? There was no sign or sound coming from there, and nobody out in the back or front yard. He walked over and called out, "Hello? Hello? Anybody in there?" Not a sound in reply. He knew there was nothing he and a younger brother could do there.

Where Mike wanted to go now was Russell Street, to see Mary Catherine Malone's house. So he and Patrick made the short walk down the hill to Albert Street. And the two boys gasped at once. There were fish lying in what was left of the road and in the rubble of the houses, and the boys saw part of the wooden bow of a boat. Patrick started to speak, but no words came. They turned right and walked to the corner of Russell Street, looked around them. Except there was no Russell Street, not if you were looking for a street in a city, with houses and trees on it. Nearly every house had been knocked down, reduced to a pile of rubble. A few had only a couple of walls still standing, but everything else about them had been destroyed. Much of what was left was ablaze. People were walking around like — what was the word? — spectres, blackened and haunted. This was a street where some of his friends — where Mary Catherine Malone — had been living up until this morning. He stared at the remains of the Malones' house. Had Mary Catherine been inside? Or had she already arrived at school? The school where Clare had seen the dead bodies of some of the girls. There was no way Mike could claw his way into that pile of smoking wreckage to search for . . . He shouted, "Mary Cath! Mary Cath!" His voice broke on the words. There was no answer.

He grabbed Pat's hand, and they walked up the hill, stumbling through the obstacle course that had been Russell Street. Mike's foot hit something, and he stopped. It was a young girl's dark blue woollen coat, her leggings and boots. Why did she leave her clothes? And then the truth hit him like a bolt to his heart: it wasn't only clothes; it was a girl without her head. The head wasn't there, wasn't anywhere. Who was she, somebody he knew? Lots of girls had blue coats like that. He didn't know; he couldn't think about it. He turned to his little brother and distracted him, pointed to the buildings ahead of them on their route, so he wouldn't see.

Ahead of them, near the top of the hill between Russell and Kaye Streets, was what remained of the convent, the school, and the church.

The convent's walls were broken and bulging out. There beside it was Saint Joe's, Mike and Patrick's school, with the roof gaping open and parts of the walls crumbling and the windows all blown out. Where some girls had died. The girls had their classes in the mornings, and the boys in the afternoons, because the boys' regular school had burned down last year, and the new one wasn't finished yet. Most of the kids lived in the neighbourhood. Were other streets flattened like these ones? Then he was gaping at his church, Saint Joseph's, its roof gone and the bare walls standing up with the pointy-topped windows empty of their glass. It looked like the ghostly places in the stories his mother liked to read; she called them gothic stories, and that always sounded like a scary word to Mike. That's what the church looked like now: gothic.

Mike's attention was caught by a sudden racket behind him. A group of people were running towards them. "Run! Run!" they were crying out. "The magazine's on fire; it's going to blow up!" Wellington Barracks was the big military base between Russell and North Streets, and Mike knew that the magazine was where the munitions were stored.

An old man stumbled towards them from Gottingen Street. His face was dark from the greasy black stuff that had been raining down from the sky, and all he had on were his underpants and one shoe. "What happened?" he called out in a croaky voice. "A bomb? They'll attack again! We'll all be killed!"

One of the women coming up the hill shouted, "Ship blew up. Caught fire, blew up! And the magazine's going to blow! It's on fire! Run!"

Mike grabbed his brother and pulled him along till they were back at his uncle and aunt's house. "Come on, Pat! Down the cellar!" They raced down the stairs and curled up under Frank's big work table. And there they waited, in terror, hoping and praying that all those munitions at the barracks would not explode.

CHAPTER IV

OCTOBER 1993

Normie

O ur play was brilliant! We only had a stage in the school auditorium so we couldn't show all that happened. But the pictures Father Burke projected above the stage showed the huge cloud over the harbour and the wrecked houses and buildings. Me and Kim and Richard had gone back to our house on Young Street in the spring to dig deep into the garden. We didn't find much, only some pieces of broken dishes. But Mrs. Stewart gave us a couple of things her family had found years ago: a silver fork and the head of a toy horse, and we put those on a table on the stage. And Dad had made photocopies of Mike and Lauchie's notes, so we went over to Miss Kavanagh's and gave her the original notes back and thanked her again.

I played the part of a mum — it was a true story, like everything else in the play — a mum who went out to the corner of her street to watch the ship on fire and then got buried in rubble when it exploded.

I had a little pillow underneath my dress, over my belly, to show that she was expecting a baby at the time. She was all banged up, cut and bruised, and had a broken hip. She lay there all day and night in pain and under all that stuff, terrified for her family back in the house. Ten kids and their dad. It wasn't till the next day that a man pulled all the junk off her, and she survived. But she found out that her husband and all ten of her kids had been killed in their house when everything blew up! It sounds like a made-up story, but it did happen! I didn't have to do any *acting* when I played the scene where the mum found out about all her family being killed. I was crying so hard I could hardly speak my lines. She gave birth to her little baby boy a few months after the explosion.

We had the littlest kids in the school bundled up in wool coats, with fake cuts painted on their faces, and we had them wandering around trying to find their parents. One of the pictures projected above the stage was of people in hospital beds with bandages on them. And another picture showed a little girl, just under two years old, sitting up in a bed. Her name was Annie, and she had been buried in the wreck — the rubble — of her apartment building for more than twenty-four hours before a soldier found her. The picture showed her in the bed with a bandage around her head and she was so sweet, everybody in the audience went, "Awww." The soldier found her under the stove, and the warm ashes in a thing called the ashpan had kept her warm. She was given the nickname Ashpan Annie! Thank God, Annie was one of the little kids who survived! But her mum and brother were killed, and her dad was overseas fighting in the war.

The explosion left a lot of kids orphans. We had bigger kids playing parents, desperately looking through the wrecked houses to find their children. Some people were never, ever found.

We had read in Mike and Lauchie's notes about a kitty named Tabby, and there was an argument at the house where all those girls had lived. I remembered the name I'd learned for a place like that: a brothel. The notes said one of the girls was arguing with "the guy with the Case" so we had him carrying a briefcase, like the ones Mum and Dad used for work. The girl was the owner of Tabby the cat, and she wanted him back, and she was hollering at a man who said she couldn't have him back. Fighting over a cat! But I remembered Daddy telling Mum one night that he had to work for somebody who was getting divorced, and they were fighting about who would get the coffee maker! Anyway, in the play, we got a fluffy little stuffed toy, a striped kitty cat, and put him in a basket and made a scene out of the argument. But the good thing was: the man took the kitty away, so it didn't get killed in the explosion!

The audience loved what we did; they gave us a standing ovation that went on and on, and we all came out and bowed. And I was really happy about that, even though I had tears in my eyes. I wasn't sure why I was crying. Important people came to see us: the mayor, the member of parliament for Halifax, and some other politicians. Our play — well, the explosion — was a big deal! I tried to make it look as if I was adjusting my glasses when I wiped my tears away, so everybody wouldn't know I'd been crying.

The mayor, Margaret Ross, had a role in the play, at the end of it. She was in it because she's the mayor of Halifax, and this was a Halifax tragedy, but also because her own grandfather's house was wrecked in the explosion and two people were killed in the house. Mayor Ross didn't have to come to our practices, because she had a paper with her lines all written out for her. At the end of the play, she stood on the stage with her gold necklace on, her "chain of office." It had big glitzy medallions on it. She said that Nova Scotia was used to responding to disasters. In 1873, it was the sinking of the SS *Atlantic* just off the coast. In 1912, ships set out from Halifax to find the *Titanic*, and over two hundred bodies were brought back to the city. A hundred and fifty were buried here. Then, less than six years later, we had the explosion.

She gave everybody some information about the blow-up. About the two ships that collided: the *Imo*, a ship full of relief supplies for Belgium, and the munitions ship *Mont Blanc*. She told the audience, "The *Mont Blanc* was loaded with high explosives, and the collision caused it to catch fire. It was about to become the most powerful bomb the world had ever known. When it detonated, the air temperature was nearly five thousand degrees Celsius, nearly as hot as the surface of the sun! No wonder the ship was vaporized in an instant. The shockwave flew through the bedrock under Halifax at around twenty-three times the speed of sound. And then there was a giant wave that came several blocks up on the land. As a result of the disaster, nearly two thousand people were killed, dozens were left completely blind, and more than two hundred survivors had an eye removed. Nine thousand people had other injuries, some of them terrible. There were thousands of people left homeless. Thank God, the munitions at Wellington Barracks did not explode and cause even more destruction. But there was a snowstorm the day after, a blizzard. It was the worst time for all that snow; the ruins were buried in snowdrifts, and relief trains were stopped or slowed down. It made it extremely difficult to help people."

And then the mayor thanked the other Canadian cities, towns, and provinces that helped our city out. She thanked the United States and other countries as well, and she told about the Christmas tree that Nova Scotia sends to Boston every year to thank them for their help. And she said a special thanks to the doctors and nurses who saw such terrible injuries as they worked long, long hours to help the people who survived.

The mayor didn't say anything about some of the bad things people did after the explosion, but me and Richard and Kim knew about them because of Mike and Lauchie's notes. There was an organization called the Halifax Relief Commission, set up to deal with all the problems. They gave out millions of dollars in payments to fix up damaged properties or replace the ones that had been destroyed. There were also courts set up to pay people for things they had lost, and there were thousands of those claims. Most people were honest, but there were some who made up stories to get more money, even though they hadn't lost as much stuff as they claimed. This was *fraud*, and they could be punished by the courts for that. There were other bad people, too, people who looted things — went into places, the wreckage of houses, and took money and jewellery and other things for themselves. Some guys even went into the morgue where all the dead people were, pretending that they were searching for members of their families. But they weren't; they were there to steal things off the dead bodies! There were also some nasty landlords who raised the rents their tenants had to pay, even if the tenants were poor; some landlords gave their tenants less space to live in and charged them more anyway. One of the members of the Relief Commission called them "vampires"! Most people were good, even after this disaster, but there are always a few bad guys anywhere.

Mrs. Graham, the director of the play, picked me to make the announcement of act two, which we would be putting on in December. I was glad we had a lot of time between the acts, because this way we could fit in more stuff from Mike and Lauchie's notes. Making an announcement was different from being in a costume and playing the part of a mother in 1917. This was me, myself, having to make a speech in public!

I took a big long breath. It was hard to see the audience because of the bright lights, but that was okay. "Thank you for coming to see *Devastated Area*. But this was only act one! You met Mike Kavanagh and Lauchie MacIntyre here tonight. Well, they'll be back in act two." I told the audience, "Act two will show what it was like for people living in the wrecked parts of our city. And it will be a bit of a *mystery* story. How come that bad guy with the funny name didn't get *blocked* from looting people's things out of the wrecked houses? Did he steal rings off the fingers of the dead people too?! And there's a mystery about that house next door to Mike's. Maybe it wasn't only the ladies who did their work there and made money out of that house; did somebody else get in on the activities there? Did somebody buy the house right out from under those ladies and make them pay him rent? And what about a *body* being taken away from that house in a *limousine*?" Mike Kavanagh's notes gave the name of the car. A Case Limousine. I'd never heard of a car like that. When Mike wrote about a "Case," I thought he meant a briefcase, so that's what we put in Act One. But it was a type of car they had back in the old days, so I said it. "A Case Limousine, very fancy! Was that the body of somebody killed in the blast? Or was there another *cause of death*?! Stay tuned!"

I'm not allowed to walk around by myself when it's dark. I'm supposed to have somebody with me or call Mum or Dad for a drive. And it gets dark early at this time of the year, this being the nineteenth of October. It was dark when we finished practising our choir music. But my house on Dresden Row isn't far from the school, only a few blocks, so I started out. I love walking around in the fall because of all the beautiful yellow and orange and red leaves on the trees. I looked down and saw a couple of perfect maple leafs — *leaves*, I mean; the Maple Leafs are the hockey team! — so I picked them up and tucked them into my schoolbag. I turned out of Byrne Street and started walking along Morris. Nobody was around to hear me, so I started practising "Jesu, rex admirabilis" by Palestrina. I love Palestrina's music!

But what was that? Footsteps? I whirled around and I saw a man a little ways behind me. He turned his head to the side and looked away. He had a heavy jacket on and his hood up and a ball cap. And he had a scarf pulled up on this face. But why wouldn't he? It was cold out. I told myself not to be scared. Why wouldn't somebody else be out on Morris Street? He was walking at the same speed as me. I started walking faster, and I could hear that he was walking faster too! A creepy man following me! Maybe a criminal! I didn't know whether to yell, but was there anybody else around who would hear me? I got to Barrington Street and I had a red light, but I ran across anyway. There weren't any cars, and I didn't see any people around to help me. And if the cops came along and caught me crossing against the light, I'd tell them about the guy. Then I heard footsteps again, and they were coming fast. Was it two men now?! I almost hollered then, but I turned and looked, and it was Richard running across the street and waving to me. Thank God! While I was looking at Richard, that man walked past me and turned in at one of the buildings at the engineering school. Good thing I hadn't made a racket, if it was just a guy studying to be an engineer. Or it might even have been a professor!

"Are you all right, Normie?" Richard asked.

"I thought . . ."

"You thought what?"

"You're going to laugh. I thought somebody was following me, but he just went in there." I pointed to the college.

"Went into the Technical College? TUNS, they call it now."

"Yeah, in there."

"What did he look like?"

"Too dark to see his face, and he had a scarf. But never mind that. I was just spooked walking alone after the sun goes down, because I'm not allowed to."

"You probably shouldn't. Anyway, I wanted to catch up to give you this. I brought it to school and then forgot about it in my locker." He held out a book. "It's really good, all about the explosion." I looked at it. It was called *Worse Than War* by Pauline Murphy Sutow. The cover showed a whole bunch of wrecked houses in the snow. "You're going to like it. Full of great info, and a few things we can add to our script for act two."

"Wow! Thanks."

"I'll get it back from you sometime, but there's no hurry. Now, I'll walk you the rest of the way home."

So we started walking, and I peeked in between some of the engineering school buildings but didn't see that man. Well, he wouldn't be standing outside. He'd be in there working. Or maybe hiding.

ço

I didn't think about the man again until two days later, when something had me scared for sure, me and Richard. Our school's secretary, Mrs. Surette, handed me an envelope that she found slipped under the door when she arrived at work. The envelope with my name on it was from Sears, the big department store. I never got a letter from them before. Did they send out ads to people in envelopes? At school? I thanked Mrs. Surette and went to my locker. I got my stuff ready for my first class, and then I opened the envelope. Oh, God! Inside was one piece of paper, and there was a message typed on it: "Do not perform any more of that play about the Halifax Explosion. Or the lawyers will take you to court. If I don't see an announcement that the play is cancelled, you will be sorry."

I showed it to Kim, and her eyes opened up wide because she was scared too. "What are we going to do?"

"I don't know! I'm going to show Richard at recess time."

I could hardly concentrate on my schoolwork. When the bell rang for recess, I went over to the grade eight class and waited for Richard. When he came out of the classroom, I waved the envelope at him and said, "We have to go outside, so I can show you this." But it turned out that Richard had got one too. Same kind of envelope and that same scary message.

Me and him went off by ourselves in the schoolyard so we could talk about what happened and what to do. "I just thought of something," Richard said. "Somebody who might want to stop our play. Remember how pissed off Brandon was when he didn't get a part in the play?" Brandon was a boy in Richard's class. Sometimes he was mean. Richard told me one time that Brandon made fun of him for hanging around with me and Kim because we're only in grade six. And Richard said something like, "Hey, I can't help it if younger women think I'm cool!" Now, Richard said, "And his dad has a new computer at home, so he could have typed the letters on that."

I looked at Richard. "I know he's jealous about not being in the play, but would he be mean enough to do this? Write these messages and put them in normal envelopes from the store so we'd be sure to open them?"

"I should grab hold of him and tell him we know!"

"No, don't do that. Dad always tells me about bad guys and the stories they make up to pretend they didn't do it, whatever it was. That's what Brandon will do, if it was him that sent them."

Richard said he was going to talk to him anyway. "But we have to be careful. If we tell Burke, he might go ahead and cancel it."

"I don't know, Richard. Father Burke's not a scaredy-cat or anything like that."

"I know, I know. And now that I think of it, maybe we should tell him. He might get together with his old man, and they might have one of those machine guns from their old rebel days. What are they called? Thompsons? And they'll find the guy who wrote the threatening notes, and they'll say, 'Either act two of our play or your brains are gonna be on that stage December the ninth!'"

I started laughing. "Richard, that was *The Godfather*, not the Irish guys! We have the video of it at home, and my dad is always quoting lines from it."

"Yeah, I know. Best movie ever. But you can be sure the Burkes would use some other scary line to get rid of the guy and make sure nobody tries to cancel our play."

"No, don't tell him, because he might tell our parents. Well, mine, because they are friends. If our parents find out, they'll get worried and they might make us cancel it. But I really am kind of scared about it. Why would somebody write something like that? Our story is about the explosion, and that was back in 1917. Who would care about that now?"

That's when Richard put on another one of his funny accents, this time German. "There was more to this than you understand, you foolish little Fräulein. Ve haff ways of stopping you from acting!"

I laughed again, but then I said, "Maybe somebody from Germany is still mad about people back then thinking the Germans did it."

"No, I have a suspect a little closer to us than Germany."

When I saw Richard again after school, he said, "I asked Brandon. 'Did you send me a letter?'

"And he said, 'What kind of a letter?'

"'Any kind,' I said.

"And Brandon said, 'If I wanted to talk to you, Robertson, I'd lean over from my desk and talk to you. But I don't.' Then he asked, 'What kind of a note are you talking about? A nasty note telling you where to go? Answers to the French exam? Or what?'

"I didn't want to tell him. He told me to piss off, and he walked away. I have to say, Normie, I don't think he sent the letters. He seemed like his regular self, not somebody who'd been caught doing something sneaky."

Then I confessed something to Richard. I said I thought I should tell my mum and dad after all. Richard said, "Okay, if you think you should. I'm not telling mine. My old man hears the word 'lawyers'? He'll come to the school and tear down the set himself!"

Everybody knew that Richard's dad was an arsehole, but I didn't say that. I just said, "I'll let you know what they say." He asked me if I wanted him to walk home with me, but it was still light out so I thanked him and said he didn't have to.

Of course, I was thinking that somebody had been following me a couple of days before. But that was probably my imagination playing tricks on me. Mum and Dad said that happened to me sometimes. But that's not always a bad thing: my imagination was part of how I got the idea for the play and wrote a lot of it myself. That was the good thing about my imagination!

℘

That night, we were going to a party, and it put those scary events out of my mind for a while. A "cast party," the grown-ups were calling it, even though Mum said cast parties are usually right after the play is over. We couldn't have it then because it would have been too late a night for us. And City Hall wasn't available that night anyway. Yes, the party was in Halifax City Hall! The mayor invited us all. So I was glad we waited and had it there. City Hall is a cool old stone building with peaks on the roof, like they'd have on a castle, and a big tower in the middle. Even though it is downtown, it had windows broken and wood splintered in the explosion. The tower has a clock and it is always set at 9:04:35. Guess why? The old City Hall clock froze that way, exactly when the explosion happened!

This was another one of those nights when the Toronto Blue Jays were playing. They were in the World Series, and they had already won three games (and lost one) against the other team, from Philadelphia. I wondered if Daddy was wishing he didn't have to go to the party so he could stay home and see the game. But he said, "We'll probably be home in time to see it. But you know what? I wouldn't miss my daughter's first cast party even if I was invited onto the field to pitch to Lenny Dykstra." (I had to ask him how to spell the guy's name, but it was great, Daddy saying that!)

Me and Richard Robertson made an agreement before we went: we wouldn't tell anybody, even our own parents, about the scary letters until after the party. We didn't want to spoil it. So, anyway, we all trooped over to City Hall. The room where we had the party had fancy chandeliers in the ceiling, the way they had at Government House, where Mr. Runcey lives. There was plenty of space at City Hall for the kids from the school and their parents and the teachers. And there were a few grandparents like my grandma Evelyn, Dad's mum. Dad introduced her to Father Burke and his father, Declan. Richard Robertson came up to us then, and I said, "Mr. Burke, this is Richard Robertson. He's the funniest guy in our school!"

"You're good craic, are you, Richard?"

"That's what your son says about me, Mr. Burke. But he keeps me in line. What do you call him? He's a priest but he's your son, so you can't call him 'Father,' eh?"

"I call him Dia Beag."

"Okay, jee-ah b'yahg, that's what I'll call him, whatever it means!" said Richard.

"I wouldn't recommend it."

I found out later it means "Little God"! When we had moved away from them, Richard said something about Father Burke and his dad. This was the first time he'd seen Declan, but he had heard all about him from me over the last couple of years. And this is what Richard said: "Maybe we should have replaced Oppenheimer in the play. Replaced him with the Burkes: 'Confidential sources say the Halifax Explosion was studied in detail by the family of exiled Irish priest Brennan Burke and his Irish republican father, Declan, to see if they could blow something up in Belfast as good as this!'"

Oh my God! If Father Burke or his father heard that . . . I looked over, and they were talking to my grandmother, so I guess we didn't get caught.

The mayor was going around the room, congratulating all of us who were involved with the play. She said it was excellent, and she'd be sure to see act two.

And then Richard was on the other side of the room and he called over to me and Kim, "Come here, you guys. There's somebody here for you to meet."

Me and Kim walked over to where Richard was talking to a man who looked like somebody's nice friendly grandfather. "Mr. Davidson, this is Normie Collins and Kim Kennedy. They wrote the play along with me."

Mr. Davidson said, "Hello, Normie and Kim. You can call me Eric."

"Really?" Kim burst out and then she turned red. It was just that you usually didn't call old people by their first name.

"Really. You kids did a wonderful job with your play. I greatly enjoyed it. I didn't see it," and then he pointed to his eyes, "but I heard every word."

Richard spoke up then. "Mr. Davidson — Eric — was two years old when the explosion happened, and he —" Richard stopped speaking. It wasn't often that he ran out of things to say or was too shy to say them.

Eric said, "Like so many other people, grown-ups and children, I was looking at the burning ship. I was looking out the window of my house and, well, there was the blast and the glass came in, and this is what happened."

"Oh, Mr. Davidson, Eric, I am so sorry about what happened to you! I can't imagine . . ." Then I stopped. Was I going to say *I* couldn't imagine living without my eyesight, because I was so *lucky*? Thank God, I didn't come out and say that.

"It's all right, Normie. I've been able to enjoy a very full life. I married and had three children. My daughter Marilyn is here tonight. And I was able to work and keep the family going. I'm grateful for the life I've had. Unlike the nearly two thousand people whose lives were extinguished that day."

Richard said, "When he says he was able to work, it wasn't just any old job. He worked as a car mechanic, got his official licence as a mechanic. And in his off hours, he fixed and restored antique cars. He could tell what kind of car it was and how the engine was working, just by the sound. And wait till you hear this! He is known as the 'Rolls-Royce Man'! He was an expert at fixing Rolls-Royces and he owned three of them himself!"

Me and Richard and Kim kept talking to Eric until other people came and wanted him to talk to them, so we said goodbye, and Richard said he'd stop by Eric's house whenever he, Richard, bought his first Rolls-Royce. Eric laughed and said, "You do that. You'll be most welcome."

A few minutes later, Mayor Ross was standing just behind Richard. And then Richard's father came over and he nearly knocked Richard off his feet trying to get close to the mayor. It's not a nice thing to say, but I don't like Richard's dad. He and Mrs. Robertson made Richard start going to a "personal coach" to make sure he "becomes one of life's success stories." Richard was always telling me about it, making fun of the coach. He told the coach that when he got old enough, he was going to run away to Newfoundland and join up with CODCO. They are a comedy group on TV, and they are so funny! Mr. Robertson wouldn't like that. He's snobby and he wants everybody to know he's rich, a big important businessman. And that's exactly what he started saying to the mayor. "Good to see you again, Your Worship." *Your Worship*, as if she was God!

"Ah, good evening, Murdoch."

"As you may have heard, I am now chief executive officer of . . ." whatever his company was. I looked over at Richard and he was rolling his eyes. He said, "Old Murdie worshipping at the mayor's feet! He'd rather do that than talk to you and me. He wasn't even interested in coming to our play. There was some fancy black-tie dinner he wanted to go to instead, but Mum talked him into 'supporting our son.' I heard them yakking about it in the kitchen."

Then Old Murdie found somebody else to gab with. A man came over to him, and Mr. Robertson kind of jerked his head in the direction of the mayor and said in a quiet voice, "Any joy?" The other man said, "Not yet. But it has to happen. Has to!" The man was big and tall and had longish grey hair pushed back over his forehead and ears. His forehead was wide and he had bushy-looking black eyebrows. I noticed a ring he had on; it looked like a pair of tweezers going down and something else in a wide *V* going up under it. And Mr. Robertson had the same ring. They must have gone to the same school.

Richard's mother walked up to them then and said to the other guy, "Good evening, Lorne."

He kind of bowed his head and said, "Lois."

"Did you see the children's play?"

The man said, "Ah, the play. No. No, I didn't."

"Oh, I thought I saw you there. I must have been mistaken."

"Must have been."

What was he doing at the party then, the *cast* party, if he had not gone to see the play? Maybe he came to City Hall just so he could look important!

Then I heard a lady burst out laughing, and I turned around. "Richard, look! Mr. Burke has got my grandmother laughing."

"I wish I could hear whatever kind of jokes *Oul Dec* would tell to somebody's grandmother!"

"Yeah, I'd like to hear them too." I watched them chatting away to one another. "He's being so polite to her, and she's from the English side of our family. Collins is an Irish name but her name before she got married to my grandfather was Chamberley. Her mum and dad came to Halifax from England before she was born."

"You're right. Oul Dec *is* being polite. I guess he doesn't think all English people are enemies. And look at the way she's looking at him. As if she thinks he's a handsome old divil!"

"Richard, you are bad!" Bad in a funny way, not evil.

Another old lady walked over then and said something to Grandma Evelyn, and Mr. Burke kind of bowed his head and went back to stand with Father Burke. And the mayor herself was looking at me and smiling, and she started coming towards me. I told myself not to be shy. She said, "Miss Collins, I'm looking forward to act two of *Devastated Area*." She leaned in towards me and said, "I cancelled a meeting scheduled for that night so that I can attend."

"Oh, wow, that's great! Thank you, Mrs. Ross, I mean Mayor, or . . ."

She wasn't the least bit mad about me not knowing what name to use for her. She just smiled and patted me on the arm.

Then Mr. Robertson came marching towards her. He caught up to her, and I moved away, but I could hear him. This time he was blabbing on about the Queen. He was telling the mayor about going to Ottawa to see Queen Elizabeth when she visited Canada last year. And then he held his glass of wine up high, and he said, "Shall I propose a toast to Her Majesty?" He didn't wait for her answer, just held his glass of wine up higher and said, "The Queen!"

I glanced over at Mum and she looked as if she was going to crack up laughing. She was staring across the room, so I looked over there. And you should have seen the face on Mr. Burke! Richard saw him, too, and he put on Father Burke's voice and said, "Will yeh look at yer man?! The face on Declan Burke! He looks as if he just took a torpedo up the rear end!" I couldn't help but laugh. Some of the people in the room raised their glasses and said, "The Queen!" The Burkes didn't.

Richard said, "I bet that's the only time the Burkes *didn't* raise a glass!"

So it was a fun night. I was able to forget for a while that somebody was trying to scare us off from the very thing we were celebrating.

Monty

When they got home, Monty turned on the television to watch Toronto play Philadelphia. Game Five of the World Series. But baseball was the last thing on his mind. He was doing his best to stay calm after hearing about the disturbing messages that had been delivered to their daughter and her friend. Normie had broken the news to them when they were in the car on the way home from City Hall.

"If there really was something to this," he said to Maura, "the warning would have come to Brennan or some other person in authority. It wouldn't have been slipped under the door for two of the students." He spoke quietly. Normie had gone upstairs to do her lessons, supposedly. She might be doing her schoolwork up there. Or she might be listening, as she sometimes did, at the floor register outside her room. She thought her parents didn't know, and for their part, they had never let on.

"If some sort of legal proceeding is being threatened in connection with the play," Monty said, "we'd be seeing a lawyer's letter setting out the reasons for the complaint, identifying the cause of action. Not this." He waved the paper at Maura.

"You're right. Imagine, something like that being sent to two young kids at school! So, is this from somebody who was sitting in the auditorium with the rest of us, watching the play? Or maybe somebody who read about it in the paper, or saw the story on television?"

The play had been covered in the local papers, and there were clips from it on the CTV regional news. The kids had been delighted with the coverage, but had the publicity now given rise to these threats?

"Wait till Brennan hears this!" Maura said. Normie had told them that she and Richard hadn't shown the letters to Father Burke, afraid they had screwed up somehow and would be in trouble.

"Well, Brennan is going to hear about it now. I'll give him a call."

Monty went to the phone and made the call, told Brennan what Normie had reported.

"What the hell?" Brennan sounded ready to bring down the wrath of God on whoever had threatened his students. "I can't have our students at risk, not even a risk of a risk!"

"I know, Brennan. Hire a security guard, maybe?"

"I'll be the security guard, and I'll *secure* that fucker if he shows up at my school with another threatening note."

"You'll keep a close watch on things, Brennan, but don't take matters into your own hands in any literal way. Call me, or call the police."

A minute or so later, Monty heard the pitter-patter of little feet descending the stairs. "Hi Dad, hi Mum."

"How's it going, sweetheart?" Maura asked. "Lessons done?"

"Almost." Their daughter looked from one to the other of them with her hazel eyes wide open. "I just remembered something."

"Oh? What's that, darlin'?" her mother asked.

"On Tuesday, when I was walking home from school, there was this guy. And I thought he was following me!"

What? Monty told himself not to react. He knew Maura would be doing the same.

"Maybe it was just my imagination. I've been using my imagination a lot lately! Writing the play and all that." Monty and Maura waited for the rest. "But I came out of school and went down Byrne Street and then to Morris, and then there was a guy behind me all the way along Morris Street. And I had my schoolbag and it was heavy, so I wasn't walking fast. And you know how men and big guys walk; they walk fast. So, why didn't he pass me instead of staying behind a slow kid with a heavy schoolbag? But when I did finally speed up, he did too."

There was a delicate balance to be maintained here: Monty had to take her story seriously but at the same time be reassuring. "Did you turn and look at him?"

"Yeah. But his face was turned away, not towards me."

"What did he look like, Normie, from what you could see?"

"I couldn't tell except that he was tall. Well, taller than me. But I'm not very tall, eh? He had on a big jacket with a hood and a ball cap, and a scarf up over most of his face. So I couldn't see what he looked like. I thought maybe it was a disguise! But I had heavy clothes on, too, because it was cold out."

"How long did he . . . How long was he behind you?"

"He went in by the engineering college when Richard came."

"Richard came?"

"Yeah, I crossed Barrington Street against the Don't Walk sign! And then I heard footsteps coming quick, quick, quick! And I was scared that the guy was running after me. But it was Richard, and he crossed the street, too, and he gave me a really good book about the explosion. And the bad guy walked in between the buildings of the engineering school. So maybe he wasn't dangerous, just a guy studying to be an engineer."

"Maybe so, darlin'," Maura said. "But, still, we'll walk you to school and come and get you after. Don't walk by yourself, just in case this was a guy with . . ." Monty could almost see her searching for the right word. "A guy with mischief on his mind! Let's go upstairs, Normie. I'd love to see that book Richard gave you."

As soon as they were gone, Monty got on the phone again. Father Brennan Burke reacted with a string of words that would never be heard during the sacred liturgy, perhaps not even on the dark side of the confession box. He would not be cancelling classes at the school, but all doors would be locked. He would not submit to threats and cancel the play, but he would be keeping a close watch on things around the school, and he would consider hiring a security firm on the night of act two of the play. He would contact the parents of all the students and obtain a commitment that their children would not be left to walk alone to school or home afterwards.

Monty paid scant attention to the baseball game on TV; in the end, he barely registered the Blue Jays' loss to the Phillies. When he got into bed, sleep would not come. His mind was filled with images of Normie walking alone, a large sinister figure stalking her along the street. And he thought about the phone conversation he had just had with Brennan Burke. He could easily imagine the priest's demeanour; the wrath of God would not be much of an exaggeration.

CHAPTER V

Brennan

On Friday evening, Brennan's father said he was up for a pint or two at O'Carroll's but, as much as Brennan would have liked to join him, he had some work to do for his music classes next morning. The choir had not sung Healey Willan's *Missa Brevis No. 3* yet this term, and Brennan wanted to refresh his memory of the music. So Declan went off to the pub, and Brennan started looking for the musical score. He could not remember when or where he had last seen it. He liked Willan's compositions, and he liked his wit. Willan once said that he was "English by birth, Irish by extraction, Canadian by adoption, and Scotch by absorption." You had to love a man who'd come up with that.

The sheet music was nowhere to be found in Brennan's room, but he had stored some of his papers in the room where his father was staying, so he went across the hall to look. He lifted Declan's suitcase away from the desk and opened the top drawer. Music, but no Willan. He opened the next drawer down and shuffled through some papers in there. And saw Declan's passport and airline ticket.

No, not Declan's. The ticket was in the name of Michael Francis O'Farrell. What the . . . Brennan picked up the American passport and opened it. There was the face of Declan Burke, and the name of Michael Francis O'Farrell, resident of Boston, Massachusetts. What in the name of God was Declan up to now? Should Brennan ask him, demand an explanation? Was it any of Brennan's business? He found the score for the Healey Willan Mass and took it to his room, and he tried to concentrate on the brilliant music. But the image of his father travelling under a false name kept intruding on his thoughts.

There was a tap on Brennan's door, and he sighed. His first unwelcome, and unwelcoming, thought was that it was Mrs. Kelly, his fidgety, cantankerous housekeeper, pestering him at a time like this. Then he remembered: Mrs. Kelly was away. There had been a death in her family in New Brunswick, and he had offered her a few weeks off to stay with her relations there. How kind of him, how blissful to have her out of the house. He called out, "Come in."

The door opened, and a woman stepped in. She was middle-aged, short and stout, and had yellow rubber gloves on her hands. She was the school's cleaner, and he had increased her pay to cover a bit of housekeeping in the parish house as well. He got up from his seat and greeted her. "Hello, Dorothy. How are you tonight?"

"I'm sorry to disturb you, Father, but something's happened at the school." Her voice was wavery, and she turned her head and looked behind her.

"Come in and have a seat, and tell me what happened."

"No, I won't stay. I put all my things in my car, and I'm afraid somebody might . . . There was a man out there!"

"A man?"

"This is what happened, Father." Her voice was even shakier now, and he walked over to her, put a gentle hand on her arm, and eased her into a chair. "I finished my cleaning and went out to my car. I began loading my things into the trunk. Then I remembered I forgot . . . I mean . . ."

"Just take your time, Dorothy."

"Okay. I'd forgotten my duster in the school, so I shut the trunk and went back inside. Unlocked the front door and went in. I turned on the light. And then I heard a rattling sound or a scrambling, something around the back door. And I looked out a side window and saw a man running from the building!"

"Is that so?"

"Yes!"

"Was he carrying anything or —"

"I couldn't tell. I don't know."

"Young fella, old? What did he look like?"

"Only saw him from the back, Father. He had a hooded jacket on. He was tall. That's all I noticed."

"All right, Dorothy. I'll take you out to your car."

He walked her to her car and looked around. No sign of anybody out there. He waited until Dorothy had pulled out of the parking lot, and then he went back inside. What now? What was that old saying? Bad news comes in threes. He rang Monty and filled him in.

"Christ! This coming on the heels of those warning letters about the play! And somebody maybe following Normie."

"Yeah," Brennan said. "Normie and Richard must be the Synge and O'Casey of their day."

"Eh?"

"J.M. Synge, Seán O'Casey. The plays they wrote got them into conflict at the Abbey Theatre in Dublin. It was 1907, I think, when there were riots over Synge's *Playboy of the Western World*. The audience were flinging things at the stage. Then, in the 1920s, it was O'Casey's *The Plough and the Stars* that caused a ruckus. And now we have our own controversy."

"We have to put an end to this."

"The play? We can't be giving in to —"

"No, put an end to the intimidation if in fact someone was trying to break in, and if it is in any way connected to the play. And with the warning notes, is it likely that the attempted break-in is just a coincidence?"

"What was the fucker trying to do, Monty, if indeed he was trying to get in? Steal the script? That wouldn't do him any good. There are, of course, several copies. And I'm sure some of the kids have them at home."

"Normie does, and I expect the others do as well."

"And what in the world would anyone want with the script of a children's play?"

"If somebody has got himself worked up about the play, chances are he's not thinking straight. Or maybe he just wants to read it himself before the next act is staged."

"I'll have to go on guard duty," Brennan said, "keeping watch at night. I can see part of the school, of course, from the parish house. But not the back of it."

"I'll join you. We'll stake out different lookout points and see what happens."

They ended their call, and Brennan thought about the lookout plan. Then he heard footsteps in the hall, and his father's door opening across the way.

Brennan got up and walked across the hall, opened the door. His concern over the break-in had left him no time to consider how to approach his father about the phony passport. So he came right out with it. "What are you doing travelling under the name Michael Francis O'Farrell?!"

His father glowered at him, the icy-blue eyes narrowed to slits.

"I'm not the enemy here, Da. What the fuck is going on?"

"Don't ask me that, Brennan. And what were you doing going through my things?"

"I wasn't going through your things; I was looking in the desk for some sheets of music."

"Let it rest, Brennan. And let me rest. I've had a few, and I'm going to sleep."

Brennan pressed his lips together so he wouldn't say something regrettable, turned, and walked out of the room. He told himself he was not a little boy who had been spurned by his father, left out of grown-up matters that were none of his affair. He was not going to revert to childhood, to childhood hurts and grudges. They were both grown men, and grown men had their secrets.

Monty

The surveillance team — Monty, Brennan, and Declan — gathered at Saint Bernadette's Choir School on Saturday night with a supply of strength-and-boldness-enhancing serums, those being whiskey and beer. Brennan had brought large padded chairs into the music room for the three of them. He had pulled down the window shades and dimmed the lights, which cast shadows of the desks and music stands on the floor and walls around them. They sipped their drinks. They waited. Nothing happened. At least not at Saint Bernie's. But something big happened in the world of baseball. Brennan had set up a television so they could watch Game Six, and the Blue Jays did it. Won the World Series on a ninth-inning home run by Joe Carter. Monty was ecstatic. Of course, his joy was tempered by the task in front of him that night: to catch whoever had attempted to breach the walls of the school. But nobody came near the place.

Monty couldn't join them the following night; he and Maura and the family had tickets to see the Barra MacNeils at the Cohn Auditorium. But it turned out that he wasn't needed; nobody tried to sneak up on the school. Even so, he assured the Burkes that he would be on duty the next night. Brennan had a commitment at Saint Mary's University where he was a part-time lecturer, but his father was locked and loaded and ready to serve.

The choir school was situated on Byrne Street near the intersection with Morris, in the southeast part of the city. It was a Second-Empire-style building made of stone with a mansard roof, dormers, and a cupola with a cross overlooking the front door. There was a newer brick extension to the older structure. They decided that anyone wanting to prowl around the building unseen would wait until fairly late at night, so Monty agreed to meet Declan at ten o'clock. There was a damp chill in the air, and he pulled the collar of his jacket up, wishing he'd worn a scarf. He waited on the front steps until he saw Declan coming across the street from the rectory. They went inside and walked to their observation post near the back of the building. They pulled down the shade and poured themselves a drink.

Monty gave voice to the thoughts uppermost in both their minds: the threats against the children's play, including the threat of legal action against it. "You know, Declan, there was a long history of legal proceedings arising out of the explosion. One after another for over two years. It all made fascinating reading for me as a law student."

"I'm sure it did. But you won't want to be reading about any lawsuits over it now!"

"No, indeed. Feelings ran high about it back then, as you can imagine. Everyone wanted revenge, someone to blame. But what in the hell has got somebody fired up seventy-six years later?"

Declan shook his head and took a sip of his drink. Monty did likewise and redirected the conversation. He asked after the Burke family in New York, and Declan filled him in on Brennan's mother, Teresa, and his sister and brothers, all of whom Monty had met over the years. Teresa was in Ireland for a long-awaited visit with family. When they took a break from conversation, Declan pointed out a pile of books Brennan had brought in to pass the time during these vigils. Monty picked up *The Collar: Stories of Irish Priests* by Frank O'Connor. Monty had read somewhere that Yeats had compared O'Connor to Chekhov. Declan had opened *Boss of Bosses*, all about the real-life New York godfather Paul Castellano. They sat in the faint light, reading and occasionally making a comment.

Then it happened: a tinkling of broken glass, just after twelve thirty. And a crash. Front of the building. Monty and Declan bolted from their seats and ran to the front of the school. Monty saw the hooded figure of a man running from the building. The man must have thought he'd blown it once again, by making noise that might be heard nearby. And he was right. He disappeared behind the church.

"He'll likely come out on Morris Street," Monty said. "He could go left or right once he gets there."

"You go left, I'll go right," Declan commanded and took off at a clip. His speed was surprising for a man in his seventies. A lifetime of being on the run? Monty made a dash for the back of the church. No sign of the man. The statue of Saint Bernadette? Monty sprinted towards it. Nobody there but the kneeling saint in white marble. Nobody behind the evergreens surrounding it. Had the guy made it to Morris Street? Monty made the short jog to the intersection, looked around in all directions. No sign of his quarry. Had he ducked in behind one of old shingled houses? Was he heading to the waterfront? Monty started left according to the plan, and he heard Declan's footsteps tapping away in the other direction. Then he heard a shout. He spun around. Declan was on the ground. A tall man was leaning down over him. Monty started towards them, and the next thing he saw was Declan rising and throwing himself at his attacker. The stranger fell backwards and Declan now loomed above him. Monty could hear Declan's voice but could not make out what he was shouting into the man's face. The fellow pushed Declan and struggled to his feet. He drew back and threw a punch, but Declan dodged it and threw a punch of his own. The man spun around and fell forward. The next sound Monty heard was a wailing siren, and he saw a police car speeding by on Hollis Street, heading south. Declan moved back, and the man in the hooded jacket got up, shook his head, and gave a panicked look around. The closest corner was Morris and Hollis, and he took off in that direction.

Monty was nearly out of breath when he reached Declan. "Are you all right?" he asked.

"I'm grand," the older man replied. "I had him down and would have kept him there. But I heard the siren and saw the peelers. Last thing I want."

The last thing Declan Burke wanted was to draw the attention of the police, regardless of the jurisdiction. Declan and many other members of the Burke clan had a long history of conflict with, or avoidance of, the authorities.

"Did he say anything?"

"Said 'fuck you' but nothing else."

Wouldn't you know it, Monty finally had a suspect who kept his mouth shut. But that was of no use to Monty in this case.

"Apart from a pair of dark eyes and light skin," Declan said, "I can't tell you anything about his appearance. He had a hat pulled down, a hood pulled up, and a scarf up around his mouth and nose. Can't even estimate the age of the fella. He's tall, strong, bit of a fearful look in his eyes, but that's all I can tell you."

Monty laughed in spite of himself. "Fearful, eh? Who wouldn't be, with you overpowering him and giving him the death stare with those baby blues of yours, Dec." Monty stopped himself from saying *Who wouldn't be fearful in the grip of a veteran soldier of the Irish Republican Army?*

"The man's eyes, I would have said they were black, but now I'm picturing them again. The pupils were big. What do they call that?"

"Dilated? Expanded?"

"That's it. Brown eyes, with big pupils. And a bit bloodshot, they were too."

"That could mean he's a cokehead, Declan. Using cocaine."

"Got himself all wired up for the job."

"Maybe so." They walked back to the school and went inside. They found one of the windows broken on a side wall of the building. And a bookshelf had been knocked over, so that would have accounted for the crash they heard.

"He was desperate to get in here," said Declan.

"He certainly was. Let's hope your tackling him will discourage any further attempts to breach the fortress."

"Let's hope so. What do you suppose he's looking for?"

"No idea."

Normie

On Tuesday at school there was a repairman fixing a broken window. And I knew why, and at recess I got to tell Kim and Richard all about it. Other kids were playing in the yard, some playing tag and some gathering leaves into a pile and jumping in them, but the three of us just stood out on the front steps.

"Last night, my dad came flying in the door at home. There was a fight!"

Richard was eating an apple. He looked up from it and said, "A fight? Who was in a fight?"

"It was about the school."

"What?" Kim and Richard asked at the same time.

"I didn't know this before, but somebody tried to break into the school a few nights ago!"

"No!" said Richard.

"Yes! And the guy took off, and nobody knew who it was. And they never told us that at school. But, anyway, Father Burke told Dad, and they decided to hang around in the school at night to see if it happened again. First couple of nights, nothing happened. But then last night, something did happen. And it wasn't Father Burke and Dad this time, because Father Burke had to be someplace else. It was my dad and Father Burke's dad."

"Oul Dec!" Richard exclaimed then, sounding like Father Burke himself.

"That's right. And a guy did try to break in, and Daddy and Mr. Burke heard the noise and they made their move! But the guy heard them, or was spooked by the noise he made when trying to get in. And he ran away, and Dad and Mr. Burke tried to catch him."

"Shit, I wish I'd've been there!"

"It might have been dangerous, Richard! Anyway, Daddy went one way looking for the guy, and Mr. Burke, Declan, went the other way, and it was Declan that found him. And caught him. And they got into a fight. And Declan, even though he's old, he won the fight. Gave the guy a big punch and knocked him down! And said stuff to him that Dad couldn't hear, but Dad figured it was something to scare the guy."

"Shit!" Richard said again. "I'd give anything to have seen that! Oul Dec is one tough hombre."

"Did Mr. Burke get hurt?" Kim asked.

"Not a scratch on him, Dad said."

"It's gotta be the same guy that followed you that day."

I knew it must have been. It gave me shivers to think about it again. "It's gotta be," I agreed. "What if the guy had started a fight with me? I could never have punched him and knocked him down."

Kim put her arms around me. "Thank God it didn't happen to you, Normie."

"I don't even want to think about it," Richard said.

એન

But the Halifax Explosion play and what Mum and Dad called "the fallout from it" were not the only things going on in Halifax, and Mum said we should go out and have some fun. Take our minds off all the trouble about the play. So, when Father Burke told us about a céilí Wednesday night at Saint Patrick's Church, we all decided to go. Me and my baby brother, Dominic, and my big brother, Tommy, and his girlfriend, Lexie. Even Grandma Evelyn said she wanted to go. Father Burke loves old buildings, and he said the céilí was a fundraiser for the old church, to make sure the place was kept in good repair. I'd been in the church before, on Brunswick Street. It has a tall steeple and pointy arches, beautiful stained-glass windows, and a lovely altar with Saint Patrick dressed in green, right up there with Jesus! But the party wasn't in there; it was in the church hall.

We went inside and met Father Burke and his dad, who was joking that "Brennan almost missed the hooley; he kept walking up and down the street here, gawping at all the grand old buildings and houses. I had to lure him inside with the promise of a pint and a tune on the fiddle." Father Burke just laughed and said that the church was a grand old building itself, and there was never any question that he'd be coming into it. There were a lot of people at the tables, and there were drinks and snacks, and a band with a fiddle, a bodhran, a guitar, and something that looked like a little accordion. The music was really lively, like the kind Mum's family would have at their kitchen parties in Cape Breton. It was Scottish and Irish music. Then a group of girls stood up and went to the middle of the floor. They all had fancy green dresses, and they had their hair done up in big curls. And they started dancing to the music. They were great! I love dancing, but I could never be as good as that even if I took the lessons.

But then Mum herself got up — she'd been a good stepdancer ever since she was a little girl in Cape Breton — and she walked over to Father Burke. He looked at her and put his whiskey glass on the table, and he went to dance with her. He was like Mum, a good stepdancer, and people started clapping in time to the music. And it was great. Even little Dominic got up! He's only two years old, and he'd been sitting on Grandma Evelyn's lap, but he squirmed away and ran over to Mum. Dominic always loved music, ever since he was a wee little baby, and he had never been shy about dancing. All the people in the hall went "Awww" and clapped for him. And he seemed to know it was for him, or maybe he was just used to everybody clapping and smiling at him; he had a big grin on his face.

Then Mum called out to the band, "Rattlin' Roarin' Willie!" That's a fun song, and she looked over at me and reached her hand out. She knew I loved to dance to it. Should I go and dance with the two of them, her and Father Burke? Would I look like an idiot in front of the girls from the real dance group? But I went anyway, and I started, and the musicians were playing the wild tune and singing about Rattlin' Roarin' Willie, who was a fiddler himself, but it's about him maybe selling his fiddle. But he didn't want to, and Mum was singing along: "But if I should sell my fiddle, the world would think I was mad, for many a rantin' day my fiddle and I have had." Except she sang it with a strong Scottish accent because Robbie Burns wrote part of the song. With her singing like that, if you didn't know the words, you wouldn't get to know them. And there I was stepdancing, and then I couldn't believe it. Mr. Burke — Declan — put down his glass and walked over to me and smiled, and started stepdancing with me, and was he ever good! Even though he's old, he looked like a young guy dancing with his feet going a mile a minute.

And it was funny. Well, not funny. I shouldn't giggle about people, especially old people. But while I was up dancing with Declan Burke, I looked around to see who was watching. And I saw my grandmother,

Evelyn, and I started thinking maybe Richard was right! What was it he said at the other party? That Grandma Evelyn thought Declan was cute? No . . . that she thought he was a "handsome old divil!" She had her eyes on Mr. Burke now as if . . . well, as if she liked him. As if he was really handsome, and she had a crush on him! Then she gawked at him even more when he got up and sang a song by himself. It was called "Mr. Maguire," and he did a great job of it, and everybody clapped and some whooped and shouted, "Yes!"

Then — I was wishing I'd brought my camera! — there was Mr. Burke putting his hand out to Grandma Evelyn, asking her on to dance! Grandma Evelyn didn't usually come to kitchen parties and céilís and things like that. That was for the Irish side of the family, the Collinses, and Mum's Scottish side from Cape Breton. So Grandma Evelyn probably didn't know how to do the dances. And now there was Mr. Burke standing in front of her, and she was shaking her head and her face was pink! Dad leaned over to her, and I heard him say, "You're not in Knightsbridge now, Mum. Give that stiff upper lip a rest, and dance with this well-mannered gentleman, why don't you?" And the next song by the band was a slow one, a waltz, and she got up and danced with Declan. Everybody — well, everybody in our family — was watching them. And Father Burke looked over at Dad and winked at him, and Dad laughed. And Grandma Evelyn was laughing, too, at whatever Declan was saying to her.

Mum leaned over to Dad and said, "Could this be the beginning of a ceasefire between the Brits and the IRA?"

CHAPTER VI

Brennan

It was great gas last night at Saint Patrick's, all the more so because his father had enjoyed himself immensely. But now Brennan had to bring him back to more troubled times. Declan had told him that the would-be burglar had broken one of the school's windows and knocked over a shelf of books before he was chased off by Declan and Monty. Declan had described the man as best he could, but Brennan wanted to hear it again. He wanted as many details as he could get about this incident and whoever was responsible.

After Brennan's two morning classes, he found Declan in his room at the parish house, sitting at his table, reading a newspaper. *The New York Times*? He must have been to the newsagent's shop a few blocks away. "You've been to Atlantic News, have you? Monty told you about the shop?"

"I have, and he did. They have newspapers from all over, including the old country."

"I know." Brennan sat down at the table. "Tell me about the man you chased, Da."

"I already told you."

"Tell me again."

"Middling tall, five ten or so. Strong and, from what I could tell, muscular. But he had on a hooded jacket, hat, scarf. I couldn't make out anything except the colour of his eyes. Brown, they were. He fucked off up the street there. Hollis Street?"

"He got away, but not before some punches were thrown."

"The gurrier thought he could knock me out of contention."

"Little did he know, eh, Dec?"

"Mm."

"You know there was some man following little Normie home from school, and then, two days later, someone sent letters to her and her friend Richard, warning them not to stage the second act."

"Monty told me."

"So, of course, some maggot trying to put the frighteners on our students, trying to break into our school, we want to know who it is. Right, Da?"

"Cinnte." Certainly.

"But neither you nor Monty could make out his features." Brennan leaned forward in his seat. "The only way I can see to identify him is to have the police conduct an investigation of an attempted break-in at the school."

"Police." Brennan's father set his face like a flint.

"Da, they can ask around to see if anyone who was out on Hollis Street Monday night saw a man in the clothing you described, running up the street. If so, did they see where he went? And — here's an aid to identification — he likely had a mark on his face or forehead from being knocked down —"

"He wouldn't have. The hat and scarf would have protected his face."

"If not a cut, a bruise then. And another bruise maybe from the thumping you were after giving him."

"What are the chances of a witness noticing that, if the fucker was running at full speed along the street?"

"Only one way to find out. I'm going to ring the peelers."

The flinty expression didn't change. But, eventually, the voice emerged. "This case, this investigation, it's just a City of Halifax investigation, is it?"

"What do you mean, Da? What else would it be?"

The father's eyes would not meet the eyes of his son. "Well, it's obviously not a *federal case*. There won't be Mounties involved, or any kind of . . ."

"You've been looking at too many Canadian postcards, Dec. This is not a matter for the Royal Canadian Mounted Police. Not a federal matter, not a drugs case, and certainly not anything with . . . with international implications, if that's what you're concerned about!" Brennan didn't know whether to laugh or start worrying about the implications of this bizarre conversation. "What's going on, Da?"

Declan shook his head, raised a hand, and got up and left the room.

Monty

On Thursday afternoon, after spending nearly two hours preparing a new client for his upcoming court appearance, Monty was sitting in the office of Saint Bernadette's Choir School with Father Brennan Burke and his father, Declan, facing two officers of the Halifax Police Department. Declan looked as if he was facing a hooded executioner. Monty was acquainted with the two cops, Sergeant Gabe Delorey and Constable Yvon Pellerin. And he made the introductions. "This is Father Brennan Burke, music director of Saint Bernadette's." That was understating things considerably; there was, nominally, a principal of Saint Bernadette's Choir School, but there was no question that it was Brennan Burke who ran the show. "And this is his father, Declan Burke, here for a visit with Brennan."

Declan gave a brief nod and said nothing.

Delorey smiled and said, "Well, this is something new for us, Mr. Collins here telling us somebody *did* commit an offence, rather than *he didn't do it*!"

"What's this? Haven't I always been happy to help the police with their inquiries?"

Both coppers laughed at that, and then Delorey proceeded with the questioning. Monty told them about the school play, and Delorey said he had seen a story about it on the news.

"Act two of the play is scheduled to be performed in December, and the kids wrapped up act one with a little teaser about what to expect. Couple of hints about the goings-on at a cathouse on Young Street, somebody guilty of looting, and the transporting of a body that might have met its end by means not related to the explosion. That was three weeks ago, seventh of this month. Then less than two weeks later, a man followed my daughter from the school, followed her along Morris Street."

Delorey took a pen and notebook out of his pocket. "What day was that?" he asked.

Monty thought for a minute. "It was a Tuesday. Would have been October nineteenth. I know, it might have been coincidence, just a man walking on the same street. We could have written that off, but two days later, Normie and Richard Robertson received letters, delivered to the school, in envelopes marked Sears department store. So they looked like a sales announcement, maybe. But sent to two students at their school? No! Richard is one of the students involved in the play." Monty handed the letters and envelopes to Sergeant Delorey. "Sorry to say, Officer, that many curious people have handled the letters and envelopes, so you may not find any useful fingerprints. Anyway, whoever did this is apparently concerned about whatever is going to be said or revealed during the December performance."

"But," said Delorey, "the play is set at the time of the explosion, in 1917. Why would anybody be concerned about any of that now, seventy-six years later? Anybody who's still alive would have been a baby or a very young kid at the time."

"We don't know, Gabe, but somebody is all worked up about something. And is trying to threaten or intimidate the school, the students — my own daughter! — into cancelling the play."

"I can understand your concern, Monty, obviously. But I have to ask some questions."

"Of course. Go ahead."

"Now, tell me what your daughter said about being followed."

Monty recounted the story of the man in the hooded jacket, cap, and scarf walking behind her, going west along Morris Street on her way home from school, the man keeping pace with her when she increased her speed. "She reached the intersection of Morris and Barrington Streets, crossed Barrington, and then turned to see her friend coming behind her. Richard. He caught up with her, had a book he wanted to lend her. And the man in the hood turned in to one of the buildings of the Technical College there by the corner. And that was that. Until the warning notes and the attempted break-in."

"And you think this is the same man."

"Hard to imagine there would be two of them worked up about events seventy-six years ago, so I'm going on the assumption that this is all one man."

"But we don't know that. Now, tell us about the attempted break-in."

Brennan answered, "The woman who cleans the school in the evenings came to me in the parish house and told me she had gone out to her car after finishing her work. She had forgotten something inside, and she went back into the school. As soon as she was inside, she heard a noise at the back door. A rattling sound or scrambling, something like that. She looked out a side window and saw a man running from the building. Same thing: tall with a jacket and a hood pulled up. She just saw him from behind. So Monty and I decided to go into the building at night and see if it happened again. First couple of nights, nothing. Then Monday night, I had to do some work at Saint Mary's University, so it was Monty and my father."

Delorey flipped a page in his notebook and said, "So, Monday night."

Monty appointed himself witness for the night's encounter. He described what he had heard just after twelve thirty, the tinkling of broken glass, he and Declan getting up and rushing to the front of the building. "He must have heard us because when we looked outside, we saw the man running away. We made a split-second decision to follow him. I figured Morris Street. I started to go left, towards Lower Water Street, Declan right towards Hollis, and then I heard something, turned, and saw the two of them."

"Mr. Burke?" Delorey said, turning to Declan.

You'd have thought, looking at him, that Declan Burke was about to have his two front teeth pulled out. But he told the police what happened. "I ran after him, and he heard me. He turned and shouted something, then came at me and knocked me down. I managed to get up and put him on the back foot, and it was him lying on the ground. I gave him a piece of my mind, and he managed to get up and he came at me with his fists. I ducked the punch and hit out at him before he could come at me again. I lamped him, and then he managed to get away. I couldn't keep up with him. There you have it."

Monty knew that Declan had not in fact tried to keep up with him; his involvement in the fray was abandoned as soon as he heard the police siren on Hollis Street.

"Did the man say anything about his purpose, anything about the school or the play?"

"He told me to eff off, but that was it."

"Any more conversation?"

"No."

"What can you tell us about his appearance, Mr. Burke?"

"He had the hood and a hat on his head. One of those knit hats. Black."

"A tuque?" Delorey asked.

"I don't know what you call them. And he had a scarf pulled up high on his face. He had brown eyes, and the centre of them, the pupils were . . . enlarged?"

"Dilated?" Delorey asked.

"Right. And a bit bloodshot as well."

Delorey exchanged a glance with his fellow cop, then Delorey asked, "Do you have a school nurse, Father Burke?"

Brennan looked surprised at that, but he just answered, "No."

"So, no nurse's office, no medical supplies." Drugs, he was asking about.

"Nothing but bandages for scraped knees."

"All right. So, Mr. Burke?" Delorey returned his attention to Declan. "Anything more you can tell us about his appearance? The Crown will need as much detail as possible if we're to make a case."

Declan's eyes darted from the cop to Monty and to Brennan. Then back to Delorey. "What did you say? The *Crown*?"

Monty and Brennan both laughed, and Brennan said, "I told you, Da, you're not in a republic now."

"All prosecutions are done in the name of the Crown," Monty explained. But it was plain to see that more was needed. "The state, except that Canada is a member of the British Commonwealth." The old republican scowled at that. Monty was having too much fun to stop there. "Prosecutors here in the province are called Crown attorneys. And if you don't behave yourself, Dec, and you're charged with a criminal offence, the case will be cited as *R. v. Burke*. R. versus Burke. The *R* stands for Regina, the Queen. And if it doesn't go well for you, and you appeal, it will be Burke versus the Queen."

Declan rolled his eyes heavenward, as if beseeching the Almighty to come down and rescue these poor colonialist children from the shackles of British imperialism.

None of this was new, in point of fact. Burke versus the British monarch accounted for much of the old rebel's life. Monty kept that to himself. But he added one more note of explanation. "If we had a king, the *R* would stand for Rex."

Gabe Delorey and Yvon Pellerin were smiling. They had enjoyed the encounter, as well they might, Pellerin being an Acadian French name, and Delorey perhaps a variation of the French as well. Then they got back to business, Delorey asking, "Any more details for us, Mr. Burke?"

"He was about five ten in height," Declan replied. "A good bit of strength in him. Can't tell you anything more than that."

"Age?"

"Not ancient, I'd say. And he was strong and quick on his feet so, as I say, not an old, old man."

Monty exchanged a look with Brennan. Declan Burke was in his seventies, and nobody could say he wasn't strong and quick on his feet. And quick with a powerful fist.

"All right, gentlemen. Thank you. We'll ask around to see if anyone noticed him, recognized him, saw where he went. Do any of you know what his beef was with the play? What he was worked up about?"

"No idea," Brennan replied, and Monty said the same.

Sergeant Delorey and Constable Pellerin thanked them and took their leave.

"That wasn't so bad, was it, Dec?" Brennan asked, and he received an icy-blue glare in return.

CHAPTER VII

Monty

The following Tuesday, Monty had an all-day trial scheduled in Kentville, for a client charged with setting fire to the place of his former employment. An all-day trial, with the verdict not seriously in doubt. Kentville was an hour outside of Halifax, and he was just about to leave the house when Maura called him back into the kitchen. She pointed to the radio. "Listen."

It was the CBC local news. "The body of a young woman was found lying on her back across the street from the Hydrostone Market on Young Street. Police say there was no identification on her body, and they have not revealed the cause of death. They described the woman as around twenty-one to twenty-five years of age, slim with blonde hair. She was wearing a white faux-fur jacket. The police are asking for the public's assistance in identifying her." The journalist read out the number to call and ended her report.

"Welcome to the neighbourhood, eh?" Maura said. "We buy a house, and there's a murder on our street."

The same street, but the body had been found some distance away, up the hill from the new house and on the other side of — west of — Gottingen. There was a triangle of land across from the Hydrostone Market, between Young Street and Kaye. "Did you ever notice the little quirk in the streets there? Young and Kaye are parallel, with Young to the north of Kaye, but west of the Hydrostone Market, they switch and Young carries on to the south of Kaye."

"Oh? I never noticed that."

"Bit of an oddity. Lots to learn about our new neighbourhood."

"Some people are getting to know it already," Maura told him. "Normie said something yesterday about the hockey player, Rhodenizer, inviting some of his pals over to the house, with Lilith away. I didn't react. We've agreed that Lilith can stay in the place for the time being, so it's up to her. But I wonder if it turned into a party, and how long it went on. Wonder if anybody heard anything."

"Let's hope not. All right. I'm off."

"Me too."

Monty leaned down and kissed their little boy, Dominic, on the top of his head. Before heading off for a day of teaching at Dalhousie Law School, Maura would be dropping the boy off with his babysitter, Lily, a mother with two other small children — playmates for Dominic. "Now, Dominic," Monty said, "don't you scare all those children at Lily's!" The little guy had gone out as a skeleton on Halloween and now, two days later, he was still in costume, still playing the role of a terrifying figure. Monty threw his hands up, in a parody of someone frightened, and the little fella laughed uproariously. Then Monty bid Dominic and Maura goodbye, got into his car, and hit the road.

Brennan

Brennan had settled into one of the empty classrooms after his first morning class and was preparing a musical score for his choir. It was

Mozart's setting of the medieval chant "Ave Verum Corpus," a hymn of veneration for the Eucharist. This was one of the many Mozart compositions Brennan treasured, for its beautiful melody and its plea to the Almighty: "Esto nobis praegustatum in mortis examine." Be for us a foretaste (of the heavenly banquet), in the trial of death.

Meditating on this led Brennan's thoughts in an unexpected direction. He had performed in the opening scene of *Devastated Area*, playing the part of the physicist Robert Oppenheimer. Oppenheimer had studied the Halifax Explosion during his research for the development of the atomic bomb. Why would this come to mind? Because of an exhibit Brennan had recently seen, a showing of Yousuf Karsh's iconic photographs of the people he had met over the course of his career. There was a portrait of Albert Einstein done in 1948, and an accompanying note Karsh had made at the time. He had asked Einstein what the world would be like if another atomic bomb were dropped. Einstein's reply: "Alas, we will no longer be able to hear the music of Mozart." Brennan's reaction was the same now as it had been when he'd first read the words: he had to blink away the tears. He welcomed the distraction when a knock came on the door. "Come in," he said and looked up to see Normie Collins.

She peered at him, concern written all over the sweet little face. She asked, "Are you all right, Father?"

You couldn't put one past the little Druid, as sensitive as she was to things seen and unseen. But he would put on a cheerful face or, at least, his version of it. "Sure, I'm grand, Normie. What's the craic?"

But it was immediately clear that she wasn't there for the craic, not that there was much in the way of rollicking fun to be had during a morning of classes at school. It was alarm Brennan was seeing in the little one's face.

"Father, I'm sorry to disturb you! Mrs. Vickers let me out of math class, because a phone call came for me."

A phone call for a student during class time? "Is something wrong, Normie?" She stood in the doorway, clearly rattled. "Have a seat, acushla, and tell me."

She sat at a desk facing him. "It's about Richard. It's him who called me, because nobody was home at my house." Brennan waited. "I mean, he said he tried calling my number at home, our number, but there was no answer. Mum and Dad had already left for work. He wanted to talk to Daddy because" — Brennan could see the fear in her eyes — "something happened right near the house where the party was."

"The party?"

"Uh, it's the new house we bought, well, not new. Old house we bought on Young Street. Richard and Kirk were there."

"Kirk?"

"The hockey player. Kirk Rhodenizer."

"Oh, yes." The lad who'd come on stage for the NHL segment of the play.

"The lady who lives in the house, she's old, and she has a girl who takes care of her. Janice somebody. And Kirk is her boyfriend. The old lady, Lilith, has gone away to visit her relatives, so Janice went with her. Kirk said he'd look after the house. Except, well . . ."

Except he hosted a party. At the Collinses' newly purchased house. Well, it was nothing Brennan and his pals hadn't done in their day. "Take your time here, Normie. Now, you said something happened. What happened?"

"A girl got killed!"

Brennan had heard the morning news. The body of a young woman had been found in the city's north end. But what did this have to do with . . .

"The dead girl, the body, was lying there across the street from the Hydrostone Market, which is on the same street as our house, but up over the hill. Richard knows about it because he saw the cop cars and a bunch of the neighbours outside this morning, and he opened a window and he heard people talking about the body."

"Ah. So Richard is not at school today, and he rang your house this morning."

"Yes! He wanted to talk to Daddy, but Daddy's at his office. Or, no, I just remembered. He's going to court somewhere else today. Out of town."

Of course, what Brennan most wanted to understand was the connection between the dead woman and Richard Robertson's efforts to call the *well-known Halifax lawyer* Monty Collins. "Where is Richard?"

"He's hiding in the house on Young Street."

"Why is he hiding, Normie?"

"I don't know." She looked him in the eye as if trying to convince him. "I don't know, honest to G— . . . honest. The cops knocked at the door, but Richard hid inside and didn't go to the door, so the cops think there's nobody home. But they'll be watching Young Street and they'll see if Richard comes out."

"I assume Richard rang his parents as well."

"Um, no. He doesn't want them to know."

"I see." And he did. Richard Robertson's parents were fixated on their money and status, and on their ambitions for their son. The one point on which he agreed with them was that Richard was a very able student, and Brennan had advanced him a grade ahead when the lad started at the choir school. He had done the same with Normie Collins. Now here was Richard wanting to "lawyer up." To protect himself from his parents as much as from the police? But why was he in fear of the police?

Normie looked miserable as she recounted her friend's troubles. "What he did was, yesterday, Richard kind of told his parents that he was going to stay over at another friend's house, a guy his parents like. He'd stay overnight because, you know, Richard and his family live a ways out of town."

Yes, Brennan had seen the ghastly, pretentious suburban pile where the Robertsons were domiciled.

Brennan's first instinct was to take himself over to the house on Young Street and talk to Richard, but he abandoned that idea the minute it came into his head. Normie was right; if the police were watching the house, Brennan's arrival would lead them straight to Richard. The question, again: why was Richard so afraid of talking to the peelers? What connection could he possibly have to the woman, God rest her, who had died?

"Normie, did Richard give you a phone number at the house where he is this morning?"

"Yes, I have it here. He wants to talk to you." She reached into the pocket of her blazer and produced a slip of paper.

"All right. I'm going to try to ring him and see what's going on. Why don't you leave it with me and go back to your classes?"

"Okay."

"Don't worry. We'll get it sorted." If it could be sorted, whatever it was.

∾

Brennan went to Richard's homeroom class and spoke to his teacher. Invented a story about hearing from Richard, that he'd be late today. Brennan hoped there was some truth in that, that Richard would arrive at school, sooner or later.

"Yes," Mrs. Chapman replied, "I tried to call his home but there was no answer."

"No worries," Brennan assured her. "I'll take care of it."

He returned to his office, picked up the phone, and punched in the number Normie had given him. The phone rang several times before it was answered, and Brennan hardly recognized the tremulous voice on the other end of the line.

"Richard. It's Father Burke."

"Oh, God. I may be in trouble here, Father! I didn't do anything, but the police are out there, and that girl is dead, and . . ."

"Normie came and talked to me, Richard. She told me you tried to reach her father. He's apparently out of town on a case. Just tell me what happened. Start from the beginning."

The young fella took a deep breath, and started talking. "I was here! With Kirk. Kirk Rhodenizer. I told my parents I was staying with another friend, Geoffrey, but I never got to Geoff's place because I got into the booze."

Brennan almost smiled in spite of himself, as he pictured his grade eight student, the acknowledged class wit, on the drink and even more comical with it. But there was obviously nothing comical about the way Richard had lived the experience. "Go on."

"Okay. Mrs. Stewart went away for the weekend to visit somebody. Her niece. And Janice went with her. Janice works for her, takes care of her, and she's Kirk's girlfriend. They left the key with Kirk to, you know, look after the house while they were gone. I met Kirk last spring. I talked to him about hockey, asked him what it was like playing Junior A here in Halifax. I told him I'd played a bit of atom and peewee."

"You played *what*?"

"Atom and peewee, you know, kids' level hockey. So, he invited me to play a few games at the Forum. And that's how he ended up with that little role in the play. Anyway, when I saw him a couple of weeks ago, he told me he was going to 'have the house' for a couple of nights, and some of his friends would be coming over for a party, and did I want to come. It sounded too cool to pass up the chance. So that's when I told my parents I was going to stay with Geoff. But I kind of knew I'd probably stay at the house with Kirk and the other guys. So I lied to my folks, and they're going to kill me. And that's just for lying. They'll take my dead body and kill it all over again if they find out I was drinking. And passed out, and missed some of what happened when a murder victim was in the house!"

Brennan's grip tightened on the receiver. "Did you say the victim was in the house?"

"Yeah, she came in for a while. Oh God, when my old man hears —"

"Let's not worry about that for now. Continue with your story."

"Yeah, well, me and Kirk and his friends — Phil somebody and Ben and I think one of them was named Donnie — were watching a game on TV, Saint Louis playing Hartford. Okay, so it wasn't as much fun as watching Montreal and Boston, but still . . . and we were drinking beer. And rum. I'm not used to it, and I got absolutely plastered. It was my first time, ever. And it was funny for a while; I was doing little skits and making the other guys crack up. They're older guys, you know, seventeen, eighteen. We were all acting crazy and falling over laughing. And then the other guys left."

"They'd had enough?"

"They . . ."

"Yes, Richard? What did they do?"

"They just left."

"You sounded a little hesitant there."

"No, no, they went off, but I was too pissed to get up and go anywhere. I kept falling asleep and waking up again; I was lying on the floor. And Kirk was razzing me about it. He was loaded too.

"And then I heard this girl outside, hollering 'No! Leave me alone!' I don't know what else she was saying, but next thing I heard, she was up on the back porch of our house, well, the house where we were. She came up the outside stairs onto the deck and started hammering at the door. It was really late by this time. Kirk got up and answered the door and he said, 'Sure, okay, come on in' or something like that. I wanted to get up and see who it was, what was going on, but I just fuckin' — sorry! — just passed out again. It could only have been a few minutes later when I came to and peered into the kitchen and saw them at the table, Kirk and this blonde one, both having a drink. And then I saw him put his arm around her, and there was a bit of smooching. She'd been drinking before she arrived. I could tell." Richard's voice caught in his throat. "Oh, Christ."

"Who was she?"

"Don't know. I'm pretty sure Kirk didn't know her. I think she said her name, but I can't remember it. Fuck! Sorry, sorry."

"Tell it your own way, Richard."

"Oh, Jesus. I have to go. Hold on . . ."

Brennan stayed on the line. He heard feet pounding along the floor, and then a retching sound that was all too familiar from Brennan's long years of overindulging. Richard was back a couple of minutes later, full of apologies.

"I understand, me lad," Brennan assured him. "I know a thing or two about the effects of strong drink."

"Right." Brennan heard the sound of liquid being gulped down. Water, he hoped. "But anyway," Richard said, "they found the girl up the street from the Collinses' new place."

"And you think this is the same person who came to the door."

"Yeah, it had to be her. What are the odds, right? I heard the neighbours out there talking, and they said she was a blonde. Long hair. Same kind of coat. So she's the same one."

"Now, about Kirk . . ."

"He didn't do anything! He's not like that, Kirk isn't. Okay, he's got a reputation as a bit of a goon — an enforcer — when he's on the ice. That's why he was let go by the Harbour Buoys, because they said he had crossed the line separating acceptable goon behaviour from what was, well, you know, over the line. It's all going to come out! About him being with her, and going after her. Except I can't remember —"

"What do you mean, going after her?" Brennan asked, more sharply than he had intended.

"No, no, not like that! She forgot her purse when she left. I saw it there on the kitchen floor, and I told Kirk about it, and he grabbed it and took off running. And that's all I remember."

"How much time passed between the time she left and the discovery of her purse?"

"Not long, I don't think."

"So, was your pal, was Kirk just out of the house for a few minutes, or . . . ?"

"I don't even remember him coming back. There's whole bits of it blanked out. Did that ever happen to you when you were drunk, Father, big blanks in your memory?"

Brennan almost joked that he couldn't remember, but stopped himself in time and said, "It happens." Then, "What time was this?"

"I haven't . . . It was late, but I just don't know."

"Is Kirk there with you now?" That was met with silence. "Richard?"

"He's gone."

Oh, God. "He left you there by yourself? When did he go?"

"I don't know. He wasn't here by the time I woke up this morning. He must have had to be somewhere this morning, I don't know. We were both too drunk to get into talking about the morning! Listen, Father, I don't want to talk to the cops! I don't want to talk about Kirk. He wouldn't do anything, I know that, but still, if they find out he went after her —"

"After her. You mean to return her handbag?"

"Yeah, just about the purse, to give it back to her, but still . . . And, oh shit, what's Mr. Collins going to say? This is his house now, and all this happened in it. And I want him to help me, you know, to fend off the cops."

"Monty should be the least of your worries, Richard. No damage to the house or anything like that?"

"No, nothing broken. Just some bottles lying around. I'll get rid of them, clean up. But . . . I sure as hell don't want my old man to know about any of this!"

Murdoch Robertson's ambitions for his son involved suits and ties and boardrooms and a briefcase filled with balance sheets and ledgers and "business models," whatever the hell those might be. His wife, Lois, was much the same. Never mind Richard's exuberant personality and his wicked sense of humour. That sort of thing is not needed in the boardroom, young man. They even had some kind of *personal coach* for the poor lad. Little wonder the young fella didn't want to face their wrath, and whatever consequences would follow. But if the girl who came into the house was the same girl whose body was found nearby, Brennan knew it was all going to come out in the open.

"Is there anything else you can tell me, Richard?" No reply. "Richard?"

"No, nothing else. I . . . I'm gonna take off, Father. The police aren't out there now. I'm going to sneak away. Maybe I should put on some of the old lady's clothes and disguise . . ." For a minute there, he sounded like the Richard that Brennan knew, but not for long. "I gotta go. I'll be at school soon. Thanks, Bren— Father, I —" And he hung up the phone.

Monty

Monty had seen Kirk Rhodenizer on the ice when he played for the Halifax Harbour Buoys; he remembered reading that he was eighteen years old when he was dropped from the team earlier this year. And

Monty had known Kirk's father when he, Monty, had played hockey back in his university days. Now, late in the afternoon after Monty returned from court in Kentville, Kirk was sitting across from his desk, telling him about the party he had hosted at Monty's newly purchased house, about the body that had been found nearby. The police had heard about the party and had tracked Kirk down and questioned him. As a witness.

"I'm sorry about the party," Kirk said. "It's just that Janice was away with Lilith, Mrs. Stewart, and I was looking after the house, and it . . . well . . ."

It was too good an opportunity to pass up. Monty had done the same in his younger days. "That's all right, Kirk. We've all been there, so to speak." Monty peered at him. "Turn your head there, Kirk. To the right."

He sighed, looked a little miffed, but he turned his head.

"What happened to your face?" There was a small cut, red and puffy on his jaw.

"Me and the other guys, we were horsing around."

"The police asked you about it, I assume."

"Yeah."

"What did you tell them?"

"Same thing I told you."

Because it was true, or was he keeping his story straight? Monty would let it go for now. "All right. Who were the cops who questioned you?"

"They told me their names, but I was all worked up. I don't remember."

"Okay. Now tell me about the woman who came to the door."

"She came flying up the back stairs, up to the back porch, and banged on the door. And I went and saw her there, and I opened the door. 'Can I come in?' she said, and she was shaking. I asked her what happened, and she said she'd been over at the house next door, and she said, 'There's a man.' And something about being scared, and could she come in for a few minutes. I guess till the guy gave up and went away."

"What time was this, Kirk?"

106

He shook his head. "I don't know. Late. The other guys were all gone by then. Except Richard Robertson. Well, you know that. I invited him to come over. Me and a couple of other guys were going to watch the game on TV, and Richard had played some hockey with us at the Forum. So I extended the invitation to him. He seems like a nice kid, good sense of humour. It was Richard who told me to come and see you."

"Right. The woman was at the door."

"Yeah, so I let her in, and I looked outside, out the back, and couldn't see anybody, but it was dark, so maybe there was somebody out there. I don't know."

"What was she doing next door?"

"She said there was something in that house. It was a cathouse back in the day. A, you know, brothel. Before it was blown up in 1917. And somebody in her family told her there was something in the house — her great-grandmother had left something there, and she wanted to see if it was still in the house somewhere."

"Hard to imagine something surviving in there after 1917."

"Yeah, I know, but she sure as heck wanted to find it. She wouldn't tell me what it was. Maybe she didn't know herself. But I know this much: she was scared shitless. Of something, or someone. That man who was out there, I guess. But she wouldn't tell me what had her so scared."

"And you told the police everything you've told me?"

"Yeah."

"Anything you told them that you haven't mentioned here?"

"Um, no."

Monty looked him in the eye. "Anything you can tell me that you didn't tell the police?" There was something; it was written all over the young guy's face. "Tell me, Kirk. It's better that I know what we're dealing with in case, well . . . I won't be of much help to you if I'm left out in the dark about what happened."

Kirk dropped his gaze to his hands and spoke in a voice Monty could hardly hear. "There was a bit of kissing. Nothing more than that! But we were both way over the limit."

"She'd been drinking too?"

"Oh, yeah, she'd been into it. She was a bit older than me, a few years maybe."

"Who was it who initiated the physical stuff?"

"It was me, I guess. I'd been drinking all night and I was hammered, and I put my arm around her, to comfort her a bit, and then I . . . Well, it was just a bit of kissing, you know."

"Nothing more?"

"No way. Look," he said, leaning forward, "I was drunk, I was an arsehole. Janice is my girlfriend, and I've never . . . hardly ever been with anybody else. I'm hoping to give her the ring someday. It was nothing, between me and that other girl. It started with me feeling sorry for her."

"How long did it last, the kissing?"

Kirk shrugged. "It couldn't have been a long time. I remember her jumping up and saying she had to leave. And I just backed off. She got up and looked out the windows, back and front, I guess to see if that guy was still out there. And then she said bye and took off."

"Where was Richard Robertson through all this?"

"He was on the dining room floor, passed out. He'd wake up once in a while and then conk out again."

Richard was what? Twelve, thirteen? "Did that cause you any concern, Kirk? An underage kid passed out on the floor?"

Kirk lowered his gaze. "Hey, I'm underage too. Won't be nineteen till next spring." Catching on that Monty was not impressed with that excuse, he said, "Sorry, sorry. I know. It was just going to be the game on TV and a couple of brew. But then, well, my buddies brought a couple of quarts of rum and . . . I wasn't operating on all cylinders. I shouldna let Richard get into the rum. And maybe not the beer. Christ, I don't know."

"All right. The young woman left. And that was the end of it?"

Once again, his witness — his client? — was ill at ease.

"Kirk?"

"She forgot her purse when she ran off from the house. I saw it and picked it up and went out after her."

"Where did you go after her?"

"Up the street, Young Street; she was running up the hill."

Monty had heard the reports; there was no handbag found with the body, nothing to identify the victim. "She didn't have her bag when they found her, Kirk."

His face flushed with anger. "I didn't fuckin' steal it!"

"What did you do with it?"

"I caught up to her, handed it to her! Said, 'Hey, you forgot this.'"

"Did you tell the police about this?"

"No."

"Did they ask if her goodbye at the back door was the last time you saw her?"

It took a few seconds, but he finally said. "Yeah. And I said it was."

"You lied to the police over returning the woman's handbag?!"

"No, I lied because she was murdered, for fuck's sake!"

"And then you were stuck with the lie."

"Yeah." His voice cracked then. "I . . . I knew how suspicious that would look, if I changed my story. Right?"

"Where was she when you caught up with her?"

"It was by that church there, the back of it."

"United Memorial Church, on Kaye Street, backing onto Young."

"Right. I think that's where I caught up. It's all pretty fuzzy." Let's hope there is nothing overly incriminating that you've forgotten, Monty thought. "When you saw her at that point, outside, what happened? Did you stay and talk with her?"

"I don't think so. I think I just went back to the house. I remember nearly tripping over Richard on the floor when I went into the dining room. He was passed out, or asleep, but he was okay. I checked. Hadn't puked up or anything. I must have passed out then. I don't know for how long."

"Where was she headed when you caught up with her? Where was she going?"

"How the Jesus would I know?"

"It was late at night. She was out on the street. There had been a man shouting at her. You didn't ask where she was going, how she would get there?"

"I told you, I was piss-drunk, okay? I wasn't thinking straight."

Monty decided to end it there. He didn't know the names of the police officers who had questioned Kirk Rhodenizer. But even if he did have their names, he preferred to stay on familiar ground, deal with the devil he knew. And liked and respected. So he said goodbye to Kirk, who mumbled a "thanks" and got up to leave. Watching him make his listless way out of the office, his head down, Monty was struck by how different Rhodenizer looked today, compared to his confidence and speed on the ice. World of difference in the young fella now.

Monty then made a call to Sergeant Gabe Delorey and left a message. He heard back from him a few minutes later. He was on friendly terms with the sergeant, yes, but he was not about to share Kirk's admissions about kissing the young one who had come to the house, or about running after her to give back her handbag. There might be a reason to disclose those facts later, but not yet. He explained that he was "assisting" the young hockey player who had hosted the party at Monty's house and had been questioned in connection with "the events of that night." He stressed to Delorey that Kirk had had nothing to do with the woman's death. Of course, Monty knew that Delorey had heard that one countless times before. Even so, he confirmed to Monty that the victim had been murdered. And he provided Monty with another, very interesting, piece of information. A piece of information that Monty, as defence counsel, would be entitled to anyway, if things were to turn more serious for his potential client. He hoped it wouldn't go that far, Rhodenizer charged with murder, but he wanted to help the guy. Monty was the owner of the house where the party had occurred, albeit without his knowledge or permission. More to the point, he felt some sympathy for Kirk. Sure, the kid was a bit surly, but that was understandable, given the disastrous turn his night had taken. That sympathy would evaporate, though, if Monty came to suspect a darker side to Kirk. He could not rule out the possibility that Kirk had committed an offence far more serious than providing liquor to a much younger boy on the night of November first.

Delorey told him that the detectives working on the case had spoken to a Diane Carmichael, who lived with her husband and young daughters in the house next door to Mrs. Stewart — Monty's house — on Young Street. The Carmichaels' house was the place that had been, until its near destruction in the explosion, a brothel. The young woman who died had come to the Carmichaels' door that night. The night she died. That jibed with what Kirk had told Monty, that she had gone to the house next door to look for something left there by a member of her family. Something left there before the explosion. Kirk also said there was a man on the scene somewhere, a man who had the young one frightened, and that's why Kirk had let her in.

Monty and Delorey ended their call, and Monty knew who he wanted to speak to next. He was anxious to hear what Diane Carmichael had to say about the young woman's visit. He got into his car and drove to Young Street, to the Carmichaels' grey wood-shingled house. It had a steeply pitched roof sloping down over the front entrance, like many of the north end houses built after the explosion. There wasn't a light on in the house, no car in the driveway. He would wait until tomorrow.

At lunchtime on Wednesday, he was on Young Street again. There was a car in the driveway this time, so he walked up the front steps and rang the bell. The door was opened by a woman who appeared to be in her mid-thirties, with short straight brown hair and glasses; she wore jeans and an Icelandic sweater. "Yes?" she said.

Monty introduced himself, handed her his business card, and explained his presence on her doorstep. He told her that he and his wife, Maura, had recently bought the Stewart house next door, that he had learned about the party, and that a couple of young fellas he knew were at the house. She said that Mrs. Stewart had told her about the sale. Like the other neighbours here, Monty said, the young guys were being questioned by the police. "So, I feel I should find out as much as I can about what happened Monday night." He gave Mrs. Carmichael what he hoped was a reassuring smile and said, "I'm a lawyer, so I take it seriously when anyone I know is questioned by the police!"

"Oh, yes, I understand."

"Thank you, Mrs. Carmichael. Now I'd just like to ask about the woman who came calling that night."

"All right. Would you like to come in?"

"Sure. Thanks."

She led him into the living room and said, "Since we are neighbours now, please call me Diane."

He smiled at her and said, "And I'm Monty."

She asked if he would like tea or something else to drink. "Thank you. That's kind of you, but I won't have anything, and I won't keep you long." He sat on the chesterfield, and she sat opposite him in an armchair and waited for his questions.

"What time did the woman come to your door?"

"It was after midnight, not long after. My kids were asleep. I'm a bit of a night owl and I was still awake, reading, so my lights were on. My husband was out at work, and I hesitated to go to the door at that time of night but, well, I did. I opened the door a crack and peered out and saw her. It was obvious she'd been drinking. You know how you can tell sometimes by the look on a person's face? And I could smell it. She was agitated, so I was a little nervous about her."

"What did she look like? How old?"

"Early twenties at most. Blonde hair to her shoulders. She was a pretty girl but looked hard in a way, or looked as if she'd had a hard life. I'm not sure why I say that, or what I saw in her. Maybe it was her clothing, a white fake-fur jacket that was soiled, skinny pants in a shiny fabric . . . Oh, listen to me. I sound like the worst kind of snob."

"No, Diane, you're trying to help with a description. What did she say to you?"

"It was weird. She was polite and all, but she asked if she could come inside and look for something."

"Look for what?"

"That was the weird part. I asked her that, and she said, 'I don't know.' And then she said she had been researching her family history. And something like, 'And I just found out the place.' She seemed to mean that 'the place' was this house. Then, 'I think my grandmother left something here.' I waited for more, and she began fumbling for a cigarette. Her hand was shaking, but she lit up the smoke and took such a long drag on it, you'd have thought she'd consume the whole cigarette in one go. Then she said, 'My great-grandmother. That's what I meant, great-grandmother. She lived here.' And I asked her when, and she said, 'Till the explosion. She was killed in it.' Killed when this house was badly damaged in the blast."

Diane raised her hands in the air and pushed them down, as if to illustrate the house crashing down from above. "I didn't know what was going on, and I'm not sure she did either. She said again that the story was her great-grandmother had left something in this house, apparently for her family. And I told her that the house was seriously damaged in the blast and had of course been rebuilt. And she took another lungful of smoke and said, 'Maybe it was in the basement.' The basement had been pretty well intact after the explosion, and the new house was built over it. But we never saw anything, a keepsake or anything, when we moved in here, so if there was something, it may have been long gone."

"And she didn't say what kind of object it was? A piece of jewellery, photo, letter?" Monty asked.

"It was obvious that she had no idea. Must have been a story or a rumour passed down the generations in her family. She asked if she could come inside and look. Well, I wasn't going to allow that. If my husband, Ron, had been home, it would have been different. But he works nights. I started to tell her she could come back in the daytime, but then I heard a man's voice. He said something like, 'Get out here!' or, well, I'm not sure. And she looked spooked, and the next thing I knew, she was running up the back stairs of Lilith Stewart's place next door. And I heard her knocking, and then she went inside. They let her in. Knew her maybe? Anyway, she went into the house. I peered out the window looking for whoever had called out to her, the man I'd heard, but I couldn't see anyone."

"Where did you think the voice had come from? The street outside? The house next door?"

She lifted her head towards the street, turned it towards Lilith's house — Monty's house. "I can't be sure at all. But after a few minutes,

I looked across at Lilith's porch, and it seemed the girl was still inside. I hadn't heard her on the stairs, going down. After I got ready for bed, I looked out again. I don't think she had come out again, and I went to sleep. And, of course, in the morning I heard the police cars and the ambulance up at the top of the street, well, where it intersects with Gottingen. And I found out she had been killed! I called the police and told them what I've told you. Oh God, I should have helped her! But you just don't know when a, well, a stranger comes to your door in the middle of the night, half-drunk and rambling about something . . . I could never have predicted that she'd be killed on that very night!"

"No, of course you couldn't, Diane. I'm sure anyone in your shoes would have done the same thing. I won't keep you any longer. Thanks for talking to me."

"I feel like a shit for not helping her out!"

"As I say, Diane, any woman in a house with her children would have been just as cautious as you were." He added some more words of reassurance, thanked her again, and left.

She called after him, "I'll look around and I'll let you know if I find anything."

What were the chances of that? An object that the young murder victim could not identify or describe, something that had supposedly been in the house before the entire neighbourhood was blown up — if such a thing had ever existed, it was highly unlikely to be in place seventy-six years later.

CHAPTER VIII

Monty

A bit of luck came Monty's way the next morning. Sergeant Gabe Delorey called his office to say that the detectives working on the suspicious death had received a response to their efforts to identify the victim. The police were confident that she was Trudi Ebbett, twenty-three years old, a resident of Saint John, New Brunswick. The cops had gone to the address obtained for Trudi Ebbett but had not yet been able to find anyone who knew her, apart from one woman who lived in the same boarding house. The woman claimed to have had little more than a passing acquaintance with her. Ebbett had lived with another woman, but nobody had seen the roommate for a while, so there was no help to be had there. At least, not yet. Perhaps the housemates, not knowing who had killed Trudi, were afraid to speak to the cops. But the police had learned this much: Trudi Ebbett had been receiving social assistance payments from the New Brunswick government.

Monty scribbled a note about Trudi Ebbett and was about to say his thanks and goodbye when Delorey said, "And there's something else, Monty. About that other incident, the attempted break-in at the school."

"Really!" Monty bent towards his note paper again. "What's the story?"

Delorey laughed. "I should be more careful with my words, especially when talking to a lawyer! This may not be 'about' that other incident at all. Just something that happened the same night."

"I'm all ears, Gabe."

"I didn't hear about this till a couple of days ago. Two of our guys out on patrol responded to a call about a car that had slammed into a telephone pole the same night you and Mr. Burke chased that guy who attempted the break-in. As expected, alcohol was involved. A witness had seen the car veering from one side of the street to the other. He'd been barrelling up Lower Water Street not long after your pal had his encounter on Hollis." The two streets were in the same area. "Did the guy park his car near the school, attempt his break-in, and then run back to the car and take off? Not much to go on, I know, but he did have a tuque on his head. Cold night, though, so lots of people did."

"Never know. The timing is certainly interesting. Were there any marks on his face, Gabe?"

"Well, he banged his face on the steering wheel. Not belted in. So, marks? Likely, but maybe from the wheel, maybe from the fisticuffs out on the street."

"Who was it?"

"Fella by the name of Benson Freling."

"There's an unusual name, at least for Nova Scotia."

"Right. Not a MacDonald or a Fraser. Anyway, my colleagues who were looking into the driving infraction found out — or Freling told them — he'd been drinking at the Lighthouse tavern earlier in the evening. Not all that far from the school. Anyway, our guys went in to find out how much he'd been quaffing down. Bartender said he'd had a few shots of rye and that he was 'all worked up about something.'"

"Did the bartender say what had him worked up?"

"No, just that he'd been going on and on to a buddy of his — bartender didn't recognize the pal — about something, someone he was pissed off about. Then he up and left. Laid a few bills on the bar and took off. His buddy was saying, 'What the eff.' But that's all we have. So, I don't imagine this is much help to you, Monty, but I wanted to mention it."

"I appreciate it, Gabe. Thanks."

Most likely a coincidence, Monty thought, but he would keep it in mind. Right now, he was more concerned about the woman who had been found dead after a brief visit to his Young Street property. With little else to go on, he decided to try for a bit more information from Saint John. So he looked up the number of an old law school buddy who practised law in that city, and he called him and asked for his help. By the end of that day, he was able to give Monty the name of a community services worker in Saint John.

He would be going out for a draft or two at the Midtown with Brennan Burke and his father, so he decided to invite them along on the trip to Saint John. Show Declan Burke a bit more of the country while he was here. When they were all seated at the tavern, with glasses in front of them, he issued his invitation. "Can you clear your schedule tomorrow, Father Burke? For a trip out of town?"

"If you give me a good reason, I can have a couple of the teachers take over my classwork. It may be a lighter work day for the students, but I wouldn't expect any complaints about that."

So Monty filled them in on the Saint John expedition.

Brennan leaned over to him and said, "Anything that gets the oul fella farther from an international airport is good by me. Keep him from hopping on a plane to New York and causing an international incident."

✧

First thing Friday morning, Monty met with a couple of clients and then made a call to a hotel in Saint John. He reserved a room for himself and a room for the two Burkes, and they were soon on the road to New Brunswick with Monty at the wheel. They broke up the four-hour drive by stopping at Hynes Restaurant in Moncton for a good down-home lunch and chocolate cake with boiled icing.

It was a bright, sunny day, perfect for a road trip. Until they approached the old port city of Saint John, where they could see a fog bank enshrouding everything that lay ahead of them. And when they arrived at their hotel and checked into their rooms, the promised harbour view was all but obscured. Monty told the Burkes he would see them after his meeting with a social worker at the community services office. He found his way to the office and asked for the woman his law school friend had mentioned. And she was able to put him in touch with the worker who had been helping Trudi Ebbett. Mary Frances Gorman was a middle-aged woman with cropped greying hair and eyeglasses with heavy black frames. She stood and invited Monty to have a seat, and he explained why he was there.

The social worker expressed her sorrow over the young woman's death. "Trudi was a troubled young person, through no fault of her own. The same sad story we see all the time, I'm afraid. Unstable home life, father in and out of the picture. *In* the picture often enough to give the mother four children she could not afford to raise. So Trudi and the other children were passed back and forth between other relatives, some of them not the best role models for a growing child. Given all that, Trudi had never been able to settle. Didn't finish school, rotated through a series of low-end jobs, struggled with addiction to alcohol. No drugs, I'm pretty sure. She receives — I'm sorry, *was receiving* — social assistance." Welfare payments.

"As you say, Ms. Gorman, the same sad story."

"I'm sure you've seen it over and over in your work, Mr. Collins. These patterns repeated."

"Oh, yes."

"And what makes this one even more heartbreaking — I hope you won't take this the wrong way, because all these stories are heartbreaking — it's just that Trudi was such a kind person. She wouldn't hurt a soul. And intelligent as well. A great natural intelligence. She could have done well in school, if she'd had the support she needed, and she would no doubt have gone on to a successful career. But she had been weakened, damaged, so extensively and so early in life that, well . . ."

"I understand, certainly. Have you any idea why she went to Halifax?"

"Sorry, I don't. I hadn't had any personal contact with her for quite a while now."

"Do you have the address where she was living?"

"Yes, I do. There are other people around her own age living there, in the rooming house, so she might have been friendly with one or more of them. Somebody might have a few answers for you."

He thanked Ms. Gorman and headed for Trudi Ebbett's last place of residence. It was on a dodgy-looking street in the north end of the city: rundown houses, many with windows boarded up. Trudi Ebbett's rooming house was one of the worst, an old wooden building with shingles that had not seen a coat of paint in decades. Monty could see faint traces of the various colours that had been applied and changed and faded over the long years of neglect. There were rusted mailboxes and doorbells for four apartments, but the names were barely legible. A couple had been crossed out. He knocked at the rusted steel door. No answer. Knocked again, then pressed all the doorbells. He could hear someone stomping down the stairs, and then the door was flung open.

"What?" demanded a young woman in a grimy brown housecoat, a plastic shower cap on her head.

"Sorry to bother you," Monty said, "but I'm looking for Trudi Ebbett's roommate, if —"

"She got shot!"

"What? Her roommate was shot?"

"No! Trudi! In Halifax!"

There had been no word of shooting as the cause of death, but Monty saw no point in arguing. "Trudi was killed, yes. Is her roommate in, can you tell me?"

"She's out. Be back tomorrow." Slam.

When tomorrow? He knocked on the door again, and the woman appeared again, obviously burdened by his persistence. "Just wondering what would be a good time to find her home."

"End of her night shift. Morning."

"Which doorbell?"

She pointed to the button and gave the door a final slam.

Brennan and Declan were in their hotel room when Monty returned.

"Did you learn anything?" Brennan asked, and Monty filled him in.

"We're no further ahead, I don't think. The worker doesn't know what motivated Trudi to travel to Halifax. What did you lads do while I was hard at work? See anything of the city? The fog lifted for a while there."

Declan answered. "Were you aware, young Collins, that two distant continents met here in this city millions of years ago?"

"I must confess ignorance here, Declan. How do you come to be so well informed?"

Declan pointed to his son. "My boy got the receptionist to ring a taxi for us, to give us a tour round the place. And we heard about some fascinating history. And geology. Tell him about it, Brennan. How old is all that rock?"

"Hundreds of millions of years. When you see a map of the world, it looks as if South America and Africa could fit together. Which of course they do because they used to be together, and Europe and North America were linked with them too. And then they all drifted apart."

"Ethnic tensions?" Monty asked.

"We might think so, given our history, Mr. Collins. But no, it was more a movement of the tectonic plates that underlie the continents. The taxi driver took us to a bridge over the Saint John River at the Reversing Falls, or Rapids, and he showed us where there is a fault line crossing the river, separating two terranes. Terranes, as I'm sure you know, are fragments that break off the tectonic plates and move independently of the plates. Scientists are saying that on one side of the fault line is Cambrian rock from Africa, and across from that is Precambrian rock from South America. Two continents meeting here in Saint John, NB!"

"That is fucking amazing!"

"It is that."

"But not everything merged so successfully in this town," said Declan. "The taxi man was one of our lads, so he had a bit of more recent history to impart. About a fault line that seemed to be wider and more impassable than the one separating those ancient rocks. The orange and the green. Sounds as if this place is a wee Belfast, at least at certain times of the year."

"From what I've heard over the years, you're not far wrong. Now, what would you like to do?"

"What do you think?" Declan asked, as if the answer was so obvious the question need not have been asked.

"We'll find one. Let's go."

The fog was thicker now than when they had arrived in the city, but they weren't put off. They headed out for a stroll through the streets of the city. Monty remembered something he had read years ago. "Saint John is famous for its fog. You two will appreciate this. More than two hundred years ago, an illustrious visitor to this province — this *colony*, as it then was — left this city for another one a hundred miles or so away. Why? Because the fogs here were so constant, the man rarely caught a glimpse of the sun. How do we know this? The man wrote a letter home to his mother. The man was Lord Edward Fitzgerald."

Declan whipped around to face Monty. "You're having us on."

"No. Lord Edward was here, with a military regiment. A British regiment, of course. But he made up for that later on, as I understand it."

"Ah, he did," Declan confirmed. "Became a leading figure in the United Irishmen, fighting for the independence of our country. A popular, witty fella as well, from all I've heard."

"We'll brave the fog in his memory," Brennan declared, as they walked along and peered at the sights around them. He was particularly taken with the streetscapes of attached red-brick houses from the nineteenth century. "This could be a street in Dublin, or in Belfast." And farther on, he admired wood-shingled houses with steeply pitched gables and decorative woodwork. "Look at the detail on those Queen Anne places."

"You missed your calling, my son," Declan said.

"When you get a call from the Man Above, that's the call you answer. The world of architecture will have to go on without me. And it has done. Probably just as well; no doubt I'd just go back and build everything in the Georgian style. No innovation for any firm of architects to boast about."

"You were just ogling the Queen Anne places," Monty said. "Asymmetrical, every one of them. Quite the opposite of Georgian, wouldn't you say?"

"I have room in my heart for all of them."

On Waterloo Street, they came upon a crowd emerging from a funeral at the cathedral. "Have we been transported back to the old country, Bren?" Declan asked. "The faces on them, you'd think they'd just got off the boat from Cobh."

"Almost certainly, they came by ship, Declan," Monty replied, "ships from various parts of Ireland, though not just last week. Long time ago. This is a very Irish city. And coming back to a hint one of you dropped earlier, there are places that pour a decent pint, if my memory serves."

"Sounds like just the thing, eh Bren?"

"It does." Then, speaking in an over-the-top brogue, "Sure, aren't we gaspin' after havin' to walk on that street you had us on? Just a block away from here?"

"What? Orange Street had you concerned?"

"If the Orangemen were looking out their windows and saw a crowd of Papists on their street, anything could have happened!"

"My dad's side of the family had cousins here," Monty began.

"The Collins side," Brennan put in.

"Right. And I remember hearing that they used to stay safely indoors on Orangemen's Day!"

"I can well believe it."

It didn't take long to find an Irish bar. O'Leary's on Princess Street. Brennan said, "A priest, a public defender, and a . . . paramilitary walk into a bar." Declan gave him the death stare.

A classic Irish pub, and yes, they poured a fine pint of Guinness. It didn't take long before they were greeted by the locals, and introductions were made. Father Burke introduced himself as a priest, and Monty allowed as how he was a lawyer, but Declan gave no hint of his own history except that he was a businessman from Dublin and latterly of New York. This was enough to get the stories going. One old fella in particular took on the role of seanchaí. Storyteller. His name was Hughie and he was in late middle age with grey hair that still showed traces of its former red. Once it was clear which side of the sectarian boundary the newcomers were from, the stories came fast and furious. There was a tale about a man, several decades in the past, who was sent to the slaughterhouse to get a bucket of blood to make "blood pudding." Monty's stomach had always recoiled at the name of it; he'd never had the guts — make that the *courage* — to sample it.

"This man," the storyteller said, "was on his way home with the bucket, when he encountered a fella sitting right there on the street. And the fella called out to our bucket man, 'To hell with the Pope!' And what did our man do when he heard that slander? He up with his bucket of blood and dashed it over the reviler's head!"

That got an appreciative laugh from all who heard it. Encouraged, the raconteur told another one. "Every year on Saint Patrick's Day, we had a little tradition. A crowd of us got together, rented a room at the Admiral Beatty Hotel here in the city to celebrate the great saint's day. One year, we got creative. Me and a pal named Bob, and some other lads, decided to do a bit of decorating, a bit of a paint job." The man smiled and raised his pint, took a long swallow, and continued, "We had a bucket of green paint. We painted the hotel room and every item in it a brilliant green. Including the toilet."

Monty and the Burkes, and others in hearing range, enjoyed the tale. Everyone laughed; some clapped and cheered. "Good work, boys! Show 'em our saint's true colour!"

"But there's always a morning after, isn't there?" the seanchaí said with a comical frown. "Always a price to be paid. Sure, we had to open our wallets and pay for our mischief. But it was effin' worth it!"

Glasses were raised in tribute, and a fresh pint was ordered for the man of the hour. And Monty and his two companions enjoyed the craic for a couple more hours before saying their goodbyes and leaving O'Leary's.

❧

The next day for Monty and his fellow travellers dawned with sore heads and queasy stomachs, but there was no getting away from it: Monty had work to do, and then there was a four-hour drive back to Halifax. Following a hotel breakfast at the table with his weary companions, he made his second visit to the city's north end. He rang the doorbell to Trudi Ebbett's former flat, waited, rang again. Finally, he heard footsteps. The door was opened by a woman who looked as if she had spent the kind of night Monty had, but with less enjoyment. Her dark eyes were bloodshot, her long brown hair uncombed. She had on a pair of faded jeans and a sweatshirt bearing a photo of the band ZZ Top.

"Yeah?"

Monty introduced himself and gave a partial explanation of why he was there; he claimed that, as a homeowner on Young Street in Halifax, he had been questioned by the police about Trudi Ebbett's death and was unable to help them. He was coming to Saint John on business anyway, so he thought he would try to find out something that might assist in the investigation. He was surprised by the woman's quick invitation to come inside. "Oh, poor Trudi. I couldn't believe when I heard. Come in and excuse the mess."

He followed her up the stairs and into a flat crammed with tattered furniture. There were plates of half-eaten food on a sagging chesterfield. An open bedroom door showed one bed in disarray, another neatly made up. The smell of cigarette smoke vied with the cloying scent of flowery perfume.

"Sorry, sorry," the woman said, "this place is a pigsty. Trudi always kept it nice, but . . . I'm Lila. Have a seat. Sorry I can't offer you anything. What the fuck happened to my friend?"

Monty told her about Trudi's appearance at the Carmichael house on Young Street; didn't mention her time in his own house with Richard and Kirk, or his role as Kirk's lawyer. "The neighbour reported hearing a man calling to her from the street or somewhere outside. She was found dead the next morning."

"What man? Who did it? You don't know, right?"

"I don't know. The police don't know. Is there anything you can tell me about Trudi? Anything that was going on recently? Anything she was worried about? Do you know why she went to Halifax?"

"She had something on her mind, no question about that."

"What did she say, or . . ."

"All she would tell me was she wanted to go to Halifax."

"Oh?"

"She had a bee in her bonnet about something. Something set her off, and she kept going to the library, looking stuff up. Went to a second-hand clothing store and got some nice things there, but she wouldn't tell me why."

"Looking what up, do you know?"

Lila gave a little shrug, then reached for a pack of cigarettes. She lit one up and took a deep drag, then offered the pack to Monty.

"No, but thanks."

"No bad habits, eh?"

"Plenty of bad habits, but I gave that one up a few years ago. Still miss it, though."

"Yeah, that's what they say. You always miss it. Anyway, like I was saying, she'd go off to the library. When I asked her about it, she just said she was doing some research."

"Didn't say what kind of research?"

"Nope, but she did say she'd tell me later. Said she had big news, a big story to tell me, and she was going to get the proof. Whatever that was, I don't know. But then there was that phone call."

"Who phoned?"

"She did. She made the call."

Monty entered that in his mental file. Phone call, phone records. Those could be checked. But his complacency was short-lived.

"I don't know where she phoned from."

"Oh? Not from here?"

Lila looked around. "Do you see a phone in here? I gave up years ago on roommates and phone bills! There's a pay phone out in the hall, but she wouldn't have used that if she was calling long distance."

"Long distance."

"Well, I mean if she was calling Halifax. So, I don't know where she made the call from. But when she came home, she was steamed. 'He can't stop me!' She was almost hissing when she said it." Lila tapped her cigarette into her ashtray. "Of course, I asked her what the fuck she was talking about, and she said, 'Later.' She meant she'd tell me later. I bugged her about it again, and she said she'd been on the phone with some guy. Who was it? All she said was, 'An asshole. But I can deal with him.' Whatever it all was, I was going to have to wait. She'd fill me in later when she got the 'proof.'"

"And you have no idea what that was all about."

A shake of the head. "Like I said, she started 'researching' something or other, and there was that phone call and there was at least one other call. And then on Halloween night, I went to stay over with my sister and her kids, and I came home next morning and found her gone. Trudi."

"Did she leave anything, any papers or something like that, which might show what she'd been researching?"

"Nothing. If there was anything like that, she took it with her when she left."

"When was it when something first set her off, do you remember?"

"It would have been, I guess almost a month ago. It was just after Thanksgiving that she started talking about doing 'research.' That's right: I remember her being pissed off — not pissed off, I'd say frustrated — on the Monday, Thanksgiving Day, because everything was closed for the holiday. She was all fired up to do her research, and she had to wait till the next day."

Monty got up to leave. "Thanks very much for speaking with me. I'm sorry about Trudi." Her eyes filled with tears as she nodded at him in reply. "I'll give you my phone number at the office, Lila, in case you think of anything else that might help. And can you give me a number where I can reach you? Something may come up, and I'll have questions for you."

"The best chance of reaching me is at my boyfriend's place." She went inside and came back with a pen and a scrap of paper, and they exchanged numbers.

Monty thanked her again and left the boarding house. He returned to the hotel to pick up his passengers for the drive home to Halifax.

Monty had enjoyed the visit to Saint John with Brennan and Declan Burke, and the chat in the car was lively once their hangovers began to dissipate. But how much had Monty accomplished in his quest for information about Trudi Ebbett? All he knew was that she had been a kind and intelligent young woman who had endured a short, unstable life. And something or someone had prompted her to embark on a course of library research, after which she had engaged in an unpleasant telephone conversation with somebody, had at least one other call, then rushed off to Halifax. There was no way for Monty to know what, or who, had set those events in motion. But he now felt he could make the argument that her death was related to all of that, whatever it was, and was not the result of an unforeseen encounter with the young hockey player, Kirk Rhodenizer.

CHAPTER IX

Monty

B ut, as it turned out, relief was not yet at hand. When Monty was back in Halifax Saturday afternoon, he dropped his passengers off at Saint Bernadette's and then stopped in at his office. He glanced through the newspapers he had missed while out of town and saw a brief story about Trudi Ebbett; the police had revealed the cause of death as strangulation. There was not much more information, except that she was from Saint John, and police were "following several leads there and in Halifax." He turned to his phone messages, nearly a dozen of them, and found one from Kirk Rhodenizer. He called the number and left a message on the answering machine. Half an hour later, Kirk returned his call, and Monty invited him to come into the office. He was at the door twenty minutes later.

"The cops had me in yesterday for questioning again."

"What?"

"I tried to call you, but you were out of town."

"Well, if it's any comfort, Kirk, I was out of town looking into the life of Trudi Ebbett. Looking into her life, hoping to find something that would account for her death." It was almost painful to see the hope in the young man's eyes. "I didn't find the answer, but I do know she was in communication with a man about something that had her upset, and whatever it was, that's why she came to Halifax. I'm assuming that man wasn't you, Kirk."

"It wasn't! I never saw her before she came up to the house that night. Never even heard of her."

That much was true, Monty believed. "All right, what did the police say to you?"

"It was the same guys, detectives, that questioned me before. They said they had a few more questions, and I was going to tell them I wouldn't speak to them until I contacted my lawyer."

"A wise decision."

"But then I thought that would make them suspicious!"

Monty tensed up. "So, what happened?"

Kirk looked down at his hands. "I told them I'd come to the police station to talk to them. Because, you know, I don't have anything to hide, right? Before I left, I called here, but you were away. So I went in."

"And?"

"They asked about her coming to the porch, me and Richard letting her in. Asked me if she had been drinking, and I said yes. They already know I was into it, had a lot of booze in me. And I went through the same things I told you. And they asked again about the cut on my face."

"And you told them . . . ?"

"What I told you! I had a little scrap with one of the other guys at the house, and then the other guys took off."

"I believe you said you and the other guy or guys were horsing around. You didn't say there was a scrap."

"Same difference, who cares? It was nothing. So, anyway, then they wanted to know if I had any 'physical contact' with her."

"Right after they asked about the cut."

"Yeah, I guess so, but I said that had nothing to do with it."

"You told me the two of you did a bit of kissing while she was in the kitchen with you."

"Yeah, so I fessed up to them about that." Monty made no comment. "Well, they might have some kind of evidence, for fuck's sake. Somebody saw us through the window, or Richard told them, or somebody saw me run out and catch up with her and give her back her purse. I grabbed onto her arm then. And if I didn't tell them any of that, they'd say I was hiding something from them and I must be fuckin' guilty! They gave me shit for not telling them all that the first time. But I said I was too hungover and scared the first time. And I told them over and over again that I didn't hurt her!"

"How did it end?"

"Well, they didn't arrest me. Said I could go. And I got the hell out of there."

"All right, Kirk. They obviously feel they don't have evidence that could implicate you in her death. And I'll contact them and tell them what I learned in Saint John, about this man, whoever he was, and her sudden trip to Halifax."

"Thanks, Monty. Really. Thanks!"

❧

"So, what have we got, Brennan?" Monty asked. The two of them were sitting in Brennan's room that evening with a copy of the script and the materials the students had used in their research for the play. They were looking for anything that might explain the warnings and the activities of the man who'd had the confrontation with Declan. "We have a description of the destruction, the wrecked houses and buildings, then the snowstorm that so severely complicated the recovery operation afterwards, the search for survivors and the bodies of the dead. And, of course, the suspicious activities the kids have highlighted in their teaser for act two. But we are still in the dark about what, specifically, gave rise to all the intimidation."

"All that aggravation, and now your young client is questioned about the murder of Trudi Ebbett. You told me about your conversation with the woman now living in the house, the former brothel; she said Trudi's great-gran was killed in the explosion. We don't know how many children she had before her death, but one of them was Trudi's grandmother. Someone in the family talked about an object of some sort left in that house. So here we have another connection to the explosion. It may be coincidence, I know, but the timing . . ."

"Yes, the timing. She came to that house for the first time — that was clear from what Diane Carmichael said — she came to the house after doing research of some kind at home in Saint John. The roommate told me that it was about a month ago that Trudi started her research. Just after Thanksgiving, and in fact Trudi had been frustrated by the timing, the holiday. She wanted to begin her research right away. Thanksgiving Day was the eleventh of October, four days after our play was performed."

"Interesting timing, for sure, Monty. But how would she have heard about the play? Somebody in Saint John, perhaps, with a Halifax connection."

"Or she heard or read about it in the news. She, or someone she knew, had a Halifax newspaper. Or she saw one of the Atlantic news broadcasts that cover the eastern provinces. The story of the play made it to the TV news. I'm intrigued by the timing, no question. But it's possible, of course, that this had nothing at all to do with the play. We're not going to come up with any answers about Trudi here today. So, let's do our own research, as best we can."

"You keep on with the script, Monty. I'll look through some of this stuff. The young lads' notes."

Some of the original pages were smudged, the handwriting faint, but the photocopies were legible enough.

Monty returned to the script as Brennan flipped through pages. Then Brennan said, "Oh! Listen to this. It's a note by young Kavanagh, two months before the explosion."

Mike Kavanagh

"How about a walk along the harbour, Lauchie, see what ships are in." Mike had all his lessons done, all finished by suppertime, and Lauchie said he'd do his later. It was warm and sunny, just like the middle of summer, so they told Mike's mum they wouldn't be gone long, and they scurried down the hill to Campbell Road, which ran along the harbour.

"Look," Mike said, "couple of merchant ships heading for the Basin."

"They won't be here long. Off to France and Belgium, they'll be."

"We should sneak on board someday. Sail over and see the action!"

"So, Mike, would we be considered war dead if we got home six months later and our parents killed us?"

"Yeah, they'd be blowing the bugles for us over our graves, and our gravestones would say *Killed in action by their dads' belts and their mums' frying pans*."

"Not much glory in that." They stood looking over the harbour, past the ships to the Dartmouth shore. Then Lauchie said, "Oh, yeah, I meant to tell you this yesterday. This is a funny one. You know the North End Reformed Presbyterian Church?"

"Why don't you guys have nice, short names for your churches, like Saint Joseph's?"

"It's because we understand more complicated things than you RCs!"

"Ha, ha. Yeah, I've seen that church. It's smaller than the one you go to."

"It's a smaller building than Grove Presbyterian, but a lot of people go there. Anyway, have you ever seen the minister?"

"Don't think so."

"Reverend MacCombie, a big tall fella with wild grey hair. His picture was in the paper a couple of weeks ago. He was praying for our sailors and soldiers and airmen, and he was raising money to help the people in Flanders and those places."

"That's good."

"Yeah, he's a good fella. But he's stern and strict, and sometimes he scares the devil out of people with his sermons."

"I suppose that's part of his job, scaring away the devil!"

"Right. So, anyway, my parents had friends over to visit, people who go to the North End church. I heard them talking about a *scandal*! The scandal was about the minister's brother, W. Bertram MacCombie."

"*Double-u* Bertram?"

"Yeah, he always uses the initial. I guess it's the *posh* thing to do."

"Posh? What does that mean?"

"I heard it from my dad. He heard it from one of the British guys. It means smart or stylish, you know, like *us*, Mikey! Anyway, the way my dad told the story to my mum, Reverend MacCombie's head nearly caught on fire, he was so angry at his brother."

"Why? What happened?"

"The minister's brother, Bertram, his business is building and buying houses and selling them again for lots of money. I guess he must fix them up or make them fancier if he gets more money when he sells them again. He's starting to get rich, and he's going to move out of Richmond and down to the south end."

"He'll start thinking he's better than everybody here, better than his own brother, the minister. But he can't be better than a minister if a minister is close to God. Are Protestants close to God, Lauchie? Or are *we* in your way when you try to get close to God? *Darn it all, Reverend, all those Catholics are in our way on the path to our Lord.* I'll have to check my catechism to find out what it says."

"Ha, ha. You're a clown, Mike. You Catholics aren't the only ones who are pals with God. We Protestants have an inside track. You'd know how to get on the track if you spent as much time reading the Bible as you spend ringing all those bells!" They both laughed, and then Lauchie said, "But here's the story. This brother is the owner of the brothel house!"

Mike turned to stare at his pal. "What? How can he be the owner of it? The girls own it, the older one, the lady who's the boss of them all there."

Lauchie was shaking his head. "Not anymore. Dad told Mum that the minister's brother bought the house 'out from under them,' for a price that was lower than what they should have got for it, and now they pay him rent every month. And he did it in some sneaky way. I didn't understand what they meant, but it's something about Reverend MacCombie's brother having a company that owns the company that owns the house! Does that make any sense?"

Mike didn't know.

"Anyway, one company owns the company that owns a bunch of houses, and that is one of them. But because of those companies, whatever they are called, the Rev's brother's name is not on it. Even though he owns it! He has some other fella doing the work, Johnny somebody, and dealing with the people in the houses. But Dad says it's him. Bertram. Mum was shocked to hear it. 'That's how he's making his money?' she said, and Dad said, 'Some of it, yes. And what I heard is that the good reverend gave him a sermon that should have sent him down to the fires of hell!'

"'His own brother,' she said, 'living off the' something — veils? — 'of prostitution. And owning a common body house!'"

"Body house? That's a good name for it!"

"That's what he said, and my mum asked him about it, and he said it's spelled b-a-w-d-y."

"I never heard of that word."

"Well, now you know. You're living next door to a *common bawdy house* owned by the brother of a respected Presbyterian minister in this very neighbourhood!"

"Ha!"

"And Dad said something else about the brother, called him a *panderer*, said the minister was going on about the disgrace of it, and the immorality of it!"

"And we have a front seat to the whole *disgraceful* show!"

"Yeah, we should start selling tickets!"

Monty

Brennan handed the note to Monty, and Monty read what the young boy had jotted down.

"Well, that's an interesting twist, the note about the MacCombies. They are the family that owns Halifax 1749 Developments Ltd. Owns it now, I mean. What do you think, Reverend Brennan Xavier Burke, does that ring any bells in the steeple for you? Minister of a north end Presbyterian church in 1917?"

"Can't say that it does. Wish I could go back in time and teach young Mike a bit of theology. Those scribblings about the Catholics and the Protestants, and the way to salvation. I'm only joking. It looks as if they had fun adding their little jibes to the notes here. But I've no doubt that Mike and Lauchie are writing their notes in Heaven now, so no harm done."

Monty was taken aback; he could not have explained why. After all, it was hardly a surprise that those two young characters, the two young diarists, were no longer among the living. Their seemingly rich lives were over. But Monty felt as if he'd come to know them, almost as if they were contemporaries of Normie and Kim and Richard. But no, they were no longer of this world.

"Are yeh all right there, Monty?" Brennan asked. He was looking at Monty with an expression of concern.

Monty shook off what he'd been feeling and said, "I'm fine. Just, well, don't you feel as if you've come to know those two little fellas, Lauchie and Mike?"

"I do. It's almost as if they're my students at the school."

"Anyway, I can look up MacCombie in records of that time. The minister and the scandalous brother. I'm aware of the present day MacCombie, but I don't know him personally. He'd be what, a grandson?" Monty did a quick calculation. "From the boys' notes, it's clear that Bertram, the minister's brother, was well-established in business, so not just a young fella back then. But, even so, the timing would be right for the current MacCombie to be a grandson. His name is Lorne. He uses the services of another law firm, the biggest firm in the province. And there are business keeners in my firm who would love to have him and his company as clients, and those fees coming our way. Which is understandable. After all, Brennan, we eat what we kill."

"Well, that certainly gets us down to the fundamentals, Mr. Barrister and Solicitor."

"I suppose it does, but my focus today is on the 1917 iteration of the MacCombie business empire."

CHAPTER X

Brennan

As Brennan tried to put aside his worries and drift off to sleep on Saturday night, his mind was assailed by an image he'd been trying to avoid since the threatening letters arrived at the school. But the image stayed at the forefront of his mind, and wouldn't *she* be pleased to know that she featured in his late-night imaginings? What if, he asked himself, the determination to close down the school play arose not out of the script or the references in it, but out of the choir school's decision to stage a play at all? The play had attracted a great deal of attention and had been featured in the news. The idea of *attracting attention* brought up memories of a specific individual whose entire raison d'être was to attract attention. At least, that had always been Brennan's impression of her. Of Abilene Hemlow.

Brennan had lived in Halifax for a brief time many years ago and had set up a choir school. Then four years ago, he had returned to the city and established Saint Bernadette's. He had hired Sister Marguerite Dunne as principal. And Brennan was the music director.

After a couple of years as principal, Sister Dunne had moved to South America to do charitable work, and Brennan had had the run of the school ever since. But before she left, Sister Dunne had undertaken a search for a drama teacher, to conduct classes and to stage theatre productions from time to time during the school year. She offered the position to Abilene Hemlow. Originally from a small town in Ontario, she had studied theatre in Toronto and then moved to Halifax. And had soon become the bane of Brennan's existence, or at least of his days and occasional evenings at the school.

During her first few weeks at the school, she played the part of a demure Catholic schoolteacher, dressed in conservative suits or matching dresses and jackets. That was how she had presented herself on the Monday morning when he first met her. But she had not been attired as a schoolmarm the following Friday night when the students had been invited to a showing of *Charlie and the Chocolate Factory* at Neptune Theatre. That night, she turned up in a long tight silky black dress with frills along the hem of it. Her light blonde hair fell to her shoulders and was done in elaborate waves, and she wore a white silk headband in the style of the flappers of the 1920s. Fair play to her, the story arose out of Roald Dahl's childhood experiences in that decade. But the evening's event was not about her. Or was he being unfair? Was she just having a bit of fun, getting into the spirit of things? Surely, that was it. But he soon came to think otherwise. He soon came to realize that in her mind, she was the central figure in any encounter with another person.

A couple of weeks after the Neptune Theatre outing, Bernie Drohan, one of Brennan's fellow priests, stopped by his office, came in and sat down. "So, Brennan, has that actressy one come on to you yet?"

"Eh?"

"Abilene."

"Ah."

Drohan then did an imitation of some typical Abilene poses, the chin lifted in defiance or cocked sideways in a pantomime of attentiveness, head and body swivelled around in a gesture of haughty dismissal. "Did she leave the stages of Ontario to come down east and impress us simple folk with her amazing talent? Who knows? But I know this much, Brennan: she's a real priest groupie. She used to go to Mass at Saint Christopher's, and she began hanging around the office of the pastor there — you know who I mean — and she'd tell him she was grateful to him, appreciated him, because he was a man who valued her for herself and not for her . . . I don't know how she put it, but her meaning was clear: men just couldn't resist her. Our friend over at Saint Chris's finally started avoiding her."

"What took him so long?" Brennan asked.

"He's the soul of kindness, doesn't see the bad side of people. And people think we Catholics see sin and devilment everywhere!"

It hadn't taken Brennan any time at all to catch on to the attention-seeker who had been hired as the school's drama teacher. She would come to his office on the flimsiest of pretexts, such as problems with a student. Or the unfriendliness of one of the other female teachers; the inference he was supposed to draw was that the other woman was jealous. You didn't have to be a psychic or a Sigmund Freud to see through that one: *They're all jealous of me and you can see why.* And any time she managed to get Brennan alone, she gave the impression that her life had been one scene after another of Sturm und Drang. Brennan knew he should be sympathetic. He, like the Lord himself, should be forgiving, not judgmental. And she was, he freely acknowledged, a fairly good teacher. But he simply could not summon the patience to deal with this pathological need for attention.

Knowing all that, however, Brennan made a big mistake. It was one of the nights he was having a few jars at O'Carroll's. He had come to know some of the regulars there as well as two talented fellas who frequently provided music: Frank the piano man, and Patrick the singer. On this night, Frank played a series of fast pieces on the piano, and that got a few people up dancing. Pat rose to his feet and sang a couple of songs from the 1940s. Brennan caught the eye of a woman he knew, a regular at the bar, and asked her on to dance. All in good fun. When the song was over, she smiled at him and returned to her seat. Then Abilene walked in. Alone. Just happened to walk into the pub that was well-known as one of Father Burke's favourite drinking spots?

When she caught sight of him, she affected to be surprised, in a way that would never have got her admitted to, or graduated from, a reputable theatre school. But a few pints of beer and a few shots of whiskey had put him in a mellow mood. So, rather than see her standing there alone, he invited her to dance. But, as luck would have it, Pat's next song was a waltz. Before Brennan could make his excuses and return to his table, Abilene reached out and drew him to her. He didn't want to pull away and leave her standing alone, embarrassed. So he succumbed. To the dance, not to the pressure of her body against his. He saw the song through and then said, "I have to go." He didn't have to go, but he wanted to get away, even if that meant leaving a half-full glass of beer on the table.

Her response was a quiet, ostensibly sympathetic, "I understand." Then, "You stay, Father. I'll go." And she turned on her heel and left the bar.

So then he didn't *have to go*. Good, he could stay on, rejoin the lads at his table, and finish his beer. And order another.

In the days after that, he was treated to what he could only have described as a regretful, almost pitying smile whenever she saw him at school.

Abilene Hemlow did her job passably well, though some of her performances brought on snickers and winks on the part of the older students. And the other teachers couldn't stand her. Oh, they were smart and discreet enough not to confess this to Father Burke, but he knew what was what. She had been hired on a yearly contract, and well in advance of the expiry date, Brennan told her he would not be renewing it. As predicted, this brought on another bout of Sturm und Drang, and threats of a lawsuit. But he had consulted Monty about the legal aspects of it — he had never told Monty about Abilene's off-stage performances — and was assured that he was within his legal rights. She did not take it well. She shouted at him that he was pathetic, that he was a drunk who used alcohol to sublimate his longing for a woman, that he had *obviously* never known a woman's love. Well, she sure as hell didn't know his history — which most assuredly did include women and love — and he wasn't about to recount it to her.

Then it was the auditions for a play she was hoping to stage, a scaled-down version of *Les Misérables*. Brennan knew that she had recently started up her own theatre company. The mother of one of the students at Saint Bernadette's, who had some acting experience and wasn't the least bit *actressy*, tried out for a part and was turned down with a spate of mean-spirited, unwarranted criticisms before she was halfway through her audition. There were a couple of other incidents that came to Brennan's attention in the weeks after he put the run to Abilene. He also knew, from the talk around the school and even from the newspapers, that her new theatre company was "struggling." It had not yet found success as a financially sound operation, and the reviews of the two last productions were mediocre.

She had shown herself to be vindictive in the months following her departure from Saint Bernadette's Choir School. And that was why she was on Brennan's mind tonight. Now the school had enjoyed a great success, a public success, the Halifax Explosion play having been covered and complimented by the news media. The school's theatrical triumph had been accomplished without the talents of its former queen of drama. Was there a chance that she had persuaded one of her male actors to intimidate the students of Saint Bernadette's so they'd cancel the play? How likely was that? Was this a product of Brennan's cynical imagination? Was he not getting enough sleep these nights?

When he awoke in the morning and reviewed the scenarios that had kept him up until the late hours of the night, he decided not to mention any of this to Monty Collins. Not for now, at least.

Monty

On Monday morning, Monty made a brief appearance in Provincial Court with a long-time client for whom the deterrence principle never seemed to work. After that, Monty was in the province's Public Archives, sifting through a pile of papers provided by a helpful member of the staff. He had asked for anything relating to the MacCombie family's businesses in the First World War era. And here were papers relating to Scotia Modern Properties Limited. A quick scan of the documents confirmed what Lauchie MacIntyre had reported to his pal back in 1917: the property development company was owned by a holding company, and it was called Scotia Victory Limited. It was clear from the documentation that W. Bertram MacCombie was the operating mind behind the holding company. The property outfit held title to a handful of single-family houses and two apartment buildings. One of the single-family places was on Young Street, and the plot plan seemed to verify Lauchie's claim that the MacCombie interests had owned the brothel. Monty recalled the young boys' notes — and, no doubt, their laughs — over the image of the preacher's brother as lord and master of a common bawdy house. Bertram the Pimp MacCombie? Embarrassing, no question, to a family of such fine, upstanding citizens.

Then he turned to another box of documents he had requested, after recalling Normie's little spiel at the closing of act one of the play. She had given the audience some tantalizing hints about what they could expect in act two, including the suggestion that some of the damage claims people had made after the explosion were fraudulent. She'd been careful to say that most people had behaved honourably, but some had not. So Monty was digging into a collection of documents that described the compensation schemes set up in the wake of the disaster. The Halifax Relief Commission had established small claims courts to handle claims for loss or damage to people's personal belongings, storeowners' supplies and merchandise, and the like. Along with the announcement of the new courts came a warning: anyone making a false or fraudulent claim would face criminal proceedings. The file contained a clipping from the *Halifax Herald* dated January 31, 1918, stating that there had been many phony claims under an earlier official body, the Halifax Relief *Committee*. In February 1918, the Commission appointed a board of appraisers to assess material damage sustained by houses, schools, churches, and other buildings. Compensation was paid in the amounts approved by the Commission.

At the bottom of the box was a sheaf of papers, somebody's handwritten notes. Some were legible, others not. But it was clear that the writer was recording the decisions made with respect to some of the claims for property damage and loss. Most of the notes contained a personal or a business name, an address or street name, and comments such as "claim accepted in full," "allowed in part," and "not allowed." Other claims were marked with exclamation points: "rejected!"; "fraud!"; "found to be exaggerated!"; "declared fraudulent!!" A quick survey of the pages showed that only a hundred or so claims were recorded by the unknown scribe, or perhaps these were the only notes that had survived. It was clear from the other documents on file that many thousands of claims had been processed. But of the ones that had been recorded here, two captured Monty's interest. One was in the name of Scotia Modern Properties Limited, the owner of a house on Young Street; the claim was "declared fraudulent!!" On another page was a claim in the name "McColbie," scratched out and replaced with "MacCombie." That claim was labelled "fraud" and "proceedings taken." So the MacCombie family and business had engaged in behaviour that would not reflect well on them, then or perhaps even today.

Now, how was Monty going to approach the current chief executive officer of Halifax 1749 Developments Ltd., the successor company to the old Bertram MacCombie business? He could hardly go up to Lorne MacCombie, confront him with the family's and the old company's shameful behaviour in 1918, committing fraud and living off the avails of prostitution, and ask Lorne, *Oh, by the way, did you follow and intimidate a young girl — my daughter — and did you write threatening letters to her and her friend, and try to break in to Saint Bernadette's Choir School?* It would be difficult enough to do that even if Monty could be sure that the past and present events were linked, but how could he possibly be sure of that? He could not. But if there was any possibility of a connection, he had to find out.

Back at Stratton Sommers, he knocked on the door of Julian MacEachern, a senior partner in the business law department. As far as Monty knew, Stratton Sommers had never represented Lorne MacCombie or his companies, but MacEachern was well informed of the activities of prominent players in the business world. Monty didn't want to show his hand to Julian, at least not yet, in case — as would likely turn out — MacCombie had had no involvement in the disturbing activities around the school. Monty asked himself, Should I cook up a story for Julian or just say I'll explain later? He decided that honesty, if not candour, was the best policy with his law partner. So he just told Julian he'd like to speak to MacCombie about something. "I'll explain later. Have you any idea where I might just 'happen' to meet up with him? I don't want to make it formal with an appointment to see him at his office, or his headquarters, whatever it might be."

If Julian was curious, he didn't let it show. He said, "You could have seen him last night, Monty, at the Halifax Club." That was a private club founded in the 1800s, catering to the business elite of Halifax. Monty knew Julian was a member.

"You were there last night?"

"Yeah, I was just leaving when MacCombie came in. But you'll still have a chance to meet the great man if you're willing to make a donation to the IWK."

That was the children's hospital in Halifax. "I make regular donations to the IWK." He did, as did everybody else he knew.

"There's a fundraiser at the Hotel Nova Scotian on Wednesday night. And you can be sure MacCombie will be there, likely on stage when it comes time for the speeches. He does a lot of good work, supports a number of charities, and that's all to the good. But it has to be said that he's not shy about getting the word out."

"To increase support for those noble institutions, you mean, Julian."

"Of course, Monty. Anything he happens to mention about himself is only incidental to his noble intentions."

Monty laughed and asked, "What time is the event Wednesday night?"

"Seven till nine, but of course these things often go into overtime."

"Thanks, Julian."

Monty hoped it would go into overtime, because he had promised Maura and Normie a night at the movies; they were going to see *The Secret Garden* at the Oxford Theatre. Luckily, it was in the city centre. He'd get home with the family and then boot it over to the Hotel

Nova Scotian and hope MacCombie was still there amongst the business elite and the generous benefactors of Halifax.

℘

The next day, he saw a number of clients, criminal and civil — in both senses of both words — in his office. In the middle of the afternoon, he received a call from Saint John. Trudi's roommate, Lila. "We had a little get-together for Trudi, a memorial service, kind of. You're looking into her death, and you asked for any information I might have. But, oh, I don't know. Maybe I shouldn't have called you about this. It's not going to give you any information about who killed her."

"Tell me anyway, Lila. I appreciate your calling me." He knew it might not provide any information about Trudi's killer, but he wanted to learn whatever he could about her life, particularly about what might have interested her in terms of her research.

"Okay, so a few of her friends and kids she used to babysit for, we went to one of the restaurants where she worked as a waitress. They liked her there, the owners did, even though . . ."

"Even though?"

"They caught her one night. She stayed on after her shift. She was supposed to lock up, but she stayed inside and sat up at the bar, drinking. And she took a bottle of rye when she left, but when she stepped outside, she slipped on a patch of ice and she fell and the bottle smashed to pieces. Somebody heard it, and . . . Well, the owner of the restaurant found out about it. But, like I said, they liked her and kept her on and tried to get help for her, for her drinking. And she really appreciated that, and she was able to get off the booze for a while afterwards. Anyway, the couple that run the restaurant, they said we could have the party room for the memorial.

"The girl who came up with the idea for the party was one of the girls Trudi used to babysit for, Shauna. She set it up and contacted people who'd known Trudi and asked them to pass on the invitation. And Shauna asked everybody to bring pictures or to remember something nice about Trudi and tell the stories. She collected all the stuff into a scrapbook, Shauna did, and some people asked for copies, and so she made them. I could send you a copy, but it's not going to help you find who did it. These are all her friends, not anybody who had it in for her."

"You never know what information might be helpful, Lila. I'd like to see the materials you have. And I'll be happy to reimburse you for the postage." He gave Lila his office mailing address, thanked her, and wished her well.

☙

On Wednesday night, he set out on his mission to the Hotel Nova Scotian. The hotel was only a few blocks from Monty's house, but he decided to take the car to save time. When he had parked and entered the grand old red-brick hotel, he saw men and women coming out. They were in suits and dresses and might well have attended the charity fundraiser. He went inside, saw a sign for the IWK event, and headed to the large ballroom where it was being held. People were standing around talking, with drinks in their hands. He knew some of them and he greeted them as he made a tour around the room. No sign of Lorne MacCombie. Monty had come too late to the party. Not too late to make a donation, though, one of the organizers assured him. So he wrote out a cheque. He spoke to a few more of the guests before turning to leave. But he spotted his quarry, striding into the room and then heading for the exit. Monty had to make his move. He circled around so he would be coming to MacCombie from the side. Now, what to say?

"Oh! Mr. MacCombie. I'm Monty Collins. We've met in the past; you may not remember." Monty wasn't sure that they had actually ever met, but it was a useful opening line.

"Of course, I remember." Did he? Had they actually met? It didn't matter either way. "How are you doing, Monty?"

"Not too bad. A little late for this gathering, unfortunately. Family commitments, you know what I mean."

"Oh, I certainly do. I have two boys, and they keep me on the hop. Tennis in the summer, ski trips in the winter."

"Yeah, tell me about it!" Monty exclaimed, joining MacCombie in the role of busy, busy parent. "Tonight it was the movies. Bit of a change, a welcome change maybe, from theatre practice, but don't tell my daughter!"

"Oh, you have a kid studying drama?"

Monty tried not to beam with satisfaction as the conversation went exactly where he wanted it to go. "No, it's a school play. Saint Bernadette's. The play is in two parts, two acts on different nights, so it's not over yet! It's all about the Halifax Explosion. You may have heard about it? The kids even made the CTV news."

MacCombie's face bespoke uncertainty. "That sounds a bit familiar."

"The play has required a lot of research on the part of the students and teachers. Parents too. I thought I was fairly well versed in explosion lore, but turns out I didn't know the half of it!"

"Oh, yeah?" And then, "I don't know much about it myself. The two ships collided, one of them blew up, and much of the city was destroyed. Great loss of life and property. But I don't know much more than that."

"Well, these young students have taught me a lot. And some of it is quite — how should I say it? — scandalous! At least for a bunch of kids in the middle school years. Lots of boozing, a bit of fighting, and a couple of scenes set in a house of ill repute! Brothel on Young Street. Who knew?"

"Really? I wouldn't know. Er, well, I mean, how could I know? It was all way before my time, eh? 1917! But," he continued, "I just don't know much more than what I said to you, the basic facts. Never knew anything more, more of the social history. I studied business, so I suppose I missed out on a lot of other stuff."

Doth he protest too much? Monty wondered. "The business degree has done well for you, from everything I've heard, Lorne! Sorry, before I got off on my own little tangent there, I meant to ask: how did things go here tonight? A success?"

"Oh, yeah! Plenty of interest, pledges of support. Great evening all round."

"Good to hear. I've made my donation, and I'll try not to miss the next event!"

"Okay, great, Monty. See you later."

Monty didn't feel he was any the wiser for having cornered Lorne MacCombie. There was a hasty denial of knowledge about the explosion and its aftermath, but there were many Haligonians who knew little more than the most basic facts about the catastrophe that befell their city. And many of those people might be quick to own up to the limitations of their knowledge when more obscure facts about the disaster were raised.

❧

The next morning, Monty decided to pay a visit to another lawyer in his firm, Blair Trites. Blair didn't regard MacCombie with the mild amusement evinced by Julian MacEachern. Blair was a fan, and for an understandable reason: Blair would love to add Lorne MacCombie and his business to his stable of corporate clients. But, for as long as Monty could remember, it was Donaldson McNabb, Stratton Sommers's largest competitor and the biggest firm in the province, which enjoyed MacCombie's patronage. Monty walked to Blair's door and was invited inside.

"Hey, Monty, how's it going?"

"Not too bad, Blair. And you?"

"Busy as hell, which can only be good, eh?"

"True enough."

Once again, Monty had to engage in a bit of subterfuge with one of his law partners. "Blair, I have a question for you. Do you know much about Lorne MacCombie and his business interests? The reason I ask —" Monty raised a hand to ward off Blair's apparent enthusiasm. "No, he hasn't come to our door, asking us to take him on as a client!"

"Damn! Story of my life, guys like MacCombie not showing up at our door."

"I know, but a friend of mine was asking about him. And I have no idea what his real interest is. But if this guy — my pal — ever needs a lawyer, I'm almost certain he'll come to us. And he will be a fine client to have on our books!" And why wouldn't this fictitious pal come to us, Monty asked himself, if all our partners and associates are as good as I am at spinning a tale and making things up on the fly? "So, anything you can tell me, or anywhere you can direct me for a bit of information on MacCombie would be a help."

"Sure. I don't have anything here. But a couple of years ago, I asked Kathryn to keep any news or journal articles she sees relating to any of the big players here in the city, in the province." Kathryn was the firm's librarian. "She has quite a file, on paper and now on her computer. I know she'd have something about MacCombie and his corporate entities."

"Great, Blair. Thanks. I'll ask her."

He headed to the firm's well-stocked library with its shelves of case reports, statute books, and legal texts. He greeted Kathryn, chatted with her a bit, and then made his request.

"I'll have a look, Monty. I know we have some material relating to those businesses. I'll buzz you when I've found something."

"Thanks, Kathryn. Appreciate it."

"Any time, Monty."

It wasn't an hour later when Kathryn called his office and reported her findings. He returned to the library and was handed a stack of papers. He thanked her again and went back to his office to do some reading. Some of the pages were clippings or photocopies; others had been printed from the library's computer. There were a few stories in the local papers and references in some journal articles. A couple of court cases: a wrongful dismissal suit by a former employee and a dispute over bylaws relating to a planned property development. There was, of course, much news coverage of the company's current development plan that was being considered by the city's Development and Planning Department. And, also to be expected, coverage of the rumours that MacCombie was being considered for the Storeyed City Award. As in "storeys" of buildings, and a pun on "storied," meaning celebrated or legendary. It was inevitably referred to as "the *coveted* Storeyed City Award." But it also had a nickname, and it, too, was inevitable: the Sore-Eyed City Award. Not everyone was a fan of some of the buildings that had been put up in recent years. In recent decades. Monty recalled Brennan's disdain for some of the brutalist concrete buildings in the city, which compared so unfavourably with the many beautiful buildings and houses that graced the streets of Halifax. The news reports made much of MacCombie's commitment to hiring people who had been disadvantaged in the course of their lives: recovering addicts, people who had been homeless, and some who had been in trouble with the law. The men, some of them quite young, were given work as labourers on the company's building sites. Monty recognized some of the names, particularly the names of ex-convicts whom he had seen in the criminal courts over the years. There was nothing in any of this that reflected badly on Lorne MacCombie or his companies, nothing like the allegations of fraud levelled against the earlier incarnation of the family's business empire.

Brennan

Brennan had been invited to a wonderful concert of sacred music performed by a choir in the town of Antigonish, about two hours east of Halifax. He enjoyed his time alone in the car, and he revelled in the exquisite sound of the choir and the organ. It was his kind of music. The program included "Panis Angelicus," music by Franck, words by Saint Thomas Aquinas, no less, and Palestrina's "Sicut Cervus." The final number was one of Brennan's most cherished pieces, Mozart's "Laudate Dominum." He had decided to stay over, and the organist–choir director, a brilliant musician named James MacPherson, arranged for him to have a room at the local university, Saint Francis Xavier. This saved him a late-night drive, and it gave him the opportunity to enjoy another event, after the concert, a spontaneous céilí (or cèilidh, as it was spelled in Scottish Gaelic) at the home of a lovely woman named Margaret MacDonald but always referred to by her original family name, Margaret MacGregor. The guests all stood around with drinks in hand and sang to her wonderful accompaniment on the piano. In between songs, the members of the choir kept Brennan entertained with stories about some of the larger-than-life characters of Antigonish. A thoroughly enjoyable evening. It was snowing when he set out for Halifax in the morning, and he had some harrowing moments during whiteouts on the Trans Canada Highway on the trip back. He had repeatedly thanked God for the ethereal music he had heard; were snow tires in the Lord's gift as well? Whatever the case, he was grateful for that so Canadian tradition of changing to snow tires before the onset of winter.

He arrived in Halifax unscathed and headed up the stairs with his travel bag, chucked it onto his bed, and went across the hall to see if his father was in.

"Da?" No reply. Brennan turned the knob and stepped into the room. No Declan, none of his belongings, no sign that the man had ever been there.

CHAPTER XI

Monty

Stratton Sommers always scheduled a staff party in mid-
November, to avoid conflicts with the many Christmas parties in
December. This year's event was on Saturday, November thirteenth,
at the Lord Nelson Hotel. Monty knew he should have laid off the
booze much earlier that night but, as Brennan would say, the craic
was mighty, and Monty hadn't wanted the fun to end. Well, the fun
was over now. Every time he drifted off to sleep, he woke up and
had to use the toilet. Rather than disturb Maura's sleep, after the
second trip to the bathroom, he retired to the guest room and got in
between the sheets there. When he finally passed out, his sleep was
disturbed by dreams, violent and unrecognizable images.

Then something came unbidden to his mind at three o'clock,
that most dread hour, thé soul's midnight. He remembered one of
the names in the laudatory article about Lorne MacCombie and his
company, about some of the disadvantaged people MacCombie had
hired to work on his building sites. One of those people was Cole

Barstead, a lifelong criminal with a history of violent offences. There was an extremely violent robbery of a young drug dealer committed many years ago, and the two men accused of the crime had turned on each other. Each claimed to be innocent; each claimed that the other had laid the horrendous beating on the victim, which left the young man with a red ragged scar across the left side of his face and a no doubt larger scar on his abdomen after his spleen had to be surgically removed. Barstead was initially represented by Nova Scotia Legal Aid, by one of the best trial lawyers in the province. But the client flew into a snit when the lawyer, speaking from long experience, outlined the situation for him, told him how slim was his chance of acquittal based on the story he insisted on telling. So Barstead fired his Legal Aid lawyer, went and hired a newbie with virtually no courtroom experience. Monty was representing the co-accused, and he was able to get his own client off, while Barstead was convicted. It was a righteous conviction — Monty had uncovered enough information to know that it was Barstead who had administered the beating — and he was sentenced to eight years in federal prison. Lying in bed at three in the morning, Monty found his mind assailed by lurid images of what Barstead had done to his victim.

And then it was Normie. As Monty tossed and turned and writhed about in bed, he formed the image of his little girl being followed and then battered and bloodied by a vengeful Cole Barstead who was, in this late-night horror show, working for Lorne MacCombie. When the sun was up, and Monty with it, he tried to shake off those fears and images. He blamed it on the hour and on the drinking. He had no reason to think that Cole Barstead would be aware of the theatrical offerings of a choir school. Equally unlikely that he would be worked up into a frenzy by an allegation against the 1917 incarnation of the MacCombie family's business interests. It was ridiculous. The notion came to him that somebody — *not* Saint Bernadette's Choir School — should stage a play based on what people imagined as they thrashed about in their unquiet beds at three o'clock in the morning. No doubt it had already been done; maybe half the films on the screens today were born out of exactly that.

Was his dream a premonition? Or was it merely a coincidence that Sergeant Gabe Delorey arrived at Monty's office Monday morning with news that he had interviewed a suspect in the Morris Street following of Normie?

"Good morning, Mr. Collins."

"Good morning, Sergeant. Can we get you a coffee?"

"No, thanks, I just had my Tims. And I won't keep you long."

"Have a seat."

"Thanks. So. We found a couple of witnesses, people who were on Morris Street at the time your daughter was followed." Monty felt a chill but didn't interrupt the cop. "Best witness was a lady who was standing across the street from your . . . Normie, is it?"

"That's right."

"Our witness is a secretary at the engineering school. That's how we found her, stopped in to some of the places around the Morris-Barrington intersection to see if anyone had noticed anything that day. Our witness had just come out of her building and started walking easterly along Morris, coming up to the intersection. As she put it, 'a young lout nearly knocked me over,' on his way by her and into the entrance there between the TUNS buildings. She also reported hearing another young guy call out to somebody, and she saw him run across Barrington to a 'young girl with the loveliest red hair,' as she put it. That jibes with what Normie reported, her friend from school hailing her to give her a book."

"Richard Robertson."

"Yes. Now, our witness from TUNS was happy to describe the lout who nearly knocked her over. His clothing was as reported by Normie, but the secretary also got a look at his face, at least the part of his face visible between the scarf and his cap." Delorey reached into his pocket and pulled out a sheet of paper. He smoothed it out on Monty's desk. "This is a photocopy of what she drew for us. At least she got the shape of the nose, kind of a short nose, and wide at the end, the nostrils." He looked up at Monty with a look of amusement. "Is that what all those writers mean, when they say somebody's nostrils flared?"

"I don't think that's what they mean," Monty replied, "though I've never been sure. Nobody's ever flared their nostrils at me!"

"That's probably a good thing. The only other feature she could sketch here was the eyes. She said they were dark, rather small and round in shape, and she tried her best to capture that in her drawing. Not much, I know, and nothing that stands out. We didn't see any point in taking this and making the rounds of the buildings and houses in that area, since nobody else had reported seeing this guy.

"But we showed it around Gottingen Street. The station, I mean." The Halifax police station on Gottingen Street. "And we may have an idea where to look."

"Really!"

"Our guys gave us a few names for a match. We had to rule a couple of them out because they aren't walking the streets these days. Thanks to the efforts of our fellow officers of the law! Anyway, what I'm thinking now is that it may be a fella we had up on a charge a few years ago. Assault, fight with another kid. He was a young oaf at the time." A young offender. "The case didn't go anywhere; clever lawyer got him off. But that's neither here nor there. We had his name. I'm going to withhold his name for now, Monty. Unless or until something comes of this. Anyway, we looked up his particulars and went to see him. Hard life, the kid had. The father vamoosed on them and the mother couldn't cope. The boy was taken into care, and then there were foster homes. The Chardley foster home, and the McCartan Street foster home. Then he was adopted, and the new parents were good folks, and there was a fairly good relationship between them and the kid. But a wild streak in him. Drinking, doing drugs, getting into minor scrapes."

"Well done, Gabe. Tell me this: have you any idea whether he ever worked for Lorne MacCombie's company, Halifax 1749 Properties Limited?"

"Don't know. He's nineteen years old now. We know he worked cleaning up at a couple of the city parks. Youth support work project of some kind."

That answered one question for Monty: Delorey didn't know of a connection, so it *was* a coincidence that the sergeant had come by after Monty's night of dreaming.

"Anyway, we had a chat with him. Now here's where I have to let you down, Monty. He denies following anybody, doesn't remember if he was on Morris Street that day. He might have been, he might have walked into the TUNS complex, doesn't recall. Sometimes he just goes out walking, likes being downtown, doesn't keep track of where he went."

"Didn't come up with an alternative, then, some other place he claims to have been at that time? Didn't think of it, or maybe smart enough to know nobody could give him an alibi for that other location."

"Yeah, I know. But here's what I'm thinking. We won't get anywhere trying to charge him with anything in relation to 'maybe following a girl or maybe not' on the nineteenth of October, 1993. But the attempted break-in at the school, damage to the property, that's another story altogether. He's an adult now, and the attempted break-in is, obviously, a serious offence. So we'd like to speak to Father Burke's dad again, pin him down a bit more on the description of the guy who tackled him. If the description matches, he'll be looking at a possible arrest."

"Good plan, Gabe. I wish I'd got a look at the guy's face that night but, unfortunately, I didn't. But Declan Burke did. I'll give Brennan a call, and we'll set it up."

Monty made the call and waited for Brennan to answer. He was about to hang up when he heard Brennan's hello. "Morning, Father. Would your dad be around? Sergeant Delorey is here, and he has somebody in his sights for the incidents relating to the school. He'd like to talk to Declan again and get his description of the man he — what?"

Declan was "gone"?

"I don't know, Monty. I don't know what the fuck's going on. I tried to ring him at his office a couple of times; didn't want to alarm the family at home if I could avoid it. No answer at the office. So I rang the house in New York yesterday, and all my sister could say was that Da had to return to his work, and he'd been busy ever since he got back."

"Thank you, Father. I'll talk to you again later."

To paraphrase the good father, what the fuck was going on? But Monty was not about to voice those concerns in the presence of Sergeant Delorey.

"Bit of bad news there, Gabe. Apparently, Mr. Burke had to return to his work in New York. But we'll get in touch with him and . . ."

"Okay, Monty. That's too bad. But we'll hope to hear from him and get his information soon. Maybe make the arrest."

"Thanks for all your work on this, Gabe. We'll hope for a quick resolution."

After the sergeant had taken his leave, Monty called Brennan again. "I'm just on my way out, Monty. But I'll talk to you later."

"How about coming over to our place for supper?"

Brennan hesitated for a moment, then said, "That would be grand. Thanks."

"See you whenever you can get there this evening."

Brennan sounded like a man with a lot on his mind.

Normie

Mum made lobster rolls and toasted the buns, the way her own mum used to do them. And there was wine, and they let me have a wee glass of it. It was called white wine but it was more like yellow, and it tasted great. We had strawberry shortcake with whipped cream for dessert. It was delicious, even though Mum said the strawberries were frozen, not fresh, because it wasn't summer anymore. Grandma Evelyn was with us, and Father Burke. My little brother, Dominic, loves Father Burke and likes to show off to him by pressing the number three button on the stereo and dancing to a song by Van Morrison. He started doing this months ago, ever since Father Burke came over and played Van on the stereo and Dominic heard it and liked it and started dancing. Then after supper, I read Dominic a story and put him to bed. Grandma Evelyn and Mum went into the living room and got out the photo albums of me and Tommy as little kids and Dominic as a baby. We have three colours of hair, the kids in my family: blond for Tommy, red or *auburn* for me, and black for Dominic, and we were so cute as little kids! Well, Dominic is still little; he's only two. Dad and Father Burke stayed in the kitchen and drank beer. I stayed upstairs and picked up one of my favourite books, a Nancy Drew mystery, *The Clue of the Whistling Bagpipes.*

I was so interested in my book and Nancy's adventures in Scotland, I didn't hear Dad and Father Burke at first. But I heard them when their voices got loud. I have a trick that I do when I'm upstairs and I want to listen to somebody's conversation down below. There's a thing called a register in the floor; it's related to the furnace and the heat, and it has metal things and holes in it. And I can hear through it what people are saying downstairs! I crouched down in front of it and listened.

Father Burke said, "I'd been to Antigonish Wednesday night for the concert — it was brilliant — and I stayed over and drove home in the morning. Skidding around through snowdrifts and at times not seeing the road at all. Halifax didn't get the storm, but it was wild out on the highway. And I got home and went to Dec's room, and he was gone. No sign he'd ever even been there! Fucked off in the middle of the night? Or did he go earlier? Flew out as Michael Francis O'Farrell, presumably."

"What did you say, Brennan? Flew out as somebody O'Farrell?"

"Ah, he . . . Never mind."

"Brennan. What did you mean?"

"I was looking for something a few weeks ago, in the room where he was staying, and didn't I find a false passport with his photograph and the name Michael Francis O'Farrell! Jesus the Christ who suffered and died on the cross!"

"What on earth accounted for that? What did he say? Did you ask him when you found it?"

"Of course I bloody well asked him. But do you think he gave me an answer?"

"So, what then?"

I stayed perfectly still by the register. I didn't want to make a move that they might hear and know I was listening.

Father Burke answered, "There was no discussion of the passport again, and now, no more Declan."

That's when I snuck down the stairs. And I could see into the living room. I wasn't the only one who couldn't believe it — you should have seen the face on Grandma Evelyn! She was staring towards the kitchen, even though she wouldn't have been able to see in there. But she could hear what they were saying. Her mouth was partway open, the way people's are when they're hearing bad news. I remembered how happy she had looked when she was dancing with Mr. Burke and when she was watching him sing. I bet she wouldn't want to dance with him now!

I heard beer cans being cracked open in the kitchen, and then Father Burke said, "Here we have the police with a suspect, and all they need is confirmation from Declan — which they'd get if Dec recognized the man in the drawing — and now we can't get that. Some scut follows Normie, tries to break into our school, and he's still out there. What's he going to do next?"

It really spooked me when he said that. Was that evil man going to hurt me? Me and the other kids who put on the play? I was scared, but I couldn't say anything about it. I couldn't admit I'd been listening in, or Mum and Dad might close up that register, or keep watching it to see if I was listening there. I looked into the living room, but Mum and Grandma Evelyn couldn't see me. I heard Grandma Evelyn say, "What sort of chicanery is Declan Burke involved in, Maura?"

Mum actually laughed! And she said, "You don't want to know, Evelyn, you don't want to know."

Monty

Monty wanted to speak to Julian MacEachern again about the MacCombie family. And it was time to be forthright about the reason for his interest. So, at work on Tuesday, he filled Julian in on what the MacCombie company had done after the explosion. And he told him about Normie being followed, the threatening letters, the attempted burglary.

"Jesus, Monty! I'd never heard any of that, the past misbehaviour. And, my God, going after your daughter and trying to break into a choir school?!"

"I'm guessing nobody knows about it, the less-than-admirable behaviour back in 1917 and 1918. And I'm sure the MacCombie clan would like to keep it that way, keep it buried."

"For sure."

"I didn't want to blacken the family's name the first time I asked you, Julian, if I could avoid it. But now you know. Would Lorne MacCombie be sensitive about how the family's company carried on back in that time?"

"I can't see it troubling Lorne MacCombie's conscience today, Monty." The word "conscience" was enclosed in fingered quotation marks. "Sure, he's a teetotaller, doesn't take a drink. He's the product of good, sober Presbyterian stock. And he has a little schtick advising young folks to stay off the demon rum and the wacky-tobacky in order to realize their ambitions for a prosperous future. But the occasional sharp business practice would not be beneath him, if he could see a benefit for himself."

"So, what you're saying, Julian, is that it's not likely he excused himself from the boardroom — or the wrecking ball — and set off to follow a little girl or break into a school. Because of something that might allude to his family's past misdemeanours?"

"Well, now, there is someone who might be sensitive to a revelation like that."

"Oh? Who would that be?"

"Our mayor will be up for re-election next year as you know, and she is much more attuned to ethical matters than Lorne. And genuinely so, I might add. She has a social conscience, and that kind of behaviour wouldn't sit well with her."

"It was more than seventy-five years ago, though, Julian."

"But in many respects it's the same company now as it was then. And from everything I've heard, MacCombie is desperate to get the city's approval for his project. It will be worth millions to his company, and to him. And he's bent on getting that Sore-Eyed City Award. So, I'd say a bad report from the past would be an unwelcome distraction."

Brennan

It had been nearly a week since Declan's furtive departure. Brennan finally reached him on the phone. Or, to be more accurate, he left a message and Declan finally returned his call. There was considerable background noise, and Brennan knew that his father was not calling from the Burke family's phone. "Imagine my surprise, Da, when I arrived home from Antigonish and you were gone. The only witness who might be able to identify our school burglar, gone."

"Brennan, I had to be here. Had to come back to New York. Now, don't be annoying me about it. I'm sorry, but it couldn't be avoided."

This was not just irascibility on the part of his father; Brennan could tell that he was deeply distressed about something. So Brennan turned the conversation away from the sudden flight from Halifax to the situation facing the man who was under threat from the drug dealer recently released from prison. "What's the latest on Flying Colum O'Flynn?"

"The situation has escalated, as they say, Brennan. Somehow, someone slipped word to the peelers that there might be questionable activity going on here at the company." Burke Transport. What kind of activity, Brennan wondered. "But McGarrity and his toadies are not the only fellas who have the ear of a member of the New York Police Department. One of my own lads has a friendly connection on the force, and my pal rang me when you were out of town for that concert and told me the cops were going to come by my office for a look at my books, my records. So I had to get the first flight out, early morning flight here to New York via Montreal and, well, get my books ready for possible prying by the peelers."

"Em, did the police show up at your office?"

"They did."

With a subpoena, or what kind of authority? Well, that didn't matter for now. Brennan merely asked, "And?"

"And they found everything to be in order."

Had everything been in order already, or had the books been put in order by Mr. Burke of Burke Transport when he got back to the office? And what kind of offence had the police been suspecting? "What were they looking for?"

"Who knows?" his father replied, in a convincing show of innocence. Was he suspected of aiding his old acquaintances in the Hell's Kitchen mob? Or was Declan doing business with a more political crowd, his Irish republican connections in New York? If that was the case, Declan would keep his cards close to his vest as he always had done. No point in Brennan trying to convince Declan to show his hand in that respect.

He had another question ready to go: "Why the false documents, Da? How long have you had the O'Farrell passport?" Silence at the other end of the line. Brennan cursed himself. He should have stuck to one question, one at a time. He could imagine Monty Collins making a critique of Brennan's interrogation methods. "Dec?" he prompted.

Finally, his father spoke. "I've had it for a while."

"Why?"

"You never know when you're going to need something like that."

Brennan tamped down the temptation to grill his father on that vague non-answer.

"And in this case?"

"I knew about the threat to O'Flynn, that the threat might come close to the company, my office. So I didn't want it known outside friendly circles that I was absent."

"But how would anyone know what flight you were on, if you went under your own name?"

"You'd be surprised, Brennan, at the connections some people have, the information they can get."

That was just one of many, many things that his father seemed to know, and that Brennan would be surprised about. And, Brennan wondered, how and why was Declan's presence in New York perceived as a deterrent to anyone who wanted to make a move against O'Flynn? Was it Declan's connections to, or acquaintance with, the Irish mob that would frighten someone off? Brennan remembered the stories of the Irish gangsters being so fearsome they even frightened members of the Mafia! Or did Declan himself have a reputation as a man to be feared?

But what had Brennan concerned now was what his father had intimated about Burke Transport. How close was Declan to O'Flynn? Was Declan himself in danger? "How well do you know O'Flynn, Da?"

"He lives here, in Queens."

"And that's how you've come to know him."

His father put on a broad New York accent. "Yeah, we're neighbours. We hail each other over the fence when we're out mowing our lawns and polishing our Buicks."

Brennan took that as a broad hint not to ask how they had in fact come to know each other, or what schemes they had been involved in together. But he did have a question. "Are you in danger yourself, Da? Is this shower of shites, McGarrity's associates, going to show up at your office?"

"We'll be ready for them if they do."

"So, what, you have measures in place to —"

His father laughed. "Measures in place. That's one way of putting it."

"How else should we put it?"

"Don't be concerning yourself, Bren."

Brennan searched for words of comfort, however insincere. He was about to try to persuade his father to alert the police about the threat against his friend and employee. But, no, O'Flynn's association with Hell's Kitchen likely meant there were outstanding matters that could come back to haunt him if he were to receive close attention from the NYPD. And, as Brennan well knew, Declan Burke was not a man for alerting the police. All Brennan could come up with was "Da, take care of yourself, for the love of God."

"I will."

Their parting words offered no comfort to Brennan or, he knew, to his father, after his unplanned return to the turbulent scene in New York.

CHAPTER XII

DECEMBER 7, 1917

Mike Kavanagh

S now was falling when Mike looked out the upstairs bedroom window of Uncle Frank's house, snow creating a white blanket over the wreckage of the houses down the hill. It was the morning after the ship blew up, and his father called him to come downstairs. When he walked into the living room, he saw all the members of his family, down on their knees. He knelt with them. They were all crying, saying the beads and praying for Ellie in the hospital, that her eyes could be saved. When she was at her cousin's place on Gottingen Street, she heard about the ship on fire and, like so many others, she had wanted to see it. She ran upstairs and watched from the window; the explosion blew pieces of glass into her eyes. The family were on their knees, praying for her and for all the other people who had been horribly injured. And they thanked God for saving their own lives and the lives of some of the other people in Richmond.

Mike's dad had to get up and go to work on his ship. *Niobe* had survived the blast but had a lot of damage from huge pieces of metal flying onto it and from a big wave splashing over it. Mike had heard Dad telling Mum that when *Mont Blanc* caught fire, *Niobe*'s captain sent seven sailors out in a boat to try to assist in some way. When the ship exploded, the men and the boat were blown to smithereens. And then a bunch of men were killed on *Niobe* itself. Mike tried not to think about what all that looked like, about the men being killed and their families being left without them. And Dad had a strange story he'd heard from a pal of his who'd been working at the drydock when the explosion occurred. The man said that for a quick moment, he could see down to the bottom of the harbour, bare rock! It had something to do with water pressure, and water had been sucked away from some of the shoreline. Thank God the Kavanaghs' dad had been aboard the ship yesterday but had come off it alive. Now, on Friday, he said he would come back from work in the early afternoon, and they would all go to their house, which wasn't a house anymore, and see if they could pull out any of their belongings. It was snowing, and they would bring a sled from Uncle Frank's to load things on, if anything could be saved.

By the time their dad returned to Frank's, it was the middle of the afternoon, and the city was being blasted again, this time by a blizzard. Aunt Mary lent their mum a heavy coat, hat, boots, and mittens, and the two ladies hugged each other, and then Mum set out in tears, trudging through the snow to the hospital to see Ellie.

Mike didn't know how many of his family's belongings were still in their own house and how much could be loaded onto the sled, but that was all they could do. He and Dad and Patrick started tramping through the snow down the hill. Mike still could not believe what his eyes were showing him, even though he had seen all the rubble yesterday after it happened. Some of his friends' and neighbours' houses were completely flattened. They were just piles of stone and shingles. Poking up through the snow were sticks of wood, some of the wood black from burning. People had their stoves lit because of the cold, and the stoves got knocked over and the fires spread all through the houses and the wreckage.

Mike and Patrick were wearing heavy coats, mittens, and boots that used to belong to their cousin Frankie Jr., but Mike's fingers were stinging with the cold as they clomped through the wind and snow, dragging the sled behind them. But Mike knew better than to complain. When they got to their own place, Dad stood there, stock-still, as if he couldn't think what to do or say now. Mike knew he was determined that their house would be rebuilt, and the family would move back in whenever it was constructed. For now, they were going to get whatever they could out of the ruins. "You boys are not to try to climb inside. If you see something, you tell me, and I'll try to get it. If you get too cold, you can go back to Frank's." And he climbed through the open window and jumped down into the cellar.

"Look what's over there!" Patrick said, and Mike turned to look at the place next door, where all those girls had lived. There was a big motor car parked right up against a snowbank in front of the girls' wrecked house. Mike knew that soldiers were going around Richmond collecting the dead people and carrying them away in their wagons or motor cars.

"That's a Case Limousine," Mike told his brother. It must be the same guy with the Case again, the same guy he and Lauchie used to see visiting the house. Mike liked motor cars and kept after his dad to save his money and get one. But he'd never be able to save enough for one like this. Yes, it was the same Case he had seen there before; one of the fenders over the front wheels was shorter than the other, as if it had been clipped. Maybe somebody drove up too close to the limousine and hit it. Looking to the back of the next-door yard, Mike saw a man in an army uniform and cap, and he was pulling a body up from the ground in the backyard of the house. He tried a couple of times and then managed to hoist the body up over his shoulder.

Mike said to Pat, "He's carrying a dead man. I'll go over and help him."

But just then, their father crawled out of the cellar. He reached around and pulled out some items from the house, then did the same again, and brought out more things. Clothes, a few books, the boys' toy soldiers and ships, a kettle and a couple of dented pots, and a cardboard box that Mike knew contained the notes he and Lauchie MacIntyre had been making for the last year or so. Dad had reassured Mike about the MacIntyre family: they had all survived. Thank Heaven! Mike hoped it wouldn't be too long before he and Lauchie were writing their "memoirs" again. "Give me the box, Dad," Mike said. His father handed it over, then climbed back down into the cellar.

Mike looked next door again and saw the soldier trying to get the body into the car. "Here, hold this and don't drop it," he instructed his brother, and handed him the box of notes. Then he ran over to the motor car. The soldier had some kind of mask on his face. A gas mask, was it? No, it didn't look like the gas masks Mike had seen; this was just made of cloth. Maybe to keep the awful smell out of his nose as he went around collecting dead people. Mike headed towards the man, who had his back to Mike now, straining to lift the body into the auto. "Do you want some help, sir?"

The man jerked his head up but didn't turn around. "No!" It was almost a shout. Then, "No, stay where you are." And he managed to get the body in, then got into the car and drove away. How many dead bodies were there? How many people had been killed? A hundred? Maybe even more. Mike wouldn't want to be a soldier doing that kind of work. But then he scolded himself for being stupid; what does a soldier do when he's out on the battlefield? His job is to kill, not to pick up the dead and carry them away.

Mike returned to the house, and his father said, "We'll come back again tomorrow and look some more." They piled their things on the sled and prepared to leave.

Mike looked over at the girls' house, its backyard. And he saw a bunch of boards stacked up beside a big gaping hole, which was filling up with snow. He remembered a garden back there, or at least the earth for a garden, with pieces of lumber lying around the four sides. Nobody had ever planted flowers in it. All he'd ever seen in it were rocks and fallen branches. Now there were pieces of lumber stacked up neatly on one side beside the hole. Stacked up? The blast sure as heck hadn't stacked wood up like that. He turned his mind to the first minutes following the enormous blast yesterday morning, which had knocked him down onto the cellar floor. After all the commotion and the screaming and crying at home, he had looked across at the girls' house next door, with its top storey smashed down. Now, a day later, Mike looked again at the house where all those girls had lived, where a man had just removed a body. And it struck Mike then: there had been no body lying in that backyard after the explosion.

NOVEMBER 1993

Monty

A week after Lila phoned Monty, a package arrived at his office. From Saint John. He tore off the packing tape and pulled out a sheaf of photocopies. Some of the pages contained handwritten notes that had been pasted in; on other pages, there were photographs. One picture showed a smiling Trudi and Lila with their arms around each other. In their free hands, each of them was holding up a lobster. Another picture was of a little blonde girl standing in front of a suburban bungalow with a woman, a man, and three other children. The name Trudi was printed below and an arrow pointed up to the blonde girl. Her own family or a family of relatives who had looked after her? There was no other information. A young teenage Trudi was photographed standing with a boy of the same age, hand in hand, on a wharf.

Another photo showed a grinning Trudi with a little boy and girl kneeling behind a couple of items made out of Tinkertoys. Monty remembered the toys from his childhood: construction sets with parts made of wood. Wheels, spools, sticks, wide blade-like parts made of plastic. In this picture, Trudi and the kids had constructed a helicopter and two people standing beside it, with foolish expressions painted on their faces: a big smile on one, a clownish frown on the other. A handwritten note read, "Trudi always brought Tinkertoys when she came to babysit. She found them out behind a store. She told us the owners had thrown them away because everybody wanted Lego! We loved the Tinkertoys!"

One of the notes struck a more sombre tone: "Trudi tried her best to give up drinking. It wasn't her fault she started drinking so much. Blame her father who kept running away. He was an alkie — maybe it runs in families. She never got nasty like him when she drank. She was a sweet girl!"

Monty brought the package home with him after work and showed it to Maura and Normie. Normie said, "It's even more sad now to think about Trudi being killed."

"Yes, it is," Maura agreed, gazing down at the representations of the young woman's short life.

"You guys had Tinkertoys when you were little, right?" Her parents nodded yes. "Maybe we can get some for Dominic."

"Good plan, darlin'," Maura agreed.

"And I know I'll think of Trudi any time we play with them."

Brennan

Brennan and Monty had arranged to get together on Wednesday to discuss the notes written by the boys in 1917 and the hints Normie had given her audience to entice them back for the second act of the play. Monty said he had an appeal factum to prepare but he could put that off. So they decided to talk things over while enjoying a beer and lunch at the Lower Deck. Brennan left his students with Mrs. Graham to study their lines for act two, in which the characters would be shown trying to grapple with the horrendous aftermath of the explosion. As harrowing as the scenes would be, he knew his young actors were keen to get back to telling their stories and showing the audience what it was like for those who had survived the blast.

The Lower Deck was located on the Halifax waterfront in a complex of stone and wooden buildings known as the Historic Properties or, alternatively, as Privateers Wharf. Brennan liked the latter designation, which reflected the city's colourful history of privateers: in other words, pirates who had the blessing of their government to sail out and prey upon another country's ships — America's, for instance. He knew that construction of these buildings had begun as early as the Napoleonic Wars.

He arrived at the waterfront just as the ferry was coming in from Dartmouth. It had been quite a while since he'd taken the ferry across the harbour; it was a fine, clear day, so that might be a pleasant little outing after lunch. Monty arrived just as Brennan was heading inside. "Greetings, Mr. Collins. I believe one of your ancestors was instrumental in founding this place wherein we shall dine and drink."

"Ah, yes, Enos Collins. I can't claim any relation, but I'm familiar with his reputation. A fearsome privateer back in the day. The only things I've ever taken off a ship are creatures with gills or claws."

"Maybe we'll enjoy a bit of the sea's bounty here today."

They found a table and ordered their drinks, seafood chowder, and fish and chips. Brennan had always liked the place, the rich colour of the wood that lined the walls, the beams of the ceiling, and, of course, the location right on the water.

Before addressing the main subject of discussion, Brennan decided to fill Monty in on the reason for Declan's vanishing act the week before. He took a sip of his beer and recounted the events that had occurred in New York.

Monty stared as Brennan told the story, then said, "I don't even know where to begin, with all that. If your father was a cat, how many lives has he gone through already?"

"I'd rather not speculate, any more than I'd be one of those people who cross out the days past, one by one, on their calendars. I try to tell myself I'm not superstitious, but I'd never do that. Must have something to do with the phrase 'Your days are numbered.' As for Declan, he certainly hasn't eased into the life we'd all wish for our fathers, a relaxing retirement, making up adventures to tell the grandchildren . . ."

"Has he any plans to retire from the company?"

"That'll never happen."

"And I guess he won't be sitting in a rocking chair, telling the grandchildren any of his *real* adventures."

"No, indeed he won't. Now, to our more immediate concerns. We haven't made any progress in our search for whoever has been putting the frighteners on our students."

"No, we're still in the dark."

"Our young thespians have tantalized their audience with the promise of scandal and intrigue in the next installment of *Devastated Area*. They read Mike Kavanagh's note about the body, the body of someone who hadn't died in the explosion and was taken away in a pricey motor car, so we may have a murder mystery. And some shameful behaviour in the form of looting, people taking advantage of the situation, stealing things from the wrecked houses. And then there's the ownership of the bordello by a family known for its rectitude and, presumably, its otherwise brothel-free lifestyle."

"And it sounds as if the outfit that bought the bawdy house took to gouging the women for the rent, overcharging them."

"What's the term for it? Making a living off the avails?"

"Of prostitution, yeah. I've been asking around, as you know, Brennan, even spoke to the present-day MacCombie. And he was unconcerned, or affected to be unconcerned, about the play. Portrayed himself as one of the many who have little knowledge of the events of that December day in 1917, beyond the most basic facts about the ships and the destruction. I was told by someone who knows Lorne MacCombie that what his family may have been up to seven decades ago might not trouble him, but he is up for a prestigious award. You'll enjoy the name of it. The Sore-Eyed City Award."

"You're having me on. And if you're not, they must be giving out loads of them every year."

"It's the Storeyed City Award, and despite the name and the nickname, there's fierce competition to win it. Lorne MacCombie is in the running for it, and he's also trying to get permission from the city for a big property development. That all depends on City Council or the Development and Planning Board, and my contact mentioned that our mayor is a person who cares about morality and reputation even if some of our business moguls do not."

"Right. And then there's the fella who engaged in the looting. Imagine taking advantage of such a catastrophic event to enrich yourself at the expense of the victims! Have you learned anything about that?"

"Not yet."

Brennan digested all this and was left uneasy. He had another idea about who might have been motivated to see the play shut down. He knew he should tell Monty, but . . . "Let's finish up here. I was thinking of hopping on the ferry for a little cruise across the harbour. Haven't done that for a while."

"Good plan. Let's go."

So they finished their lunch, polished off their beer, and left for the ferry terminal. They bought their tickets and waited as the blue and white passenger boat put in at the dock. Monty said, "Have you ever taken the ferry 'cross the Mersey?"

"I've been known to belt out the song in a crowded bar in the late hours of the night. But that's the extent of my knowledge."

"Well, that ferry from Liverpool across the Mersey to Birkenhead is the only saltwater ferry service in the world that is older than this one."

"Is that so?"

"It is. We also, as you may know, have a town named Liverpool on a river named the Mersey. South shore of the province."

"I've been there. Lovely town, lovely houses."

"Good, I knew it would please the architect manqué in you, Brennan."

They boarded the boat and seated themselves on the deck, and the fifteen-minute crossing from Halifax to Dartmouth began. They had a fine view, the early afternoon sun shining down on the blue water, the waves with an occasional whitecap. Brennan was enjoying the little voyage, but less pleasant matters intruded on his enjoyment. He knew he had to tell Monty about Abilene Hemlow, and the grudge she might still be holding against Saint Bernadette's Choir School. There was nobody seated near them, so he couldn't use lack of privacy as an excuse.

"Do you know who I mean by Abilene Hemlow? Do you remember her?"

Monty turned from staring out at the Atlantic to look at his friend. "Yeah, she was the drama teacher at the school. You asked my advice about not renewing her contract. I never knew what had gone wrong there; you didn't say much at the time."

"Didn't want to get into it." He then proceeded to tell Monty about her, the theatrical poses, her fixation on priests, her attention-seeking behaviour.

"Christ, Brennan. I never met her. Was she really like that?"

"She was."

"I know you're not one to castigate others without cause. But there must be more to this woman than that."

"Of course, there must be. But I never saw it. And to hear the talk around Saint Bernadette's, nobody at the school ever saw it. I'm sure there is a reason. Deep-seated insecurities, to state the obvious. But, anyway, my point is —"

"That Abilene Hemlow did not take kindly to her contract not being renewed."

"Did not take kindly. That's putting it mildly. What's the expression? She threw a hissy fit. She gave out to me that I was a drunk, that I used drink to drown my sorrows over my frustrated longings for a woman. Including herself in the longed-for category, presumably."

"Ha. From what I know of your history, Burke," and here Monty put on a stereotypical Irish brogue, "you did more shaggin' and ridin' before you entered the priesthood than the rest of us porr divils get to enjoy in a lifetime."

"Sure I was just a lad out to experience the world and its delights as God created them."

"You're a saint, Father."

"Ah, now, I'm a couple of miracles short of sainthood. But I can tell you I wasn't tempted for an instant by that one, Abilene."

"How's the drama teacher you have now? Is Mrs. Graham giving you any trouble?"

"Mary Fiona Graham. She is class. Talented, fine sense of humour, knows everything there is to know about theatre, and is not the least bit theatrical herself."

"Good. That was my impression of her as well."

They were coming close to the Dartmouth shore, and Brennan took a look around. He saw an enormous container ship passing under the Macdonald Bridge on its way out to sea. He said, "Can you imagine, Monty, living in the middle of the continent somewhere, out on the prairie, a thousand miles or more from any sight of an ocean?"

"I couldn't fathom it, Brennan. Father, forgive me for the bad pun."

"Te absolvo, my son. How about a walk along the waterfront here before we sail back?"

"Sure. You'll get a fine view of Halifax from over here."

"That's what we'll do. I'll wrap up that unwelcome conversation I initiated, and then we'll enjoy our walk and try to forget all that shite. What I'm wondering, obviously, is whether that one's resentment against the school might be behind the attempts at intimidation. I've heard from teachers and parents that she expressed, or demonstrated, considerable bitterness about being cast out. Did she convince, or entice, some male actor to do her bidding, carry out those attempts to frighten or intimidate our students and scuttle act two of the play?"

"You're going to have to talk to her."

"I appoint you for that task, blue eyes. But keep a grip on your belt when you see her."

"You're not going to weasel out of it that easily, you old heartbreaker. If the two of us show up, like a pair of detectives, she might come down with a case of the vapours, affect a nervous collapse. So, you're on your own. But why don't you leave it till we've checked out some of the other angles first."

❧

Monty and Brennan might not be a pair of detectives, but such a pair arrived on Brennan's doorstep not long after he returned home from his harbour cruise. They introduced themselves as Detective Sergeant Lennox MacPhee and Detective Constable Shaughnessy Doyle. He invited them into the office, and they sat down.

"We won't take up a lot of your time, Father," said MacPhee. "We are here in reference to the death of Trudi Ebbett on the night of November the first, or early morning of November the second. We know that Mr. Collins has been looking into links among three incidents that seem to be related to the play your students put on in early October. One incident, in particular: the letters sent to two of your students. As for the death of Trudi Ebbett, we have learned that she embarked on some kind of quest or research shortly after the play, and we know that some excerpts from the play made it to the CTV regional news broadcasts. Then she came here to Halifax and approached the resident of a house in the north end, asking if she could enter the house and search for something she believed a family member had left there not long before the Halifax Explosion. None of this points to a certain link between the play and her death, but the timing suggests that it should be looked into, if only to dismiss it from our investigation. So, we are here to ask you for a copy of the script for the play."

"Certainly. I have copies of the script for the first act and a draft script for the second, which is scheduled to be performed next month. Hold on and I'll get them for you."

He returned seconds later with the copies and handed them over. They thanked Brennan for his assistance and went on their way. As the detectives would no doubt have predicted, Brennan got on the phone and relayed to Monty the entire conversation.

Monty said, "That sounds like good news and bad news, Brennan. They are open to the idea of a link between the play and Trudi's death, which brings the school's production into the mess again. But it should be good news for Kirk Rhodenizer; he may not have to fear another visit from the coppers."

CHAPTER XIII

Monty

M onty was just about to leave work for the day when Julian MacEachern appeared in his doorway with a newspaper in his hand. "Have you seen this, Monty? Drunk driving case."

"No, I haven't. Is somebody in need of my services?"

Julian laughed. "Maybe so. The guy was loaded and rammed his car into a telephone pole on Lower Water Street." That struck a chord with Monty. What had he heard about an incident on Lower Water? "When was that, Julian?"

Julian looked Monty in the eye. "Monday night, twenty-fifth of October."

"Ah." The night Declan had chased down the would-be burglar.

"Police found him in the car, and he's facing an over-eighty charge, impaired driving, and some related charges as well. He appeared in court and told the judge he needed time to consult a lawyer. So he's set to appear again on Friday. Not sure what his insurance company might have to say about the damage to his car! But here's the point. The man's name is Benson Freling."

Yes, Monty remembered the name Sergeant Delorey had given him for the drunk driver.

"Actually," Julian said, "it's Benson Freling Junior. You were asking me about Lorne MacCombie and his corporate interests. The story here says the guy is an ironworker; no other details on that. But right after this happened, my sister's husband Robert was over at the house, and he said a guy he'd been in architecture with at Dal had wrapped himself around a pole downtown. I asked him who, and that's the name he gave. Benson Freling."

"Architecture? Didn't you just say ironworker?"

"Yeah, poor old Benson never made it past his first year in architecture. Drank away a promising career. Robert said he was bright and capable, had great ideas and skill, but couldn't handle the booze or the morning classes that Dalhousie University insists on scheduling in spite of the painful hangovers suffered by some of its students! Apparently, his family was none too pleased. Furious, the way Robert described it. Benson Senior is an engineer, and the mother 'came from money,' as my sister put it."

"Of course, Julian, being an ironworker is nothing to sneeze at. We all rely on their skill every time we enter a building, whether we think about the structural steel, the strength of the bolts, all that, or whether we never give it a thought."

"No, no, I didn't mean it that way. If you're anything like me, you'd give your eye teeth for some skill around the house. I can barely hammer a nail, so I'm in awe of anybody with carpentry or construction skills. No, I just meant to say that the parents had loftier goals for Benson Junior. Anyway, Ben works as an ironworker for Halifax 1749 Developments. There's your connection with MacCombie."

So. A connection with Lorne MacCombie. And a tendency to go off in a temper when he's on the booze, the way Sergeant Delorey described him. "If you hear anything else about him, Julian, I'd appreciate it if you'd pass it along."

"Sure thing, Monty. I'll be seeing Rob sometime in the next couple of days. Or I can give him a call."

"Whatever suits you best, Julian. Thanks."

☙

Monty and the family had just finished their supper when the phone rang. "Hi, Monty, it's Kirk." He sounded rattled. "The police are here again, and I told them I wanted to call you to come over."

So much for Monty's impression that Kirk must now be in the clear. What about his impression that Kirk had nothing to do with the strangulation of Trudi Ebbett? Was Monty, after more than twenty years in the criminal courts, now wearing rose-coloured glasses when in fact he should be looking through a glass, darkly? But he had committed himself to assisting Kirk, and that's what he would do. For now.

"Good, Kirk. I'm leaving right now. Don't tell them anything, anything at all, until I get there."

"Okay. Get here as fast as you can."

"I'll be about fifteen minutes."

He headed out immediately for the drive to the Clayton Park subdivision. He pulled up to Kirk Rhodenizer's four-storey apartment block well within the fifteen-minute estimate, and Kirk buzzed him in. Kirk was wearing a pair of black sweatpants and a grey sweatshirt that showed a guy in a hockey helmet, no face mask; his mouth was a wide open black hole. Beneath it were the words *Puck Off!* The two detectives were sitting across from him in a cluttered living room that smelled of fried food and cigarette smoke. They introduced themselves as Detective Sergeant MacPhee and Detective Constable Doyle. Monty recognized them from various court appearances. He greeted them and sat next to Kirk on an old plaid chesterfield.

"We just have a couple of questions for you, Mr. Rhodenizer. We have a copy of the script for" — MacPhee peered at the papers in his hand — "*Devastated Area*. And we'll be reading through it. But maybe you can just tell us a bit about your role in the play."

179

What? But Monty would let this one go. He'd jump in if the questioning turned dangerous.

Kirk looked across at Monty, then said, "I was over at the house on Young Street. The one where the party was. But it was before that. Sometime in the spring. And this young guy was with two girls at the house next door. Richard, his name was. And they came out of the house and saw me there, and Richard recognized me from hockey and started talking to me. And I invited him to a pickup game at the Forum."

"Right," MacPhee said. "So, then what happened?"

"We had our game, and a few more games, one in September. And Richard invited me to have a bit part in the play he and the other kids were doing for their school."

"Oh yeah? What part did you play?"

"Back during the first season of the NHL — the league was brand new back then — Montreal had two teams. Montreal Canadiens and the Montreal Wanderers."

"I'm a Habs fan myself," MacPhee said. The nickname for the Canadiens.

"Bruins," said the other cop, declaring his loyalty to the Boston team.

"Right, Doyle. We'll see who'll be hoisting the cup next spring."

Kirk gave a little laugh and said, "So, the two Montreal teams played an exhibition game back in the day, after the explosion, and they donated the money from the game to the Halifax Relief Fund. To help people after the disaster. Richard said it would be cool if I put on a Canadiens jersey and read out a few lines about that game and the donation to the fund. I did that. It was the only role I had in the play."

"Great." MacPhee smiled and said, "Maybe you'll be wearing a Habs jersey someday."

"Ha. Doubt it."

The detective sergeant looked more serious then. "In your conversations with Trudi Ebbett the night of November first, did she say anything about her boyfriend?"

Kirk shot a look Monty's way, didn't know what he should say. His face turned a bit pink. But all he said was "No. Never said anything about a boyfriend."

MacPhee leaned ahead in his seat. "You looked a little uncomfortable with that question, Kirk. Any reason for that?"

"She might have had a boyfriend, I don't know. Probably. She was older than me, in her twenties. And I . . . I have a girlfriend, and I didn't say anything about her to . . . to Trudi."

"Why would you have said anything about your girlfriend to Trudi? Or why would you *not* have said anything?"

Kirk's face was flushed a brighter pink now. Again, he looked over at Monty, who nodded at him to answer the question.

The police were obviously working their own angle on this.

Kirk went on to elaborate about the events of that night. "I was sloshed. Been drinking all night. And she had a few in her too. And we ended up kissing, only for a few seconds or so, till she got up and ran out of the house."

"And what was your reaction to that? You've got something going with this 'older woman,' starting to kiss each other, and then she up and leaves. How did you feel about that?"

Kirk responded with a nonchalant shrug.

"It pissed you off, maybe? Anger fuelled by all the booze? Is that how you got the cut on your face? You struck out at her, and she struck back?"

"No!" It was almost a shout.

MacPhee smiled, a look of satisfaction on his face. He waited a few seconds before continuing. "And then, as you said in an earlier interview, you ran after her, up Young Street."

"Yeah, to give her back her purse!"

"Her purse. She didn't have a purse on or near her when her body was found."

"I didn't steal it, I gave it to her!"

"All right. Let's get back to the scene in the kitchen . . ."

"It wasn't a scene! It was just nothing. I have a girlfriend, and if she found out somehow, she might dump me. All I did was put my arm around this Trudi one because she was upset about whatever she wanted to find in the house next door. And because of that guy outside hollering at her."

"What did the man outside say to her?"

"Told her to come out of the house, something like that. And she was scared of him." Kirk raised his voice then, "And she was right to be scared, eh? He fuckin' killed her!"

"Did she say who he was?"

"No, she didn't. I asked her, and she wouldn't say."

"Did she say anything about Saint John, maybe a guy followed her to Halifax, anything like that?"

"No, nothing about him at all."

This conversation, as distressing as it was to Kirk, gave Monty hope. It was a good sign, the reference to a boyfriend, a guy following Trudi from Saint John. That was the theory the police were working with, or one theory anyway: perhaps Trudi had been killed by a jealous boyfriend. And they must have learned something in Saint John that pointed to the existence of just such a man. Just such a suspect. The detectives took their leave then with, Monty hoped, more interest in a Saint John boyfriend than in a drunken young hockey player in Halifax.

☙

As was their habit whenever they were in for the evening, Monty and Maura were watching Peter Mansbridge deliver the news on CBC television. It was one of the few things they ever watched on TV. On this night, there were stories about the continuing fallout after the Liberals' rout of the Progressive Conservatives in the October election, an update on the mission of the space shuttle *Endeavour*, then this: "And now, David McGibbin reports from New York in our continuing series on organized crime in Canada and the United States, and the cross-border links between the Mafia and Irish crime groups in the two countries." The reporter spoke of the assassination, a few years ago, of the leader of Montreal's West End Gang and the revenge killings that followed. "This kind of life is not for the faint-hearted, Peter! There was a harrowing attack recently on a family in New York City, and a rumoured connection with what was once a powerful Irish criminal gang operating out of Hell's Kitchen on New York's West Side."

"Press record!" Monty said to Maura, who had the remote control in her hand.

"What?"

"Tape this. Brennan might be interested in a story about Hell's Kitchen! As might any son of a man with Hell's Kitchen connections, who recently used a phony passport and then vanished into the night."

"All right." She pressed the button. "But you're going to be in trouble if I'm taping over one of Normie's shows."

The next morning, after his early Mass, Brennan arrived at the Collins-MacNeil house on Dresden Row. Monty had invited him over to watch the tape. The recording began just as the reporter launched into the story of the attack in New York City.

"The family whose home was attacked in Queens are believed to be safe, Peter, but they are not taking calls or answering their door. Understandably, given the circumstances. A gang of men arrived at the house late last night and fired shots at the door and windows, before shouting threats and disappearing into the darkness. The threats are believed to have been directed at the owner of the house, a man named Fiach O'Flynn. O'Flynn immigrated to New York from Dublin, Ireland, twenty-five years ago as a young man. He lives in the borough of Queens with his wife, one of his daughters, and her three children. Fortunately, none of the women or children were hurt. But Mr. O'Flynn has not been seen since the attack. Police are not speculating as to his whereabouts or what might have happened to him. He is rumoured to have been associated with the Hell's Kitchen Irish mob when it was a powerful force in the city. Police are not saying what might have motivated the assault on the family home, but sources tell us that there has been a long-simmering conflict between Mr. O'Flynn and another faction of the Irish criminal organization. So, Peter, we'll continue to follow events in New York as they unfold."

The reporter signed off, and Brennan sat with his elbows on the arms of his chair, head in his hands. Monty resisted the temptation to question him. But finally, Brennan spoke. "What are we going to hear next, that Declan is involved in this clusterfuck? His headquarters shot up? Is he at risk? Again?"

Again. Declan Burke had been shot at a family wedding a few years before.

Brennan sighed, got up from his seat, and said, "And as for our troubles closer to home here, I guess we won't be able to count on him to return to Halifax and testify if we catch that blaggard who tried to break into the school."

Monty had been thinking the same thing. Declan Burke was the one and only witness who might be able to recognize the man who had made the attempt on the school.

∽

Julian MacEachern stopped by Monty's office later that morning and had this to say: "Another tidbit about Benson Freling, Monty. I was talking to my brother-in-law again. Rob. And he told me that sometime in the last year or so, Benson applied to the university again. Applied to Dal to get readmitted to the architecture program. Rob is still involved with the school in various ways, and he knew about the application. And here is what might be of interest to you: one of the people who wrote a letter of reference for him was Lorne MacCombie."

"Interesting indeed! Thanks for letting me know, Julian."

"Any time."

Monty twisted his chair around and looked out the window, forming a picture in his mind of Benson Freling drinking at the Lighthouse tavern, getting worked up about something, bolting up from his barstool, and running to Saint Bernadette's Choir School with the intention of breaking in and removing a play script that might offend his benefactor, Lorne MacCombie. Is that what happened? Had Freling heard grumbling about the play from MacCombie or somebody close to the family?

Then Monty brought to mind the man who had messed with Declan Burke and had got the worst of it, running away up Hollis Street. Did he turn towards the harbour, to wherever he had parked his car? Had he driven off in such a state that he ran himself up against a telephone pole and ended up with criminal charges as a result? Should there be more charges added to his sheet?

That was getting ahead of things, but one thing Monty could do was go to the courthouse to have a look at Freling when he appeared with his lawyer to face the charges. On Friday morning, Monty set off for the short walk from his office on Salter Street to the Halifax Provincial Courthouse on Spring Garden Road. Like any defence lawyer in Halifax, Monty had known victory and defeat in the court, but he never tired of looking at the nineteenth-century sandstone courthouse with its columns and fanged faces set in the building's front elevation. He went inside and entered the familiar courtroom and mouthed a silent greeting to the clerk and the lawyers he knew. Then he found a seat in the gallery and waited through several arraignments until Benson Freling's name was called. Saul Green, one of the city's most prominent lawyers, rose to inform the court that he would be representing Mr. Freling. The client was a tall, muscular man in his mid-thirties with dark brown hair, cut short in a military-looking style. Of course, all Monty had seen of him — if it was him — the night of the attempted break-in was a man in winter clothing fleeing the building. Today, Freling was dressed for court in a suit and tie. He looked to be the same size as the man Monty had seen, but other than that, Monty had no frame of reference to assess his appearance. Freling looked about him with a scowl on his face and then returned his attention to the proceedings, as his counsel waived reading of the charges and informed the judge that his client wished to enter a plea of not guilty to all charges. There was no need for Monty to stay around; he had what he wanted, a sighting of Benson Freling. So, he rose and quietly left the courtroom.

Monty mulled over the idea of getting in touch with Sergeant Delorey, to talk again about Benson Freling's actions the night of October twenty-fifth. Freling was all the more a person of interest in the break-in, now that Monty knew of his connection with Lorne MacCombie. But he knew what the policeman's response would be. He would more than likely be interested in Freling as a suspect. But Monty had not had a good look at the man when he and Declan had chased him. So he knew, as Sergeant Delorey would know, that the Crown would require much more cogent evidence in order to make a case. The Crown prosecutor would want the evidence of the man who had fought with the suspect, had seen him up close. The case would be going nowhere without the eyewitness evidence of Declan Burke.

CHAPTER XIV

Brennan

Brennan was in the school auditorium Friday morning with his choir. He always started rehearsing for Christmas well ahead of time, and this year was no exception. The choir was singing Victoria's "O Magnum Mysterium," one of the most beautiful, most sublime pieces of music ever composed. Victoria was born in Ávila, Spain; what was it about that city that produced a mystic like Saint Teresa and a composer like Victoria, whose music . . . What was it Huxley had said? "After silence, that which comes nearest to expressing the inexpressible is music." Tomás Luis de Victoria's music did exactly that: it expressed the inexpressible. Brennan was moved, as always, by the brilliant Renaissance piece and his choir's performance of it. He stayed silent for a long moment, revelling in the sound, before he praised his students and sent them off to the more mundane work of their school day.

When he was leaving the auditorium, Richard Robertson caught up with him. "I have something to show you, Father. It's in my locker. Have you got a minute?"

"Always have time for you, my lad. Let's go."

So they headed for the locker room, Richard keeping up a line of patter as they walked along. Had Father Burke seen *National Lampoon's Christmas Vacation*? Even better, the sad Christmas portrayed by the hilarious Newfoundland comedy troupe, CODCO? Brennan had not seen them but hoped that sometime he would.

When they arrived at Richard's locker, he opened it and pulled out an old leather-bound photo album. "Me and my dad, we don't have — I guess you could say we don't have a lot in common! The things he's interested in aren't the things I'm interested in." That was true, as Brennan knew all too well. "But one thing we're both keen on is cars, especially old ones. Not that I'd say no if somebody offered to buy me a brand-new MGB convertible! Dad took me to a car show last year. A bunch of guys had driven their old cars out to a place in the country. Chevies from the fifties and sixties, a 1962 Triumph Spitfire, and some antique cars too. A Model T Ford! Of course, Dad likes the really expensive ones, the Mercs and the Porsches. And he likes to know who owns them."

"But anyway, about this." He pointed to the photo album. "My father has lots of these albums full of car pictures. I look through them sometimes. And last night I was thinking about Mike and Lauchie's notes from the old days, and one of them wrote about a Case Limousine. They talked about a guy who was a regular at the bawdy house next door to Mike's. Drove a Case Limousine."

Brennan remembered. "Right." And he remembered something else. "That was the fella who —"

"Took the dead body away from the house, the body that Mike said hadn't been there right after the explosion. The mysterious death! And so I wondered if there might be a picture of it in one of Dad's collections." Richard turned the album so Brennan could see it and flipped through the pages. There were black and white photos of cars on every page.

"So you found a Case Limousine in here?"

"Um, no, sorry. But look." Richard's face brightened then. "Some of the cars have the plate number showing. Some even have the owner's name with them. If Dad has these pictures, other antique car guys must have them too." He turned to the front inside cover of the book. "Here's the car club he belongs to. Timberlea Timeless Wheels."

If there was something in this that would provide a clue to the intimidation of his students, Brennan wanted that information right away. Now. "What are the chances those fellas would be available today? Or would they have meetings at this time of year?"

"Doesn't matter if they do or they don't." Richard poked a finger at the address. "This is the guy's house." And there was a phone number given as well.

"Go maith." Good. "Thank you, Richard. I'll be looking into it."

☙

Brennan went into his office before his next class and rang the car club man, Curtis Van Galen. His wife answered and said Curtis would be home between five thirty and six, so Brennan called back then and received a friendly invitation to come and see Curtis's collection of photos. Brennan asked for directions, said his thanks, and headed out for the drive to the western Halifax suburb. He found the Van Galens' small one-storey house and saw an old-model Mercedes and a new-looking pickup truck in the driveway. Van Galen came to the door and ushered him inside. He introduced himself and his wife, Lina, and directed Brennan to follow him downstairs. One half of the basement was a wood-panelled room with model cars on the shelves and framed pictures of cars on the walls. "My headquarters," Curtis said, smiling. "Now, what is it you're looking for?"

Brennan gave an edited version of the story, telling Curtis that he was trying to trace the owner of a Case Limousine, a man who had helped recover bodies after the explosion. Curtis walked over to a file cabinet and withdrew several scrapbooks.

He laid them out on a table and said, "They're organized by date. This one is 1910 to 1930." He opened the book and flipped through the pages, and Brennan saw photos and newspaper clippings showing old cars. In some of the pictures, the car's owners were seated inside or standing by the doors. "Ah. Here's a Case from 1912." The car was shown in a news clipping. "Hey, the man is named here. Robert somebody, from Stewiacke. Oh, no, the story says he was killed in the war, in 1915. So, that's no help to you. Here's one, same year. No, not a Case. It's a Packard." Brennan looked at the car. No owner identified, but it wasn't a Packard Brennan was looking for.

"Ah, here we are, Father. Finally, a 1914 Case Limo and a face to go with it." The driver and passenger compartment was rectangular with large windows. Brennan had always associated the word "limousine" with the long stretch limos used to transport high-paying passengers around, but the 1914 limo had a boxy shape to it. "I've always liked those open spoke wheels," Curtis said. "What we're interested in is this fella." The proud owner of the vehicle was wearing a long overcoat with what Brennan's mother called a notched collar and a bowler-type hat. Curtis lifted the book and peered closely at the image.

"Do you know who he was?" Brennan asked.

"Sorry, no idea. I was hoping there might be a name. Let's see what else we can find." He turned all the remaining pages, but there were no more Case Limousines. He shook his head. "No luck, Father Burke. Just one 1914 Case Limo and no name with it."

"That's all right. It was a long shot. I appreciate your efforts here, Curtis."

"You're welcome." He picked up the scrapbooks and replaced them in the shelves. "Hey, wait a minute! I have a fax machine." Brennan waited. "I can fax that pic to a buddy of mine, older guy, been at this a lot longer than I have. He's got a great set-up at his house, has all the same stuff I have and more. And he knows more about the old autos and who owned them. He was one of the first guys I ever heard of who had a fax machine. How about I send him that picture and see what he says."

"That would be great, Curtis."

"Tell you what. I won't keep you waiting here. It might take him awhile to get back to me, but if you give me your phone number, I'll let you know if I have any luck."

Brennan thanked Curtis again and drove back to the city. Two hours or so later, he was in his room when the phone rang. It was Curtis and he had a name for him, the owner of the 1914 Case Limousine shown in his scrapbook. "Does that name mean anything to you, Father?"

Yes, the name meant something.

Monty

Monty's mother was a friend of Abigail Runcey, wife of the lieutenant governor of Nova Scotia. Ever since Monty's father died six years ago, his mother had been living in Chester, where her family had always maintained a summer home. Often when she came to Halifax, she called on Mrs. Runcey. And she was a close enough friend that Monty's family had been invited, along with two hundred other guests, to the wedding party for the Runceys' son, Thane, last month. So Monty was acquainted with Thompson Runcey. When Monty showed up at Government House and was admitted for his appointment with the lieutenant governor, he hoped the LG would look upon him as the son of Evelyn Chamberley Collins, rather than the father of the young girl who had tried to procure his assistance for a member of the Hell's Kitchen Irish mob.

Runcey came into the foyer and welcomed him to the house.

"I am very sorry to disturb you, Your Honour."

"Tom. And you are Montague. And you go by Monty, I know."

"That's right. I'm sorry to disturb you, especially about this, but I don't see that I have a choice. The children at my daughter's school have written a play, *Devastated Area*, about the Halifax Explosion."

"Oh, yes, I heard about that. Good for them. Come in, Monty."

"Thank you."

Runcey directed him into a cheerful brightly lit room and invited him to have a seat. "Can I get you anything? Tea? Something a bit livelier?" The lieutenant governor was smiling as he said it.

"Sure."

"Scotch? Gin?"

"A wee glass of Scotch would be nice."

A member of the LG's staff entered the room, but Runcey thanked her and told her he would get the drinks. He went out, and Monty peered after him. He couldn't see whatever bar set-up the LG had, but he tried to remember where Normie had seen the dollhouse that had so thrilled her at the wedding party here at the house. When Runcey returned and handed Monty his glass, Monty said, "My daughter was entranced by that wonderful dollhouse she saw when we attended Thane's wedding party."

"Oh, it is magnificent. It's a replica of a place owned by members of our family in England. Oxfordshire. My mother's family."

Monty knew that the LG's mother's family, the Rayworths, were even grander than the Runceys. "Have you been there?"

"We've had the occasional visit. Splendid place, I have to say. My mother always said how much she missed the place when she came over here with my father before the war. First war, of course. My dad was an *Oxford man*, don't you know," he said with a laugh. "Spent more time in the gin mills than in his classes. Let's just say he didn't *get a first at Oxford*! But he met my mother, so all's well, as they say."

Then his expression saddened. "It's a shame that she didn't live to . . . Well, the family property has been handed down, in the old way, to the first son. But Mum had no brothers, so as the eldest daughter she would have . . . Oh, forgive me for going off on family history here, Monty. Now, this may be of interest to you and your little girl. That dollhouse was made by a man here in Nova Scotia. Lawrence Clarke, lives in Annapolis Royal. He has made replicas of some of the lovely houses in that part of the province. I'm sure he'd be happy to make one for your daughter."

"Oh, she would be overjoyed. Thank you, Tom. I'll get in touch with Mr. Clarke and look into it."

It was time to get to the point, however painful that might be for the lieutenant governor. "The school play is in two parts, two acts. They performed act one on October seventh. And at the end of the show, they did a little teaser about what to expect in act two." There was no avoiding it any longer; Normie had to be named, and the Hell's Kitchen gaffe might come to the LG's mind, if it hadn't already. "Two weeks after the performance, Normie — my daughter — and another of the students received anonymous notes at the school. The notes had a threatening tone and were designed to frighten the kids out of showing the second part of the play. If they didn't cancel it, they would be sorry."

"Good Heavens! Who would do a thing like that?"

"Hard to imagine, isn't it? And on another occasion, a man followed Normie home from school. One of her friends happened to come along, and the man took off. But two disturbing incidents, and in light of the notes, I think we can assume the following of my daughter had something to do with the play as well. Especially in light of what happened after the threats: a man tried to break into the school."

Runcey's astonishment looked genuine. "This is terrible, Monty. I assume you have brought in the police."

"Yes, we have. Now, as distasteful as this is, I have to bring up something we learned at the school. One of the sources of information for the students' play was a series of notes made in 1917 and 1918 by a couple of young boys who used to get together at the home of one of them, kid named Mike Kavanagh. His house was next door to a place on Young Street, which, at the time, was a brothel."

"Ah."

"Now, as I say, at the end of the first performance of the play in October, the kids announced that act two would take place on December ninth, and Normie offered a couple of little hints about what the audience could expect in that second performance. She tried to build up a bit of suspense by referring to a 'mysterious death,' a death that did not appear to be a result of the explosion. And they've been enjoying a bit of mischief about the 'house of ill repute.'"

The lieutenant governor looked more amused than worried. "I see. And what has this to do with me, may I ask?"

"Not you, personally, sir. Tom." Or so Monty hoped. "But the hint about the mysterious death came from Mike Kavanagh's notes. In a note written the day after the explosion, Mike described a man retrieving a body from the backyard of the property I mentioned, the brothel. The man was in uniform, army uniform, and he carried the body to a car. Of course, many soldiers and others had the harrowing task of searching for the bodies of those who had been killed during the blast, or burnt to death in the fires that followed. People's wood stoves had set fire to the remains of many of the houses. But according to this note, there had been no sign of that body in the yard right after the explosion. So this raised the suspicion that the person had been killed some time before December sixth, and the body concealed. The suggestion was that the man who retrieved the body the following day had some involvement in the death or, at the very least, was aware of it."

"Well, it wasn't me, Mr. Collins. Monty. I was only a babe in arms at the time!"

"Oh, I know that, sir. But the Kavanagh boy had taken notice of the car into which the man laid the body. Of course, motor cars weren't all that common at the time, and this one stood out even more. It was a high-end model, an expensive car. Now, the father of one of the students involved in the play is an antique car buff. Has a keen interest in the old cars, particularly the pricier models. He has scrapbooks and collections of photos and, for some, photos or names of the owners."

For the first time, Runcey looked uneasy. His eyes avoided Monty's.

"The student's father, of course, knows other people engaged in the same hobby. And with one thing and another, we came upon a picture of a 1914 Case Limousine, the kind of car the young boy saw on the day in question. I don't imagine there were many such cars in Halifax at the time. Maybe only one." Runcey opened his mouth to speak but closed it again. Said nothing. He knew where this was going. "And the owner is pictured beside the car. The owner was Harrison Runcey." The lieutenant governor's father.

There was a quick intake of breath, and Runcey moved back in his seat. After only a brief moment of silence, he said, "My father certainly would not have been . . . involved in anything of the sort you are describing. You are right about one thing. My father had a Case

Limousine. He bought it in Ottawa during the first war. He spent a few months up there working with the Department of National Defence. It went well for him, from everything I heard. We have a photo of my father with Sir Robert. Robert had known my grandfather when they were both lawyers here in Halifax."

"Sir Robert Borden?" Monty asked, in a display of polite interest. He assumed Runcey was referring to the prime minister of Canada during the First World War; Borden had been born and raised in Nova Scotia.

"That's right. He invited my parents to a reception of some kind, and the photo shows my dad and my very pregnant mother. They returned home to Halifax not long after I was born. So I had early experience of motor cars!" The LG smiled, but the smile was fleeting. "Montague, I cannot imagine, for one instant, that my father would have been involved in anything like what you have described. If he had been assisting in the recovery efforts after the explosion, as were so many other good citizens and soldiers, if he picked up a body, that hardly means he had anything to do with whatever happened to the person whose body was found. Someone may have told him there was a body in that location."

Perhaps, or perhaps the fact that he knew the location of the body implied some involvement. But there was nothing to be gained by giving voice to that argument.

"I suppose," Runcey said, "I should be grateful that my father wasn't named in the school play. Or at least I assume he wasn't!"

"He wasn't named in the play or in the little hints about act two, and he won't be named when the second act is performed."

Monty saw no reason to tell Runcey that Normie had mentioned the Case Limousine when giving her little promotional spiel for act two. If, as unlikely as it seemed, Runcey had something to do with the intimidation, that meant he knew the car had been mentioned. If he was innocent in all this, there was no need to cause him any further distress on that account.

"So," Runcey said, "who is this car enthusiast? I wonder if it's some-body I know."

Monty shrugged off the question. "Just one of the parents, and he didn't have the photo himself. It was somebody else who had it. I didn't recognize the name."

Runcey placed his glass on a side table and leaned forward in his seat. "And you may be sure of something else: even if I had known about this old limousine being seen at the house in question, I would not have been writing anonymous notes to a bunch of children putting on a school play."

"No, no, I'm sure you wouldn't," Monty said. Surely, he reasoned, if Lieutenant Governor Runcey had taken issue with something he'd heard about the play or the teaser for the next act, he would not have skulked around and sent threatening notes. He would have gone through proper channels and had someone contact the school to protest the insinuation against a (long dead) member of his family. Or he would have asked, in a most courteous way, that the man's name not be used.

"And," the LG continued, "this should go without saying, but I feel compelled to say it nonetheless: I was not out stalking a young girl along the streets of Halifax or breaking into a school!"

"I know. And I'm sorry to have confronted you with this, sir, but I have to investigate these incidents as best I can."

"I understand." The LG rose, gave Monty a quick nod of the head, and left the room.

CHAPTER XV

DECEMBER II, 1917

Lauchie MacIntyre

Five days after everything blew up, Lauchie was sitting in the living room of a big house in the south end of the city. The chair he was sitting in was made of soft gold and white material, and its legs were curved and made of dark wood. Across from him was a piano, with family pictures in silver frames. There were other pictures on the walls; they had silver frames, too, but were paintings done by artists.

Two north end Presbyterian churches had been destroyed in the blast, Lauchie's church, Grove Presbyterian, and Reverend MacCombie's church, North End Reformed. People were saying that more than one hundred and fifty Grove Presbyterian parishioners had been killed. Lauchie hadn't heard the numbers for the other parish. Lauchie's minister, Reverend Murray, had arranged for the MacIntyres to stay in this south end house while the owners were away visiting their daughter and grandchildren in Toronto. Reverend Murray was with them now;

he had stopped in to pray with the family, to give thanks for their survival and to pray for the dead and injured.

Lauchie hadn't always been good about saying his prayers, but he was truly prayerful now. His family had been spared by a stroke of luck. Or by the grace of God. On the morning of the explosion, Lauchie had come down from Needham Hill to find his house on Duffus Street, like so many others, slammed to the ground, and debris all over the yard. But nobody had been in the house when the blast occurred. His dad had been working at the drydock, and he had survived with a few minor burns from bits of white-hot metal flying through the air. His mum had taken his sister to a doctor's office on Windsor Street, so nobody was home when the roof and top floor had been blown off the house.

If only his friends had been this lucky. But no. Karl Neumann had run down the hill to Veith Street to find his house destroyed and on fire. The fire was started either by sparks from the explosion or by the family's stove being knocked over. Lauchie heard that Karl had been screaming and trying to bat the flames out with his coat, trying to get in to rescue his mum and Johann and the two little brothers, Stefan and Friedrich, but it was impossible. If Karl had stayed home to do his lessons that morning instead of running up the hill with Lauchie to watch the ship burning, Karl, too, would have been killed. And Mr. Neumann had been killed when the nearby Acadia Sugar Refinery was destroyed. Lauchie could not begin to imagine what his friend was going through now. He hadn't seen Karl; his aunt and uncle had taken him to their home in Lunenburg. When would Lauchie see Karl again? Would he ever? Karl had no family left in Halifax now.

The day after the explosion, Lauchie had heard the news that Mike Kavanagh and his family had lived through the disaster, but that his little sister, Ellie, had injured her eyes. He'd also heard that the Kavanaghs were staying with Mike's uncle Frank. On the day Lauchie and his family were being moved to the south end house, he told his parents he had to see Mike before they left, so they let him go up to Frank's place. It was a quiet visit; Lauchie and his best pal didn't have anything to joke or laugh about. One thing they would do, though: Lauchie said they should both continue writing their notes. Not that they would ever forget what had happened to their city! But there were lots of other things, and lots of people, they would want to remember later. Mike said yes, they would definitely keep writing the notes, and they would see each other again soon. Now, in the MacIntyres' temporary home in the south end, Lauchie added Ellie Kavanagh to the people he was praying for, with Reverend Murray.

Lauchie hadn't heard any news about Mary Catherine Malone, the girl Mike Kavanagh liked. It was probably more accurate to say Mike *loved* Mary Catherine; Mike lived for those days when they went roller skating down the Russell Street hill. Lauchie didn't want to think that she might have ended up like so many others, the many, many people, including kids and mums and babies, who had been killed. But after what he had seen with his own eyes in the first days after the blast, he knew all too well that horrible things had happened to people. He'd seen a man's body with only half his head still on, and a gooey grey lump lying beside the hole in his skull. And Lauchie had overheard his mother crying, telling his father about a lady who'd been killed while holding her two little babies in her arms; all three of them had died. And there were mums or dads who had survived and were walking all over Richmond like ghosts, or going to the morgue, searching for their little boy or girl or baby that they couldn't find. Lauchie had cried himself to sleep every night since the explosion.

Lauchie's dad had been reading the newspapers, and he'd pointed out the names or pictures of some of the navy and army men he had known, men who were now listed among the dead. Lauchie had met some of them; he remembered thinking that someday he'd be hearing that one or more of them had been killed in the war. Now they'd been killed in their own city. And he recognized another man in one of the photos: the fellow he and Mike had spotted at the brothel house, the guy who looked like Charlie Chaplin. He remembered something about him having a row with somebody else. The guy with the Case? The Case Limousine. Whatever that was about, "Charlie C" wouldn't have bothered with an argument if he could have foreseen what was going to happen. Of course, you could say that about everybody:

nothing in their everyday lives could be seen as important compared to surviving what was to come.

Now, on Tuesday evening, sitting in the grand south end house after Reverend Murray had left, Lauchie pretended to be reading one of the books he'd found on the bookshelf, all about horse racing at a place called Ascot in England. But what he was really doing was listening in on the conversation between his father and mother at the dining room table.

His dad said to his mum, "That story I told you about in yesterday's paper, about fellows being caught looting?"

"Yes?"

"Well, he wasn't named in the paper, but I happen to know that Blocker Steadman was one of them!"

"Blocker?"

"Morley Steadman. Blocker's his nickname. He's from one of the rental places up here in Richmond, but some of the members of the rugby club let him play. Welcome to the team, old chap. His father is with the First Regiment here, artillery. Maybe knew one of the rugby dads from there. Anyway, one time Morley was playing rugby, and he tripped and fell on his face in the middle of a play, and he blocked it. Not the way a rugby blocker is supposed to do it! Anyway, everybody started calling him Blocker, and the name has stuck."

"Right. So, what did he do? You said looting?"

"Yeah. His old man will tan the hide off him. After everything people have suffered here, those louts go out and steal stuff. And with Blocker, it wasn't just the shops or taverns or places like that. He went into people's houses, where people had been killed, houses that are half-wrecked and abandoned. And he took the families' treasures, things that survived the blast. Silver and jewellery, tools, all kinds of stuff. I don't know if he was into the rum or what, to have done things like that. Some fellows even robbed the corpses over there at the morgue that's been set up at Chebucto School. Pulled rings off fingers! The morgue!"

"Oh Lord, how can people behave like that?"

"I don't know if Blocker actually went into the morgue and robbed the dead, but it's a known fact that he engaged in some looting. As I say, Steadman Senior will have his hide."

Hearing this, Lauchie made a note in his mind to write this down for Michael K. Then maybe the two of them could find this Blocker and take him down in a rugby tackle and give him a black eye or two.

Mike Kavanagh

All the information that Mike had been missing, he now had. And wished he'd never heard any of it. His little sister, Ellie, only six years old, was blind. The doctors said her eyes had been destroyed and had to be removed! Someday later, she'd be given artificial eyes! But they won't make her see. The whole family was, as his mum said, "devastated." The flames and smoke of the burning ship, those were the last things Ellie ever saw. Mike could not imagine what her life would be like now, whenever the doctors let her out of the hospital. Dad told him there were hundreds of people with eye injuries, and doctors were working with them day and night. Some of the people would be left totally blind, like Ellie. Nearly five hundred members of Saint Joseph's parish — church and school — were dead. Saint Joe's had lost more people than any of the other parishes. But there were losses for the other churches in the neighbourhood too: Saint Mark's at the corner of Russell and Gottingen, and Kaye Street Methodist.

And there was more. Mike and Lauchie's pal, Karl Neumann, was an orphan now. All his family had been killed, his dad at the sugar refinery, the rest of the family at their house on Veith Street. And on that same street, more than twenty kids had been killed at the Protestant Orphanage. And there was news from the girls' house next door on Young Street, the *common bawdy house*, as Lauchie's mum or dad called it. Three of the girls were killed when the second storey of their house crashed down into the first floor. But one lady in the house survived and was rescued along with her daughter, who was just a little girl.

And Mary Catherine. Mike had always secretly hoped that they would start going out together when they were old enough, and then get engaged and married. He used to joke to himself that they would roller skate up the aisle at Saint Joe's, Mike in his fancy suit and Mary Catherine in her wedding dress. Their parents wouldn't approve of the skates, but the bride and groom would do it anyway. But there was never going to be a wedding now, only a funeral. Mike had seen the Malones' house on Russell Street, completely flattened and burnt out. Gerry and Sean Malone, the two oldest boys, weren't home when it happened; they were down near the harbour watching the burning ship. They weren't hurt except for being knocked down and bruised, and they had some burns from the pieces of hot metal flying around. Their dad was working over at the railway station in Rockingham, so he didn't get hurt. But Mrs. Malone and the three youngest kids were in the house and were killed when it was blasted apart. Where was Mary Catherine at the time? She had been on her way up the street to school, and now nobody would even tell Mike how she died.

But Mr. Malone came to Uncle Frank's house and told him about the funeral for Mary Catherine and her mum and brother and sisters. It would not be in Saint Joseph's church because there was hardly anything left of it, and all the other churches were overwhelmed with funerals. So the funeral was going to be at the home of Mary Catherine's aunt, who lived alone across the harbour in Dartmouth. And Father McManus, the priest from Saint Joe's, was going to do the Mass. And the Kavanaghs were invited to come — if that's what you did with funerals, invited people.

Mike dreaded going to it, but he had to. There was Mrs. Malone in a coffin with her face all cut and bruised. And there were the three youngest kids all together in a big coffin. You could only see their battered and cut little faces; everything below their necks was covered with a shiny cloth. As for Mary Catherine, Mike was told she was in the third coffin, but the cover was closed on it. He had heard whispers about closed coffins. He'd never been told what that meant, but he'd always believed it was something bad. The family didn't want people to see the dead member of the family. Why? Why was Mary Catherine in a closed coffin? He asked his mum and dad, and they didn't give him a direct answer. All his mum said was "She died instantly, Michael dear; they say she didn't suffer at all. And, of course, she's in Heaven now with her mummy and brother and sisters." But what had really happened to her that nobody wanted her to be seen? Had she been ripped apart like the other kids and babies and grown-ups Mike had heard about? Had her arms or legs been torn off? Her head? What happened to the girl who loved to go flying down Russell Street on her skates, his future roller-skating *bride*, the girl he loved? Mike didn't even care that Lauchie and everybody else saw him standing before the coffin, crying as if he would never stop.

After the service, Mike was standing alone by the front window, gazing out at the harbour, at his ruined city across the water, when Lauchie came up to him and said, "I hope the police and the judges get the men who are responsible for that collision, and that explosion, and put them in jail for the rest of their lives!"

Mike replied, "I wish me and you could find them first, and —" And what? What could he or Lauchie, or the men of Halifax, ever do to get real revenge against the men who let this happen? What could the city or the police or the courts ever do to make up for the death of Mary Catherine?

NOVEMBER 1993

Monty

Monty sat at his kitchen table and peered at the copies of the Mike Kavanagh and Lauchie MacIntyre notes before him. He remembered the stories he'd heard about the explosion and its aftermath, the rage of the people of Halifax, the incendiary news editorials, thirst for revenge. At first, the blame was heaped upon the Kaiser and, by association, any Halifax resident with a German surname. Some of these people were attacked by their neighbours, and there was even a mass arrest of people with German citizenship. But it soon became apparent to most people that the explosion was not the result of a German plot. The blame then attached to two men: the local harbour pilot, Francis Mackey, who had guided the *Mont Blanc*, the French munitions ship, into Halifax harbour, and the ship's captain, Aimé Le Médec. It didn't help the French crew's case in the public mind that many French Canadians had resisted the wartime government's imposition of conscription; they did not want to be forced to fight alongside Britain in a European war. So some English Canadians held a grudge against French-speaking people.

Before the explosion, very few people — even those who should have been told — knew what the *Mont Blanc* was carrying in her holds. It was not unusual in wartime to have a munitions ship in port, but this was a ship loaded with highly explosive materials. The ship had not been flying a red flag to signal its dangerous cargo because this could have been seen by any of the German submarines that were attacking ships in the western Atlantic. The *Mont Blanc* was following the rules of navigation and entering the harbour on its proper side, the eastern side, of the harbour. The *Imo* was a Norwegian ship leaving Halifax for New York to pick up relief supplies for Belgium. It was the *Imo* that was steaming out of the harbour on the wrong side when the collision occurred. She should have been staying to her right, on the western side. But it was argued on the *Imo*'s behalf that there were other ships in her way; in order to avoid them, she had no choice but to move out of her proper lane.

There were several proceedings dealing with the collision. The first was the Wreck Commission Inquiry, headed by an admiralty judge of the Exchequer Court of Canada. At the end of the hearing, which was memorable for an abundance of courtroom grandstanding and inflammatory reporting by the newspapers, the commissioners placed all the blame on the *Mont Blanc* — Captain Le Médec, the pilot Mackey — and on Evan Wyatt, an Englishman, a commander in the Royal Navy, who was in charge of traffic in the Halifax port. To all reports, Wyatt was touchy about his reputation as "an officer and a gentleman." Gentleman or not, he was one of the three men declared responsible for the collision; Wyatt, Le Médec, and Mackey were arrested and charged with manslaughter, for the deaths of the *Imo*'s captain and pilot. After a protracted series of legal proceedings, the three men were eventually free of any criminal responsibility.

There followed a royal commission examining the role of pilots in the harbour. And then there was a lawsuit with the owners of the two ships claiming damages against one another. This was heard before the same judge who had held the Wreck Commissioners hearing and found against the *Mont Blanc*. With limited exceptions, the same evidence was used again. Same judge, same evidence. Not surprisingly, the French ship was again assessed all the blame. The decision was overturned on appeal to the Supreme Court of Canada. It was a split and — to all appearances — a political decision. Two Anglo-Canadian judges sided with the decision to blame the *Mont Blanc*. Two Franco-Canadian judges rejected this. The tie-breaking judge found that the captains and pilots of both ships had been at fault. The owners of the relief ship, the *Imo*, appealed this decision to what was then the highest court for Canadian cases, the Privy Council in London, England. The law lords unanimously upheld the ruling that both ships were equally at fault. The judges focused on the fact that, however it was allowed to happen, the two ships had "allowed themselves to get within five hundred feet of each other." Each ship should have "reversed her engines and gone full speed astern long before they were allowed to approach so close to each other as five hundred feet . . . both Masters were to blame for not having prevented their respective ships from getting into it."

Monty had always felt that this was the best decision that could have been made in such difficult circumstances. Over the years, he had read reams of documents and articles about the collision and explosion, and he had always been outraged at the treatment of the local pilot, Mackey, who in the end was completely exonerated, as well he should have been. Monty also believed that some blame was attributable to the various military and civilian authorities that regulated ship traffic in the harbour, given how easy it was for a floating bomb like the *Mont Blanc* to enter the harbour. But for the students putting on a play at Saint Bernadette's Choir School, he advised Normie and Father Burke to avoid getting into all the legal complications and the nastiness associated with them. Just make the point that the crews of the two ships were found equally responsible for Canada's worst-ever disaster.

＃

Monty turned from the heartbreaking note Mike Kavanagh had written about the death of Mary Catherine Malone and his other friends, the destruction of the homes of family and friends, the blindness of his little sister. He picked up Lauchie MacIntyre's note of December 11, 1917. There was that Case Limousine again, and reference to the row between the owner of the limo and the sailor who looked like Charlie Chaplin. And then, according to Lauchie's note, that sailor's picture was in the paper along with other military personnel who had been killed in the explosion. But what had Mike Kavanagh written about the limousine and a body? Monty flipped through the photocopies of the pages and found Mike's note again, written the day after the explosion. A man had loaded a body into the limo, but Mike had been convinced that the victim had not died as a result of the blast. There had been no body lying in the yard after the explosion. And what else? Right. Lumber neatly stacked up, which had not been stacked up before. Mike had suspected that the body had been concealed, presumably under the boards, and had been dug up and removed on December seventh. And loaded into the Case Limousine. Monty would have to process all this again.

But there was something else in Lauchie's December eleventh note. A name familiar to Monty. Blocker Steadman! That would be another family who might be red-faced if named in the students' play. Colonel "Blocker" Steadman was mentioned in the news every Remembrance Day, not for his service during the final year of the First World War, but for his service in the Second World War. Monty's father had often told him stories about soldiers and airmen he had known during and after the war, and Steadman was one of them. Monty recalled that Steadman had served with the First Canadian Army in the Battle of the Rhineland, near the end of the European war in 1945. He was with the troops that had penetrated as far as Düsseldorf, and the fighting was bitter, the casualty figures high. If Monty remembered correctly, the Canadians lost something like five thousand men, the Germans something like eighty to one hundred thousand — either killed or taken prisoner. And Steadman received a medal of some sort. Monty had seen Steadman's grave, among others, when his father had taken him for walks through the Camp Hill Cemetery when Monty was in his teens. He decided to take a detour on his way to work the next morning and have a look.

There was a light dusting of snow on the grass and grave markers when he entered the cemetery next to the Halifax Public Gardens. He walked through the cemetery and remembered many of the gravestones he had seen on previous visits, particularly the towering memorial to Alexander Keith, the great Scottish-born former mayor more famous as the brewer whose products were still being enjoyed more than one hundred years after his death. There would often be a bottle or can of beer left by the grave to honour the great man. It took some searching but Monty found Steadman's monument, showing that he was born in 1898 and died in 1974. The inscription read, "Colonel Morley L. Steadman, MBE, known as 'Blocker' since his rugby days, fought valiantly in both world wars. Served with the First Canadian Army in the Battle of the Rhineland, February–March, 1945. Decorated by the King in December 1945."

Yes, the Steadman family would be justifiably proud of their father. But, Monty asked himself, would they be upset about the colonel's past antics, his looting back in 1917? True, it was not a flattering story: a young soldier stealing from people who had lost members of their family, lost limbs or eyes, lost their homes in the disaster. But, surely, the man had more than made up for that with his war service. Hadn't he? Monty shook his head to clear away an image of Steadman looting the bodies of men lying dead on a European battlefield.

CHAPTER XVI

Brennan

Brennan was standing by his window, looking across at his church in the falling snow. How beautiful it was, especially with the church lit up inside and the reds, golds, greens, and blues of the stained-glass windows shining out on the delicate white flakes. If life could always be this peaceful. But, of course, it could not. The bell of a phone would shrill out, as now, and break the spell.

"Hello," he said, in what must have been heard at the other end as a less-than-welcoming tone.

"This is your captain speaking." It was Brennan's brother Terry, a commercial airline pilot and the life of every party.

"Terry! How's the form?"

"Just grand, Brennan, and yourself?"

"I'm standing here mesmerized by a lovely fall of snow."

"Well, I have something to tell you. And I'm not speaking as Terry the barstool bon vivant and raconteur now, though what I have to say might sound like a tale fabricated after a few too many pints of porter."

"Let's hear it."

"Is it safe to assume that your telephone conversations are not of interest to the Mounties or the Canadian security services, whoever they might be?"

"It is safe. We've had no taps on our lines since we caught the papal security services at it, and removed all the bugs, and received assurances from the Holy Father that the Vatican spooks had been chastised and would sin no more."

"Good. Then I shall speak freely. You will be receiving a visitor sometime in the next couple of days."

"And who might that be?"

"Our OC." Officer Commanding, Brennan translated, a military term used by, among others, the IRA. Terry meant their father.

"Ah, the dear man," Brennan said, "coming to me with a little card, perhaps with a pressed flower in it, apologizing for his abrupt departure from my home and hearth. When does he fly in?"

"He'll not be flying in. He'll be coming in one of the company vehicles, travelling by himself to and across the Canadian border, and 'Sure, I may as well go on to Halifax, see Brennan again while I'm at it.'"

Declan's company, like the one operated by a branch of the Burke family in Ireland, hired out trucks, lorries, vans, and other vehicles. The company also transported goods from place to place, as part of its service. "Driving, not flying? Why? Is he delivering something to a customer here in the Maritimes?"

"Yes, but there's more to it."

"Isn't there always?"

"There is, right enough. You know about the guy who works for him, the fella who's being threatened by that convicted drug dealer."

"Flying Colum O'Flynn."

"Right. O'Flynn who, whatever else he might have done while in league with our co-ethnics in Hell's Kitchen, was dead set against the drug trade. So, I think Dec's always wanted to reward him for taking that stance. Hiring him at the family firm and now . . ."

"Now what?"

"You've heard what happened at O'Flynn's house?"

"I have. It even made the news here. There's a series about the Canadian and American crime . . . communities, and this came up in one of the broadcasts."

"Well, after those shots were fired at his house, O'Flynn apparently caught up with the guy who carried out that ill-advised attack. McGarrity, the drug lord. O'Flynn inflicted some injuries on him, but apparently McGarrity survived and got away. So O'Flynn is now wanted for assault causing serious bodily injury. Little wonder he went after the guy!"

"Wouldn't we all?"

"Except your good self, Father. Turn the other cheek and all that."

"Sometimes I fail to be the forgiving priest of God I'm supposed to be. So, O'Flynn?"

"He's on the lam." Brennan had been staring out the window, hardly aware of the falling snow. Now he dropped down into his chair. "Please don't tell me Declan is transporting the man across the U.S.-Canadian border."

"No, no, you can rest easy on that score. And if all this wasn't bizarre enough, here's the plan for getting him out of the USA: rumours are going to be put about that somebody will be helping to spirit him out of the country, either by air or by land across the border into Canada or Mexico. And a few men are going to head out to various border crossings to set up false trails, put the cops on the wrong track. The police will be checking the border crossings, questioning the Canadian and Mexican border authorities, and they'll find nothing suspicious at all. Just innocent men like our oul fella transporting goods across the border, travelling to visit family or friends. And while this is going on, O'Flynn — disguised, no doubt, and with false papers — will board a cruise ship with his wife, or someone posing as his wife, for a transatlantic voyage to Spain. As you know, there are a lot of Irishmen in certain parts of Spain, not all of them on innocent holidays abroad. And some of those guys will presumably handle things from there. I have no idea what plans his family has in all this."

"Christ almighty, Terry, this is wild!"

"I know, I know. But when you think of it, it's no more crazy than some of the lads in the old country thinking they could hijack a helicopter and land it in the yard of Mountjoy Prison."

"And lift three IRA men out."

"Exactly. What were the chances of that working out? And yet it did."

That is exactly what happened in the Dublin prison in 1973. Brennan well remembered his father's glee when he heard the story.

"So, Brennan, our da is on his way to you even as we speak."

"What?!"

"He'll be crossing the border, and his vehicle will no doubt be searched, and there will be nobody but Da in the vehicle, and nothing but the parts for a river dredger leaving the States for the city of Moncton, New Brunswick. A genuine delivery, all the requisite papers in order. The driver, our father, innocent and completely unaware of why his crossing is of so much interest to the authorities."

"Just when I think I've heard it all."

"We've never heard it all, Brennan, not with a paterfamilias like our own."

"Which passport is he using, I wonder?"

"What do you mean?"

"I'm talking about his phony passport."

"His *what*?!"

"Yeah, you heard me right. The lads at passport control in this country and yours know him — or have known him — as Michael Francis O'Farrell."

"Maybe they know him better than we do, Brennan!"

"Maybe so. I came upon it when I was looking for something in his room."

"Well, this time, Bren, he's heading across the border in a Burke Transport vehicle with a real item to be delivered, so he'll be travelling under his own name."

"Good. Sounds as if he'll be as clean as a tin whistle still in the package from Walton's when he crosses into Canada this time, as Declan Burke."

"Now that we have you here, Declan." Declan met this with a wary look. They were sitting in Declan's room at Saint Bernadette's rectory. Monty had welcomed Brennan's father back to Halifax but restrained himself from comment or question about Declan's sudden disappearance earlier in the month or the reason for his return to Canada now. "How would you like to accompany me to a construction site?"

"And I'd be doing that for what reason, Monty?"

"You'd be helping the authorities solve a crime."

"Helping the authorities? You must have me confused with somebody else."

"It's the guy, or it may be the guy, who tried to break into the school."

"Ah."

"I'm hoping you'll be able to recognize the man you confronted, if this is indeed the right man. His name is Freling."

"I didn't see much of him that night, Monty, him with his face mostly covered."

"I know, but it's the best we can do."

Monty stopped short of laying it on too thick; he didn't say *I'm afraid of what he might do next, if we don't stop him.* Monty was afraid of exactly that, but he didn't want to put that burden onto Declan's shoulders.

"All right then. Should I be covering my own face for this adventure now, Monty?"

"That tweed cap" — Monty pointed to it on the table — "pull that down a bit, and that should do it, especially if you're not seen with me. I'll point Freling out and then leave you to have a look."

Declan pulled on his winter jacket and tweed cap, and the two of them went out to Monty's car for the drive to the building site on the western mainland of Halifax. Monty had already checked out the project and knew that steel beams were being erected that week, so ironworkers like Freling would be on the site. When they arrived, Monty parked a good distance away from the building, which at this point was only a structure of steel columns and beams rising above the foundation.

Monty said, "I'll go first and find our man."

He reached into the glove compartment and pulled out a Toronto Blue Jays baseball cap, and put it on, tugging the brim down low over his face, then began walking towards the building. He hoped there were enough people on the periphery of the site that his arrival would not give rise to curiosity on the part of the crew. They were all wearing hard hats, of course, and none of them were gazing in Monty's direction, so he began to despair of picking Freling out of the crowd. He was about to give up and return to the car when he caught sight of Freling. He was instructing a couple of the younger men, pointing upwards at a beam being put into place. Now, how was Monty going to describe him to Declan so Declan would be able to pick him out? There was nothing about his clothing that differentiated him from the other members of the crew. Or wait, there was something after all, which Monty could see when Freling moved a little closer. He was wearing a pair of workboots that had a logo or a tag on the side, a blue cross on a white background, in the shape of the flag of Finland. As far as Monty could tell, none of the other men had the same boots. He walked casually back to the car and told Declan what to look for.

Declan made a wry face as he pulled his tweed cap down and set out to find his man. Monty put his key in the ignition, turned it, and listened to the latest CD he had put into the stereo: Luciano Pavarotti singing a selection of songs and arias. The last glorious notes of "Non ti scordar di me" were playing when Declan returned to the car and got in. "It's not him."

"What?" Monty swatted at the stereo to turn it off.

"That wasn't the man I grappled with that night."

Monty was reluctant to give up. "Tall muscular fella with the workboots with the blue and white flag?"

"That's who I looked at, and it's not our man, Monty." Declan twisted in his seat and faced Monty as they drove away from the site. "I'm picturing the scene in my mind, that night at the school, and my encounter with the fucker out on the street. He was fairly tall.

But not six feet, a bit under. Muscular, strong; I could feel that as I tussled with him! I can picture thick eyebrows, dark in colour. Eyes were dark; I'm quite sure of that. And those wide-open pupils. Drugs is the theory there. Can't recall, or couldn't see, anything more than that. But I know that wasn't the face I saw here today."

"That's helpful. Thanks, Declan."

When they returned to Saint Bernadette's, they found Brennan and told them that Benson Freling was not their man. Declan again recited the description of the man he'd fought with. Monty and Brennan exchanged a glance, and Monty said, "That doesn't sound like the same guy in the drawing made by the Morris Street witness, the woman who saw the guy following Normie."

"The last thing we effin' needed," Brennan muttered, "two different men, two of these maggots out there."

☙

Monty returned to his office and sat down to prepare a statement of defence for a doctor being sued for malpractice. It was a welcome interruption — Monty needed a break from the gruesome details of the medical case — when Julian MacEachern popped in and said he had news.

"Just wanted to give you the heads-up. You were asking about Lorne MacCombie. The city just rejected his development plan, the big one with the shopping centre, condos, and all that."

"Whoa! That's a big blow to him."

"He'll be steaming, and you may be sure he'll find somebody to blame. Heads will roll, as they say. Not a man accustomed to hearing the word 'no.' And you can imagine the expense he's gone to with architects and purchase of land, and all that. But, still, it's not over for him yet. Or it may not be. The city has offered him another chance if he makes some changes to his proposal and makes a new application. That will cost him a bundle, too, the changes to be scoped out. Blair Trites just filled me in; he attended a press conference MacCombie gave following the decision."

"Shit. I'd have been there if I'd known."

"Well, if you're still curious about the guy, watch the local supper-time news. I imagine this will make the broadcast."

"I'll be sure to watch it. Thanks, Julian."

So that's what Monty did. He and Maura planted themselves in front of the television to watch the local CTV news. The city's decision and MacCombie's press conference were the third story in, and Monty pressed the record button. "The proposed development was not acceptable to the city because of the height of the condominium buildings, which would cause too much shadowing of neighbouring properties, and because the plan would require that a nearby lake be partially infilled, leading to an obvious deterioration of the lake itself and of the surrounding countryside and associated wildlife. But the city has left the door open to Lorne MacCombie and his company if he is able to submit a revised plan to take account of the defects and flaws identified by the city. MacCombie held a press conference at his recently constructed downtown hotel."

Lorne MacCombie was a big man, with longish grey hair brushed back from a prominent forehead. Sitting at a long table, he was flanked by a half-dozen men and women who were presumably officers of the company. MacCombie put on a smile, which did not look all that natural on him, and said, "Any time you have a plan you think is a good one, and then permission is denied, you're disappointed. No question. But we at Halifax 1749 are grateful to our city planners for their invitation to put forward a new proposal for the lands. We'll be sitting down to work on that without delay. We like to think that our property developments are good for everyone: for the City of Halifax and its residents, for all those people and businesses that will lease space in our magnificent buildings, for all our dedicated managers and employees. And for our young people as well. Halifax 1749 takes its community responsibilities seriously, and one of the ways we do that is to employ young people who have had a rough start in life. Guys who had perhaps unstable family lives, guys who have run into trouble with the law. Let me show you."

Maura said, "Oh, lovely. A moment of glory for yet another greedy landlord who expected to profit from throwing shade over the properties of his neighbours, while destroying a lake and its surroundings. How many times have we heard that story?"

"Now, Maura, don't be so cynical. We're about to see what a good citizen he is!"

"Oh, yer arse, but yeah, let's see what kind of a saint he claims to be."

MacCombie turned and signalled to one of his staffers, and a video came up on a screen behind the table. It showed a group of young boys and a couple of girls on a summer outing. They were standing on the deck of a big three-masted sailboat. Monty had seen it in the harbour from time to time. The kids were smiling and waving, and then there were close-ups. Someone was on board the yacht with a video camera. One teenage girl thanked MacCombie for hiring her the previous summer, after she narrowly escaped being "put out to work the streets. Mr. MacCombie has shown me that life doesn't have to be like that. I can do whatever I put my mind to doing!" Then it was a boy who spoke of getting in with the wrong crowd and selling drugs for a scary guy who kept him under threat, until the boy was discovered by MacCombie and offered a chance at something better. The scene switched to the courthouse on Spring Garden Road where, presumably, the boy had been charged as a young offender. A few more young people were shown briefly, and there were a few images of rundown houses, garbage-strewn parking lots, a jail cell. Something flashed by that looked familiar, and Monty would watch the recording again. It was a house and a street sign, and it came up just after the face of one of the boys was shown.

The presser ended with MacCombie thanking the city's Development and Planning Department and Mayor Margaret Ross for having enough faith — "and I know something about faith myself!" MacCombie declared with a smile — having enough faith in MacCombie and his company to give them a second chance to propose a development that would benefit everyone in Halifax. Monty was surprised at how much coverage the press conference received; he figured it must have been because of MacCombie's assurance in saying all the right things about protecting the environment, respecting the designated space, and his willingness to give troubled young people a chance at a better future.

"I got a kick out of that little shout-out to his family history, their faith," Maura said, "good Presbyterian stock, the MacCombies. Are they really teetotallers, do you know?"

"Hard for the likes of us to imagine people who never take a drink, but that's what I've heard about them. There have been ministers in their family line, in the past and in the present, as well. Now, I'm going to rewind and play part of it again. There's something I want to see."

He rewound the tape until he found what he was looking for. And there it was. He paused the tape on one of the boys MacCombie employed in his charitable outreach to the disadvantaged. The kid looked quite similar to the face that had been sketched by the secretary at the engineering college, the woman who had witnessed the man following Normie. Monty could not be certain, since the woman had been limited to his small dark eyes and his nose that looked wide at the end. But the similarity was there. And then there was the house and street sign: McCartan Street. Monty had seen the house in his days as a lawyer with Nova Scotia Legal Aid. The McCartan Street foster home. Sergeant Gabe Delorey had told him that the boy he had tentatively identified from Normie's drawing — identified but not (yet) named — had once been a resident of the McCartan Street foster home. Would his gratitude to MacCombie inspire him to try to shut down the next performance? To make sure nobody saw what seemed to be billed as an unsavoury revelation about the MacCombie family and its companies in the past? Would the kid be afraid that such a revelation would scotch the current company's chance to win city contracts in the future? Or had the whole thing been engineered by MacCombie, using the kid to do his dirty work?

Normie had been at Kim Kennedy's for supper. Monty didn't pounce the minute she came in the door; he waited for her to settle in and describe her day, the highlight of which was the students' rehearsal for the second act of their play.

"Everybody's excited about it," she said, her eyes shining. "We're showing how brave people were, and how hard they kept working to help the ones who got hurt and lost their houses. Of course, it's very sad, but it's going to be just as good as act one!"

"That's great, sweetheart. We're all looking forward to it." Then he said, "I want to show you something I recorded on the TV."

"Okay!"

He turned on the set and the recording, and located the fleeting picture of the young guy who had, presumably, spent time in the foster home. He hit "pause" on the remote control. "Take a look at that boy, would you, sweetheart? I'm wondering whether he looks like the guy you . . . saw on Morris Street."

"Oh, God! I don't know if I want to see him!"

"I understand," Maura said, "but this is only TV. You won't be out walking by yourself until all this goes away."

"I guess so."

"Is it him?" Monty asked.

"It looks something like him, I think. But I only saw between his hat and the scarf he had pulled up, so I'm not sure. I want to help find that guy!"

"I know you do, sweetheart."

"I just can't tell for sure."

She couldn't say yes for sure, but she couldn't say no. Monty put down the remote control. And tried to reassure his daughter. "We'll find him, Normie. And don't worry; he won't follow you again." He invented a principle supposedly learned from long experience with the kind of guy who had followed Normie. "They don't do it again, guys like that. They're too afraid of being recognized."

"What's going to happen to our play, Dad? Some of the kids at school are saying we have to cancel it. We went to all that work to write it, and get the costumes, and learn all the lines, and practise it. And everybody loved act one! Well, I mean, everybody we know. And Father Burke loved it, too, and he keeps telling us the problems will be solved and the show will go on. But what if it doesn't? We're so lucky that we're having it in December, because that's when the Halifax Explosion was. And we're doing all the practising for it, and we're so happy doing it. But what if we have to cancel it? Or put it off till later? Nobody will come and see it if we have to wait and put it on in January!"

"Sure they will, Normie. They came to see act one in October. And they'll want to see act two no matter when you perform it. Now, let's look at this again, see if any of the other kids . . . look familiar." See if one of the other boys in MacCombie's orbit might have been the follower. He picked up the remote control again and pressed play. He kept an eye on Normie as she watched the press conference with obvious reluctance. A couple more young guys were shown, with no reaction from Normie.

The tape rolled for a few more seconds. Then, "I saw him!" Normie exclaimed.

Monty peered at the image of a young man running towards the camera with a grin on his face. "Is that —"

"No, not him!" She was pointing to the television. "Rewind it!"

Monty pressed rewind.

"Stop, there he is!"

He stopped the rewinding. The news report had switched from the young employees back to the employer. Lorne MacCombie. "You've seen that man, Normie?"

"Yeah!"

"On the street that day?"

"No, no, at the mayor's party. The cast party. He was talking to Richard's dad."

Monty did his best not to overreact. "So, the man you see there, Mr. MacCombie, he was at your play?"

"Nope. I remember thinking it wasn't very nice. Somebody asked him if he liked the play, and he said he had not gone to see it! And he came to the mayor's cast party anyway! Maybe just to get the food. Or the booze!"

"That's what he said, Normie? He hadn't seen the play?"

"Yeah. But maybe he didn't like it and didn't want to say anything mean about it so he just said he'd never seen it!"

Monty thought back to his encounter with MacCombie. What had he said about the play? He had acknowledged that he'd heard about it. But he certainly had not revealed that he had attended the cast party. Why not? Had he seen the play after all? Had he heard Normie's little promotional spiel about the dark deeds that would be revealed in act two?

Brennan

Brennan said — or, rather, sang — his morning Mass on Wednesday, and prayed for his students, that they would be kept safe from harm. Then he led them in a rehearsal for their Christmas concert. One of his favourite pieces, and theirs, was "In the Bleak Midwinter," Gustav Holst's setting of the Christina Rossetti poem. "Let's hear a good, sharp *K* in the word 'bleak,'" he requested of his choristers. "All else will follow from there." Many of the children loved the image of angels and archangels, cherubim and seraphim thronging the air. Brennan's own favourite lines were "Our God, Heaven cannot hold Him, nor earth sustain / Heaven and earth shall flee away when He comes to reign."

But earth was very much with him, and he was smacked down upon it again when he returned to his office and started returning the calls that had come in from parents of his students. Brennan had sent letters to all the parents, informing them of what had happened. He had, of course, tried to be as reassuring as possible, claiming to be confident that he and the police would get the problem sorted. He could only imagine the version of events that had been passed around by the students themselves. So the parents were understandably concerned about the threats made against the play, and some pleaded with him to cancel it. All were driving or accompanying their children on the way to and from school. Brennan didn't tell them that he had conscripted his father as a fellow security guard on the property during school hours. Some parents said they would pull their son or daughter from the production. He understood all this and told them so. And he thought they were probably right; act two should be cancelled, or postponed until the source of the threats had been uncovered and blocked from any further harassment. He assured them repeatedly that he had the students' best interests at heart, and that he would postpone the production if the matter had not been settled a few days before the performance. Brennan was not a man to give in to threats, to intimidation of any kind, and he loathed the idea of giving in to the sort of blaggard who would do this to a group of school children. He knew that the students were divided over whether to cancel or to publish and be damned. Well, a couple of weeks to go yet.

He and Monty had to identify this fucker and shut him down.

CHAPTER XVII

Monty

Monty's mother, Evelyn, was over for supper on Wednesday evening. It was November twenty-fourth, his late father's birthday, and they all exchanged some cherished memories of Marshall Collins. Monty wanted to enjoy the tales about his father, rather than dwell on Normie's worries — everyone's worries — about the play, the alarming events it had spawned, and whether it would be shut down altogether. He prompted his mother to talk about Marshall's days at the Bletchley Park code-breaking centre, the crucial work he had assisted in during the Second World War, cracking the German codes. She spoke about her impromptu flight to England to be with him, the secrecy around his work, her admiration for the brilliant women she met there, and what she later learned when their work as code breakers was made public.

But the fun — the respite from anxiety — was brief. After their meal, Evelyn said, "Monty, I heard you and Maura speaking about 'suspects' in relation to the school play, and the distressing events that followed the performance. And one of the names I heard was Steadman. Why the reference to Steadman?"

"The boys' notes from after the explosion say that Blocker Steadman had been looting, going in to what remained of people's homes and helping himself to their belongings."

"Oh, I don't believe it, Monty. Your father and I knew Blocker; he wouldn't have behaved in such a way."

"Not by the time you knew him, Mum, but before the Second World War forged his character for the better, he may have been a hoodlum."

"I can't imagine it. And his character must have been forged well before the second war. He was considerably older than most of the soldiers he served with in that conflict. He fought in the first war as well, joined the fray in 1918."

"Maybe the Steadman family today can't imagine it either. How would they react if the play suggested that he was less than a stellar citizen back in the day?"

"Well, he didn't look the least bit put out at the play."

"What? Who? What are you saying, Mum?"

"His grandson was there. Did you not see him?"

"Whose grandson?"

"Blocker Steadman's. Allister. Blocker and his wife had one son, and then the marriage broke up. The son died a few years ago. Motorcycle accident, if I remember correctly. So there's only the grandson, Allister, and his sister, Cheryl. I think she's living out west now."

"You're saying Blocker's grandson was at the play?"

"Yes, with his wife and two little girls. I saw them on their way out. Didn't have a chance to say hello. Well, he would not have known me, I'm sure. But he was there and he was smiling at the girls as they left the auditorium."

Smiling because he didn't have a care? Or because he hadn't recognized the reference to his family, or he didn't want to let on that he had heard something unsavoury about his grandfather? How had Normie phrased it in her little promotional talk? Somebody with a funny name hadn't been "blocked" from a looting spree, something like that. Had he perhaps mentioned it to someone else in the family, who hadn't taken it so calmly?

Evelyn looked at Monty and obviously noticed his concern. "If you want to know more about Blocker, Monty, why don't you speak to Bill MacKenzie?" Major Billy "King" MacKenzie was an old friend of Monty's dad. The nickname "King" derived from the name of Canada's tenth prime minister, William Lyon MacKenzie King. "Did you see the piece in the paper the other day, about the Battle of the Bulge? There's going to be a ceremony to commemorate it next month. Bill's name was mentioned, as it is every year. Bill would know the Steadman family well. But" — she placed a gentle hand on Monty's cheek — "I know you'll be discreet, darling."

"When have I ever been anything other than discreet, Mother?"

She smiled and said, "We'll leave it at that."

℃

Monty knew he still had the newspapers for the last couple of weeks; keeping them was an old habit, since he didn't always have time to read them through on the day they arrived. He found the article his mother mentioned, about the Battle of the Bulge, which piqued his interest as a history buff and as someone who was running out of ideas about what his next move should be. The story was about the upcoming anniversary of the battle in mid-December. Major MacKenzie had been with the Canadian Parachute Battalion in the latter days of the battle, and then in the Netherlands. King MacKenzie and Marshall Collins used to get together with other veterans of the Second World War to share their reminiscences. Marshall had not been in battle himself; he had been recruited for his mathematical abilities to work at the code-breaking operation at Bletchley Park. Monty had always assumed that these gentlemen's conversations consisted of, yes, war stories. But he'd never known for sure because, whenever Monty or any other civilian came within hearing range, the talk was — or suddenly became — about hockey, baseball, or soccer. Monty hadn't seen much of MacKenzie since

Marshall's death in 1987, but he was keen to contact him now. Ask him what he knew, if anything, about the highly decorated Second World War veteran Blocker Steadman.

Monty looked up MacKenzie's number and gave him a call. His wife answered, and Monty asked after her and the family. She, in turn, asked about Monty's wife and kids. Then she handed the phone to her husband. After some preliminary chat, Monty told MacKenzie he had a couple of questions for him and wondered if they could get together at a time convenient for MacKenzie. He replied that his dance card was not as full these days as it had been while he was stationed in England awaiting return to Canada in May of 1945. Monty laughed and said, "Your secrets are safe from me."

"Oh, I can't be sure of that if you have inherited the talents of your old man, breaking codes and unearthing the Reich's secrets."

They agreed to meet the next morning at the Young Street Tim Hortons. MacKenzie was already stirring his coffee when Monty arrived. The old army man looked rugged and fit, younger than his seventy-five years, with a full head of cropped grey hair and eyes of almost the same colour. They talked a bit about the news of the day.

Then it was time to get to the point, and Monty had no desire to deceive the old soldier. "King, you may have heard about the play put on by the students at Saint Bernadette's Choir School. All about what happened here in December 1917."

"Oh, yes, I heard about it but too late. Wish I hadn't missed it."

"Well, there's a second act coming up on December ninth. My daughter is a student there, and she was instrumental in writing the script and getting the play organized. My daughter, Normie, and a couple of her close friends."

"Good for her, Monty! I'm even sorrier now about missing it, but I'll try for act two."

"Aye, there's the rub." And he gave MacKenzie a précis of the situation, the attempts to derail part two of the play. He did not mention the death of Trudi Ebbett, an event Monty fervently hoped had no connection to the play.

"Somebody is doing this to a group of children putting on a play?!"

Major MacKenzie looked as if he would meet the culprit on the field of battle and slay him in a hail of bullets.

"Yeah, I know. It's outrageous. Now, the man in charge at the choir school is a close friend of mine, Father Brennan Burke."

"I've heard that name."

"He's a brilliant, talented man. He set up the choir school, and —"

"Music, right. That's what I heard."

"And he's supported the students' play one hundred percent. He is wild about these threats to his students, to their production of the play. Let's just say he's not willing to 'turn the other cheek' in this matter."

"Little wonder."

"Anyway, Brennan and I have gone through the script and the little teasers the kids put out there about what to expect in act two. Much of the material comes from notes we were able to obtain, written by two young boys back in 1917 and 1918. And we've come up with three families who might have had reason to be . . . embarrassed by something done by an earlier member of the family back in 1917. And we're wondering if it's a member of one of these families who is determined to shut the thing down, so as not to bring shame on the family."

"What the hell kind of shame could equal the shame of threatening and intimidating a group of school children?"

"Exactly, King. Whoever it is hasn't thought that through! Now, here's the person I wanted to ask you about, someone who was known to have done some looting in the aftermath of the explosion. This was one of the things the kids alluded to, something that would be featured in act two. And the man who had done the looting was Morley 'Blocker' Steadman."

"Blocker! He's been dead for something like twenty years!"

"I know, I know. But I'm wondering whether someone in his family would be jealous enough of his reputation to . . . act out, if they heard about the play, and the hints the kids put out there about the next performance. I've never heard anything negative about any of the Steadman family, never heard anything in my work as a —"

"Criminal lawyer!"

"Yes, nothing in that context. Or never heard any talk among the older generation. So I know this is a long shot. But, well, I felt I should ask, given what has happened to the kids at the school."

"You're right, of course, Monty. You have to look into all the possibilities. And you're right that the Steadmans are good citizens who have never brought scandal upon themselves." MacKenzie leaned in closer then and said, "But that stellar reputation is something they are fiercely protective of."

"I suppose they are."

"Don't know if you'd have seen this, or remembered it, but there was a letter in the paper a few years back, from Blocker's grand-daughter. Cheryl. I can't recall her married name, but I knew at the time it was her. She wrote to protest an opinion column in the paper, criticizing some of the actions our men undertook in the war. The columnist had written about the Allies' bombing raids over Germany. Dresden, Hamburg, all that. I believe the phrase 'war crimes' was used. And Cheryl wrote a blistering reply, about Hitler, his atrocities, the occupation of so much of Europe, the concentration camps and all of it, and said the writer had no business criticizing the Allies' conduct of the war."

"Really! I don't remember seeing that."

"It was a few years ago. She's living in Alberta now. And I know that she and her brother have written a couple of times to *Legion Magazine*, not to complain about anything in that fine publication, but to praise Canadians' contribution to the war effort, to tell a little story or two about Blocker in the Rhineland in '45. I suspect they wouldn't take kindly to anything that might impugn the reputation of the family. But in the same vein, I can't imagine them doing anything of the sort you've described! I don't know everyone in the family, the younger set particularly, but if they're of the same calibre as the Steadmans I know, they wouldn't be out there acting like hooligans."

Given all this, Monty wanted to have a chat with Allister Steadman. "King, can you suggest a place where I could oh-so-accidentally bump into Morley's grandson, Allister?"

"I've heard he's a frequent visitor at RA Park. In the bar downstairs."

"Good to know." Royal Artillery Park was the officers' mess in the centre of the city across from Citadel Hill, established in the early 1800s.

"Now, I'd rather not accompany you there, Monty. I'm not there very often, so if I show up all of a sudden with you, and you want to question Allister . . ."

"No worries. I understand. I'll come up with another battle plan, another way to get myself in there."

Monty thanked King MacKenzie, and they went their separate ways. There was another friend of Monty's father that he could call upon. Colonel Stuart Forsythe had often been a guest of the Collins family when Monty was growing up. And Monty had seen him at various events in recent years, so a call to Forsythe would not be considered odd. The subject of the call might be, but Monty would handle that.

When he arrived at his office, he learned that a client had been ordered to appear in court that morning but had neglected to inform his lawyer until the last minute. So he rushed over to the Spring Garden Road courthouse, arranged a future court date for the client, and returned to the office. He picked up the phone and called Colonel Forsythe, told him about the school play and the unnerving events that followed it, and explained his reason for hoping to meet up with the grandson of Blocker Steadman.

"Sounds a little thin to me, Montague."

"I know it does, Stuart. But I feel we have to check out every possible connection, however tenuous. I'm sure we both hope there is nothing to it, as far as the Steadman family is concerned."

"I hope so, yes. But that being said, I'll certainly be happy to help you out. I see Allister from time to time at RA Park. Are you available on short notice? Not much point in you coming along evening after evening if he's not there. But I could give you a call if and when I spot him in the bar."

"That would be fine." Monty gave him his home number. "Much appreciated, Stuart. Thanks."

ജ

Monty had some free time after lunch, so he took a walk over to Saint Bernadette's to tell Brennan about the latest plan. Brennan greeted him, invited him up to his room, and, without question or comment, poured them each a shot of Jameson.

"A little early in the day for me to start on the whiskey, Brennan."

"Eh? Have yeh never heard of a liquid lunch being enjoyed by those who have work to do in the afternoon?"

"It's not unknown to me, I admit."

"Perhaps what's missing, then, is a prayer. The prayer of our great Irish Saint Brigid, she who miraculously turned bathwater into beer. Let us pray." He bowed his head and recited:

> I would wish a great lake of ale for the King of kings.
> I would wish the angels of Heaven to be drinking it through time eternal.
> I would wish cheerfulness in their drinking.
> I would wish Jesus to be there among them.
> Amen.

Monty stared at him, then said, "You are in the company of the saints, Father Burke. Let me never doubt you again."

"Ego te absolvo for your lapse in faith, Mr. Collins. Go and sin no more. And enjoy your little glass of spirit."

Monty raised his glass to Brennan, smiled, and took a sip of the blessed liquid. Then he got down to more earthly matters.

"What do we have, Brennan? We have three families — three that we know of — who would have reason to be embarrassed or ashamed of things done by an earlier generation of the family. And we also have the classic disgruntled ex-employee, the forced exit of your school's drama teacher. But would those past deeds or resentments prompt someone to commit a break-in, send threatening notes, intimidate a young girl?"

"All those things happened, Monty. Somebody carried out those actions."

"That's right. But wouldn't there have to be a stronger motive?"

"Not necessarily. You've often meditated on . . . what would we call it? The evil that men do. How many times have the pair of us got onto that subject, after lifting a few jars down the pub? Neither of us can be considered naive about human behaviour, Monty. There is nothing that people won't do, no depths to which someone or other will not sink."

"Yeah, yeah, I know." He suddenly felt as if he had put away half a dozen shots of whiskey and was morose with it, even though he'd only had the one. All it took was to consider some of the things he had seen in the courts over his many years in criminal law. "But then there's Trudi Ebbett, Brennan. Did somebody commit murder as a result of something in the play? She appeared in Halifax shortly after the publicity about the play, and whatever she hoped to find at the Carmichaels' house was related to the explosion, but . . ."

"But," said Brennan, "the warning notes came from someone desperate to stop act two of the play from being performed. Do you think maybe it was somebody we haven't considered yet, somebody we're not aware of?"

"Is it remotely possible that we have two different motives here, two different players? One who went after Trudi, the other who issued the warnings? The warnings were deliberate, of course. But the killing of Trudi appears to have been spontaneous, not premeditated."

"But two motives, two different players? That would offend against the Occam's razor principle, Monty. The oul razor shaves off any unlikely explanations."

Monty was familiar with the argument, that when there are competing explanations for something, the simplest is likely the right one. The best explanation is the one that makes the fewest assumptions. He desperately hoped that one of their assumptions would pay off, sooner rather than later, so he and Brennan could rest assured that the school and the students would be safe.

CHAPTER XVIII

Brennan

B rennan had seen an announcement in the local paper, the *Chronicle Herald*, about a performance of *Steel Magnolias* at the Uncut Boards Theatre. Uncut Boards, he knew, was the community theatre company established by Abilene Hemlow following her unwilling departure from Saint Bernadette's Choir School. He'd liked the name of the company, a bit of local wit; he'd heard it had been chosen by one of the members to reflect the fact that it was located out beyond the city, virtually surrounded by forest. Brennan knew he had to speak to Abilene, and he certainly did not want to accost her at her home. So he decided to seek her out after tonight's performance. He had spared her an interruption on opening night, but this was night three. He knew that *Steel Magnolias* was a play with an all-female cast, the characters being women in the Southern USA. He nearly shuddered when he pictured Abilene as a Southern belle: the accent, the mannerisms. But it had to be done, and he was enough of a gentleman not to disrupt the performance by walking in near the end, so he would sit through the thing and see Abilene when the audience had departed.

The theatre was somewhere to the west of Halifax, and Brennan needed to consult a map in order to locate it. After a couple of wrong turns, he found the place. The theatre was in a charming small white wooden building that had formerly been a schoolhouse. There were around a dozen cars in the parking lot, and people were heading in for the performance. Brennan waited a few minutes, until it was almost curtain time, and then went in and bought his ticket. The house was about half-full. Shortly after Brennan took his seat, the curtains parted and Abilene emerged on the stage, decked out as expected, as what Brennan would imagine to be the quintessential Southern belle. Her blonde hair was puffed up into a "big hair" style and she wore a shiny pink dress with frills on it. Brennan expected that, somehow, she would combine directing the play with acting in it. But she surprised him: she was not a member of the cast. She was the director, and only the director; others would have the pleasure of being seen and admired on the stage. She welcomed the audience, introduced the play, and then retreated behind the curtains.

And the performance was good, well above par. Southern American characters almost call out for overacting, but most of the actresses resisted the temptation. Brennan joined the audience at the end in a round of heartfelt applause. Now, no evening with Abilene Hemlow would be complete without something or other being overdone, and this was the case with a surfeit of curtain calls. Members of the audience began shifting in their places and getting up to leave before the cast came out for the fourth time. Brennan waited until all the spectators had left. He wasn't sure where the actors and others involved in the production would come out, so he left the building and stood in the parking lot where he'd be able to see Abilene make her exit. It was a clear November night, stars bright in the sky.

Finally, she emerged, wearing a long cream-coloured coat with a white fur collar. She caught sight of him and reared back, her hand flying to her heart. He stood and said, "That was excellent, Abilene. Well done."

She looked as if she didn't know quite what to do with a compliment from such an unlikely source. But she wasn't long in coming up with a response. "Could this, Father Burke, be a case of *Who's sorry now?*"

He made no answer to that, and he could almost see her trying to decide what tack to take next. What came now was her eyes taking in the look of him from head to toe and back. Then she cocked her head in the way he remembered all too well and said in a flirtatious voice, "No collar tonight, Father." His winter jacket was unbuttoned, and she eyed his blue shirt and navy blazer, apparently liking what she saw. "Does this mean you've put aside your priestly responsibilities for the evening? Or, now that you've seen how talented I really am, you want me back, at your choir school."

What to say? He started with "You are indeed very talented. You've done an extraordinary job with your cast and staging."

"Perhaps we could go for a drink, Brennan, and talk over old times." What old times? There hadn't been any.

It was time to get down to the unpleasant business at hand. "Abilene."

"Yes?"

"You know the school staged a play about the Halifax Explosion, *Devastated Area.*"

She arranged her features in a look of confusion, but then thought the better of it. "Oh, yes, I heard about that."

"We performed the first act on October seventh, and the second act is to take place in December. But somebody wants to shut the play down."

"What do you mean, Brennan?"

"There has been a campaign of threats and intimidation against the students, to frighten them out of staging act two."

"Oh, that's terrible!"

"Somebody even attempted to break into the school."

Her jaw dropped at that revelation and then, "That's outrageous, Brennan! Who would do such a thing?"

"That's what we're determined to find out. It's either someone who was offended by something in act one, or fearful of something coming up in act two."

She placed a hand on his arm and gazed at him with soulful eyes. "I'm so sorry to hear it, Brennan."

He didn't think he'd ever heard his name voiced so frequently in so short a time. Now, for the brief interrogation. And he wasn't looking forward to it. "We have to consider every possible angle, everyone we can think of who might have a grudge or a grievance against the play. Or against the school. Someone who would commit these acts of intimidation or persuade someone else to commit them on his or her behalf. I know you were upset, angry, about us not renewing your contract."

Cue the hissy fit. But she surprised him, played against type. She answered coolly, "I hope you're not thinking of me in that role, Father Burke. I'm an accomplished actor, but I don't think I'd be convincing as a real-life burglar, or an intimidating figure who could sneak up and say 'Boo!' to frighten the children out of performing their play."

Sneak up? Did that encompass following a student? He hadn't said anything about sneaking up.

"Now, if you'll excuse me, Father. I'll take a pass on that drink. Good night. I'm glad you enjoyed *Steel Magnolias*." And she turned and walked away. She didn't whirl about and flounce off. She just quietly exited the stage of their conversation.

This was Abilene the Drama Queen being undramatic, quietly dismissive, unconcerned. Did this mean she had indeed had nothing to do with the campaign of intimidation that followed the play? Or had she at last mastered the skill of understatement? Why had she not asked for any details of the intimidation? Would she not have been curious as to how the acts of intimidation had been staged? As a theatre director, would this not strike a chord, raise concerns for her and her group, in case they ever offended a member of the audience? Brennan had always seen her as a *Do tell!* type, wanting to hear *all the dirt*. Had Abilene Hemlow at last learned to act the part of an innocent person reacting with quiet dignity instead of loud and strident histrionics?

CHAPTER XIX

Monty

M onty and Maura were home on Saturday night, getting Normie ready for a skating party at the Halifax Forum. They had taken little Dominic over to spend the evening with family friends who had a two-year-old girl, his favourite playmate. The event at the Forum was more than just a skating party; it was a chance for Normie to look at some of the young guys employed by Lorne MacCombie. MacCombie had rented the rink for a hockey game, and in between periods, the ice would be used for other guests to enjoy some regular skating. Brennan and Declan were going to join in, not on the ice but in the hospitality section MacCombie was setting up to overlook the ice. Normie was all ready to go, skates slung over her shoulder, when the phone rang.

Monty answered but he could barely make out what the caller was saying because he was speaking in a whisper, and there was a great deal of noise in the background. Eventually, though, he caught on that it was Colonel Stuart Forsythe calling to tell him that he was at

Royal Artillery Park and Allister Steadman was downstairs in the bar. Monty made a quick decision; this was his chance to suss out Blocker Steadman's grandson, so he told Forsythe he'd be there in twenty minutes. He promised to make it up to Normie, whose only response was a quiet "okay."

RA Park was across from Citadel Hill; it was bounded by Queen, Sackville, and Brunswick Streets and wasn't far from the Collins house on Dresden Row. Monty changed from jeans and an old sweater to khakis and a crisp white shirt and dark green sweater, pulled on a winter jacket, and sprinted through downtown Halifax to arrive at the army mess well within his twenty-minute estimate. The building was long and low, white with a black gabled roof. He was admitted and immediately headed downstairs to the dark-panelled Noon Gun Room. The walls were decorated with photographs, and guns, from various times in history. The bar was named after a Halifax tradition over two hundred years old: every day but Christmas, a cannon on Citadel Hill fired a one-pound charge of black powder at exactly twelve noon. Monty had once been walking by the foot of Citadel Hill and had seen a small group of American tourists drop and flatten themselves on the pavement when they heard the cannon fire.

Monty spotted Stuart Forsythe standing alone by the bar, so he walked over to join him. "Beer?" asked Stuart.

"Sure."

"Two Keiths, Shirley," he asked the woman tending the bar.

"Coming right up, sir."

Shirley handed them their glasses, and Stuart asked, "How are you doing, Monty? Still busy putting the bad guys back out on the street, I suppose."

"If you turn bad, Stuart, and you want to be put out on the street, I'm your man."

Colonel Forsythe laughed and clinked his glass against Monty's. The colonel was noticeably more frail than he had been last time Monty had seen him, likely seven or eight months ago. He was balding, and his face was thin and lined. But his voice was strong enough to command attention, or to command a troop of soldiers in the field. A few seconds passed and then he lowered his voice, saying, "That's young Steadman over there."

Monty followed his gaze and saw a man in his early forties, tall, wide-shouldered, with cropped black hair. He was sitting at a table by himself. "How should we work this?" Monty asked Forsythe.

"I'd rather not be the one to introduce you. After all, I have to live here!" Forsythe laughed as he said it.

"I understand, Stuart. I'll take this on myself. He will have noticed you and me together, but once I've broached the subject of the play, I'll tell him that I did not disclose to you my real reason for seeing you here, and looking for him." He looked at his target and saw him lifting a glass of beer to his lips, tilting it up and draining it. Was he about to leave? Monty would have to make his move. "Off I go," he said, and carried his beer over to where Steadman was sitting.

"Excuse me," he said, "are you Allister Steadman?"

"Yes."

Now what? He didn't see how he could ease into it, make it look like a coincidental meeting. He was going to have to wing it, as if one of his witnesses in court had just, without warning, gone off-script.

"This is going to sound odd, I know, but I'm here on a bit of a diplomatic mission!" He smiled in a way he hoped was self-deprecating.

"Oh? Is there an international crisis I haven't heard about? Should we mobilize the troops?"

"No, nothing like that. It's a little closer to home. My daughter is a student at Saint Bernadette's Choir School." No reaction from Steadman. "And they recently staged a play about the Halifax Explosion."

"Yes, I saw it. My wife and I attended with our two children."

"How did you like it?"

"I thought it was well done. Excellent."

"Thank you. That's nice to hear. Now, here's the diplomatic aspect. Some real-life people were included in the script. Two boys who survived the explosion, others who survived but lost family members. Of course, one of the boys had a sister who was blinded."

"I know. Terrible."

"And at the end of the play, as you may recall, there was an announcement of more to come. Act two. And there were a few little hints meant to entice the audience to come back and see the next installment." Steadman said nothing, so Monty continued, "The kids promised a 'murder mystery' and revelations about some questionable property dealings, specifically relating to the brothel that featured in the play. And then a reference to some of the less-than-honourable activities carried out by some in the days after the disaster."

Steadman looked at his glass as if ready to take a drink and saw that it was empty. He looked at Monty and said, "Yes, I remember some of that. Where are you going with this?"

Where indeed? "Well, having seen the play and heard those little promotional tidbits, you'll know that several families were referenced, by name or otherwise, in the play and in that promotional spiel. Apparently, somebody took issue with something that was said, or portrayed, on the stage." Monty then engaged in a bit of story-telling, purely fictional. "What happened was, the director of the school, Father Brennan Burke, received an anonymous phone call from someone who had taken offence at something in the play. The person did not specify what had upset him. As I say, he did not identify himself. But he stated quite forcefully that, in his opinion, any further performance should be cancelled, so as not to cause any more hurt or offence."

"No!" Steadman looked, or managed to look, genuinely surprised at this.

"So, a few of the parents at the school are going around trying to find members of any family that might have been affected or upset. And we'll do our best to make amends. Now, I should point out that I asked Colonel Forsythe" — he turned his head in the direction of Forsythe at the bar — "if he knew where I might find you. I can assure you that he knows nothing about the reason for my request. So," Monty said, with deliberate awkwardness, "this is my diplomatic mission: to find out who might have been angry or hurt by something in the play."

Steadman merely shrugged. "Not me," he said. "Now, I'm about to head home. Uh, good luck with your mission." And he got up and left the room.

Monty watched him leave. And wondered why Allister Steadman had not made a point of saying that, as far as he knew, there had been no reference to his family in *Devastated Area*.

Normie

I went to a skating party on Saturday night, but I wasn't there only to skate. I was also going to be a sleuth! Like Nancy Drew. That man I saw at the cast party, Mr. MacCombie, had a whole bunch of young guys working for him. They were guys who had a hard life, sometimes even "trouble with the law," so it was nice for somebody to give them jobs. Give them "another chance" in life. But my dad thought maybe, just maybe, it was one of those guys who followed me from school that time. So he wanted me to look at them all and see if I recognized one of them. It was in the news that Mr. MacCombie had rented the Halifax Forum to let the guys play a game of hockey. And between periods of the game — hockey has three periods — other kids would have the ice for regular skating, even figure skating. I love figure skating, even if I'm not very good. Anybody who wanted to come was invited, not just people who worked for the company. So it wouldn't look weird if I was there. Unless the creepy guy saw me and remembered me. But that would be okay because, even though Dad ended up having to go someplace else, Mum and Grandma Evelyn were coming. Father Burke and his father were coming too. There was a party for the older folks who could be up above in the seats and watch the skating. The people who organized it set up a special place where those people could look down and see the rink, and also drink beer and wine while they were doing it. So, if I saw the bad guy and he saw me, Mum and Grandma and Father Burke and Mr. Burke would protect me. (Unless they all got drunk!)

Father Burke brought something really cool for me to use in my work as a sleuth. No, not a magnifying glass. It was a little set of binoculars called opera glasses. So, when the hockey players came out on the ice, I looked at them through the special glasses. The players all had hockey helmets on, but when I was followed that day back in October, the bad guy was wearing a scarf pulled up and a cap pulled down, so this wasn't any worse than that. It was better; you could see their faces. I looked down at all the guys, and I couldn't tell if the follower was there. But I would keep watching as they sped around the ice. Hockey is a fast game, so the players are always zooming around. Hard to see if the bad guy was out there. And I didn't know whether I hoped the guy was there, or he wasn't!

Each period of hockey is supposed to be only twenty minutes, but it always goes on longer than that because the referee keeps blowing the whistle for icing or being offside — I'm not sure what those things are, but you're not allowed to do them — and the play stops. But that was okay. It wasn't "all work and no play" for me, as the grown-ups sometimes say. Because, while I was spying on the hockey players, I was hearing all kinds of funny talk from Mum and Grandma Evelyn and the Burkes. I think maybe they all had a drink of booze before they came, and they had glasses of stuff again now. Father Burke said, "You're doing a good job as a detective here tonight, Normie. You did a brilliant job acting as a mother in the school play. So it's no surprise that you're playing this part to perfection as well."

And I said, "Thank you, Father. Now, don't anybody clap for me. Because I'm working under the covers!" They all looked at each other and smiled, and I wondered if I'd said it wrong. But that was okay, because he said I was doing a good job.

I turned my attention back to the guys on the ice, but I heard Father Burke telling Mum and them about somebody. He said, "Speaking of acting," and went on to talk about this girl he knew. Mum asked him who she was, but he wouldn't give her name. "I'd never have given her a role in the explosion play, unless she was to be the explosion itself. The flash-bang, the roar heard dozens of miles away — some say over a hundred miles away — and the heat so intense it vaporized the

French ship. The role of a lifetime for her and there's no way you can be said to overact that! What do they say about actors who overact, ham it up?"

"I believe it's 'chewing up the scenery,' Brennan," my grandma said.

"Right, that's it. Well, maybe someone should give her a role as one of those stone-faced fellas that stand round Buckingham Palace, or wherever the Queen is, and wouldn't change their expression if a helicopter flew over and dropped a load of hot porridge all over them."

Then Grandma Evelyn was funny because she started talking the way the English people do — that's how her own parents talked, so she knew how to do it — and she said, "I assume you are referring to the Queen's Foot Guards. Next time one of those stoic gentlemen pops his clogs, that stage-struck woman should take over his role. Liven things up a bit round Buck House."

Everybody laughed, except me because I was pretending to do my work with the spy glasses. But I was laughing to myself.

"Yer one had a thing for priests," Father Burke said then. "I think she was hoping to have the excitement with one of us." I didn't know what kind of excitement he meant, but they all laughed again. And Father Burke said, "Any one of us would have sufficed. In that role."

"Ah, now, Brennan," Mum said to him, "surely *yer one* was after you, and you alone, you handsome oul divil."

Declan said, "Sure all the girls were mad for him. Long before he became a holy priest of God, and long after that as well."

"The girls mad for me, is it? From what I've heard about you, Da, the girls have been mad for you since Holy Mary was out at the clothesline, pegging up the swaddling clothes."

"Ah, now, even looking back at the far distant past, I don't recall ever being the centre of attention."

Mum made a snickering sound. "I've been under the impression you've spent much of your life avoiding attention, Dec."

Turning to Father Burke, Declan said, "She must be a trial to you, my son, this strap of a girl here."

"There's no denying it: she has a mouth on her, and she's not afraid to use it. But let's get back to yourself, Da. Never the centre of attention? Tell about the time you worked the land, up there — where was it? Up near the partition, I believe? Your brief stint as a farmer."

"Ah," his father protested, "don't be telling that oul tale."

Brennan

Brennan was going to tell it, though he would be careful in the telling of it. "Declan was up in County Monaghan, close to the border between Monaghan and Armagh, between the Irish Republic and the northern . . . state." The British-occupied territory. "This happened during the Emergency, known to the rest of the world as the Second World War. Now, I didn't hear any of this from Declan, but from somebody who travelled in the same circles. Up there he was, doing some, em, work, or research. And he came upon the village pub. So why not take a break and enjoy a couple of jars? There was a session on and a bit of dancing. Dec has a fine pair of feet for the dancing."

Evelyn smiled in Declan's direction and said, "I know."

"And there was a young lady who, so the story goes, liked the cut of this fella when he took to the dance floor."

"Now, Brennan, any newcomer to the village would have drawn a bit of attention. And I was already an oul married man at the time."

"Young married man, but go on."

"So I wasn't going to be playing away in any real sense of the phrase, but . . ."

"But?"

"I received an invitation to visit the family farm. Family of this young one, Clodagh. And she had come to the village on her father's tractor! Now, us Burkes aren't country lads, so —"

Brennan said, "I'm trying to picture the scene. Dec sitting up on a piece of farm equipment with a comely country maiden."

"Mmm" was all Declan said.

"Then you got an idea in your head."

"I did. I wanted to find a way to the border that was less . . ."

"The road less travelled, I assume, Da. Less likely to be patrolled by the authorities in the North." The authorities being the British Army.

"She said she'd show me. But I was to drive the feckin' tractor. I knew she was just, well, taking the piss out of me. But I claimed I could drive a tractor as well as any culchie lad. Or lass." The word "culchie" was a slur against country people in Ireland.

"Anyway, she explained the controls, and I took over. I sent us lurching forward and nearly ran us into a tree. But off we went, her giving directions to the border, telling me tall tales about life on the farm, and about her da and brothers and their work as Volunteers." Volunteers were republicans, IRA like Dec. "And I was driving the thing along a little path and then a boreen, and I was quite chuffed with myself until I made a turn and had to swerve to avoid hitting something. We nearly went arse over kettle. 'You're making a right bollix of it!' says Clodagh."

Brennan saw Normie's eyes as wide as English pennies. She was seeing Declan Burke in an entirely new light. Brennan turned back to his father and said, "What was it you nearly hit, Dec?"

"British Army vehicle. One soldier. I didn't know why he was alone out there, away from his unit, but there he was."

An enemy soldier. Was he avoiding the eyes of Evelyn Chamberley Collins as he said this?

"You approached the man, did you, Da?"

"I did."

"Did he welcome your approach?"

"He looked a little concerned."

"Terrified, the way I heard it. You had taken something out of your jacket pocket by this time, I believe."

"Didn't know what I might be facing up there near the partition."

"How did Clodagh respond to that?"

Declan took a sip of his beer, then said, "Just nodded her head as if she was saying, 'Proper thing.'"

Brennan left it to his listeners to infer what the object was, which was no doubt being pointed at the soldier.

"The lad was lost. He'd crossed the border without realizing it. By the look on his face, I knew he'd copped on to his mistake. He was maybe nineteen years old. Conscripted into the army and posted to that troublesome colony. He had the janglers; I could see the shaky hands on him, on the wheel. He called out to me, wouldn't open the window, but said, 'I'm not, I'm not going to . . .' He had one of those London accents. Cockney, is it? 'I'm leaving, but . . .' But he was stuck in soft ground, and he needed a push. I didn't see a weapon, so I put away my . . . I told him I'd help him out and show him the way to the border. I now knew it was two miles away. I told the squaddie to come out and push; I'd take the wheel. He didn't like it, but he saw no alternative. So, Clodagh helped push, and we got the thing out of the rut."

Brennan didn't know what exactly Declan had in mind when he'd gone searching for a way to the border: a raid on a British barracks, perhaps?

"I told him I'd go with him, guide him to the border, and walk back. He looked at me as if I was a spectre risen from the depths below. But he was in a cleft stick: if he didn't let me help him, he might never find his way. So, he steeled up his nerve and got into the car. I moved to the passenger side. Clodagh wanted to come along, but I told her no. I'd walk back to the village myself. I didn't want her there."

Maura, her manner uncharacteristically subdued, said, "You didn't want her to see what you were going to do."

Declan looked at her and said, equally subdued, "I didn't want her to see what I wasn't going to do."

"You let him live," Brennan said.

Declan merely nodded his head.

Normie

I got so interested in the story Father Burke and his dad were telling that I forgot to use my opera glasses, my *spy* glasses, to watch the hockey game. What would Nancy Drew say about that?! But then the first period was over, and it was time for other kids to go skating.

Mum said, "Let's get down there and put your skates on, Normie."

She came down and helped me lace up my skates good and tight, tighter than I can do it myself. And I went out on the ice. There were a few other kids, and some of them were girls, so I didn't feel I was in the middle of a boys-only party! I skated from one end of the ice to the other. I love skating! I thought about doing a twirl, but if I fell, it might hurt, and the other kids might laugh at me, so I just did regular skating. I noticed one of the hockey guys skating close behind me, and then he went out to the side and came over in front and made a circle around me. He had a hockey helmet on, but I could see his face. He was laughing, but I didn't think he was laughing in a mean way. Maybe just playing a joke. Why wasn't he zooming around any of the other girls? When he went behind me again, I looked around. And I saw that all the other girls had friends with them; I was the only one on my own. So maybe that was why. I hoped it was.

He was as tall as the guy who followed me along Morris Street that day, but he had skates on, so that makes everybody taller. But I had skates on, too, so maybe that didn't make a difference. As for his face, I just couldn't tell, because I had seen so little of his face that day in October. This guy had brown eyes, and I think the follower did too. But lots of people have brown eyes.

Then I heard a man's voice, and I saw Mr. MacCombie coming out on the ice with just his shoes on. I knew his name because of the time I saw him on TV and told Daddy I'd seen him at the cast party. And he was in charge of this party today. He walked up to the guy who was teasing me, and he said, "Come on, no more clowning around. It's almost time for second period." And he signalled for the guy to follow him off the ice. Then he got the other guys off the ice too.

When I was back up in the special seats with Mum and them, Mum was looking at the drawing made by the lady on Morris Street. The *witness*. "He looked something like this drawing, the eyes and nose — which, unfortunately, is all we have for comparison — but there were a couple of boys or young men down there who could have matched this as well." She looked up at me. "What do you think, Normie?"

She was right; it wasn't just one guy who sort of matched the picture. "Daddy would say we don't have enough *evidence*." The grown-ups smiled at that, but they knew I was right. "But you guys saw how he kept skating around me." I tried to sound as if I wasn't scared.

"Yes," Mum said. "But, you know, boys do that. They like to tease girls, and you were on your own, so maybe that's all it was."

"Yes, maybe you're right. Boys act like that sometimes!"

"We do," Father Burke said, and everybody laughed. I felt better then. It was probably just some boy playing tricks.

CHAPTER XX

Brennan

When Brennan wound up his grade eight music theory class on Monday morning, Richard Robertson stayed behind in the classroom.

"Is there something I can help you with, Mr. Robertson?" Brennan asked him. "Having trouble identifying the subdominant in the diatonic scale, something like that?"

"Not at all, Father Burke. It's something else I want to talk about. But I should check with you first. Is it a sin to talk to a priest about prostitution?"

"Ah, it's confession you're looking for, is it?"

"Nope. Just something I heard from somebody else."

"Right, the old story. It was 'somebody else.'"

"It's my mother, and she's not walking the streets trying to pick up men, or anything like that. It's this: I remembered one time she was reading the paper and she said to my father, 'How much do they pay these professors to research such filth? Well, I suppose this is the sort of thing they do with four months off every year.' It was something like that she said. And I asked myself, 'What filth is that?' Of course I wanted to see for myself. This was a few weeks ago. I picked up the paper after she put it away and saw that there was a prof at the Mount who wrote a paper on prostitution here in Halifax. The history of it. And something about 'girls' in the north end. And that, of course, is where Young Street is."

"It is, right."

"And then later, with all the stuff that's happened, I started thinking. This professor might know something about the place on Young Street, the *brothel*. If somebody today is upset or pissed off — oh, sorry, Father — about the play, and it's the prostitution angle that's got them wrapped around the axle, this prof may have some information. Oh, I don't know. As soon as I say it like that, it seems like a dumb idea."

"Not necessarily. Anything we can find out might help us. Can't hurt, can it? Thanks, Richard. Any time I need information about the ladies of the night, I'll ring the Robertson residence for the scoop."

"Jeez, if my old man or my mother answers, hang up the phone!"

"Duly noted. Do you have the article?"

"Uh, no. My mother puts the papers out, so we don't have it anymore."

"No bother. I'll track it down. Thanks, Richard."

At lunchtime, Brennan walked over to the city library on Spring Garden Road, asked for assistance, and soon found himself reading the story about Professor Betty Louise Rossiter at Mount Saint Vincent University. She had indeed done a study and written a paper about the history of prostitution in Halifax. So Brennan got in touch with Monty, and they made an appointment to go to the university and speak with her. The campus was high on a hill overlooking the Bedford Basin, which, as Monty pointed out, was the bay where ships had gathered to form convoys to head overseas during the two world wars. Hundreds of convoys during the Second World War alone. He and Brennan found Professor Rossiter's office and knocked on the door. She opened it and indicated that she was with a student but would be available shortly.

Less than five minutes later, the student emerged from the office, and the prof stood in the doorway, smiling at her two new visitors. They introduced themselves, and she invited them inside.

"Thanks, Professor Rossiter," Monty said.

"Betty Louise," she said, "or Betty. Have a seat." There were two chairs opposite her desk, and they sat down. "Tea?" she asked. "I have some made. I always do!"

"Sure," they both said. "Thanks."

She turned and picked up a large ornate-looking teapot patterned with blueberries, poured them all a cup, passed around the milk and sugar, and sat down. "You said on the phone you are interested in my work on the sex trade here in the city."

"That's right," Brennan replied, "and here's why." He told her about the play, the Young Street brothel, and the events that had unfolded after the performance of act one.

"That's appalling, trying to shut down someone's work, intimidating young students. What is wrong with people? How many times have I asked myself that question?"

"We've all asked ourselves the same question," Brennan remarked.

Monty said, "Of course, the play is set in December 1917, and our students had the good fortune to come upon some notes written by two young boys in 1917 and 1918. They wrote about the days before and after the explosion, and one of the boys, Michael Kavanagh, lived next door to a brothel on Young Street. He had lots to say about that!"

Betty Rossiter stared at him, and he was able to read the expression on her face. "We would be happy to provide you with copies of all the notes, Betty. Michael Kavanagh's sister, Ellie, still alive in her eighties, handed the notes over to my daughter for the play, and we made photocopies."

"Oh! Thank you, Monty. I would be most interested in reading them."

"We'll get them to you right away." He made a mental note to bring copies to the professor.

"And I think I'll be able to help you with your research," Betty said. "A woman named Alma has helped me with my own work. She told me she remembers some of the people in the Young Street house."

"Remembers?" Monty asked. "She's still alive? Well, Ellie Kavanagh is still alive, as are many people from that time, so why not Alma?"

"Why not, indeed!" Betty smiled. "Her name is Alma Senns. Still hale and hearty at the age of eighty-six. I wouldn't suggest turning up on her doorstep unannounced, but I'll be happy to call her and ask if she'd be willing to talk to you."

"That would be grand," Brennan said.

They thanked Betty Louise, gave her Monty's phone numbers, and said goodbye. When they had left the building, Brennan exchanged a look with Monty. He figured Monty had been thinking along the same lines as Brennan had done before they met her, expecting either a flamboyantly dressed prossie-wannabe, or a disapproving, puritanical nun. Betty Louise was neither; she was in fact a serious but friendly scholar and what one would call a motherly type of woman. "Aren't we a pair of gobshites?" Brennan said.

"Yep, that's what we are."

"So, are we going to see Alma?"

"Damn right."

And that's how it went. Betty Rossiter called Monty that evening and told him she had spoken with Alma Senns, had filled her in on Monty and Brennan's interest in the Young Street house. So, the following afternoon, Brennan and Monty walked into a three-storey brick apartment building in Fairview on the Halifax mainland. Alma's face showed every one of her eighty-six years, but her voice was strong, and her welcome seemed genuine. She was wearing a loose-fitting dress, brown with a pattern of small yellow and white flowers. The apartment was small and cramped with overstuffed chairs, but it was clean and had a view of the water. Brennan and Monty introduced themselves, told her their story, and explained their interest in anything that might have happened on Young Street in 1917, which might be disturbing to somebody after all this time. Alma pointed to two armchairs and invited them to sit.

She remained standing as she said, "I lived there, in that house. Or stayed there, I should say. Twice, I think it was. Would you like a cup of tea or coffee? The water's already boiled."

Monty and Brennan looked at each other, and Monty said, "Sure, coffee for me." And Brennan opted for tea.

Alma asked for their milk and sugar preferences, then went into her kitchen and prepared their drinks. Returning to the living room, she handed them each a cup, went back for her own, and sat down. "My mother — well, those were hard times for a young woman with a daughter to raise and no husband to support her. My father had abandoned us when I was a baby. So my mother had to get money for us in any way she could. There were two other kids who stayed there on Young Street with their mothers once in while, another girl and a boy. The women in the house took turns looking after us when our mothers were, you know, busy. Those other kids were probably in the same situation we were in; other relatives usually looked after us but were occasionally unavailable.

"As I say, I remember two spells in there, a few months at a time. First when I was little, four or so. It was funny: they were really strict, the women. Strict about us children. When they gave us baths, they wouldn't let the boy in the tub with me and the other girl, or us in with him, even though we were just little. Everything had to be proper. You'd think it was a daycare centre operated by a church! I was there again when I was around ten or eleven. Just for a couple of weeks."

"Did you see anything that might account for the reaction we've described to you?" Monty asked. "Hard to imagine something festering all these years, I know."

She leaned over and put her teacup on a side table. She said, "Well, I saw a couple of fights. You know, fellas would be drinking. Partying with the girls if the madam was out for the evening. There was one guy — I later learned he was a cop! — and one of the other men recognized him, had a beef with him, and they threw a few punches at one another. This had spilled out into the front yard. My mother found me at the window, all eyes, and pulled me away from the sight. And there was a time when one of the men got rough with one of the girls at the house, one of the women working there. Two of the other girls got on top of the guy and yanked him away from her and sent him packing, with a black eye! So there were things like that once in a while, but would anybody care about that today? All those people would be long in their graves by now."

"I know," Monty agreed. "But somebody now, seventy-six years later, is bent out of shape over something that happened then and wants the play shut down."

"Somebody's son worried about the family's reputation? Maybe the cop's family."

"Probably something like that. A son or daughter or other family member, quite likely."

"I do remember another fight. No, not a fight but an argument. That wouldn't have been too long before the explosion. My mother had me out of there before that happened, before the explosion, thank God! There weren't any little kids in there at the time. But three of the women were killed when the house blew up." She raised her head and looked out the window, as if she might still see the cloud of smoke rising more than two miles into the sky. Then she turned back to her visitors. "What was I saying?"

"You were telling us about an argument," Monty replied.

"Right. There was a man who was always dressed to the nines when he came to the house. I don't mean flashy clothes, the kind that would attract attention, but high-quality clothes. Expensive. Even as young as I was, ten or eleven, I got the impression that he was some-body important or thought he was! And, as they say in the stories, 'money changed hands.' Well, money changed hands in that place every night, obviously! But the other fella in this was a sailor I'd seen a few times. Saw him once in his uniform, so I knew he was a sailor. I was sitting at the kitchen table, and the sailor and the well-dressed guy were in the backyard, and they were squabbling. I saw the expen-sive guy hold out an envelope to the sailor, who had a smile on his face when he grabbed the envelope. The well-dressed guy sure wasn't smiling; his face said, 'If looks could kill!' Now, I couldn't hear what the snooty-looking man said, or I've forgotten, but the sailor smirked at him and said something like, 'When enough is enough!' That's all I could make out, and the sailor walked away, and the other fella stood there fuming. Then he came into the house, and I ducked down under the table so he wouldn't know I'd seen him. I'm not sure why I did that. And well, that's all I can recall."

"You've a good memory, Alma, after all these years," Brennan said to her. "Thank you for giving us your time."

"Oh, you're welcome. I don't get that much company! I'm not sure if any of that will help you."

"It could be helpful, and we appreciate it. God bless you."

And they took their leave of Alma Senns. There were dark clouds overhead, but the rain had held off, and Monty suggested that they take a drive around Bedford Basin. "Enjoy the view of the water, maybe see a ship or two."

"Good plan," Brennan agreed.

So they drove out the Bedford Highway skirting the water, which was a deep greyish blue, with ripples on the surface. Brennan looked back and saw a container ship being unloaded at the Fairview Cove container terminal. "I'm fascinated by operations like that," he said. "Goods coming into a country from all over the world."

"You come by it naturally, Brennan, living in so many port cities during your lifetime. Dublin, New York, Halifax."

"True enough."

"So, what can we take from our conversation with Alma?"

"We have a cop using the facilities on Young Street. Would his descendants be sensitive about that?"

"Could be. And there's the sharp dresser, someone from the moneyed classes. And the sailor. Canadians were very attuned to our country's reputation during and after the First World War. It was sort of a coming of age — a brutal way to come of age, for sure — for our country in that war. We were recognized for our great contribution, more than sixty thousand dead and many more wounded. Canada was regarded as an independent country after that. Rather than just a British colony."

"To quote Yeats out of context, 'a terrible beauty is born.' It was a terrible way to gain respect. A war that turned out to be for nothing. Millions of military and civilian deaths, millions wounded. All for absolutely nothing, Monty, given that it started up again a mere twenty-one years later."

"Yeah, one of those brutally painful facts of human history. Are we any the wiser, do you think?"

"In a general sense, or are you talking about our investigation?"

"Let's not get into the larger question. We'll stick to our current inquiries."

"Time will tell. I'm not all that hopeful. But, of course, time is what we don't have. Just over a week till act two. I am hell-bent against cancelling it. The kids would be broken-hearted. But their safety comes first."

They were silent for a while as they contemplated the folly of mankind and the dark cloud hanging over the students' play. But at the same time, they could appreciate the beauty of their surroundings. When they arrived at the main thoroughfare in Bedford, Monty said, "Chickenburger?"

"That sounds like just the thing."

So Monty pulled into the much-loved Chickenburger Restaurant, and they came away with bags of chickenburgers and fries, and hit the road again.

Monty said, "What about that money changing hands outside the brothel? Money changing hands at a brothel is par for the course, but that exchange was a little heated, to hear Alma tell it."

"Somebody being paid off for something or other."

"Or perhaps being paid in installments. Sounds as if the conversation might have gone like this, the sailor receiving the cash saying, '*I'll* let *you* know when enough is enough.' And the man doing the paying was kitted out in expensive clothing, so was a source to be tapped."

"Extortion? Blackmail?"

"Chances are. Does this get us any further ahead, Brennan?"

"Not as far as I can tell. But we are seeing through a glass, darkly. Not discerning what surely is there to be seen. If only we could see it."

"Great help you are. Call upon a higher power to assist us, would you, Father?"

"Ah, now, I don't want to push my luck. I've a pile of requests in His inbox already, Montague."

CHAPTER XXI

Normie

I kept thinking about the house next door to our new one, the Carmichaels' house that used to be the brothel. That house played a big role in our play, if you can say a house played a role! The girl who got killed, Trudi, she had told Mrs. Carmichael there was something in that house that her great-grandmother had kept in there. Is that what got her killed, whatever was in the house? I wanted to find out! If we solved the mystery of her death, that would be great. Good in a way for the people who loved and missed Trudi, like all those friends and the kids she used to babysit for, who made the scrapbook about her. She would never come back, but at least they would know what happened to her. But it would also be good to have such an exciting story in act two of *Devastated Area*. The grown-ups, our parents, would say no if me and Kim and Richard asked them if we could go to the Carmichaels' house and hunt for whatever Trudi wanted to find. But sometimes amateur sleuths like us have to do things our own way! That's what Nancy Drew would do, and the Hardy Boys too. The case must be solved! The first thing I thought of was me and Richard going to the house and asking if we could go in and look around. But Richard is kind of big, and if the lady of the house was alone . . . I thought of another plan. It would just be me and Kim, and we'd go to Mrs. Carmichael's door in the daytime, not at night, and ask if we could look.

I told Kim about my plan right after school on Tuesday. I didn't want Mum and Dad to know about this part of my investigation because they'd say no. So I had to make up a story. What to say? I decided to call Mum's office and tell her I was going over to Kim's house, and that her parents were going to drive us there. Kim would tell *her* parents that she was coming to *my* house. I knew we'd both make up for the lie later by telling the truth about where we went, when it would be too late for them to say no! I made the call from the school's phone but Mum wasn't in her office, so I left a message on her answering machine. That was good; it was easier than talking to Mum herself. Kim got her mum on the phone and sounded like she really was coming to my house.

Then we took the bus up to Young Street, walked to the Carmichaels' house, and knocked on the door. Mrs. Carmichael answered our knock; she had short brown hair and glasses, and there was a little girl with her, about five years old. She had on a sweater that was the colours of a ladybug; she was really sweet. I said, "Hello, Mrs. Carmichael. I know you don't know me, but I'm not a stranger!" She kind of smiled when I said that. "My mum and dad bought the house next door to you. My name is Normie Collins, and this is my friend Kim Kennedy." Then I went on to tell her how my dad was a lawyer and he was involved in the case of the young girl being killed. I didn't mention Kirk. So it may not have made much sense to her! But I told her about our play and the notes we found that were written by two boys back in the old days, Mike and Lauchie. And that they had heard one of the . . . ladies that lived in this house telling her friend to "hide" something for her. And I said I had heard about the girl coming to Mrs. Carmichael's door that night looking for something in this house, and that it might be an *important clue* to the murder. She smiled again but not in a sarcastic way.

"Mrs. Carmichael, did you ever find anything that might have been about that girl's great-grandmother?"

"No, dear, but I can't imagine anything being left in here after all these years and after the place was mostly wrecked in the explosion. Though, um, if somebody wanted to hide something in . . . in a house of that kind back then, the rooms might not have been the best hiding place. A lot of people would have been, well, in and out of the rooms here. So maybe the basement or the attic. But, of course, the attic didn't survive the blast."

"Was the basement wrecked too?"

The little girl started tugging at Mrs. Carmichael's sweater and saying, "Mummy! Mummy!"

"It's all right, sweetheart. We have to wait for Daddy to come home." Mrs. Carmichael turned to me and said, "This is Lucy. Our older daughter, Sophie, has a piano recital over in Dartmouth. There's a gathering at the home of one of Sophie's friends, at Megan's, before the recital. And Lucy is keen to go. Why don't you get your xylophone, Lucy, and play with that until we go."

She scampered away.

Mrs. Carmichael turned back to me and Kim. "What were you asking? The basement, was it? No, the basement wasn't destroyed, though everything else fell into it when much of the house collapsed. The people who bought this house before us, after it was rebuilt, they just put wood panelling over the old stone walls of the basement. I had a look around after . . . at some old things we have piled on a shelf, but I didn't find anything that the poor girl's great-grandmother might have left behind. Just our own things."

"Oh, okay," I said.

"Now, when we bought the place, we tore the panelling off, so much of the old stone is still there. Well, we didn't do the work. We had a contractor in. But I'm sure if he'd found anything interesting like that, like what you're looking for, he would have told us."

Probably, I thought, unless it was something valuable. Like jewellery. Maybe the guy stole it! I told myself not to think such nasty thoughts about people.

Kim spoke up then. "You're probably right, Mrs. Carmichael, but . . . could we come in and look anyway?"

She looked as if she was thinking about it, then she said, "I'll tell you what. I don't like bringing Lucy down there. It's damp and, well, not all that clean! But my husband will be home any minute. He works nights, and right now, he's out looking at snow blowers. Doesn't want to have to shovel all that snow like he's done the last couple of years! Anyway, he'll be home soon. Would you like to come in and wait, or . . ."

I figured we shouldn't go in and hang around; we might "wear out our welcome" as my mum says. "Maybe we should come back another time, Mrs. Carmichael. You've got the piano recital to go to and —"

"No, no, today is fine. Ron will be back soon."

"Okay, it's a nice day. We'll go out and walk around, and we'll come back. We'll see a car in the driveway?"

"That's right," she said. "And maybe a snow blower!"

So we left and walked up the hill to the Hydrostone area. That's one of the main parts of the city that was destroyed, and they built new houses out of Hydro-Stone, which doesn't burn. I especially like the houses that have long sloping roofs in the front. We walked around the blocks and went to Young Street a couple of times, and there was no car in the Carmichaels' driveway. Then there was, so we walked back to the house. Mr. Carmichael met us at the door. He looked a little older than Mrs. Carmichael; he had curly dark hair with a lot of grey in it. "Did you get a snow blower?" I blurted out.

He laughed and said, "I've got one on order. Have to build a shed for it now! So you girls want to search our cellar, eh?"

"Yes, please!" me and Kim both said.

"Come on in."

We walked inside and waved to Mrs. Carmichael, and we could hear the plinking of the xylophone. We followed Mr. Carmichael to the basement stairs.

"Careful now, the steps are steep."

There was all kinds of stuff down there. Tires, Christmas decorations, an old tricycle, a cooler for picnics, the same kind of things we have in our basement. The walls were made of big stones with grey stuff in between them, holding them together.

There was a set of shelves that took up most of one wall, and there were old books on the shelves, some old cups and saucers, two tool boxes and a metal box that had a label taped to it: "Family." The box was around the size of the big five-pound boxes of chocolates we usually got for Christmas. They were called Ganongs, and I loved them.

I asked Mr. Carmichael, "Whose family is this box for?"

"Diane's and mine. You can open it if you like. You'll see some old pictures, black and white, of our parents and grandparents, their old Chevs and Pontiacs. I don't know what all else; it's been awhile since I opened it."

"So it's your own family's things."

"Right. The guys who did the work down here, the contractors who removed the panelling, they'd come upstairs and say they found an old picture, or a death notice from the paper years and years ago, things like that. We just told them, 'Anything like that you find, just put it in that box marked Family.' So that's what they did. I don't remember us ever looking in the box again, after the guys finished their work down here. Some of that stuff may be from the previous owners, for all I know."

"Ron!" That was Mrs. Carmichael calling from upstairs. "We have to get going. Traffic will be heavy going to Dartmouth if we wait too much longer."

"She's right," he said. That meant we'd have to leave without finishing our search. But he looked as if he was thinking about it, and then he called up the stairs. "You and Lucy go now, go to Megan's," he said, "and I'll borrow Doug's car and meet you at the recital." He turned to me and Kim and said, "My uncle, couple of blocks over, hardly ever drives anymore. I can use his car any time I like."

Mrs. Carmichael called down, "Okay, we'll do that." And then she said, "Good luck, girls! Hope you find something."

And I said, "Good luck to" — what was the girl's name? — "Meg— . . . Good luck to Sophie!" And Mrs. Carmichael said thanks, and I heard them go out a few seconds later.

Mr. Carmichael smiled and pointed a finger at us. "I'll be upstairs, so don't you girls think you can steal any of my tools or my nuts and bolts!"

"We won't!"

"I know you won't. If you need anything, just holler for me. Good luck with your search. Oh, I'll give you a flashlight, and you can peek in where the mortar is cracked, in case somebody shoved something in between the stones. I don't think so, but here you go." And he picked a flashlight up off a shelf and handed it to Kim. Then he went upstairs.

Kim turned on the light and pointed it at one of the cracks between the stones. "Nothing in that one," she said and moved on to another crack. Again, nothing there.

Then, "Look! Can you see something?" I peered in; it looked like a green piece of paper. "Can you get your hand in?" I couldn't but I saw a big flat thing on the shelf, something like a knife, only wider, so I went over and got it, and we stuck it into the crack. Tried to pull the green thing out. Couldn't get it.

"You try," I said to Kim, so she did. And she had better luck. She slowly pulled it out.

"Aw," she said. It was only a leaf. "I'll keep looking around the other stones.

"Normie!" she yelled then and jumped backwards, pointing at the bottom of the wall where it met the floor. "A spiderweb!"

We both stared down at it. Then I said, "There's no spider."

"Whew, I'm glad. I hate them! Do you want to see what's in that box?"

I turned and looked at the grey metal box on the shelf. It was covered with dust, and I blew the dust off. That made me sneeze, and I had to rub my eyes. But I opened the box, and it was like Mr. Carmichael said. Those old black and white pictures like the ones Mum and Dad have at home, ladies in flowery hats, men in those hats men used to wear when they were dressed up, little kids in beautiful winter coats. There was even a bundle of report cards in the names of Ronald Carmichael and Diane MacKay. That would be her name before she got married. The cards were when they were in the little grades, and they got marks of A and B on most of their subjects. I put those on the shelf.

Then partway down in the box was a little blue folder with pictures of knives and forks and silver teapots, and their prices listed. The name "Birks" was stamped on the folder. I knew that Birks was a jewellery store, jewellery and silver and fancy things like that. This could be what the great-grandmother left! Maybe the real silver stuff, the things on this list, had been in the house to be left for her family!

I was really excited about it, and I turned to Kim. "Look at this!"

"Oh, nice. But, you know, Normie, it may just be the Carmichaels' own stuff."

I turned the folder over and read, "Oh, shoot. It says 1959, so it wasn't left here before the explosion. Maybe it didn't even belong to the Carmichaels, being that old. Left over from somebody who lived in the house before them."

But we kept looking. Further down in the collection of things, I saw a little square brown box. I pulled it out and saw that it had pictures of flowers drawn on it. Scratched into the wood. When I rubbed my fingers along the designs, I realized that it was made of metal. What did you call that, when silver turned all brown or black? I couldn't remember, but I had seen Mum polishing all the dirty stuff away from her silver teapot and spoons, and the silver would be shining. I noticed there was a little clip, and I pushed at it, and the box opened up. There were little papers in it. I was careful when I started to pull them out, and then I saw something else. An envelope with a name on it: "Irene." The envelope was yellowish, and the sticky stuff on the back was undone. I opened it, and there was a piece of paper inside. I looked at it and saw the date and I said, "Wow! This is dated November the tenth, back in 1917, even before the explosion. It's to somebody named Irene."

"Read it, Normie!"

Halifax, 10 November 1917. To my darling Irene. This is a lock of your brother's hair. If anything happens to

261

me before I can make a proper home for you, I want you to know this. Life has not been easy for me and I have done things that would not make you proud. But you are my daughter and I love you. You have a brother you will never know, born in October. This is all I have of him.

I looked up at Kim. "It's a lock of a baby's hair!" Then the letter said,

Beautiful. He had a full head of hair when he was born. They call this strawberry blond. He has been given to a *very important family* and he will have a good life. His father paid me money for the baby, for me not to be with any other man, and money to go away to New Brunswick for many months, till I gave birth. His wife knows all about it, except he told her he had fathered the child on the daughter of another *important family*. So many lies! Stephen will always be *my* baby and I miss him terribly! I don't like the new names they gave him. They make me think of Tabby, like a cat! He will always be Stephen to me. I did it for money, so I can give *you* a good life. Your loving mother, Minnie.

"Tabby!" Kim said, her eyes about to pop out of her head.

"Oh my God!" I said. "Tabby wasn't a kitten; he was a baby!"

"No wonder that lady was so upset," said Kim. "The lady Mike used to see at that house — this house — she was the little baby's mum and she wanted him back! And that man stole him!"

Wow! I didn't want to brag out loud, even to Kim, but look what we did: we solved the mystery! Well, part of it. We knew Tabby was a baby, and a man took him from his mother. But we didn't know who Tabby really was. Nancy Drew would never have stopped before getting the whole story.

"Is that why the girl was killed here last — when was it?" Kim asked.

"First of this month."

"But why would somebody kill her about something that happened that long ago? Seventy-six years ago."

"I don't know. But wait till my parents and Father Burke hear about this!"

We went upstairs and told Mr. Carmichael that we had found the secret that had been hidden. We thought it would be rude not to show it to him. "Look what we found!"

He stared at the dirty little silver case and said, "I never saw that before. The contractors must have just put it in the box with the other things; well, that's what we told them to do."

"Open it up," I told him, and he did. He picked up the letter and read it. He had been smiling, but now he looked sad. He put it back in the case and closed it. He gave it back to me and said, "You take care of that." We said we would, and we thanked him and left the house.

Monty

Monty was still at his office when he got a call from Normie asking him to come and pick her up at the school. The school? He had heard from Maura just after three thirty that Normie was going over to Kim's house. Well, now it was Saint Bernadette's. There was no more walking home alone, never mind that the school was only a few blocks from the house, so either Monty or Maura had been collecting her in the car or meeting her for the walk home. Monty had the car today, so off he went. As soon as Normie climbed into the seat and closed the door, she announced that she was going to "call a meeting."

"A meeting, sweetheart?" He looked over at her.

"Yes." He could see that she was bursting to tell him something. But she surprised him with her ability to keep the agenda to herself when he asked what it was about. "You and Mum have to be there, and Father Burke, and Kim and Richard."

"This is about the school? About the play?"

She nodded her head and pressed her lips together, as if to avoid the temptation to blurt out her news, whatever it was.

"If it's connected not only to the play but to the . . . any criminal behaviour, Normie, I have to know about it."

"I know, Daddy, so can we have the meeting early tomorrow? At lunchtime?"

Monty didn't know what his schedule would be like, but he wanted to hear this. It could well turn out to be irrelevant, of course, but he wanted to hear it. "Lunchtime, it is. How about tomorrow at the school?"

"Good. That way, Father Burke and Kim and Richard will be there. And you and Mum."

℃

At twelve fifteen the next day, Monty, Maura, Normie, her two friends, and Brennan Burke were seated around a table in Saint Bernadette's rectory. Normie was beside herself with excitement, as was Kim, but nobody spoke until Father Burke opened the proceedings.

"I believe it's Normie who'll be chairing the meeting today. Go ahead, Normie," Father Burke urged her.

"All right, here we go." She launched into her story, larding it with a great many details about the Carmichaels' family, their daughters, their basement. Monty avoided catching Maura's eye. The amateur sleuths had been doing an independent investigation. Monty knew that Maura would be as impatient as he was to find out what had Normie and her friends so chuffed with themselves. Monty saw Brennan twisting around in his seat. Ah! A pack of smokes on the table behind them. But he held off, as the young detective kept them in suspense with a surfeit of irrelevant information.

But Brennan knew as well as did Monty and Maura that Normie deserved her moment in the spotlight and that she was sensitive enough to be troubled by any suggestion that she was not running a meeting as she should. When Monty reflected on it, he'd probably never been to a meeting in his life when the chairman had got to the point right away.

"Mr. Carmichael showed us a metal box with family pictures and letters and report cards in it, stuff that was really old. He said he hadn't looked in the box for ages, and when the men came to take the wood panels off the basement walls and they found old photos or papers, they could just put them in that box."

Normie's eyes were gleaming now; she was getting to the big revelation. "So Mr. and Mrs. Carmichael never knew about *this*!" And she pulled the rabbit out of the hat — or the little silver case out of her pocket. She showed it around to the group. "I snuck into the silver polish at home and polished it."

"An old cigarette case," Maura said.

"Is that what it is?" Normie asked.

"It used to be quite fashionable to carry your smokes in an elegant little case. So this was what Trudi Ebbett had been looking for?"

"No, I don't think so," Normie replied. "It's this letter! It was in the case under some other little papers. I'll read it to you." And she read them a letter that had been written in November 1917, pausing after "This is all I have of him."

Normie looked up at her spellbound audience. "It's a lock of a baby's hair!" She went on to read about the baby who was given up to an *important family*, given up by a mother who thought she was giving her child a better future than she herself could ever have provided. And she was paid for her efforts. But she had come to regret her decision and confronted the new father, to no avail.

"Jeez!" Richard exclaimed. "It was a baby, not just a kitten! Good work, Nancy Drews."

Monty's mind was reeling from the revelations.

"Remember, Daddy? The part of the play we did from Mike's notes of what they saw happening at that house? The girl was all upset with that man, whoever it was she was hollering at. She wanted him to give Tabby back! She wanted her own little baby back!"

Monty caught Brennan's eye. They wanted to talk and *not in front of the children*.

"Good work, Normie and Kim!" Monty said. "You've found out what 'Tabby' meant. That letter is evidence, maybe evidence in the murder case."

The three young people stared at him, wide-eyed.

"Brennan, we'll want some photocopies of this. And Normie, you and Kim and Richard have to keep this to yourselves. You haven't told anyone else, have you?"

"They didn't even tell me till now!" That was Richard, and he didn't look aggrieved. It was more like admiration than resentment.

"Well," Normie said, looking a little embarrassed, "we did show it to Mr. Carmichael."

"Fair enough, sweetheart. It was in his house, after all. I know you won't tell anybody else."

"We won't!" Kim and Normie assured him.

"Good. It's important information." He didn't want to say it might be dangerous information. "Now, Father Burke and I will go and make the copies, and I'll be keeping the original."

"I know," said Normie.

"So why don't you adjourn the meeting now, Normie? Whenever we get more information, we'll meet again."

Maura congratulated the young sleuths and reluctantly left for work. The three kids trooped off, excited but conspiratorial. Monty was confident that they would keep the information to themselves, at least for now.

And now it was Brennan and Monty in the office by themselves, with the letter and several photocopies. "What in the name of God do we do now, Monty? Who the hell was Tabby? Is this what the Ebbett girl was killed over?"

"It could very well have been."

"But why, after all this time has passed?"

"Why indeed? The only names we've uncovered since this began are Runcey, MacCombie, and Steadman. Allister Steadman is the grandson of Blocker; Lorne MacCombie, the grandson of Bertram MacCombie. So a few generations removed. They might be prickly about their family's standing in the community. But the lieutenant governor is the *son* of Harrison Runcey. It was Harrison's car on Young Street, the car Mike Kavanagh noticed because it was unusual. And that was the car into which the body was loaded, the body of the person who had apparently died before the explosion, not during or after it."

"The porridge thickens."

"But, Brennan, when I spoke to Runcey, he was not overly concerned about it."

"We have to find out who Tabby was, the baby. His mother was Minnie. According to the boys' notes in 1917, Minnie was one of the girls living in the brothel. The lads' notes say she had a row with a man, demanding that Tabby be returned to her. And he made a nasty reply to her, called her a whore or something. This letter says she had originally named the boy Stephen, and she was writing to her daughter Irene."

"Well, we'll be keeping all those names in mind. But we'll start with Runcey to see if he has any information, because that's the only connection we have so far, Harrison Runcey and his car. But, as I say, Runcey didn't seem worried about it when I spoke to him." Monty thought for a minute. "You have the *Canadian Encyclopedia* in the school library, I think. The kids used it for information about the explosion."

"We have it, yes."

"How up-to-date is your copy?"

"Not sure. A few years old, maybe. Certainly newer than 1917!"

"It's only a few years old anyway; the encyclopedia was created in the 1980s. I want to check something."

They walked to the school's library and found the encyclopedia on the shelf. Monty reached over and pulled out a volume. "This is 1988, so it probably won't have . . ." He turned the pages. "No." He closed it and returned it to the shelf. He looked around the library. "I don't suppose you have a volume of *Who's Who?*"

"As a matter of fact, we have *Canadian Who's Who 1992*. It was donated to us by a Mr. Murdoch Robertson."

"Why doesn't that surprise me? You may be sure he's featured in it. Well, it does have a lot of useful information. Let's see if it will aid our work today." Brennan fetched the volume. "So, is he listed in here? Robertson?"

"I've no idea. Didn't bother me arse to look him up."

"He'd be disappointed in you, Brennan."

"Not for the first time or, I dare say, the last."

Monty opened the book and thumbed through the pages. "Let's see what it says about the Runceys. Yes, here — Oh, Christ! Lieutenant governor of Nova Scotia since 1989." He looked over at Brennan. "Thompson Abbott Runcey, born in Ottawa on October 27, 1917."

"Thompson Abbott. T-A-B-B. Tabby."

"I'm trying not to say 'Son of a . . .'" Monty handed the book back to Brennan. "T.A. Runcey is our man."

"But, Monty, it wasn't a seventy-six-year-old man you and my father tangled with after the break-in here."

"No, although he was quite an athlete in his day. Tennis, rowing. But no, I can't see the LG donning a hooded jacket and heading out to intimidate a child or break into a school."

"The question comes up again: is it possible that there are two people with grudges over the play, or one with a beef about the play and another with a more personal motive relating to the young one who was killed? I know it offends the Occam's razor principle, but we have to consider the possibility. The school burglar wanted to see what was in the script, or even to steal it — though he should have sussed out the fact that we'd have more than one copy of it. Or that we could just write it again. As for the killing of the Ebbett girl, yes, she might well have gone to Young Street because of something she heard about, something about the play. But the killing may have been a spontaneous action by somebody she met that night. The play brought her to Young Street, but it did not account for her death."

Monty shook his head. "You're not convinced by that suggestion, I don't think, Brennan."

"There has to be a better explanation. And about the car that Robertson identified. How many other people would have made that connection? If someone did, why not come to us and ask us not to include that in the play? For that matter, why not get the lawyers onto us? Not just threaten legal action in a note slipped into the school for the students."

"The owner of that car, Harrison Runcey, is long dead. His corpse won't be suing anybody. And just because the man was out there in his car helping to recover the dead after the blast, that doesn't necessarily mean he had anything to do with the death. He may have been told there was a body there. It's all too speculative."

"It is that."

"We just don't know. It's time for another chat at Government House. I'd like to get over there right away. But if Runcey does have something to hide, he may be spooked by me turning up on his doorstep again. Might refuse to see me. Who knows? I do know there's a reception for some visiting dignitaries, a delegation from the Netherlands, and that's tomorrow night. I don't have an invitation, never thought about attending. But I could easily wangle an invitation through my office. Or from my mother, for that matter. Abigail Runcey sends her invitations to these things, so she'll almost certainly be going."

"Right. And you'd get Runcey alone at some point. Maybe show up near the end of the event." Brennan laughed then. "And take a look around, see if he's got a bodyguard or some other fella on his staff who looks the part of a school burglar. Someone he sends out on less-than-dignified errands. An undercover man to do his dirty work. God forgive me, I shouldn't be laughing."

Monty said, "Sometimes, Brennan, you just have to laugh. It eases the tension, as they say. And, yeah, I'll keep an eye out at Government House. We'll bring your old man along to identify the man, if he exists."

"I'd love to see that. Me oul Irish republican da in the lieutenant governor's residence, shaking the hand of the British monarch's man in Nova Scotia. Or would he have to bow and curtsy?"

"No, that wouldn't be required, though I'd love to tell him otherwise, wouldn't you? But the shaking of hands would suffice. Anything more than that would be considered vulgar. And protocol precludes the capping of knees, the lobbing of cherry bombs. That sort of thing is frowned upon, don't you know. No, we'll leave your father out of it. We'll spare him an introduction to the Queen's representative. When

I think of it, though, why don't you come along yourself? You've been in City Hall. Why not see the interior of one of the greatest buildings in Canada, you being such an architecture buff?"

"Sure, why not?"

CHAPTER XXII

Monty

Monty's mother did indeed receive an invitation to the event at Government House, and once Normie got wind of it, she was keen to see the place again. So, it was Evelyn and Normie, Monty and Brennan in the delegation. Maura had to host an evening lecture at the law school, so she had to miss the LG's reception. Monty and his companions were ushered into the ballroom, a big airy room with heavy gold curtains cinched at the sides of the enormous windows. There were close to a hundred other guests standing around in stylish dresses, suits and ties, some of them with wineglasses in hand. Runcey was at the far end of the room with his aide-de-camp beside him.

"There's Mr. Runcey," Normie said, smiling. Monty reminded himself that she knew nothing of the Runcey connection to the letter she had discovered at the Carmichaels' house. "Who's that beside him," she asked, "the guy in the uniform?"

"That's his aide-de-camp. That means he's a serving or former member of the armed forces, the Mounties, or a municipal police force, and he helps the lieutenant governor at official events like this one." The man wore a uniform with a distinctive gold braid on the right shoulder. Thompson Runcey was talking to a tall fair-haired man wearing some kind of medallion. One of the Dutch guests of honour, Monty assumed.

Normie announced that she wanted to "go and see something." Monty assumed she meant the dollhouse, and he said, "Sure, you go right ahead." He went for a little walk around, greeting a few lawyers and other people he knew.

Then he left the room and wandered about the first floor until he saw Normie once again ogling the magnificent English dollhouse. Evelyn was there with her, and there were others admiring it as well. Unbeknownst to Normie, Monty and Maura had arranged with the builder in Annapolis Royal to make a similar dollhouse for her for Christmas. Thane Runcey, the LG's recently married son, was chatting with two middle-aged women with strong Dutch accents. "Yes, it's a replica of the house you saw in the painting out there." He meant the painting of the great stone house in England, with its peaks and chimney pots. "It's the property of relations of ours, my paternal grandmother's family." One of the women looked confused, so he said, "The family of my dad's mother."

That twigged something in Monty's memory. On a previous visit — it must have been the wedding party for Thane and Caroline — Normie had heard someone say that the English estate passed down the LG's mother's line. What else had Normie said? Or was it Maura? A remark at the party, something gauche. About the price of the estate; had somebody asked how much it was worth? Monty could think of more than one person who would have been appalled at a gaffe like that. *Not our sort, darling.*

Monty returned to the ballroom and watched as Thompson Runcey — *Thompson Abbott* Runcey — circulated among his guests with his aide-de-camp, making the visitors all feel welcome in their grand surroundings. Monty felt a pang of guilt, knowing that Runcey's cheerful mood would soon be shattered.

The reception lasted for about an hour and a half before the crowd began to thin out and the guests said their thanks and goodbyes. A young guy with dark shaggy hair was going around, picking up plates and glasses. Brennan was seated by the wall, gazing about him at the architectural splendour.

Monty saw his chance when the last of the guests departed and Runcey was alone, so he approached him and said, "This has been most enjoyable, Your Honour, but I'm afraid I have some questions for you again."

Monty could see the man making an effort to keep a pleasant expression on his face. "All right, have a seat, Mr. Collins, and ask your questions."

The aide-de-camp approached them, but Runcey thanked him and said he would not be needed now, so he could go home to his family and enjoy the rest of his evening.

"A bit of an update, first," Monty said when they were alone. "The young woman who was killed, Trudi Ebbett, had gone to the house we spoke of last time, on Young Street."

"The house of *ill repute*," he said, putting an ironic twist on the words.

"Yes. And the reason Ms. Ebbett went to the house was to ask the current owners, the Carmichaels, if she could go inside and look for something. She said that her great-grandmother had lived in the house up to the time of the explosion — she was killed in it — and that she had left something in the house for members of her family. Trudi Ebbett did not know what the object was — a keepsake of some kind, a piece of jewellery, she had never heard what it was. Just that the great-grandmother had left something to be found by, or given to, someone in her family later on. We now know that the great-grandmother's name was Minnie."

Thompson Runcey heard the name without any sign of recognition or concern.

"A search of the property, the basement, turned up the item Minnie had left in the house." Monty was not about to say that his own daughter had found it. "It was a short letter written by Minnie to her daughter, whose name was Irene."

Again, no reaction from Runcey. Was Monty on the wrong track here? Should he have looked up the name MacCombie in the *Who's*

Who? Was there a Thompson or a Timothy or a Terence A. MacCombie in this saga somewhere?

But it was T.A. Runcey he had before him now, so he carried on with the conversation. "Minnie told Irene that she had given birth to a baby boy and had given the baby up, given him to a 'very important family' so he would have a better life than she could provide." Monty remembered then the lock of hair, which Minnie had described as "strawberry blond." Runcey's hair was grey now, but his colouring was the kind often seen on people with red hair: light skin, a faint hint of freckles, and hazel eyes. "She had called her baby Stephen."

Runcey waited with a bland expression on his face.

"She said in her letter that she didn't like the names the new family had given the boy, which she mocked as 'Tabby.'"

"Tabby?" Runcey asked. "What kind of name is that? Sounds more like a cat's name."

"That's what the kids wrote into the play. Michael Kavanagh, one of the boys who wrote the notes in 1917, recounted an argument between Minnie and the man to whom she had given her child. She had regretted giving him up and was desperate to get him back. The man — who was apparently the child's father — was having none of it. The students at Saint Bernadette's had no idea that the name Tabby referred to a baby; they, too, thought it must be a pet. From what I've been able to piece together, Trudi Ebbett saw a news story about the play. There were a couple of little excerpts from the play itself on CTV, across the Atlantic provinces. The tie-in, of course, was the upcoming anniversary of the Halifax Explosion. And she caught the Tabby reference; it was a word or a name she had heard from her family. She put two and two together and identified the house on Young Street as the house where her great-grandmother Minnie had lived."

Monty turned his head and saw Brennan looking at him. He was too far away to hear the conversation, but he certainly knew what was being discussed. Or revealed. And it did seem to be a revelation. There was no indication that Thompson Runcey had known any of this history.

"Tom," Monty said, "it seems to me that the word 'Tabby' came from the sound of the names the new family had given the baby. Names like Thompson Abbott." Runcey reared back at that. "The child had strawberry blond hair — there is a lock of it attached to the letter. And he was born in October 1917."

The change in Runcey was remarkable. Monty could actually see the colour draining from his naturally pale face. There was no need to remind him that the argument about Tabby had taken place between the young woman and the man with the Case Limousine. Runcey's father.

"Was there an adoption, Tom?" Harrison Runcey was his biological father, but had there been an adoption to make Cordelia Runcey, in a legal sense, his mother? Of course, if all this had come as a shock, the man certainly did not know he was adopted, if in fact he was.

Runcey gave a definitive shake of his head. His voice was barely audible. "I have seen all my parents' — all my father's — papers, all his belongings, legal documents. No adoption papers."

And then Monty remembered what Runcey had said about his mother — the woman he thought was his mother — in the months before he was born. His father had been working with the Department of National Defence in Ottawa. There was a party or a reception with Prime Minister Borden, and a photograph of Runcey's pregnant mother, or "my mother looking very pregnant," something like that. So the couple had put on an act, staged a fake pregnancy to explain the birth of Thompson Abbott. A birth stated to have taken place in Ottawa. Thompson was the Runceys' only child. Was this by choice, or had Cordelia never been able to conceive? In late 1917, she must have put padding in her clothes to look the part of an expectant mother. As for the other woman, Minnie, had Runcey Senior taken precautions — that is, had he insisted that Minnie take precautions — to ensure that there would not be any uncertainty as to the paternity of this child born to the working girl on Young Street? Yes, according to Minnie's letter, that was a condition of the deal. She was not to be with any other man. In the event that she hadn't lived up to that part of the arrangement, Monty knew from ribald conversations as a teenager that birth control methods were nothing new; rubber condoms had been around since the 1800s. Women in the prostitution trade would be well familiar with those. But Monty figured she had forsaken all others for that stretch of time; she was being paid, no doubt handsomely, so would not have needed to ply her trade. And according to the letter, once her pregnancy was confirmed, the father had paid her to spend the months of her pregnancy in New Brunswick. The situation had been carefully managed to hide the truth. Thompson was not, in any legal sense, Cordelia Rayworth's son.

Monty thought of the painting of the grand estate in England. The woman who had given birth to Thompson was a prostitute working and apparently living at the house on Young Street. Minnie had given the baby up — and then regretted it. Monty recalled one of the boys' notes describing a "barnburner of a fight" when she confronted the man at the brothel and demanded that "Tabby" be returned to her. But the baby remained with his new family, and Minnie wrote to her daughter that she had given him to a "very important family" so he could have a better life. Would one aspect of that better life now be denied him, the grand estate in England that was passed down the Rayworth side of the family? He had no Rayworth blood in him at all, and there had been no adoption.

What was Monty going to do now? Make an accusation against the lieutenant governor on suspicion of . . . The silence was shattered by the crash of breaking glass. Followed by a scream. It sounded like . . . Monty bolted up from his chair, and Runcey did the same. And here came Normie, running into the ballroom, a look of terror on her face. Monty reached her and clasped her to him. Then, from the same direction, came the young guy who had been doing the cleanup. His eyes were wide. With what? Fear? Anger? Runcey called out to him, "Jared, what are you doing?" But the kid turned and ran to the front door, wrenched it open, and left the mansion.

"Daddy! That's him, the guy who foll—"

"Brennan!" Monty called out and sprinted to the door and out across the front lawn onto Barrington Street.

The boy was a fast runner, heading south on Barrington, but Monty urged himself on, and Brennan was close behind him. Monty called out, "Stop! You won't get away!"

And he might have, if it hadn't been for a car that screeched to a halt in Bishop Street, after nearly hitting the kid. He leapt back against a volley of curses from the driver, and this gave Monty and Brennan the chance to reach him and nab him before he got away again. They each took one of his arms and walked him to the sidewalk, all the while maintaining their grip on him.

"I didn't do nothin'!"

How many times had Monty heard that in his long criminal law career? "If you didn't do anything, why did you run?"

"Fuck you!"

"I'll ask you again: why did you run?"

"Because she thought it was me, but it wasn't!"

"She thought it was you who did what?" Monty surprised himself; he was moved with an unexpected feeling of pity for this young boy. Monty knew nothing about him, but he reminded him of so many others he had met over the years. Disadvantages in life, lack of opportunity to develop the person's natural intelligence, accounted for much of the criminal behaviour he had seen. Also familiar was a complete lack of sophistication, or imagination, when a guy was caught or cornered. Monty asked again in a softer tone, "What do you think she thought about you? She thought you had done something?"

He tried to recover. "I don't know. The way she looked at me, like she thought I did something."

Monty was anxious to get back to the big house, back to Normie. He turned to Brennan and said, "I'm going back to see about —"

"The little one," Brennan answered. "Go ahead. I'll handle things here."

The captive turned his face from Monty to Brennan, and there was no mistaking the fear in his face. Brennan Burke, with his chiselled face and penetrating black eyes, was without question a more intimidating figure than was Monty. He didn't know what to advise

Brennan, or what to expect of him, with respect to *handling things here*, but he took off at a clip to the lieutenant governor's house to be at his daughter's side.

Brennan

Brennan kept hold of the boy's arm and looked into his eyes. "What was that all about? We're going to find out now or later. So, let's hear it."

"Who are you?"

"You'll answer my questions, and then I'll answer yours."

"Yeah, right."

The lad raised his chin and ran his free hand through his shaggy mop of hair. He stared, unblinking, at Brennan. An attempt at a look of defiance. How was Brennan going to deal with this? If he was the little gurrier who had followed Normie — and Normie's reaction indicated that he was — the lad was not acting like someone who had merely been walking behind the little girl. If that had been the case, he would not even have remembered it. So, he had been following her and it had to have been in relation to the play. The following and the warning notes were an unlikely coincidence of events.

Brennan held the boy's gaze and said, "What bothered you about the play?"

There was little doubt; the word "play" had hit a nerve. All doubt was removed when he sneered at Brennan and said, "What play? What the fuck are you talking about? I don't go to kids' *plays!*" And he flapped his free arm around in an attempt to imitate a child making a dramatic gesture on the stage.

Brennan saw no need to belabour the point the boy had unintentionally made, so he did not ask *How do you know I'm talking about a kids' play?* Instead, he said, "I'm Father Brennan Burke."

"Father?"

"I'm a priest. I run Saint Bernadette's Choir School." The boy's lip quivered at that, but he said not a word. "Your turn now."

"I'm freezing to death."

So was Brennan. It could not have been much above zero. He took this as an opening. "Sure, you'd be more comfortable with a heavy jacket, a cap, and a scarf pulled up over your face."

"I . . . What the fuck are you talking about?"

"You're not going to be arrested for following someone." Unless there was intimidation, a threat; Brennan didn't know the law on it, but he was going to wing it. "So" — he smiled at the lad in what he hoped was a friendly way — "let's hear your confession." The boy looked uncertain then, weighing what he must have conceived as his options. "Let's hear it before I take you back to the big house. Why did you follow the little girl?"

Brennan could feel his captive go slack. The idea of going back to the big house seemed worse than standing out here in the cold, talking to a stranger who seemed to know exactly what had happened.

"They were going to lose it all!"

Brennan started to interrupt, then thought the better of it. Let the witness give his own testimony, in his own way. Don't make the mistake of cutting it off.

"I bet you didn't grow up in a foster home! Right, *Father*? I didn't have a father, just that old bastard who took the money the government gives out to guys like him, who talk their wives into running foster homes. He thought there was no problem he couldn't solve by using his fists. Who's that boxer that won all the awards?"

There were many, Brennan knew, just as he knew there were many good, loving foster parents, but this was no time to go off on a tangent. "You were in a foster home?"

"Yeah, I got dumped by my real family. Not good enough for them. Well, guess what? I have a chance to be good enough. Way better than them! But now we could lose the whole fuckin' thing."

An unstable life, a foster home. That hockey game at the Halifax Forum was part of a program to offer young fellas a chance at a better life. But there was a work project, too, wasn't there? Then he had it. MacCombie. "You worked for one of the MacCombie companies, did you?"

"No!" Then, "Who?"

"MacCombie. You obviously know the name."

Then came the attempt to dismiss MacCombie as irrelevant. "Yeah, so what?"

"When did you work for him?"

"I never."

Brennan returned to another track. "What did you mean when you said you could lose everything? Lose what?"

He took his time coming up with an answer. "What do you fuckin' think? I'll lose everything if I get arrested and put in jail!"

"That won't happen." Brennan wasn't sure about an arrest, but surely jail was unlikely. He turned the conversation to something else the lad had said. "You said 'we' could lose everything. Not just you, but others. Who did you mean by 'we'?"

"Just my . . . nobody. I just meant me. Now, fuck off!" And with that, he squirmed around and tried to free himself from Brennan's grip. But he was no match for his captor.

The young fella was shivering now with the cold, as was Brennan himself. He couldn't keep him out here. "We're going back to the big house," Brennan announced and marched his sullen prisoner back towards the mansion from which he had fled.

When Brennan drew close to the entrance, he looked to the house, and what to his wondering eyes should appear but his father, standing just outside the door, face to face with another man. Behind the man stood Monty. The tension among the three of them was evident from their postures even from Brennan's position at the edge of the property. He still had a grip on the boy.

Monty

When Monty left Brennan and the young guy out on the street, he had returned to the house. It was in chaos. Monty's mother had her arms around a weeping Normie. There was no sign of Thompson Abbott

Runcey. But Monty could hear a heated argument taking place somewhere in an adjoining room.

A man's voice. "Did you send him out?"

A woman's reply. "What do you mean, did I send him? You saw him; he just took off!"

"I don't mean this time; I mean the other time. The time you blabbed everything to him!"

"I never! He overheard us talking about it. About losing our chance."

"Oh yeah? Well, it isn't *our* chance yet, is it? I'm not fucking chained to you yet!"

"Fuck you! You're not chained to me at all. Who wants to be married to a guy who gets fired from every single job as soon as the boss finds out what kind of idiot you really are. That's your resumé your new boss reads every time: *He can cook, 'cause look at all the restaurants he's worked in. But when he gets all coked up, he's a friggin' asshole who —*"

Something crashed to the ground, and Monty was about to go and investigate. But then from farther away, he heard her again. The same woman, her voice quiet but somehow, at the same time, shrill. Frightened. "Don't you fucking dare! I'm outta here! Don't ever call me or come near me again!" There were footsteps, but they seemed to change direction.

That was all Monty heard, but it was enough. The man bickering with the woman was a cook. Thompson Runcey's oldest son was a cook, a chef. His employment profile was apparently an inglorious history of being hired and fired. And his fiancée, at least in the heat of the moment, was having none of it. And he had mocked her about her "chance." Her chance to what? Acquire wealth, social status as a member of the Runcey family? A chance that was now lost? Was Edwin Runcey the man who had tried to scotch the children's play, tried to prevent the truth about the Runceys' family tree from being revealed to one and all? Monty had seen Edwin in passing, earlier in the evening. He was just under six feet in height, in good shape. He had long wavy light brown hair; Monty hadn't noted his eye colour.

He could not tell one way or the other whether this was the man he and Declan Burke had chased that night, but then Monty wouldn't have recognized whoever it was. He had not had a good look at the man's face, obscured as it was by hat and scarf. But Monty was not the only witness; Declan had seen enough of him to give the police a description. And Monty knew where Declan was this evening: a short distance away at the Saint Bernadette's rectory on Byrne Street.

Monty had made his decision. He saw a phone on the wall across from him. He walked over to Normie, gave her a hug and offered her some words of comfort, and told her he had a phone call to make.

When he had made his call and hung up the phone, he saw Thompson Runcey walking towards him. The man's face was drawn and pale, his eyes red as if he had been weeping. He signalled towards a seat down at the end of the room, so Monty followed him. There was no preamble. "My son's girlfriend, Wanda, hasn't had an easy time of it. The father of the family abandoned them, abandoned the three children, and the mother was unable to cope. She gave Jared, the youngest boy, up for adoption. He spent some years in a foster home before another family came forward and adopted him. He was a handful, but the new parents were good to him. They did their best."

A door creaked somewhere in the house, and Runcey whirled around, but there was nobody to be seen. He took a deep breath and loosened his tie. "Wanda managed to locate the boy's new family, find her brother a couple of years ago. Wanda . . ." He looked around as if she might have tiptoed into the room behind them. "Wanda, with her disadvantages, obviously sees an advantage in hitching her wagon to my son's star."

Monty kept his own thoughts to himself, that Edwin Runcey's celestial identity might be better termed a dark blot on the sun, an unstable magnetic field. What Monty had once overheard as "being hired away from one restaurant to another because of his talents" was in fact a history of being unable to hold a job.

He tuned back in to what the lieutenant governor was saying. And that's when Runcey made a slip. "If Wanda was concerned that something might threaten what she hoped to attain by — yes, it sounds crass — but what she hoped to attain by marrying into this family, she would not have been shy about expressing herself. And her young brother could well have been in on those conversations, or overheard them. If your daughter believes that he is the boy who followed her that day, and I think we can infer that from her reaction, it would suggest that he had heard something about the play, and a slur on our family. A threat to our reputation, and . . . and . . ."

It was obvious to Monty that the man did not know how to finish the thought. If Monty's head was spinning from all this information, what must Runcey be feeling? The "Tabby" revelation had dropped like a bombshell on Thompson Runcey tonight. If this was the information that had led to the attempts at intimidation, it meant that a member of the Runcey family, or someone close to the family, had learned or heard about that damaging information well before the lieutenant governor had done so. And if —

Just then, Monty heard the front door open and looked over. His mother and Normie also turned to see who had arrived. Hard to say whose face showed the most surprise: Normie's or her Grandma Evelyn's as Declan Burke strode in and stopped at the threshold of the room. Normie brushed a hand across her eyes and stood up, saying, "Hi, Mr. Burke!"

Evelyn rose at the same time. "Good evening, Declan."

"Ladies," he said, nodding at them both.

Monty rose to go and meet him.

Then it all happened in an instant. Edwin Runcey came flying into the room. He took a hurried glance around, and his eyes locked on Declan. Edwin's eyes widened in alarm, and he rushed forward. But Declan was standing in the entranceway, partly facing away from Edwin, and didn't see him coming. Monty couldn't believe what he saw next. As Edwin bore down on Declan, Monty's mother stepped into his path to block him. Edwin kept coming and shoved Evelyn down. She fell to the floor but with astonishing speed thrust her leg out and tripped Edwin, who crash-landed just beyond where she lay.

Monty made a beeline for this mother. When he reached her, Declan was looking down at her, his eyes and mouth open wide with astonishment. It was the most expressive look Monty had ever seen on the man's customary poker face. Here was an elderly woman who had never, to Monty's knowledge, had a violent encounter in her entire life. An elderly English lady stepping up to protect an IRA warrior whose history had certainly included numerous violent encounters, many no doubt with English opponents. Monty could easily have imagined Declan fighting off someone who posed a threat to a woman, but he would not have imagined the reverse.

Declan reached down, and he and Monty gently helped Evelyn to her feet. But Edwin Runcey had reached the front door of the building, about to escape. Monty shouted, "I'll take care of her, Dec. Go after him!" And Declan, looking from Evelyn to the door, made his decision: he bolted for the door in pursuit of Edwin.

Monty eased his mother into a chair. She was trembling, and as much as he wanted to go outside and see what had become of Edwin and Declan, he wanted to make sure his mum was all right. She didn't appear to be injured; her expression was not that of someone in pain. All he could think of was the age-old English remedy for an unpleasant episode. "Would you like a cup of tea, Mum?"

She actually laughed at that and replied, "That would be just the thing. But not right now. I'm fine, darling."

"You're sure?"

"I'm sure."

Monty looked up from his mother and saw Thompson Runcey walking towards a room off to the side. He went in and quietly closed the door behind him.

Peace and quiet at last? It was not to be. The next character to make an entrance on stage was a young woman wearing a red silky dress with wide puffy shoulders; her dark hair was done in the big style you'd have seen in the last decade, with curls bunched up on her forehead. Monty couldn't help but think of Brennan's description of the drama queen who had taught theatre at his school; could she have staged anything more theatrical than tonight's events at Government House? Monty recognized the new arrival as Edwin Runcey's girlfriend, Wanda. When he looked more closely, he saw a narrow stream of blood dribbling from her lip. To no one in particular, she cried out, "He hit me!" Edwin, presumably; the row between them had turned physical. With Edwin gone out, Monty saw Wanda as his best source of information about all the turmoil that had erupted tonight, and maybe some of the factors that had led up to it. He walked towards her, introduced himself, and asked her to tell him what had happened.

There is a term used frequently in the law: floodgates. If a certain claim were allowed, this might open the floodgates, might encourage an untold number of claimants to come forward and overwhelm the courts of justice. Well, one look at Wanda's outraged, bleeding face told Monty that the floodgates were about to open here tonight.

"He did this!" she exclaimed again.

Hell hath no fury, Monty remarked to himself as he faced the woman scorned. He took her by the arm and led her to a seat as far as he could get from Normie and Evelyn. "Tell me what's happened, Wanda. I'm sorry, I don't have a handkerchief." She gave a dismissive shrug and lifted her arm, used the sleeve of her dress to wipe away the blood. "Who hit you?" As if Monty couldn't guess.

"He did, of course. Edwin. He did it before, too, just after that night."

Monty kept his tone gentle, unthreatening. "Which night?"

"When she called again. He gave her his home number that time."

"Who?" She looked away then and put a tentative finger on the cut lip. "Who called?"

"He was all coked up."

Monty took a deep breath and told himself to be patient. "Let's start from the beginning, Wanda. You mentioned a phone call."

"Yeah, he was here one night. Typical. He'd go to the bars downtown and get plastered and then come and stay here, instead of driving out to our own place in Herring Cove. It was back, I think . . . yeah, sometime after Thanksgiving, the week after, maybe. The call was for his father, but he was out at some la-dee-da dinner, so Edwin took the call. And the one on the phone told him that she'd done all this research. After that kiddies' play was on the news. About the explosion, and she saw the news about it in New Brunswick and said she already knew about it."

"Already knew?"

"About the funny name. Tippy. Or, no, Tabby. She already knew about that name. Somebody in her family said it sometime. Told her about it. And there it was in the play. And she went and did *research*."

Monty took a glance around and pleaded with the fates not to cause any interruption as this narrative unfolded. His mother held his gaze, and he knew she had caught on that something important was keeping Monty at the other end of the room. This was going beyond the incidents of intimidation. Edwin's reaction to seeing Declan, recognizing him, put Edwin in the frame for the attempted break-in. And now Monty had learned that Trudi had put Edwin in the know about "Tabby."

For now, he would stick to the chronology of events as Wanda was relaying them. "And what about her research?" he asked.

"She said she found out from some book that the name Tabby and the timing of the baby's birth actually meant Mr. Runcey! That he was somebody else's son, and not who he said he was. Even loonier was that she said her grandmother or great-grandmother got killed in the explosion. And that she was a hooker! That Mr. Runcey's real mother was a ho! It doesn't get any wackier than that, eh? I didn't get it. If some woman was killed in the explosion, how could this girl be a descendant of her? But I guess the woman had had another kid before, before 1917. So this girl was descended from that one." Wanda rolled her eyes skyward. "I don't friggin' know!"

Monty thought through it all, and he reasoned that Trudi Ebbett had done what Monty and Brennan had done. She knew there was a baby with a name that led to the nickname Tabby, born in October 1917 to an important family. She did some research. Maybe she found several possible matches, important families and names, checked them out. Whatever the case, she had narrowed it down to Runcey.

"And all this wacky shit," Wanda groused, "and she was coming to Halifax to find the proof!"

"Did Edwin know why she wanted to find the proof?"

"She said Tabby was really in *her* family, not the Runceys! And I told Edwin this was all crazy shit, and he should just ignore her. But he was all upset and obsessed about it, and he phoned her from our apartment and told her off and told her not to come to Halifax."

So that was one of the phone calls that Trudi's roommate had told him about in Saint John. "What did she do then, the girl from New Brunswick?" Wanda's damaged mouth twitched, and she sent a fearful look around the elegant room. "Wanda?"

"She came anyway! She phoned him and said she was going to get the proof, whatever the hell it was, at some house in the north end. And Edwin was drinking, as usual, and he'd done a line of coke, and he — he got into his car, even though he was high and drunk, and he went roaring off to that street to tell her to back off and get lost."

Monty finished the story for himself: Edwin took off for Young Street, saw Trudi at the Carmichaels' house where she asked to be admitted to search for the proof, and he stood outside shouting at her. She was frightened enough to take refuge in the house next door — Monty's house where Kirk and Richard were drunk after their party. And the next morning, Trudi was found near the top of Young Street, lying dead in the grass.

"Her name was Trudi," Monty said softly.

There was a long moment of silence. Then came a scream of denial: "He wouldn't do that! There's no way! He's not —"

"Wanda, he did. You know it. And he's hurt you. Your lip —" he began, but she cut him off.

"No! I'm not gonna listen to this! He didn't mean — He needs help. I have to phone —" And with that, she rose and headed back towards the room from which she had emerged.

Now she was defending him. But it was too late for that. Edwin may not have gone to Young Street with the intention of killing Trudi Ebbett, or even hurting her. Persuading her to drop her quest, threatening her, no doubt. The killing was likely not planned. An altercation gone wrong. There was no doubt in Monty's mind about who had killed Trudi. And there was no doubt that Edwin's dreams, and Wanda's, of inheriting that sumptuous country house in England had died before Trudi took her last breath.

And had there been another murder? Monty replayed what he had read in Mike Kavanagh's notes, about the person who had not died in the blast but whose body had been dug up and taken away in a Case Limousine the day after the explosion. Harrison Runcey had a Case Limousine, and he had something to hide, the secret of his son's conception and birth. The 1917 notes made reference to a row outside the brothel, between the owner of the pricey car and another man. There was also Alma Senns's story from her time living in the brothel house with her mother, a story about a quarrel and the suggestion of blackmail. Had Trudi told Edwin that Harrison Runcey may have killed a man to protect his secret? How likely was it that she, a great-grandchild, would have heard or learned about that? Not very likely, Monty figured.

But what about Normie's promotional spiel for act two? What had she said? That there was a murder mystery coming up, that a body had been taken away in a Case Limousine. Monty knew that the limo story had been mentioned in at least one of the news reports after the play in October. Had Edwin heard or read about it? Or was Edwin afraid of more secrets coming out about the infant Tabby? Whatever the situation, Edwin was bound and determined that there would be no more revelations blackening the name of his family and threatening his own future prospects.

Monty stood for a moment, marvelling at the stunning events of the evening. The revelations about the Runcey family, the truth about the murder of Trudi Ebbett, the apparent identification of the boy who had followed Normie on the street. And he couldn't help but smile at this one, his elderly mum — an English lady "of good family" — stepping up in an effort to save IRA hard man Declan Burke when a wrathful Edwin Runcey came barrelling across the room. Monty shook off his ruminations and headed for the door.

The drama continued when he opened the door and stepped outside. There, on the front lawn, were Brennan and Declan holding down a raging, struggling Edwin. The boy who had fled earlier was standing off to the side, staring wide-eyed at the scene. And what a scene it was: there was Declan Burke interrogating Edwin Runcey in a tone of cold fury. The Dublin inflections in his voice were more pronounced than ever. "It was you. I saw yeh. We had a little barney out in the street, do yeh not remember? So why don't you grow a pair and own up to it?"

"Fuck you, you're out of your mind!"

"Goin' after a bunch of children and their school play. What did yeh think yeh were goin' to get by breakin' into the school, yeh louser? The script, was it? Did yeh not think there would be several copies of it? Or that they could just sit down and write the thing again? Or were you going to plant more threatening notes? Or write them on the chalkboard? Well, you're fucked now."

There followed a string of furious denials in language and tone that one would not expect of the first son of the Queen's representative. But then again, Edwin Runcey's dismal employment history, his drug use, and who knew what else hardly lived up to the expectations — the stereotype — of the dutiful, successful first son of a prominent man. It was about to get far worse for the Runcey family.

And it was Declan Burke, of all people, doing the interrogation. Declan Burke, interrogating a suspect! Perhaps he had done this sort of thing before, in a far different context. Questioning a traitor to the movement? An informer? But now he was taking the part of a police officer, certainly a novel role for him to play. What would his reaction be when it dawned on him that he would be called as a witness for the prosecution? A witness for the *Crown*?!

Monty walked over to the Burkes and said to them, "Keep him here. He killed Trudi."

Brennan and Declan stared at him, their muted version of astonishment showing on their faces. Edwin shouted, "I didn't kill anyone!" and made a lunge towards Brennan, but Brennan was well able for him, and he and his dad forced their captive down again.

"I'm calling the police," Monty said and went inside to make his call.

Normie was standing off to the side, but close enough to the doorway to have heard the commotion outside the house. When she saw Monty, she rushed to him and said, "You're calling the police now?"

"Yes, I'm going to tell them what we learned here tonight, and they're going to arrest Edwin Runcey."

"Because he's the one who killed Trudi! And broke into our school!"

"He's the one. And, Normie, if it hadn't been for you — you and Kim, carrying out your investigation — we wouldn't know who had killed Trudi, or why he did it. I'm so proud of you, sweetheart. Or should that be *Detective Collins*?" He and Maura would be having a talk with her, warning her against courting danger by getting involved in any more criminal investigations. But that had to wait. "Now, you go over to your grandma and keep her company. I have to make that call."

He went to the phone and called the police, gave them a condensed version of the story, and went outside again, to wait. A short few minutes later, a police car pulled up, roof lights flashing blue and red. Another arrived seconds later.

The occasion would have called for a crash of thunder, a bolt of lightning from the sky. But instead a gentle snow began to fall as the curtain rang down on the final scene. Monty saw his daughter staring out one of the front windows, and his mother staring out another. He turned, and what was this? Declan Burke was looking towards Evelyn at the window, and he raised his hand to his forehead in a salute. To Evelyn Chamberley Collins! The veteran soldier of the Irish Republican Army saluting the English lady who had stepped forward to save him from harm! Monty started to smile, then he found there was a catch in his throat.

And standing in front of his magnificent Georgian house, Lieutenant Governor Runcey stared out from the front entrance, his face slack and pale, his wife shell-shocked by his side, as their son was placed in a police car, to be charged with murder and the attempted burglary of the choir school. None of this was Thompson Runcey's fault. Monty could hardly bear to look at him, the lieutenant governor, whose mother was not his mother, whose great house in England was not his house, whose father may have committed murder back in 1917 to cover up the truth. Thompson Abbott Runcey, a good man whose entire family history had been revealed as a lie.

EPILOGUE

Normie

We put on act two of our play, *Devastated Area*, just as we had planned it, on December 9, 1993. We got a standing ovation at the end! We didn't put in anything more about "Tabby," and we didn't give the names of those people who had done bad things back in 1917 and 1918. We talked about the bad things but didn't name names. And we showed that most of the people in Halifax were good and did their best to help families after the disaster. Oh, and Kirk Rhodenizer got to recite his lines again about the Montreal Canadiens and the Montreal Wanderers giving all the money from their game to the Halifax Relief Fund. After the play, Kirk apologized to Richard for being "a useless arsehole" the night they had the party at our new house. Richard told me he had to "fess up" to his parents about where he'd been that night, and about "having a beer." As if he only had one drink! He said they "freaked out" but "there was no violence," so I guess they didn't hit him!

Me and Richard and Kim were really sad about Trudi Ebbett and her great-grandmother who gave up her baby, and we were sad about Mr. Runcey. He is such a nice man, and it's awful what he found out about his family. His son Edwin is going to be in court charged with killing Trudi. My dad is not his lawyer.

And last but not least: rest in peace, Mike Kavanagh and Lauchie MacIntyre. You have been good friends to us, and we wish you could have been on stage with us to get your share of the applause!

AUTHOR'S NOTE
&
ACKNOWLEDGEMENTS

S aint Bernadette's Church and Choir School are fictional, as is Byrne
  Street. North End Reformed Presbyterian Church is fictional. I have
taken liberties with the descriptions of some houses in Halifax's north
end. The Halifax Harbour Buoys are a fictional hockey team.

❧

I would like to thank the following people for their kind assistance
in researching and writing this book: Joe A. Cameron; Joan Butcher;
Rhea McGarva; Marilyn Davidson Elliott, daughter of Eric Davidson;
Barry Cahill; Matt Stimson; the New Brunswick Museum; Dr. Sandra
Barr; my aunt Pauline, God rest her, and our cousin Bob, for the
true Saint John stories, as told here in O'Leary's Pub. And, as always,
many thanks to my wonderful editors, Cat London, Crissy Boylan,
and Rachel Ironstone. Any errors are, of course, mine alone.

SOURCES

Adams, Sharon. "The Halifax Explosion: Our Deadliest Wartime Accident." *Legion Magazine*. November–December 2017.

Bird, Michael J. *The Town That Died: A Chronicle of the Halifax Explosion*. Halifax: Nimbus Publishing, 1995, 2011.

Cahill, Barry. *Rebuilding Halifax: A History of the Halifax Relief Commission*. Halifax: Formac Publishing, 2020.

Canadian Institute for the Blind (CNIB). "War Years and the Birth of CNIB: Halifax Explosion." Accessed April 29, 2024. https://thatallmayread.ca/explore-history/wwi-cnib/halifax-explosion/.

Cuthbertson, Ken. *The Halifax Explosion: Canada's Worst Disaster*. Toronto: HarperCollins, 2017.

Elliott, Marilyn Davidson. *The Blind Mechanic*. Halifax: Nimbus, 2018.

Erickson, Paul A. *Historic North End Halifax*. Halifax: Nimbus, 2004.

Flemming, David B. *Explosion in Halifax Harbour: The Illustrated Account of a Disaster That Shook the World*. Halifax: Formac, 2004.

Kitz, Janet F. *Shattered City: The Halifax Explosion and the Road to Recovery*. Halifax: Nimbus, 1989, 2008.

MacDonald, Laura M. *The Curse of the Narrows: The Halifax Explosion of 1917*. Toronto: HarperCollins, 2005.

Scanlon, T. Joseph, and Roger Sarty. *Catastrophe: Stories and Lessons from the Halifax Explosion*. Waterloo, ON: Wilfrid Laurier University Press, 2020.

Sutow, M. Pauline Murphy. *Worse than War: The Halifax Explosion*. Tantallon, NS: Four East Publications, 1992.

Waterson, Sam, title role. *Oppenheimer: The Father of the Atomic Bomb*. Directed by Barry Davis. Aired October 29–December 10, 1980, on BBC Two. DVD. London, UK: BBC Worldwide Ltd., 2008.

Entertainment. Writing. Culture. ────────────

ECW is a proudly independent, Canadian-owned book publisher. We know great writing can improve people's lives, and we're passionate about sharing original, exciting, and insightful writing across genres.

──────────────────────── **Thanks for reading along!**

Certified

Corporation

We want our books not just to sustain our imaginations, but to help construct a healthier, more just world, and so we've become a certified B Corporation, meaning we meet a high standard of social and environmental responsibility — and we're going to keep aiming higher. We believe books can drive change, but the way we make them can too.

Being a B Corp means that the act of publishing this book should be a force for good – for the planet, for our communities, and for the people that worked to make this book. For example, everyone who worked on this book was paid at least a living wage. You can learn more at the Ontario Living Wage Network.

This book is also available as a Global Certified Accessible™ (GCA) ebook. ECW Press's ebooks are screen reader friendly and are built to meet the needs of those who are unable to read standard print due to blindness, low vision, dyslexia, or a physical disability.

FSC
www.fsc.org
MIX
Paper | Supporting
responsible forestry
FSC® C103567

This book is printed on Sustana EnviroBook™, a recycled paper, and other controlled sources that are certified by the Forest Stewardship Council®.

ECW's office is situated on land that was the traditional territory of many nations including the Wendat, the Anishnaabeg, Haudenosaunee, Chippewa, Métis, and current treaty holders the Mississaugas of the Credit. In the 1880s, the land was developed as part of a growing community around St. Matthew's Anglican and other churches. Starting in the 1950s, our neighbourhood was transformed by immigrants fleeing the Vietnam War and Chinese Canadians dispossessed by the building of Nathan Phillips Square and the subsequent rise in real estate value in other Chinatowns. We are grateful to those who cared for the land before us and are proud to be working amidst this mix of cultures.

ecwpress.com